Bonchi

Bonchi

a novel by
Toyoko Yamasaki

TRANSLATED BY
HARUE AND TRAVIS SUMMERSGILL

UNIVERSITY OF HAWAII PRESS
Honolulu

PUBLISHED UNDER THE AUSPICES OF THE KAMIGATA
BUNKA KENKYŪKAI AT THE UNIVERSITY OF HAWAII
AND SUPPORTED BY GRANTS FROM SUMITOMO METAL
INDUSTRIES, LTD., SUNTORY LIMITED, MATSUSHITA
ELECTRIC INDUSTRIAL CO., LTD., SUMITOMO BANK,
LTD., AND KANSAI ELECTRIC POWER CO., INC.

JACKET AND TITLE PAGE ILLUSTRATIONS
BY TEII NAKAMURA

FIRST PRINTING APRIL 1982
SECOND PRINTING SEPTEMBER 1982

Translators' Note

Toyoko Yamasaki is the author of twelve popular Japanese novels, the first of which was published in 1957. She defines her early concerns as a writer when, in discussing her first novel, *Noren* ("The Merchant Tradition"), she says, "I was born in Osaka and grew up there. It is in my blood. And the concentrated essence of Osaka is to be found in the long and distinguished tradition of its merchant aristocracy." The financial overlords, male and female, of the famed Osaka business district called the Semba are portrayed both accurately and affectionately in her first five novels. *Bonchi* is the third of these. In it, the special customs of the wealthy merchant class—customs which even between the world wars had begun to disintegrate and were largely to disappear under the triple impact of aerial bombardment, defeat, and occupation—are a significant part of the story line. Many of these customs are strange and exotic to present-day Japanese, but in *Bonchi* they are presented in colorful detail and interwoven with the story of a successful Semba merchant.

Easily as vital as the titular hero of the novel are the many women he associates with. In Japanese social lore the women of Osaka have always constituted a special breed, and from this novel one can, we think, understand why. Mrs. Yamasaki in an early work remarks that the traditional Osaka woman is, in appearance and behavior, "an amiable, courteous lady . . . but, under this genteel facade, she conceals the strength and endurance of one who will, if necessary, pull an ox-cart to market." Whatever the variety of characterization, great lady, geisha, or flapper, the women in *Bonchi* show this strength. In the Heian period of the eleventh century Japanese society had a strongly matriarchal cast; the reader of *Bonchi* may well wonder if in some ways it is not so still.

This translation was undertaken while Mrs. Yamasaki was resident in Hawaii during the years 1979–80. We consulted with her from week to week concerning the text, suiting our practice to her desire that we translate not only words but whole situations and scenes so that they would be understood and enjoyed by western readers much as they had been earlier by her Japanese audience. In Japan the readers of her novels consist of the large middle class which, despite the excellence of Japanese television, still reads books and magazines with avidity. Nearly all her novels first appeared in serial form. Although originally a journalist, Mrs. Yamasaki's preferred narrative unit is the dramatic scene, and some of her success may be attributed to her use of cinematic techniques. *Bonchi*, in any case, was so popular that it was made into a movie and two different films for television, one in 1962, the other a decade later. The reasons for this popularity will, we think, be easily apparent to the western reader.

Bonchi

One

The fifteenth of each month was Kimono Changing Day for all the great houses of the Semba District. The Imperial Court had its customs, and the merchant princes of Osaka had theirs. On such days the Kawachiya household was extremely busy. The three family seamstresses worked from morning to night in their small, dark sewing room, taking apart the squares of rich silk which formed the kimono and sewing them together again. Each member of the family would receive a new wardrobe suitable to all occasions for the coming month, and then take off the previous month's Oshima kimono of matted silk and underkimono of *habutae* silk, bathe, and dress again in clothing from the new wardrobe.

Kikuji, looking at the newly sewn Oshima silk in the seamstress's tray, yearned to be elsewhere. He had a hangover. Wearily, he kept his unresponsive body straight to its full height, letting the chambermaid tend to him. O-Toki, divorced and experienced, could hardly be expected to blink her eyes at the sight of Kikuji's naked body just out of the bath. Unprotestingly, she leaned down and helped him put on his shorts, and then slipped the cotton underwear top over his neck. Then, after draping the silk underkimono, light as cicada's wing, over his shoulders, she handed him a cigarette. He held it absent-mindedly between his lips, and, for the sake of something to say, asked, "How's everything going at the store?"

"Same as ever, sir," she replied briefly, attuning herself easily to his mood, realizing that he didn't much care what she said.

Kikuji didn't trust himself to speak further. He gazed inattentively out at the garden in the little courtyard, his wandering attention caught by the faint spring sunshine. The upper part of the sliding door was covered with paper panelling, the lower section with glass. Through it, he saw the half-gloom of the courtyard. The trees in it were Chinese black pines, and, since most Japanese find colorful flowers vulgar, the garden was all green. Only the gray of the granite stone lantern and the red carp in the pond gave an accent of color.

From a distance, he heard the soft sound of white silk tabi as they came sliding gently over the hall floor, within each a small foot, belonging either to his grandmother, Kino, or his mother, Sei. They had, he knew, just come from his grandmother's detached room at the rear of the house, facing on the courtyard. O-Toki, standing behind him, helped him into the outer kimono of Oshima silk. She tied a narrow sash at the level of his hips, the silk making a soft, rich sound as she squeezed it with her hands; then she hurried to put on the stiff, striped Hakata waistband. From her haste, he realized that she too had perceived the approach of Kino and Sei. Just as she finished tying the stiff sash tightly, the glass door slid open behind Kikuji. He turned around.

"Ah, my ladies. Both of you together. Good morning," said O-Toki. She picked three cushions from the pile in the corner of the room, placed them on the woven tatami mats carpeting the room, and retreated toward the door. Her manner of placing the cushions, Kikuji observed, was very precise: he sat down quietly on the one nearest the door; his grandmother, although the retired lady, took the one in the center of the room; and his mother, though lady of the house, seated herself on the cushion which was least conspicuous. His grandmother curtly told O-Toki to leave, and, after the maid had slid the door shut behind her, turned to her grandson.

"Kiku-bon, aren't you playing around too much these days?" Her sharp eyes gleamed with curiosity under the still unwrinkled forehead. Perhaps, Kikuji thought, her smooth skin resulted from her daily use of the little red silk rubbing sack filled with perfumed rice grains. An imperial luxury. But his mother, as always, was picking up Grandmother Kino's opening, adding, "Of course, we know you're all grown up by now. But to anyone outside the family, you look like a hanger-on, a perfect lounge lizard. Surely, you can see this?"

Kikuji, without replying, adjusted the collar of his kimono unconcernedly. He stood with a relaxed grace almost girlish in its quality. Thick eyebrows and large eyes cut strongly across the long face, and his mouth was large and sensual.

"Quite apart from what we in the family may think," his mother went on, "it's not at all good to have our employees hearing about your playboy stunts."

Kikuji moved his lips slightly, as if intending to speak, but still said nothing.

Grandmother Kino went on to complete the analysis of his conduct as though delivering the *coup de grâce*. "I wouldn't mind if it were only a matter of splurging at restaurants and teahouses, but you are going in for womanizing, I hear, and it's most embarrassing. It affects the reputation of our family business. You simply must make up your mind either to stop playing around in this unseemly manner or else get married. I can't stand this kind of behavior any longer!"

Still Kikuji remained silent as a stone. He sat nonchalantly, cigarette in mouth, not exactly watching the faces of his grandmother and mother, but not looking away either.

"Kiku-bon! Are you listening to what we are saying?" Kino asked impatiently.

Kikuji nodded slightly.

"Then will you be so good as to give your opinion of this whole unpleasant matter?"

"My opinion?" Kikuji spoke for the first time, reluctantly. "It doesn't matter what I say. Isn't that so?"

He stretched wearily. At twenty-one he felt totally out of condition, slowed down by too many beers on too many nights.

"Are you complaining?" asked Grandmother Kino sternly, taking a long, slim pipe from her sleeve. But before a quarrel could develop, Sei exclaimed, "Mother! You'll get nowhere talking so impatiently to Kiku-bon." He always responds well if only you speak nicely to him."

"So! If I speak *nicely*. You have brought him up so peculiarly that I can't make him out. Is he a gentleman or a spoiled brat? I certainly didn't raise you in this muddled fashion, did I?"

"It's all right, Mother," Sei replied. "Kiku-bon, why don't you tell your grandmother you're sorry you were rude?"

Sei tried to smooth over the awkward situation by placing her

3

hand on his shoulder as though massaging it. Kikuji realized irritably that it was just a tactical gesture. In his early morning mood, he despised them from the depths of his being. They were not, he reflected, submissive bride and dominant mother-in-law, but mother and daughter. They worked together. Their pretense of restraining each other was too practiced and obvious for Kikuji not to recognize it. This sort of thing wasn't new. It was a standard mode of behavior for these two women of Kawachiya's. It was good for business.

The family enterprise had been in Osaka for many generations. Kawachiya Kihei, the founder, had come to Osaka as a peddler in 1765. He had obtained a job with a tabi wholesaler in the Motomachi District, and his employer had ultimately allowed him to go into business on his own by opening a store on West Yokobori Street. From that time on, the family had prospered. In 1830, however, a genetic difficulty peculiar to the Kawachiya line first made its appearance. The wife of Kawachiya Kihei III gave birth to a girl, Kino's mother. There were no other children. The family, acting in accordance with traditional practice in such a situation, selected for their daughter a husband from among the most diligent clerks in their employ. The groom gave up his name and much of his male dominance to become Kawachiya Kihei IV. His wife in turn gave birth to only one daughter, whom she named Kino. Sei likewise had been an only child, and her husband had been picked for her from among the most intelligent and hard-working clerks in the firm. In this manner, the family name had been perpetuated.

But Kikuji had been born into a matriarchy. Grandmother Kino and his mother shared the same attitudes. His father, Kawachiya Kihei VI, could not, even now at forty-eight, hold up his head with any dignity before Mother or Grandmother. When his grandfather, Kawachiya Kihei V, was still alive, Kikuji remembered hearing his father called by his real name, Isuke. In his old age, Grandfather, perhaps trying to forget his own humble origins, had not been at all sympathetic to Isuke, his adoptive son and Sei's husband. In Isuke's every effort to adapt, he saw his own humiliating past as in a mirror. Kikuji recalled that, ever since early childhood, he had been called Kiku-bon by his grandfather. The "bon," of course, was indicative of Kikuji's status as heir to the family business. But, although Grandfather always greeted the child with the suffix of dig-

4

nity and affection, he continued to address his adoptive son merely as Isuke. When in elementary school, Kikuji had been invited to visit a friend's house, and he suddenly realized that many of the modes of behavior in his own home were very strange. He asked his mother why this was so. She had replied, "Of course our way of living is much different from that of your friends. Both your grandmother and I are direct descendants in a line of distinguished merchants. Your father came here to work in our store, and he eventually became my husband, without, however, acquiring any ultimate control over the family's business. You are next in line to inherit ownership of our firm after me. That is why your grandfather calls you Kiku-*bon*, but continues calling your father merely Isuke, just as he used to call him when he was a promising young clerk in our firm."

The full implication of all this hadn't registered with Kikuji for a long time, and yet it had been apparent to him that everyone from Grandfather to Grandmother on down, including all the store employees, treated him with deference, and spoke to him always as Kiku-*bon*. By the time he had entered high school, he had begun to realize that Grandfather, though he persisted in calling Kikuji's father merely Isuke, was nevertheless very deferential toward Grandmother, and even toward Mother, who was, after all, his own daughter.

During Kikuji's third year in high school, a great-uncle, Grandfather's older brother, had come to visit them, bringing with him a large, ceremonial rice cake for the New Year holiday. He had been there once before when his nephew was in elementary school. Kikuji regarded this broad-shouldered, deeply tanned great-uncle as all-capable and ever-ready, a hero from the outside world of romance. He was said to be nearly seventy, but he seemed much more youthful and lively than Grandfather. He had noticed at the time that Grandfather for some reason hadn't welcomed his brother with much enthusiasm, even though he had come all the way from distant Wakayama. When he first arrived, Mother had greeted him very briefly, and then turned him over to the care of the chambermaid. When he went off one night to see the kabuki play in the Dotombori District, it was the maid who showed him how to get there.

To Kikuji, his uncle smelled of the sea. For a child never allowed to go into the offices of the store in the front of their house, who had lived largely in the company of his grandmother, his mother and their maids, the tales of this seaman were indescribably fascinating. One day he was lounging comfortably in his uncle's room, listening to lively yarns of fishermen throwing their nets at sea, when suddenly the door slid open revealing his mother.

"Good morning, Uncle. I thought I would stop by to see how you were making out," she said. "I'm sorry not to have done more to make you feel at home. But I've been so busy. You know how it is. If you want anything, though, just ask the maids. They'll take care of you." Then she turned carefully to her son and said, "Kiku-bon, I have some things I want you to take care of now."

This, he realized, was her real objective: to get him away from his uncle. The formal civilities were merely window dressing. But the old fisherman, if he noticed anything strained in her behavior, gave no sign.

"It is good of you to take care of me so nicely," he said. "This may be the last time I'll be able to visit your fine family. Our boy Kikuji has certainly grown tall, hasn't he?"

Put off by his unceremonious reference to her son as "our boy Kikuji," Sei replied stiffly, "We are glad to have had you with us. Kiku-*bon* has enjoyed it too. And now, shall we . . .?" She turned to Kikuji, expecting him to accompany her. But her distant manner with his uncle had offended the fifteen-year-old deeply.

"Thank you, Mother. I'll come later," he said firmly. "Uncle's stories about deep-sea fishing are far more interesting and educational than a lot of dull schoolbooks. And anyway, I've done my homework."

Sei's smooth white face reddened slightly. The door closed with a perceptible bang as she departed. That evening, Kikuji ate his supper in a strained atmosphere. His great-uncle had gone out for the evening, having been (fortunately, all things considered) invited to the home of an old friend who had grown up with him in Wakayama.

On the wooden floor of the kitchen in a space of about ten mats, individual trays with legs were placed for the highest ranking employees of the firm. Led by Wasuke, the manager, the chief clerks filed in in order of seniority and sat down on cushions. Before beginning to eat, they placed their hands on the floor, and, facing the raised and tatami-matted dining room of the Kawachiya family, chorused, "Our thanks to you for your many favors." After the senior employees had finished, the junior clerks came in, and, after them, the lowly apprentices, each group performing the same ritual before eating. When finished, each person took his tray to the kitchen sink on his way out.

In the family dining room, the menu was more elaborate, consisting of five courses. Kikuji, as he ate, noticed that a faint taste of fish lingered in his mouth. Much as he loved sliced raw fish, too much of a delicacy is still too much, and he had had more than his share during the last four days of the New Year holiday. How the apprentices would have loved it. From time to time during the meal, he cast a quick look at his grandmother. She sat moving her mouth to circulate the last of the tea around her false teeth, making more noise at it than usual. Now and again she looked severely at Grandfather. Could it be that she was angry because he ignored the problems brought on by his brother's visit?

"My dear, I understand that your brother has been telling his fish stories to Kiku-bon again."

"Um-humh."

"Please do not just say, 'Um-humh.' This is a serious matter! Your brother kept his hold on your son even after Sei went to get him. I should like to make clear that, since Kiku-bon is going to be the head of an important commercial house, there is no need to give him all this sardine-and-octopus talk!"

Grandfather had looked helplessly about him, not knowing what to say. Kikuji's father bowed his head and stared down at the table, avoiding Grandmother's eye.

"Surely, part of our agreement when you moved from the role of clerk to that of my husband was that you should see the members of your own family as little as possible? As I recall, your association with your kinfolk was to have been limited to paying your respects at the family grave once a year. No visits from fisherman brothers!"

Her tone was as sharp as a blow, but Grandfather just blinked his eyes meekly.

Suddenly, Kikuji threw his chopsticks onto his tray. "Grandma, you're crazy!" he shouted. But his grandfather had ignored the outburst, and, seated as he was, bowed low to his wife. "I must apologize for my brother from Wakayama," he said calmly. "He meant no harm. He's a very good-hearted sort, and his whole life has been fishing and the sea. He just got carried away in talking about it. It isn't worth fretting about, really. Try to forget it. You too, Sei. All right?"

The "you" he used to address his own daughter, Kikuji recalled, was the formal rather than the intimate pronoun. His manner of speaking to her was not that of father to daughter, but of subordinate to mistress.

"If you, my father, say so, I shall certainly go along," Sei had replied, and, catching her mother's eye, she nodded amiably. Then she turned to her husband, and said quietly, "I hope you've been paying attention to all this too, my dear. As with Father's family, so with yours, you know." Kikuji's father, who had hoped not to be drawn into the discussion, had nodded in embarrassment.

This was the family situation throughout Kikuji's boyhood. Three generations of matriarchal dominance had produced a domestic pattern in which the man of the house was in fact a mere servant to his wife, a stud.

In the year of Kikuji's graduation from high school, his grandfather had been paralyzed by a stroke, and his father became Kawachiya Kihei VI. But, although his title had changed, the family organization remained the same. Kihei was master only when he was attending to the firm's business in the offices at the front of the house. The little dyed curtain with the firm's insignia over the door marked the line of division between the place of business and the family's living quarters, and once his head brushed through it he reverted to his status of subordinate, and behaved with careful humility.

After Grandfather's death, Grandmother and Mother had suddenly begun to spend money very freely. Grandmother was fifty-three, but kept her head high, her fine, almond-shaped eyes flashing often with the special arrogance of the wealthy. Although austere, her face, with the hair drawn up tightly after the fashion of retired ladies, was striking. Sei too was beautiful, although her face was more rounded, and her mouth with its full lower lip gave her an expression of youthful innocence. Perhaps her special beauty was softer and less intense than her mother's because Kino had always been the cutting edge for the two of them. With such a defender to clear away difficulties, Sei could afford to seem the more gracious and easygoing.

8

The Great War in Europe had begun soon after Grandfather's death and the family business was more prosperous than ever before, but, as the ladies' shopping trips became more frequent, Kikuji's father had some difficulty in paying all the bills. When the deadline for payment came at the end of the month, Grandmother would say to him in unexpectedly soft and amiable tones, "Please, old dear, take care of the Kodaimaru bill for me, will you? Like a nice boy."

And he always answered, "Yes, Ma'am" from the latticed accounting room, and soon after sent payment. If it was not Grandmother, it was Sei. She came to him often with a pleasant, absent-minded expression on her face to tell him that she needed more money for household expenses. Always he gave without demanding any explanation. The two women always showed slight embarrassment, and phrased their requests with increasingly synthetic smiles, but Kihei with no expression at all on his face simply said, "Yes," and gave the money they asked for.

This was the image of his father which Kikuji had had from his earliest years until now. He was, he realized, witnessing the operation of a special Semba custom: it was not at all uncommon in this very tightly organized commercial area of Osaka, a world in itself, really, for the authority of the daughter of the house to exceed that of her adoptive husband. In the Semba money talked, and the trademark of a great commercial house was almost an imperial crest. In the case of Kikuji's own family, however, where daughter had succeeded daughter in matriarchal succession for three generations, the authority of the women had about it something mysterious, an almost divine sanction. It could not be questioned, since behind it lay nearly a hundred years of customary obedience.

Kikuji tended to regard his father as spineless and weak, and yet, mindful of family tradition, managed to keep his youthful feelings of revolt against the women's authority under control and hidden from their eyes. But, if there was no flame, the embers were always there, smoldering.

The sun went suddenly behind a cloud, and the room, never very bright, was darkened. Grandmother Kino and Sei remained sitting with the tigerish perseverance of the mature stalking the young, waiting for Kikuji's answer to their criticism of his conduct.

9

He turned at last toward them. "So what would you have me do?" he asked.

Sei beamed at him. "Get yourself a nice girl and get married," she said. "That's what we would have you do."

He looked at her in alarm, opened his mouth to speak, but what he said was not what he had intended. "A wife? In this house? *Another* woman? I don't see—" He stopped in confusion.

Kino looked at him, the forced smile of the professional plotter creasing the sides of her eyes, and said reproachfully, "Now, now, don't you say such a thing. You're a real catch for any girl. You're going to be head of this house. You just let us find you some young creature who'll keep you busy of nights so that you won't get tripped up by some shady lady. Eh?" She laughed, but her eyes were studying him with care. This was one of those piercing appraisals which the maids and apprentices had learned to fear. Kikuji felt suddenly beaten down. He wondered angrily who had told tales about his doings, and then bit his own tongue, realizing that it must have wagged once too often to someone who liked dealing in others' scandals.

It was when he was about to graduate from a business college two years before that he had begun to play around a bit. His studies hadn't taken up much of his time; whatever his grades, he was still destined to become the fifth master of Kawachiya's. He was among the lowest tenth of his class. He accounted for his neglect of studies by saying that the others needed a strong academic showing if they were to get jobs, and so he had considerately stepped out of their way.

His friends consisted mostly of the sons of long-established commercial families in the Semba. Initially, they had hung around the movie theaters and coffee shops in the Sennichimae or Dotombori Districts, but within a short time they were frequenting the Tobita, a section of town well known for its brothels. By the time he graduated, Kikuji knew, as he put it to his friends, what a girl was.

His school friend, Sasagawa Shigezo, who was heir to a lumber business, had first taken him to one of the houses in the Tobita District. Kikuji had been surprised to find that the girl he had selected was humbly attentive to his every wish. Grateful, he had paid her double the standard fee. The woman was overwhelmed at this generosity and gave herself to him freely from then on.

So Kikuji came to his unexpected discovery, a much greater revelation to him than to most boys. Raised by a grandmother who was routinely addressed as "my lady" and a mother who was constantly deferred to as "lady of the house," both of whom were regarded as unquestioned superiors by their employees as well as by their husbands, he felt dazed at having for the first time encountered a woman who behaved in quite a different way. In her world, he was master and she his willing servant.

But now he had been found out. It occurred to him that his friend, Sasagawa, who had initiated him into the mysteries of the Tobita District, was a loudmouth, and probably at least indirectly responsible for Grandmother and Mother finding out. Damn the man!

Kino and his mother sat with patient alertness awaiting his response to their suggestion. He decided to clear up any misapprehensions.

"You're telling me this because you've made a thorough investigation of all my activities this past year, isn't that right?"

His grandmother looked at him with faint amusement. "Yes, of course. We had to protect family interests—*your* interests." She tapped her pipe into the ashtray. "You must let us take charge from now on. A good marriage is the safest course for a boy like you."

Kikuji's silence was regarded as consent by the two women. From that day on, they frequently went out or were engaged in long conversations with visitors in the parlor. Among them was a woman of dark complexion around fifty with a pleasant air about her. She was Uchida Masa, and she was performing the office of go-between on behalf of the elder daughter of Takano Ichizo, a sugar wholesaler with a firm at Koraibashi. Ichizo was something of a legend in the Semba. By astute trading in sugar stocks, he had gone from the rank of a lowly apprentice to that of a rich and powerful merchant. Since 1914 his name had been included in every list of the very rich in Osaka. He naturally wished for a social position as firmly established as his fortune, and, to gain this, he wished to marry his two daughters off to sons of long-established commercial families with solid reputations. He had enough money; he sought now through his daughters to achieve respectability.

Uchida Masa proved so diligent in her visits to Kawachiya's that Kikuji wondered just how huge a fee Takano Ichizo must have promised her. The go-between, a well-esteemed retired lady from a very small house of notions wholesalers in the Horie District, started negotiations off skillfully by setting both Grandmother Kino and his mother on a pedestal, addressing them as "my lady" or "worthy madam" with every other sentence. Both the ladies grew visibly more refined each time Uchida Masa spoke with them, as though feeding on her constant respectfulness. In her professional capacity, she saw them as very special customers, since not only were they heiresses to considerable wealth, but the owners of an old, established firm which was both a steady source of income and a sign of exalted social status. Also, she shrewdly noted that these two still-beautiful women had been spoiled fairly completely as a result of being born into a family which for three generations had been a matriarchy. They were used to having their own way in everything. They kept reminding her of "the customs of the Semba," or "the ways of a Semba household." Uchida Masa's adroit stroking of their fur, however, converted their pride to a naive trust. When she sensed that she had them deeply involved, she said, "The Takano family, you must realize, is receptive to your every wish. They fully understand that their daughter is most fortunate to be received into a house with a tradition and reputation which money cannot buy."

She spoke persuasively, smiling pleasantly and rubbing her hands together in an almost supplicating manner. Both Kino and Sei were completely won over. The two women discussed the matter with each other as though Uchida Masa were not there in the room, listening.

"Then let us hold a *miai* for our son and the young lady to meet each other and talk things over," said Kino. "We can let the go-between take care of the details. She seems very well aware that the Takano daughter will be marrying our Kiku-bon because of the great name of our house, and she and her family will always have reason to feel gratitude and appreciation."

Sei agreed, and they gave their instructions to Uchida Masa to set up the *miai*.

Kikuji dutifully went to this premarital interview, and met Takano Hiroko for the first time. The meeting took place, as often was the case with such delicate arrangements, at the Nakaza Theater in the Dotombori District. It was a rainy day and the theater was not crowded. In seeming defiance of the weather, Hiroko wore a very elaborate kimono with long and full sleeves. He looked at her searchingly, but her face was as expressionless as a doll's. At the time, she was just twenty, almost two years younger than he.

Throughout the elaborate negotiations, the two ladies of the house never talked over the idea of prospective marriage with Kihei, Sei's adoptive husband and the master of the family business. When the wedding was almost at hand, they reported the substance of their planning to him, and then gave him a number of large bills which had accumulated in the course of their conferences and parleys. He took them and paid them without comment.

In October, the wedding took place at Naniwa Shrine, and the reception at the Shibau, a restaurant in Kitahama. Kikuji, though inexperienced in such matters, thought the reception magnificent in every way, and his judgement was confirmed when he overheard one of the waitresses saying to another, "These people must be made of money. Have you ever seen a fancier show?" There were two hundred guests, and each individual serving, he learned from his father, cost twenty yen. (At this time the train fare from Osaka to Hakodate in Northern Hokkaido was twenty-seven yen.) The expense had been divided according to the thrifty custom of the Semba: the groom's family paid sixty percent, the bride's, forty percent. The expensive reception had originally been suggested by the Takano family, and Kihei, who felt it to be extravagant, was initially reluctant to pay so much. But Kino and Sei angrily scolded him for his miserly attitude.

"How could we possibly play second fiddle to this newly rich fellow, this first-generation Semba success? No economizing! We'll outdo his most extravagant gesture with a more extravagant one, even if we have to sell one of our five storehouses to pay for it," Kino urged. Then she looked coldly at Kihei and said, "This is no marriage with an adoptive groom, I hope you realize."

In his usual taciturn and inscrutable fashion, Kihei counted out the money and gave it to the women.

As for Takano Ichizo, the bride's father, he was not trying to overawe them with his wealth. His carefree spending was a sign of his elation at joining his family by marriage to the name of a great firm with an illustrious tradition. The joyous event, however, was a prelude to much unhappiness for his daughter.

On the day set for inventorying the trousseau Kino carefully inspected the eleven wagonloads of boxes and chests of all sizes and descriptions which had come to the Kawachiya home. Then Sei turned to her new daughter-in-law. "Hiroko, is this all you have brought with you?"

"Yes, my lady," replied Hiroko, looking puzzled.

"Well, I'm sorry to say, it just won't do."

Hiroko paled, and sat silent, waiting.

"Of course, your folks have paid a fortune for all this stuff, but nowhere do I see any linen kimono or any of the thin, silk dress *haori* which in summer distinguish residents of the Semba from other people living in Osaka. You surely know that in the Semba it is the rule to have many changes of clothing for each season of the year? On June first we must have linen kimono, and you have none at all. On July first we are required by the custom of centuries to wear the thin, silk *haori*. And you have none of them either."

"I am very sorry, my lady," said Hiroko, bowing low, placing her hands before her on the floor. "I'll have someone bring them over right away."

But Kino wouldn't let her off so easily.

"I don't hold with last minute additions just tossed in any old way. Tonight, after the store closes, please have all this stuff taken back to your father's place, get him to supply a complete inventory, and return it to us in proper order. These things must be done right or not at all!"

Tears appeared in Hiroko's rounded eyes, and fell on her lap, but neither Sei nor Kino paid any attention as they left the room.

Kikuji at the time of this confrontation had been lounging in the living room, chatting with a former classmate of business college days. But he learned about it from Hiroko after going to bed. His young wife wept silently, her thin shoulders shaking, and she took some of the heavy quilt into her mouth to stifle the sobs. Several times during the night she said angrily through her tears, "All this fuss about changing clothes, changing clothes! The custom of centuries! Can it be so important?"

Kikuji was surprised to find that Hiroko, despite her frail appearance, was in actuality a person of strong temperament. As he felt her restless body tossing next to him, he sensed a strange chill entering him from the contact of his skin with hers. He felt goose pimples under his newly sewn night kimono. This unpleasant sensation,

14

he thought, must surely be a portent of strife between his wife and the other two ladies of the gloomy old house in the Semba. Nor, as events soon made clear, was he mistaken. Difficulties arose from all sorts of small problems. In early December, two months after their wedding, Hiroko was directing the maids in preparing dinner for the employees. The menu called for a stew of turnips and fried tofu. As she was adding seasoning to the large, five-gallon pot of turnips, she noticed the scent of perfume. Startled, she looked behind her and saw her mother-in-law at her elbow.

"Oh, Mother Sei. Excuse me for not seeing you," she stammered. "I was just preparing—" Her voice trailed away. Wiping her hands on her apron, she bowed low to her mother-in-law. The perfume came from Sei's newly done hairdo, a coiffeur looped impressively in the *marumage* style of married ladies. She looked into the large container.

"Who cut the turnips into such big, round pieces?" she asked severely.

Onatsu, the kitchenmaid, said mindlessly, "The one who cut the turnips? I did, my lady."

"And why did you make the pieces so big?" pursued Sei. "You are expected to cut food into small bits in this house. Don't you know that?"

"Yes, my lady. But the young mistress said this would be more appetizing, and so—" Onatsu was just sixteen, and anxious to please.

Sei's finely formed face under the stately hairdo took on a grim look. "The young mistress said you should do it that way?" She paused, then turned to Kikuji's wife. "Hiroko, surely you didn't tell her to cut the turnips into chunks that big?"

"Well, yes. I did tell her," she replied softly.

"But why?"

"I thought that larger pieces looked more appetizing and tasted better."

"Please keep in mind from now on that for our employees the appearance of quantity is more important than the taste. They find it much more satisfying to see lots of small bits on a dish than just a few big chunks. I do hope you can get it right in the future. If you can't conform in matters of this sort, I simply do not see how you can be regarded as part of a long-established family such as ours. Newly rich people, I realize, often manage things in this helter-skelter fashion. We never do. We have our house rules, and they cover just about everything, even the slicing of potatoes and turnips. You must learn our ways if you are ever to become in reality the young mistress of this house."

She turned away so quickly that the inner hems of her kimono fluttered, and she had left the kitchen before Hiroko could muster a reply. After her imposing figure had disappeared, Hiroko plunged the blade of the large vegetable knife into the boiling stew, trying to slice the large pieces of turnip into the traditional small bits. Onatsu rushed to her and cried, "Ah, mistress. You'll hurt yourself. Do be careful!" But, blinded with tears and indignation, she kept stabbing ineffectively at the turnips bobbing on the boiling surface of the stew.

Just before dinnertime, she signaled to Kikuji, who had returned from an afternoon's work in the offices at the front of the house, to join her in his room. She told him about the encounter with Sei in the kitchen.

"Your father is such a nice man," she said finally. "He never complains, and always manages to keep everything going smoothly. Even back here." She motioned toward the family living quarters. "But I can't stand your grandmother and your mother! Goodness knows, I've tried. But they keep on telling me the custom of the centuries for everything down to how to cut up a turnip. They dress every sneeze in some Semba ritual. How can I retain my sanity in such an atmosphere? I can't eat a thing tonight. They never rest from disliking me. I almost wish I could—" But she stopped in mid-sentence, realizing the danger of telling her husband that she wished she could go home.

Some months later, Hiroko became aware of more strange behavior on the part of the two ladies of the house. What ancient Semba ritual would they invoke to justify themselves this time? Over a period of weeks she had come to notice that every time she used the toilet, either Sei or Kino would soon after go into the restroom and remain there for a long time. Suddenly, a suspicion came to her which made her cheeks flame red. No. They had their bizarre customs, but they were not animals. She put the thought out of her mind. But the suspicion kept returning with ever-increasing sharpness. She decided to test it.

On a cold February day, when Kino had her sliding door open to

16

let the charcoal fumes escape from her room, and could see down the hall toward the restroom, Hiroko, hunched over as though in pain, went along the hall, entered the toilet chamber and closed the sliding door. After a lengthy interval, she left, banging the panel shut as she came out. Then she walked slowly around the hall corner, out of sight of Kino's room, but still within view of the restroom door. Instead of going to her room as Kino would expect, she remained there in the dark corner of the hall, waiting, hardly daring to breathe. Soon she heard the shuffle of tabi on the wooden floor, and Kino came up the hall to the restroom entrance. She looked around to be sure that no one was in sight, and then picked a branch of hemp palm from the courtyard garden before entering the toilet chamber and closing the door. Quickly and silently, Hiroko went to the entrance panel and, holding her breath, slid it open a crack. There was Kino, her back to the door, bending over the toilet, covering her nose with one hand and with the other holding the stick and probing the bucket of excrement under the toilet seat.

Hiroko boldly slid the door wide open.

"Eh? What—" Kino looked back, startled for an instant. Then she tried to make the best of a bad situation. "Surely you know better than to open the restroom door without knocking! Where is your sense of etiquette in these matters?"

Hiroko looked at her squarely for an instant, then said with assurance, "Excuse me. But I sensed that you were in some unusual predicament. May I assist you?"

Kino laughed nervously. "The older I get, the more visits I make to this place. And then, of course, it's chilly today, don't you think? Well, and so I came here to relieve myself, and somehow dropped my purse into the privy. So I'm looking for it. Do you see?"

"Yes. I see." With the confidence of one who knows she has the advantage, she continued, "Please go back to your room, my lady, and rest. I will take care of this."

"Yes. Yes. Perhaps that would be best," answered Kino. "But be sure you look carefully for it. And remember what I said about knocking on the door in the future." Kino left without so much as a backward glance.

Hiroko drew out the branch Kino had left. At its tip was the red-stained bit of toilet paper which Hiroko had used a short time before. Her suspicion had not been too outlandish. These women were

17

determined to control every intimate detail of her life. With insatiable curiosity, they had wished to determine if she had become pregnant, and had spied on her revoltingly to find out.

Nearly blinded by her embarrassment and humiliation, she tottered into Kikuji's room and collapsed on the tatami mat in front of him. Her husband was startled and put his arms around her to support her.

"What *is* the matter? What has happened?"

Impeded by tears and embarrassment, she managed to tell him what had occurred. But Kikuji wasn't much help. He was so disgusted that he could find no words to express himself. That his mother and grandmother, dressed as always in their magnificent silks and fragrant with rare perfumes, should strip off all normal human decency and behave little better than beasts was impossible for him to grasp fully. And in his eyes she could see that there was nothing more to be done about the matter.

Though the long rainy season was supposed to have ended some weeks before, it had been raining off and on for the last three days. Even the earth inside the hedge and under the eaves was wet. And when wet, far from cooling off, the ground seemed to give off hot vapors. Inside the house, it was humid and stuffy.

The weather fitted Hiroko's mood. She felt completely apathetic as she sat watching the gloomy, windless courtyard where every leaf of every tree was frozen in dreamlike stasis. She was conscious again of the bitter taste in her mouth which she had been noticing for the past several weeks. And once more she felt a twinge of nausea.

Kikuji was working constantly in the front offices, but, whenever he could manage time off, he came back to her room to have tea with her. When he appeared this hot afternoon, she had a special sweet which he liked, called "Night-blooming Plum." She had gone to Tsuruya Hachiman Sweet Shop to get it for him. Unlike most sake drinkers, Kikuji couldn't do without sweets.

Hiroko tried to put the sweet bean paste into her mouth, but found the exertion in the thick heat almost too much. She looked down at her hands in her lap, and said in a low voice, "I guess it's time to tell you, Kikuji. I am going to have a baby." Her face was a deep red.

"A baby, you say? Really!" Kikuji didn't quite seem to be taking it all in. He too was deadened by the heat. Her blushing face made her seem elated, and yet, as he studied her eyes, he realized that she was frightened. "What's the matter?"

"Let me go home to have the baby."

"But why?"

"I don't know what might go wrong in this house," she replied. "I don't know how to have a baby in accordance with the custom of the Semba. This place isn't right for a baby. The way they wax the hallway, I might slip and kill both myself and the baby!"

Kikuji made a reproachful clucking noise. "You feel persecuted, and that makes you see things wrong. Look at it this way: that unpleasant business in the toilet may simply have been the result of Grandmother's and Mother's envy of you, a younger woman, who could still have children—"

Hiroko flared up. "I can think of no more loathsome an attitude than that! You can't explain them away. I wish you could. In this matter you must do as I say. For the next two or three months I am going to tie my waistband in such a way as to hide my condition. When the sixth month comes around, I shall return home, pretending that I have caught an infection of some sort. Do you understand?"

She was tense and haggard with fear, and reluctantly he agreed. Next day, telling Sei and Kino that they were going to the theater, he took Hiroko to the doctor's office for the initial consultation. Since the episode of the toilet, he had been compelled continually to choose between his wife and the two ladies of his family. Kino and Sei, since being found out by Hiroko, had been cautious and distant. Hence they did not detect her condition. Hiroko, moreover, was remarkably skillful in concealing her increasing girth.

In December, her sixth month, Hiroko pleaded illness and remained in bed most of the time. The doctor gave in to Kikuji's insistence, and allowed him to report that Hiroko was suffering from a recurrence of an old kidney ailment. Learning of her illness, Sei and Kino became thoughtful, and paid her many visits. They came always very silently along the polished wooden floor of the hall, and slid open the doors very suddenly. She on her part was always listening. When she caught the faint sibilance of tabi softly moving in the hallway, she would pull the heavy quilt up to her chin and close her

19

eyes. After two weeks of thus outwitting the two keen-eyed ladies of the house, Hiroko went back to the home of her father and mother.

A few days after her departure, Kikuji told his grandmother and mother that Hiroko's kidney infection had been brought on by pregnancy. When she heard this, Kino's eyebrows went up in astonishment.

"Well! She pulled the wool over our eyes. And we had a right to know! How long has this great actress been performing her play?" In her great irritation, she clacked her false teeth about in her mouth.

Sei was equally uncompromising. "Our family tradition requires that the birth must take place in the room where our ancestors are enshrined. At that time the bride's mother is welcome to join us. But to think that she didn't even tell us—" She broke off and bit her lip.

In their anger at being tricked by Hiroko, they remained ominously silent. The apprentices who came every ten days from Hiroko's house to report on her progress were sent away without any tip. The baby which was soon to come was never mentioned by the ladies. One day O-Toki, the chambermaid, seeing the two in a good mood, said carefully, "Some of the seamstresses are not busy now. Shall we sew some clothes for the baby?"

Sei looked at her. "That is a matter for us to decide. You will please keep your nose out of it!"

O-Toki retreated in distress.

The child was born on March third, the day of the Doll Festival honoring all young girls. It was a boy. As soon as Kikuji, at work in the firm's offices, heard the news by phone, he went rushing to his father.

"It's a boy! It's a boy, Father! He knew what he wanted! He decided to be born even if it *was* Girls' Day!" Kikuji was very excited.

Kihei, balancing accounts in the latticed business office, looked up with a sudden smile so big that the corners of his eyes were creased. He looked much older than his fifty years.

"I am so glad for you, my son. Now we have an heir for the family name." He looked toward the curtain over the doorway leading to the living quarters and made a gesture with his head, motioning Kikuji to go in and inform his mother and grandmother. Kikuji nodded, and the small curtain brushed his head as he went to tell the ladies the good news. But Sei was not in her room. Walking across the outside courtyard, he reached the detached rooms of his grandmother. He stopped abruptly. Through the glass door panels he could see that they had unrolled a pure red carpet right across the room. On the exhibit shelf of the art alcove, they were setting up the dolls for the Girls' Festival. Both women were elaborately dressed in woven silk kimono. Kino had her hair arranged in the style of an elder woman, with a tortoise-shell ornament. Sei's hair was done with equal care in the *marumage* style of the younger matron. They had placed five different dishes on the red doll table which they had set up in the display area. They offered each other sweet wine in small red ceremonial cups. As they drank it, they looked at one another and giggled. In half-fantasy, they were playing at dolls; more seriously, they were expressing by means of the festival their hopes and prayers for a girl. Kikuji stood looking as the spring sun cast its light on the red carpet and on the two women, one sixty, the other forty, innocently playing with dolls as young girls might do at the festival. He did not dare slide open the glass door without warning. He retreated a little and made a noise. From inside came a soft call.

"Who's there? Is it you, Kiku-bon?" It was Sei's voice.

"Yes, Mother." He opened the door and entered the room. "The baby has been born. I just received the phone call."

Kino and Sei looked at him in suspense. They wished to appear calm, but could not quite manage it.

"And—? Did you—did you find out what sex the child is?" asked Kino.

"Yes, I did." He took a deep breath. "It's a boy."

There was a long silence. Finally Kino flexed her eyebrow and laughed discordantly. "What would you expect? An unmannerly boy who gets himself born on Girls' Day just to spite us the more!"

"Well, there's the answer to our prayers," said Sei, absent-mindedly staring at the festival dolls.

As he looked at the two women, Kikuji suddenly remembered his old nurse, O-Ushi. She had taken full charge of him from earliest infancy on through primary school. Even when he had gone to kindergarten, she hadn't left him. While he folded colored paper at his tiny desk, she would crouch watchfully behind the desk. No matter how many times the teacher told her that attendants should wait outside the classroom, O-Ushi stayed near her young master. She

21

said that if he ever cut his fingers on the scissors or tore a fingernail on the large blocks the children tumbled about, she would never be able to forgive herself. Kikuji had been greatly embarrassed by this faithfulness, and the other children in the class had made fun of him, calling him "Nurse-child," "Nurse's Pet," and other still less pleasant names.

He recalled especially a time when he must have been about six years old. It was the evening of the Summer Lantern Festival, and he noticed that O-Ushi, dressed in her light kimono, was crying silently.

"What's the matter, O-Ushi?" he asked.

Her crying became a wail. Finally, she managed to speak.

"Oh, young master. You are the heir of a great family. And yet, even at festival time, when everyone else is putting out lanterns for each boy in the family, even then the two respected ladies of the house do not celebrate their good fortune in having such a nice boy." She wiped her eyes with her handkerchief, and blew her nose. "I know I shouldn't be saying so, but the respected ladies of the house are a strange lot. But excuse me. My tongue runs away with me. I was just talking to make a noise."

He knew vaguely what the lanterns were which she had been talking about. At the time of the Summer Festival, he had noticed that the lanterns had been hung, one for each son, in front of the heavy curtain dyed with the family crest distinguishing each storefront. But they hadn't made much of an impression on him until O-Ushi spoke because he seldom left his home during festival time except to make a visit to the local shrine at night, accompanied by Sei, Kino, and all the household servants. Then he realized that other boys in the neighborhood set great store by the Summer Festival lanterns, and counted them carefully as they swayed in the wind over each doorway. But at the door of his family's store, there was no lantern in front of the dyed family crest.

O-Ushi on another occasion moved close to him and whispered in his ear in a breath smelling heavily of tobacco, "Bon-bon, when you were born, your respected mother, I've been told, carried on like a crazy woman because she hadn't produced a girl. Your family is just upside down from all other families, that's the way it is."

The spring after that, O-Ushi suddenly left the Kawachiya family. Her place was taken by her divorced daughter, O-Toki.

22

Now he remembered O-Ushi's words about his mother's strange behavior at the time of his birth. It was as though he were seeing the film of the past unreel all over again as he watched their bitter reception of the news that his son had been born. His knees shook, and he walked unsteadily along the corridor after closing the door on his mother and grandmother.

When he came back to the store, his father, as usual, was in the accounting room, bent over his abacus. Noticing Kikuji, he raised his head, and widened his eyes in silent question, "How did it go?"

"They didn't seem very happy."

Kihei sighed and put down the abacus. "Too bad, too bad," he said softly. "Not all things go as they have planned."

"They seem to have had their hearts set on another heiress," said Kikuji.

Kihei looked silently at his son, then nodded. He picked up the abacus again, gave it a click or two, then looked up at Kikuji once more. "You must go to your wife and son. Now! Don't hang around here."

Kikuji suddenly felt suffocated in the house. He had an apprentice bring him his wooden clogs at the entrance of the store and asked him to call a taxi. He went outside, got into the cab, and was driven slowly off. The road from West Yokobori was about twenty-four feet wide, and it went straight to Imabashi, the eastern section of town. On both sides of the road were the storefronts so typical of the Semba District: low, one-story structures, side by side, extending far back, with the family quarters at the rear. Fencing each house off from the road were the unpainted lattice fences that traditionally marked these long-established commercial houses. Inside his own family's store, as in most of the others he looked at as he drove past, the merchandise was piled high, and clerks were working busily counting and storing the various bales.

Behind each of these facades of business respectability was there a home life essentially like his? Were all Semba commercial families regulated by customs unknown to the rest of the nation? In this area, bounded by the four rivers, did the heavy traditions accumulate like silt at the river mouth, eventually burying all normal human impulses under the heavy weight of dead custom? With such thoughts weighing on his mind, Kikuji went to visit his wife and son.

In the inner room of the Takano house, as he tiptoed softly in, he saw the baby sleeping quietly beside Hiroko. It had fine black hair, and the eyebrows on its tiny wrinkled face were firmly marked. Hiroko saw him kneeling beside her looking at the baby.

"Well, my dear, I have given you a boy." She was moved by her words, and tears came to her eyes. She shifted the position of the child so that he could see it more clearly. He understood how proud she was. In the Semba generally, a son is thought a great asset to a commercial family, a crown prince in a merchant dynasty. Hence their bragging lanterns in the Summer Festival. Kikuji smiled gently at her, concealing the apprehensions in his heart.

"Thank you, Hiroko. I am very proud. And I'm relieved that you came through it without any trouble." He reached for her hand, stroked it and kissed it.

"Hisajiro" was the name he selected for the boy. When grown, he would sooner or later succeed to the ownership of the Kawachiya enterprises, and at that time would become Kihei VIII. So Kikuji didn't worry too much about the name. Hiroko wanted something more exotic as a name for her first child, but she too realized that, whatever they called him, he was really still another Kihei.

A month later, Hisajiro was brought back to Kawachiya House in the arms of his nurse, accompanying Hiroko. The nurse, Tome, was from Nara. She had been selected by Hiroko's parents. As soon as she sat down in the inner room, her good-natured face softened, and she held the baby toward Sei.

"Hisa-bon, this is your real home. Say hello to your Grandma," she said, smiling.

Sei looked appraisingly at the child held in Tome's extended arms, and said without interest, "He takes after his mother."

Kino initially did not even come in for a look. But Tome reported to Hiroko and Kikuji that, when they were not around, she had come in to look at her great-grandson, and had tried to talk to him, saying, "Poor little Hisa-bon. Even if you are a boy, your face is delicate and gentle like a girl's." And she then played with his tiny hands. This was the first of a number of visits to the baby by Kino.

Three months after Hiroko returned with the baby, Sei and Kino suggested divorce. With the start of July, Hiroko went to Naniwa Shrine to offer prayers, as was usual at the first of each month. With her went Tome, carrying Hisajiro. Kino and Sei had completed their visit to the shrine earlier. When they were sure that Hiroko had left, they summoned Kikuji to the inner room. They looked, he thought, very cool and elegant in their summer kimono, now that the monthly change in wardrobe had taken place.

Kino came directly to the point as soon as Kikuji was seated. "Kiku-bon, I have been wanting to discuss this matter with you for some time," she said. "But I haven't had time. Now that the seasonal wardrobe change is finished, I am free. So I want to tell you. Your mother and I have decided that Hiroko should go back home."

"You want—what?" exclaimed Kikuji, pretending a surprise he did not feel. He remembered too well Hiroko's passionate statement, "I cannot stand your grandmother and your mother!" followed by her half-spoken wish to go back to her family home permanently.

"I know you're not going to like this," continued his grandmother matter-of-factly, "but, since she cannot follow the established Semba customs, there is nothing else to do." Kino was not arguing so much as stating the law. Hiroko had broken it. Hiroko must go. It was very clear, very simple.

Sei filled in the particulars.

"It isn't that we don't like the girl. It's not that she's not bright or hasn't a good disposition. She's a good girl. But she can't possibly adapt herself to our ways." She paused for a moment, waiting for her words to sink in.

"The day before yesterday, which was the day for the monthly clearing of accounts, the uniform she gave the apprentice who was to make the rounds to collect on the various outstanding bills was all wrong."

"All wrong?" repeated Kikuji dully.

"All wrong!" his mother insisted. "A beginning apprentice, a boy under sixteen, wears, you will remember, an outfit of plain striped cotton. The full apprentice, on reaching the age of sixteen, is given a much better uniform. She confused the two outfits, and sent the unskilled boy off in a uniform always reserved for the fully trained workman. What were our customers to think, now, I ask you? She had overturned the custom of centuries. Our major clients, on seeing the fellow in the wrong outfit, must simply have laughed at him. We were made ridiculous! Ask anybody. Confusing uniforms in this independent and even obstinate way undermines the reputation of Kawachiya's. We can no longer entrust her with our good name." She reasoned the matter out with the calmness of a logician.

Kikuji already knew about the uniform mix-up. Hiroko had told him about it that evening, just after it had happened. She said that she had inquired of Sei as to the proper uniform for the boy who did the bill collecting, and that Sei had not mentioned that there were separate uniforms for the two kinds of apprentice.

"Did you make sure that she knew about the proper outfit for the apprentice doing the collecting?"

"Why, of course." Sei looked at him closely, narrowing her eyes. "Ah! So she has talked to you about this catastrophe and is trying to place the blame on your old mother."

"No," said Kikuji hastily. "But, Mother, you make too much of this. Our customers surely were not upset because of a slight discrepancy in a uniform. The world won't come to an end if all apprentices wear the same outfit."

"My world would," his mother replied angrily. " 'Slight discrepancy' indeed! She has been giving you these notions. She talks like an anarchist. 'Slight discrepancy'! She is not fit to be the mistress of our fine old house. We have gone on now many generations, but only by being tough and practical. Be sensible, Kikuji. We have our heir now. We no longer need her. She must leave."

He shook his head as though to rid it of confusion. "I just don't understand you. Now that she has produced an heir, you are ready to discard her, like something that has been used up."

"Exactly so! We brought in an outsider for just that purpose, didn't we? And now we have the successor to the family line. I would have infinitely preferred a girl, but one can't have everything in this life, and I've got used to one man-child, so maybe I'll learn to get used to still another. But do be realistic, Kiku-bon, my dear. It takes a certain kind of fierce watchfulness to keep an ancient name spotless. That name is a shield and protection to us who bear it. It gives us our wealth and our reputation, and we can depend on it, generation after generation, as long as we serve it well. And so, to protect our name, she must go."

Kikuji sat looking into space. The interior of the house was completely quiet. The sounds of daily business taking place in the offices of the store at the front of the house did not reach the inner rooms.

Kino's high-pitched voice broke the stillness, but he paid no attention. It would be more of the same. He was feeling the weight and stillness of the house, the undeviating pressure of three generations of women building opinion into custom and custom into law. The darkly shimmering posts of the inner room, polished each morning with the juices from tofu, took the full heaviness of the one-hundred-and-fifty-year-old house upon themselves. Sometimes the posts would shift infinitesimally, and the whole house would groan and creak. He too felt the enormous weight of the old house on his shoulders, and, whenever he shifted his ideas or attitudes, no matter how slightly, there were groans and sighs. The blood and sweat of three generations of industrious and ambitious women had permeated every corner of the house.

The musty smell of female domination deadened Kikuji's senses. Had he ever really escaped from the womb? Was he not even now being slowly strangled by an invisible umbilical cord? He felt himself soiled, diminished, unable to breathe. He bowed his head to conceal the tears in his eyes.

"It shall be as you wish," he said, with the simplicity of total surrender. "We will send her back to her home."

Despite the heat of early August, Takano Ichizo, fat though he was, did not seem to be sweating as he sat on his cushion next to Uchida Masa waiting for the discussion to begin. The go-between was silent, motionless, her bony face masklike in its severity. They had come to take Hiroko home. The divorce arrangements were almost complete. The two sat facing Kino, Sei, and Kikuji in a room which had been opened to the inner courtyard in the hope of catching any stray breeze. Kihei, on learning of the meeting, had gone off to a business conference, saying that, since they hadn't consulted him on any aspect of the marriage before now, he saw no reason why he should get involved at this crucial time.

Kino and Sei held their heads high and tried to achieve a kind of remote, aristocratic courtesy. Everyone was uneasy. Sei smiled amiably at her guests.

"It was good of you to come on such a very hot day. Please try one of our fans to cool off," she said, more stiffly than she had intended. Then she paused, not quite knowing how to start the meeting to the best advantage.

27

Kikuji sat with his head bowed and eyes downcast. After a time, he began to look absently out at the inner courtyard. No one said anything. It was too hot even for polite conversation. The sun shone oppressively down on the courtyard. The dusty leaves of the bushes in the garden looked parched. The pond in the center reflected the light blindingly. All the bustle of the street outside with its cries of peddlers seemed suddenly lost in the stillness of the terribly hot midday.

Takano Ichizo moved his plump frame uncomfortably and read-justed his feet. Then he took a deep breath and began to say what he had prepared carefully beforehand.

"I have received a detailed report concerning the difficulties of this marriage from Mrs. Uchida, our go-between." He gave a har-ried look at the two ladies of the house. "I feel that I must say that, if you had given any other reason than the one which you did give for dissolving the marriage of these two young people, I would have questioned your wisdom. They seemed to me very well matched." And he gave a deep sigh before going on. "As a businessman I know the great importance one must attach to keeping the name of the firm unblemished. Since somehow, without intending to, my daugh-ter has so conspicuously failed to adapt herself to the customs of your house that she has damaged your reputation—well, what can I say? I am very sorry this has happened. But I love my daughter and will certainly take her back."

Having finished his speech, Takano Ichizo perspired profusely, and fanned himself vigorously.

Kino nodded in gracious approbation. Things were going well, she thought.

"It is good of you to see our point so readily," she said. "We are, of course, concerned for our continuing reputation, and, as the unfor-tunate incident with the apprentice's uniform shows, your daughter just can't, I'm afraid, conform to our ways and needs. But I do hope you'll understand that this is not a case of a dictatorial mother-in-law tormenting the bride of her son from motives of jealousy. In every other way she's a very pleasant young lady, this daughter of yours. I'm sorry she can't bend and adapt more, but we all have our weak points, now, don't we?"

She glanced at Sei, who picked up the refrain.

"Yes, it's just as Mother says. It breaks my heart to have to make this decision. I came to it most unwillingly. If it were only my convenience to be affected, I wouldn't raise a finger. But it's our customers who have had to suffer from our mix-up, and that, I am afraid, is contrary to the centuries-old tradition of our house. Do you see what I mean?" And she leaned forward toward the old man beseechingly, her brows contorted with the distress of her unpleasant duty.

Kikuji fixed his eyes on his mother as she spoke. These two hunters, he thought, have trapped poor Hiroko without a single regret, and now they put on this absurd play for the benefit of the Takano family so that Hiroko will be blamed for causing our separation and divorce. But he said nothing, and once more studied the two women. They sat, confident now, the only ones in the room not crumpled and sweating, cool and resplendent in their well-pressed summer kimono secured with the crisp Hakata waistband.

Takano Ichizo moved restlessly again. "Yes, yes, of course," he said. "Even we relative newcomers to the business scene, without any very old tradition to protect, understand that a firm must safeguard its reputation. Oh, my, yes." And he gulped down the already cold Uji tea at one swallow, as though to conclude matters.

But Uchida Masa, silent up to this point, now put her hands on her knees and leaned forward assertively.

"I'd be dense in the head not to see what the respected ladies are getting at: the bride did not fit in with the traditions of this distinguished Semba family. That I can understand. Such adaptations are not easy. That is why I asked you to teach this young Hiroko. I told you and you knew anyway that she was not born into the Semba, although her father came to it later. Even without teaching I thought her very willing, and I cannot for the life of me understand—"

But Sei interrupted her excitedly. "Who *told* you we didn't try to help her? At every turn! Has she been talking? Is this what she says of us?" She stared formidably at Uchida Masa. "Well, just you let me tell *you* a thing or two—"

But Kikuji cut in on her. "I—I understand, Mrs. Uchida, how you feel. But it's already finished. For Hiroko's sake and for mine, please let us not continue this meaningless autopsy. You want to know whose fault it was. It was my fault. I was supposed to have protected her—"

There was a pause. Uchida Masa then nodded slowly.

"Very well," she replied. "If you, Kiku-bon, take the blame, there is nothing more to be said. But," she frowned angrily, "I shall never again act as go-between for any family of the Semba District. With all your money and your old reputations, you ought to provide good mates for boys or girls of suitable family. But no outsider can ever be accepted by you. You are the ones who are rigid and incapable of adapting. If the poor creature breaks a chopstick you act as though the end of the world had come. Rules and customs are to help people in their dealing with each other, not to kill them!"

Kino delicately tapped her thin gold pipe with her hand, and said absent-mindedly, "Is that so?"

Uchida Masa stared at her. "And that's all you can say? A fine young girl is tortured throughout two years of marriage, and then, after she has given her husband an heir, she is simply dumped, thrown out, discarded. And the two of you who do this sit there so cool, so immaculate. It is incredible! Never have I come across such insensitivity! But, of course, I am not a native of the Semba." And she mopped her hot red face with her handkerchief.

"Who are you calling insensitive, you old bag, you!" snapped Kino, putting aside her pipe. "I'll tell you a thing or two—"

"Please, ladies, please!" said Takano Ichizo loudly. "We have already finished our business. Please do not make this more painful by emotional talk. It won't change a thing. So let me take my daughter home."

Kikuji stood up abruptly. "I'll get Hiroko," he said, and then left quickly.

She was in her room, staring blankly out the window. The leaves of the trees outside reflected a greenish tint on the whiteness of her kimono. Seeing Kikuji, she started and squinted for an instant as though looking into a sudden glare.

"Is the discussion in the inner room finished yet?" she asked. At his nod, she went on, "Then let me leave now." She put her hands on the floor and bowed toward him. Her shoulders seemed thinner than they had a few months before. He felt the sudden impulse to take her in his arms. But recollection of the scene he had just left restrained him.

He thought of their last night together, just before this morning's horrible meeting. Her verdict on his behavior had been no less final and crushing than Uchida Masa's judgement of the two ladies. Following long conversation within the hot, airless mosquito netting, they had fallen silent, weary of talk which led nowhere. After a while, Hiroko spoke in a small, faraway voice: "When a man is twenty-four, he is supposed to be fully grown and mature. But you have been raised in a bon-bon way, Kiku-bon. Though you seem resourceful and dependable as far as anyone can see, yet, when strength is called for, you are suddenly very vulnerable and frail. You are a Semba bon-bon."

"A Semba bon-bon," repeated Kikuji thoughtfully. "Bon means one who is resourceful, a manager, a person of great potential. But in French a bonbon is a soft, sweet sort of candy, I think. Surely one can't be both vigorous and soft at the same time?"

"In the Semba, one can."

As he looked back over their marriage, he realized that he had never defended Hiroko against the constant pressure of Sei and Kino's hostility. He had let the inexperienced girl fend for herself. He felt sorry for her, and very guilty. And yet, and yet— He had been with her a mere two years, and, because of family demands, it had not been a time of harmony. The bond between them had been too fragile. It is easier to depend childishly on someone than manfully accept responsibility for another. Was it that? She had leaned on him, and he had not been strong enough to help. Semba bon-bon! Was his feeling for her to be thus easily extinguished?

"I couldn't help it," he said in a low voice, more to himself than to her. From across the hall he could hear the crying of five-month-old Hisajiro, whom Hiroko would leave behind. He watched her face become keenly attentive on hearing the noise, but then Tome's low, soothing voice, pacifying him, sounded, and Hiroko said nothing. Tome, who was being left behind, was a good nurse, and she trusted her.

He knelt on the tatami mat in front of her. "Hiroko—forgive, forgive—" he said, his voice trailing off.

She nodded coolly, and turned her eyes away. He saw aloofness in her every gesture, in the rigidity of her posture, in her eyes, which looked at him now only to measure him. It was the same coolness he had seen in her last night. He knew now that she had already left him. The physical departure was but the drab completion of a profound inward abandonment. She didn't touch him, look to him in her need, or even want him. This rejection hurt him, and he tried once more to explain what he didn't understand himself.

"This is a wrangling of three women! How can a man disentangle it all? The emotions of women fighting among themselves are very hard for anyone to deal with. If I had stood out against Kino and Sei, do you think it would've made any difference? One can't fight them and their three centuries of tradition. Twenty-four years of life isn't enough to do much good, you know."

Again she nodded disinterestedly.

"You and I can do nothing, don't you see? And even Grandmother and Mother aren't entirely responsible. It was the way they were brought up: to worship the family firm as though it were a nation or a kingdom requiring their absolute loyalty. That's the way it is, don't you see?"

Just then there was the sound of feet moving softly along the corridor. It was Sei. Looking in at the door, she said to Hiroko, "Your father is waiting for you."

"Mother! For God's sake, leave us alone," Kikuji exclaimed.

She stared at him for an instant, offended, and then walked off in small, rapid steps, returning to the living room.

Hiroko, however, waited no longer. She quickly went to the open door of the room in which her father and the go-between sat, along with Kino and Sei, in silence. She knelt by the open door, and, turning to the ladies, said, "I am sorry that I have been unable to fulfill your expectations. Please take good care of Hisajiro." It was a speech of formal politeness. She bowed so that her forehead touched the tatami; as she raised her head she looked quickly at Kikuji. There were tears brimming in her eyes for the first time since last night. She had wanted to leave without shedding one tear, but the consciousness of all that she was leaving hit her forcefully now, and she wept quietly. Kikuji suddenly realized that by her coolness she had been striving for control over her emotions.

At that point, she stood up tall and straight; her father and Uchida Masa both prepared to rise.

"Please excuse us for causing you all this trouble," they said in formal fashion. Then they struggled to their feet. Hiroko walked the long corridor toward the door with her eyes downcast, not looking back. At the steps of the entryway she stopped. The wooden clogs of her father and the go-between were there, but she didn't see hers. She turned to O-Toki, the chambermaid, who was crouched to assist the departing visitors with their footwear.

"O-Toki, I don't see my clogs anywhere—"

O-Toki jumped up and said quickly in a low voice, "My lady, they were placed at the kitchen entrance."

"What on earth—?"

"I am so sorry. The respected ladies of the house have read the omens, and they find that if their daughter-in-law departs from the front entrance, then misfortune will visit them twice. So they ordered me to place your clogs at the kitchen door."

Hiroko turned deathly pale, and her lips trembled slightly. She seemed on the verge of fainting. Kikuji, who was at the rear of the group crowding the entryway, pushed through and stepped down on the cement floor. He placed his own clogs in front of Hiroko, while from the corridor he heard Kino and Sei talking excitedly. Still trembling, Hiroko placed her foot on the wooden clogs. Kikuji carefully guided her toes around the straps. Hiroko left from the front entrance in the oversized footwear, supported by her father. Sei and Kino came out in front of the store to watch them as they went down the street.

Three days later, in the evening, Uchida Masa came to take back Hiroko's trousseau. Kino, not wishing to see her, pretended illness. Sei and Kikuji met the go-between in the living room. In an awkward attempt to show her appreciation for the go-between's efforts, Sei offered Uchida Masa supper, but the invitation was declined.

"I'm sorry. I'm feeling unwell all of a sudden, and not at all hungry."

At this, Sei became distant and even brusque. She told O-Toki to take the tray away, and then began hurrying her visitor to get the job done. But the more she hurried her, the more Uchida Masa took her time.

"Aren't you going to start getting this stuff out of here?" asked Sei.

But Uchida Masa only smiled and opened a notebook.

"All in good time." she said. "We must have a complete inventory so that the goods are returned in proper order. These things must be done right or not at all, my lady." She went on sorting her inventory sheets. "I've got five men waiting outside, and once I have checked off everything and made sure that the various items are in good condition, I'll have the boxes taken away."

Sei managed a tight smile, and said, "Well, as you please. Kikubon here will assist you in your figuring."

And without more ceremony, she turned and left, trailing behind the scent of her perfume.

Kikuji, embarrassed at his mother's discourtesy, said, "Please excuse her. I realize, of course, as you do, that they have several times acted badly before you. They don't get around much, you know, and sometimes they forget their going-out manners. They mean no harm."

She stuck out her chin and made no reply. On entering Hiroko's room, she pulled out her lists for the trousseau, balanced her reading glasses on her nose, and began to itemize the contents of the room. Since the marriage had lasted only one year and ten months, the chests, the mirror and lacquered dressing table were still in perfect condition. Uchida Masa slowly and systematically took out the contents of the chests, first counting and then examining the bedding, the cushions, and the many kimono. She went on then to check everything right down to the number of thin sashes and small towels. Kikuji sat at the center of the room, watching the woman's efficient procedure. O-Toki came in with tea, and, hesitating a little on her way out, said shyly, "I would be glad to help you—" But Uchida Masa replied tersely, "No, thanks. I must do it all carefully myself. I'm responsible." She gave the girl a quick glance and a nod, and went on studying her inventory, squinting through her small spectacles at her lists.

After checking off the various items, she carefully repacked them. Then she took the bride's curtain with its family crest off the door, and, following prescribed convention, turned it inside out so that the crest did not show before placing it on top of one of the boxes. Then she ordered her workmen to carry their load out through the kitchen entrance and place it on the carts in front of the house.

Kikuji stood in the narrow alley leading from the door, and watched the possessions of his divorced wife being carried away. It was now three days since Hiroko's departure. As the bearers emerged with their loads from the kitchen door to disappear into the darkness, Kikuji felt that the whole procedure was almost surreptitious, a stealthy concealment of shame. To the world the shame, perhaps, was hers; but to those who knew the facts, his was the shame, his the blame. Just a little while ago she had come happily and expectantly as his bride to this house, bringing her carefully selected, wonderfully sewn treasures with her in the various chests of her trousseau; and now, she was dismissed like an erring servant maid, and her trousseau dispatched scornfully in the dark after her.

A whiff of sweat and a respectful grunt told him that the man carrying the last bundle was behind him, about to leave the house. He turned quickly to the bearer. "Wait just a moment, please. I have something here which my wife—which she forgot. I'll put it right in here at the top of the chest—"

As he did so, the silk bedding packed tightly in the box clung softly to his hand.

"Kiku-bon, you're taking all this hard, aren't you? You do feel something still for your poor wife." It was Uchida Masa, who had been observing him. "You've just put a little something in the chest for her to remember you by, eh? You're all right, I guess. It's those two in there"—she motioned with her chin toward the nearly darkened house—"who give people like me a pain in the backside!" She laughed harshly, clapped him on the arm in farewell, and walked toward the bearers and their carts waiting in the darkness.

As she had guessed, he had added a memento of his own to the trousseau so sadly departing. It consisted of two thousand yen wrapped in a silken cloth. This, he thought, would keep her comfortable for two or three years.

Strictly speaking, Kikuji realized, this large sum did not belong to him to give as he pleased. Several days earlier, he had asked Kihei, while the two of them were alone in the front offices, "Father, would you be willing to lend me a large amount of money?"

"How much?"

When told the amount, Kihei had sucked in his breath sharply, as he often did when faced with a difficult business decision.

"Well! That's a lot of money. Enough to start a new business, I should think. In these days fifty yen a year is a good salary for anyone, you realize?"

Kihei looked at him, waiting for an explanation. But his son had merely replied with quiet earnestness, "I really need it, very much. At the very latest, the day after tomorrow."

"The day after tomorrow?" Kihei had repeated thoughtfully. And suddenly his careworn business frown evaporated and was replaced by a gentle, almost shy smile. "It's all right, Kikuji. I'll get it together tomorrow. Since it's a lot of money, though, we'll do it in proper fashion, and make it a loan and not a gift—even if you are my own son."

He nodded at his small joke, and looked again at Kikuji. "Just— use it well, Kikuji. Use it well."

Kikuji had bowed and had left quickly. He knew, of course, that even though the ladies of the house were the heiresses, the business practices observed in the Semba District did not allow them to participate directly in the activities of the firm. Kihei alone had charge of the company's finances. He alone controlled the cash in the big safe in the front office. Hence his freedom in deciding to help his son—

Kikuji watched Uchida Masa disappear in the darkness as she went to meet the bearers awaiting her. He held his right palm as though to recall the strange, clinging sensation of the silk on his hand as he had stuffed the packet of money into the chest. From a distance came the noises of Uchida Masa's group. It sounded as though they had finished loading all the chests onto their carts.

Suddenly, there was the protesting creak of wood, the squeaking of wheels as the carts began to move. Slowly the alien murmur of the men faded away on the night air as the carts moved further off, leaving Kikuji alone in the silence of the little alley, contemplating the looming darkness of the eaves.

TWO

U p to the dismal summer of Hiroko's departure, the most meaningful part of Kikuji's life had taken place in the family area at the rear of the big old Kawachiya mansion. With the coming of autumn, however, Kikuji began working regularly in the store at the front, learning the business.

Until now, he had, as children often do, taken the house he had grown up in completely for granted. It was, he realized as he thought about its design, as different from other houses as the people who lived in it were unlike other families. He saw it now not merely as a home, but as a compound of interrelated activities and interests, housing a family, a business establishment, and a large number of employees. It had grown from a simple store with the family living behind into a rich and elaborate complex in which the emotions of a family and the schemes of business had become confused and intertwined.

He tried to study the whole establishment with the eye of a stranger, as though seeing it for the first time. Much of its special quality, he could see, was shared by other long-established business houses of the Semba. Like them, it was separated from the dusty street by the unpainted, latticed fence which was almost a trademark of Semba firms. The frontage was an imposing sixty feet. Like them too, the Kawachiya mansion combined business efficiency with esthetic considerations.

To the right as he faced the property, Kikuji looked on the large, paved area, often used for loading and unloading merchandise. This yard was bounded by a wall, and against it was the dormitory of the clerks and apprentices, along with their outhouses, plus several concrete storage vaults, immune to fire and most natural shocks. On the left side of the house, extending halfway down the property, was a carefully tended garden with several stone lanterns and finely shaped pines. The rear boundary was the West Yokobori River. Their lot was separated from it by a little embankment and a wall. Just inside this rear wall were Grandmother Kino's separate rooms, connected to the main house by a walkway, along which was situated the restroom. To one side of the walkway was the oblong inner courtyard, which, extending between Kino's rooms and the main house, was, Kikuji thought, the more intimate and beautiful of the two gardens.

If in the organization of the grounds one sensed a diversity of uses and purposes, the same was true of the interior. When he entered at the front door, Kikuji was in the two large rooms which they called the store, although they filled the many functions of a highly complex business. There was a small, latticed enclosure for accounting and bookkeeping. There was a space for the temporary storage of their product, and, should an important business conference be required, Kihei, or his manager, Wasuke, was free to take clients into one of the three luxurious and spotlessly clean parlors immediately behind the store. When Kikuji's head brushed the small doorway curtain at the rear of the two front rooms of the store, he was in the family area, but the three parlors could be put to use either by the family for social occasions or by the business for its needs.

A gleaming, polished hallway extended down the middle of the house. On the left side, overlooking the garden of the middle courtyard, were the best rooms of the house; his father's, his mother's, and the family shrine room. On the right side of the hallway as one went beyond the store and parlors was the kitchen with its elevated family dining area, and a lower space just above the level of the courtyard outside where the cooking took place and where the clerks and apprentices dined. Next to the kitchen was the maids' workroom (their bedrooms just above were reached by a stairway of ladderlike steepness), followed by the quarters of Kikuji and his one-time wife. Kikuji had felt ever since his childhood that the center of beauty and authority was in the detached rooms of his grandmother at the rear of the house. But it seemed to him that the house had all the variations of a social spectrum: the public, efficient, masculine business facade at the front, the exclusive and aristocratic feminine presence at the rear. In between were the lesser functionaries, the clerks, the apprentices, the chambermaids, and the seamstresses. It was a little world in itself, and quite as complicated in its desires and ambitions as the great outer world.

Kikuji, rendered incapable of controlling his life under the eyes of Kino and Sei in the family area, had determined to try his luck in the world of men. He gave the daily processes of the business his complete attention, and gradually found himself becoming more and more deeply interested in them. In the year between his graduation from college and his marriage, he had only dabbled in the complex but orderly round of activity which took place under Kihei's watchful eye. After his marriage, he had been too preoccupied with domestic strife to be of much use in the store. Now, however, he found in it the escape he needed from dependency on his mother and grandmother. Still, the adjustment to a regular schedule of unvarying industry was not easy for him. He had grown up in a household of women and had rarely during his school years even been allowed in the store. Now that he had made his commitment to it, he found its atmosphere masculine and demanding.

Each morning under Kihei's and Wasuke's guidance, he worked out the amounts to be delivered to the retail stores. Since most of these were customers of many years, he knew about how many pairs of tabi they would need on any given day. So he ordered the appropriate quantities to be packaged and labeled for pickup. When the merchants came for their supplies, Kikuji sat at the edge of the loading platform, ledger in hand, to supervise and assist in the process. The customers, seeing him at work in his cotton kimono, a rough apron tied in front, complimented Kihei on having a son who worked as hard as any apprentice. Kihei liked hearing these praises, and the merchants knew it. They did not know, and nobody but one of the seamstresses did, that Kikuji could not for the sake of his work give up the soft silken touch of his *habutae* underkimono; and, to conceal this touch of luxury, had asked the seamstress to face the sleeves and hem them with cotton material so that his silken comfort would pass unobserved.

He had been initially surprised and continued to be impressed by the fact that Kihei, so ineffective in the family quarters, had only to make the mildest and most courteous suggestion to have the whole

39

work force accept it as absolute law. The daily routine of the store had long been the special province of Wasuke, the elderly store manager. An assistant manager, a thin and precise young man named Hidesuke, helped to oversee the activities of the thirty apprentices and clerks who ran the store.

Hidesuke bothered him. Kikuji thought he must have been born old and sharp eyed. His efficiency in handling fussy customers was indisputable. When they complained about the tardy delivery of an order, he would agree with them entirely. Kawachiya's reputation, he would say, depended on its promptitude. Then, at great length, he would explain to the customers, with much clucking and exclamation, what they surely must already have known: that Kawachiya's put out its orders to various small subcontractors, who made tabi in their own shops according to the parent firm's specifications. But (here Hidesuke would roll his eyes and lean close to his customers, speaking in a sepulchral whisper) these craftsmen were not as dependable as they might be. Sometimes, they would surprise you by working overtime four or five nights in a row to produce a special order. But most of the time, as soon as they had any money, they got drunk. And when they were drunk, they stayed drunk until the money was all gone. Then, and, alas, only then, would they come back to Kawachiya's with the completed order. At this point in his talk Hidesuke would take off his glasses and wipe them with his handkerchief while he shook his head sadly and said unflattering things about the character of today's workmen, adding with a smile that it wasn't like that in the old days, now, was it. He could spin this sort of thing out endlessly until the merchants, dazed into a state of amiable resignation, would go away quite convinced that Kawachiya's was a solid organization dedicated to the completion of their orders with a speed which would not sacrifice durability and skill. And in general, this was true. There was no question about Hidesuke's enormous loyalty to the firm and his belief in its importance.

One day Kikuji happened to be within earshot when Hidesuke was instructing a terrified new apprentice on his duties and obligations.

"First of all, you must understand that what we make here at Kawachiya's is symbolic of Japanese culture at its best. It is shapely, it has comfort, it is supportive of the complex beauty of the human

40

form. Don't you agree?" Here Hidesuke looked over the rims of his glasses at the apprentice.

"Oh. Oh, yes! Very much so!" said the young man earnestly.

"I have heard westerners referring to the Japanese tabi as a 'sock'. That is because they have never worn tabi and don't know the difference. Any savage might have invented the sock. It has no style. It is meant to be largely hidden within the shoe, as though it were, you might say, the underwear of the arches."

Hidesuke paused to smile delicately at his joke. The apprentice, who had been listening with great attention, smiled slowly.

"But the tabi is meant to grace the feet, not hide them. In total design it has an esthetic beauty of which the wearer of the lowly sock may be completely unaware. Look at its flat sole of heavy cloth, meant for maximum comfort and usefulness as the wearer moves over the tatami mats of a Japanese room. And within the tabi, the big toe is king, separated from the other toes by his own private enclosure. Only so are we able to grasp the thongs of the wooden clogs when we go out to walk over mud and filth without soiling our feet. How carefully the tops are sewn to the sole! The secret of our Kawachiya tabi is precisely in that sewing, discovered for us by that original genius of tabi design, Kawachiya Kihei I. Without our special craftsmanship, the whole thing might soon pull apart or become shapeless, as cheaper wares do. And look at the modest, yet graceful clasps which hook through loops at the back of the ankle, pulling the whole foot-garment into a thing of beauty, framing a man's appendages, or a woman's, so that all beholders look twice with enjoyment. In short, the tabi is a great technical feat and an esthetic triumph. And hence the Kawachiya motto, 'You can tell them by the big toe!' It has taken four generations of craftsmen to produce the perfection of our present-day tabi!"

The apprentice said nothing, and Hidesuke frowned.

"Do you follow me, young man?"

"How could I fail to do so, eloquent sir? How stimulating your talk is. It is like being washed in a great waterfall of words."

"Be that as it may," replied Hidesuke modestly, "I want you to understand that you are about to participate in no ordinary industry. We spend our energies in perfecting this inconspicuous aspect of Japanese dress, just as some Japanese artists carve deathless lines in ice or even in sand. One pair of tabi wears away, but the ideal remains, to be perpetuated by succeeding generations. That is the way business at its best works. An everlasting process of renewal and improvement!"

The apprentice radiated agreement.

Hidesuke's cleverness in manipulating people vaguely disturbed Kikuji. He knew that the assistant manager's single-mindedness and skill had been acquired over years of experience and that Kihei often found him even more useful than the elderly Wasuke. Nevertheless, he found he could never do anything right in Hidesuke's presence. When the assistant manager was around, Kikuji refrained from working on the orders of major customers. If he made a mistake with a minor client, Hidesuke perhaps wouldn't see it or make much of it.

One of Kikuji's tasks was to inspect the finished pairs of tabi after they came in from the subcontractor's workshop. The motto of Kawachiya's was "You can tell them by the big toe!" As Hidesuke had explained to the apprentice, tabi bearing the firm's brand name were famous for the care and precision with which the space for the big toe was sewn. The big toe, of course, was separated from the others by the gap required for the wearer to grip the thong of the wooden walking clogs firmly. Kawachiya Kihei I, the founder of the firm almost two hundred years ago, had left careful written instructions on the proper sewing of tabi, stressing that the secret of durability and shapeliness even after repeated washing was in the special sewing of the big toe. On this small matter was based the continuing prosperity of the firm. Hence the managers of the firm took great pains to instruct their subcontractors carefully on the correct way to sew the famous Kawachiya toe. And, when the finished product was returned, it was inspected closely before being shipped to the retail stores.

When Kikuji sat down with a pile of tabi in his lap, he would first study the shape of each one. Then he would inspect the sewing of the side and bottom pieces. Finally, and most important, he would place a bamboo stretcher in the tabi and examine the toe area. If the seam stretched well, without bunching, he would pass it, but, if there was evidence of an uneven or weak seam, then he knew the toe would not last long and would reject the pair, placing them in a box at his left to be returned to the subcontractor.

Like much important work, the examination of the tabi was monotonous. One day, after he had inspected thirty or more pairs, Kikuji heard a low voice at his shoulder. "Sir, may I be of assistance? You see, these are substandard—" And Hidesuke, reaching deftly into the pile of tabi which Kikuji had just approved, stretched them with the ease of long experience to show the defects which he had missed. Kikuji looked at the tabi and then at Hidesuke with embarrassment. The assistant manager smiled and gave his master's son a tactful wink.

"Don't give it a second thought. Anyone misses some until he knows almost by instinct what to look for. Just do a little bit today and a little tomorrow, and you'll soon get the hang of it. And now why don't you go and take a break? I'll finish these up for you."

This was not the way Hidesuke spoke to the clerks and apprentices when they made mistakes. Missing three bad pairs out of thirty was a poor showing. He clicked his tongue in embarrassment, nodded, and walked off. After this incident he was wary of the assistant manager, and more careful than ever in performing his tasks. He did not want this special treatment.

Kino and Sei, as they observed Kikuji's sudden diligence, were puzzled. At first, they thought it a temporary alienation from them because they had brought about his divorce. But as time passed and there was no letup in his interest in the family business, they became uneasy. All through the fall and winter he had spent his time working in the store. After talking it over, they decided that they would have to do something to divert his attention from the routine of business. So they made plans to make him some new clothes and take him with them to a kabuki play. Kikuji was none too enthusiastic about accompanying them on what obviously would be an elaborate excursion, but he didn't wish to keep alive his resentment about the divorce, and saw this invitation as a way of burying the past.

Reservations were made for a day in mid-April. Busy as he was in the store, Kikuji could sense the atmosphere of tension and suspense emanating from the maids' room. With only one day of vacation each year (plus another day for travel time to and from their homes) the maids were much excited at the prospect of two of their number being selected to accompany the ladies and O-Toki, the head chambermaid, to the theater. There were two chambermaids, four kitch-

43

enmaids and three seamstresses to choose from, and all were in a state of despairing anticipation at the prospect of going to see a great play and famous actors.

Kino and Sei finally, on the day before the play, named the lucky two who would accompany them. Immediately the two maids went first to the public bath, and then to the hairdresser's. That night, since they wished to preserve the freshness of their special hairdo for ladies' maids, they resisted the urge to lie down and sleep normally on the bedding spread on the floor. Instead, they sat up all night, leaning as best they could against a pile of quilts, dozing fitfully. It was a small price to pay for such an outing. Next morning their hair glistened immaculately, although occasionally they had to stifle a yawn.

On the day of the play, the Kawachiya household was busy at five in the morning, preparing the hot bath for the lady of the house and her mother. The lucky servants who had been selected to accompany them tried to do as much work as they could before leaving so that the other servants could not complain that they had in any way neglected their duties. Then, when the ladies were taken care of, the two maids went to their room, took out their dress kimono from the chest, and put them on while the other servants looked on in a mixture of envy and admiration.

Meanwhile, in Sei's room, the hairdresser carefully combed over her hair once more, setting in perfect order again the magnificently upswept hairdo he had given her the day before. The maids helped her into a full-dress kimono. But trying on one kimono before the mirror was not enough. Just as a young girl restlessly and excitedly tries on her whole wardrobe before sallying forth to meet a prospective husband at an arranged interview, so Sei stared critically at herself, now in this kimono, now in that, unable to decide which was the more impressive and suitable. She draped one over one shoulder, another over the other, faced the mirror, smoothed the silk with her fingers, frowned thoughtfully, and finally, with a sigh of resignation, made her decision. She put on the kimono, the maids painstakingly tied the brocaded waistband and adjusted its folds. Then Kino entered the room, and with the air of a connoisseur, criticized this fold, that shade of red, the line of the hair. All this took some time.

Kikuji had been awakened by the commotion the ladies were

making as they organized their appearances. He ate his breakfast quietly, and was just finishing the first cigarette of the day when the servants excitedly announced that a graceful Yakata boat, sent from the Marugame Teahouse, had arrived at the rear entrance of the mansion, on the Yokobori River, and was waiting to take them to the play. They could, of course, have taken a taxi and arrived in fifteen minutes. But Kino and Sei relished the grand and ceremonious manner of the old courtly days in Nara and Kyoto. Theirs was no mere trip to the playhouse; it was a stately procession by water, a leisurely and colorful celebration of their family, as esthetically necessary to them as the kabuki play itself, to which it was the only appropriate prelude. The Yakata boat was a long, slender craft with a high, curving prow. At its center was a cabin in the shape of a little teahouse. Although the number of these boats had declined considerably in recent years, Kino, as a longtime, free-spending customer at the Marugame Teahouse, had no difficulty in arranging the elaborate river trip.

The servants opened the rear gate and escorted the ladies down to the boarding platform. The women, excitedly laughing and chattering with each other, held up their kimono and cautiously balanced themselves on their wooden clogs as they crossed the platform into the boat. They bowed their heads carefully as they entered the little cabin amidships, the floor of which was covered with a thick red carpet. The maids who had to stay at home loaded on the boxes of extra kimono needed for the evening performance. Then they stood, hands clasped in front of them, looking sadly and speculatively at the boat that was leaving them behind. Along both banks, the houses of the wealthy extended, and occasionally the voyagers could see a maid on an upstairs veranda spreading a quilt out to air. It was a clear, windless spring day. Just after going under the Nigiwai Bridge, they came to the junction with the Dotombori River on their right, and, turning into it, they arrived soon after at the dock of the Marugame Teahouse, which had the special distinction of being situated directly across the street from the Nakazu Kabuki Theater.

The boatman, who was wearing a tunic with the crest of the teahouse, put down his oar and shouted, "Those of you inside! Quickly, now! The illustrious Kawachiya family has arrived!"

Immediately girls wearing the red teahouse apron came running out with tiny steps, bowed deeply, while one of them said, in sing-song cadence, "We are privileged to serve you once again. Thank you for your continued patronage." Then they helped them out of the boat and escorted them to a room looking out over the river. Here the ladies rested, nibbled at some cakes and drank tea, and had their hairdos and makeup checked once more: they were more like actresses preparing to make an entrance onstage than members of an audience about to take seats in the theater. Just before curtain time, the teahouse servants escorted them across the street and into the Nakazu Theater.

In all this, Kikuji felt like a stray afterthought.

Their compartment was a tatami-matted area large enough to seat six people comfortably. It was, like all the other reserved areas in the theater, surrounded by a low railing, over which was draped a cloth dyed with the crest of their teahouse. Kikuji noted that, since the program was a very special one, featuring the great actor, Nari-komaya, there were no unreserved seats, the teahouses having early snapped up all tickets for their special customers.

When the curtain was drawn shut at the end of the first act, wait-resses from the teahouses moved carefully through and around the various compartments, carrying many red lacquer boxes of food stacked one on top of the other. "Excuse me, excuse me," they kept chirping, sounding, Kikuji thought, like birds in spring. But they worked hard, serving up the various orders quickly and courteously. From now on during the performance most of the audience were busy eating and drinking while they watched, listened, and com-mented.

Kikuji's compartment was near the long walkway extending out from the stage on the left side which the actors used for some of the most spectacular moments of the kabuki plays. In the box immedi-ately in front of theirs was an old gentleman with four geisha and numerous bottles of sake. Kikuji assumed from his authoritative manner that he was probably a retired owner of some large Osaka firm who had come to the theater for a good time. The geisha with him watched the play with interest, now and again picking up some tidbit with their chopsticks and putting it in their mouths without ever taking their eyes off the action on the stage.

Suddenly the old man with many grunts and exclamations turned his back to the stage and gave his undivided attention to

46

drinking. The four geisha were horrified, and looked at each other in consternation.

"Please, my dear sir," pleaded one, "the next performer will be Narikomaya-han. You mustn't turn your back on him without even seeing him."

The old man snorted angrily. "What's so good about Narikomaya? He's paid to entertain me! I paid. I paid a tremendous amount to your old teahouse just to be here. And now that I've paid, I'll look at him if I want, and I won't look at him if I don't want. It's entirely up to me. Let him do his dance. I'm not bothering him!"

And he poured himself more sake while the geisha stared in confusion at each other, wondering what to do. After a moment of indecision, the youngest of them stood up and said in a low voice to the others, "Let me sit in front of our worthy guest so that his inattentiveness will not be visible from the stage." She tried in the narrow space available to change her seat, but, in the process, she tripped over the hem of her kimono, and for an instant lost her balance. She put her arms out to recover herself, and, as she did so, the corner of her sleeve brushed Sei's cheek.

Immediately Sei stiffened with irritation.

"How disgusting," she said in a loud voice to Kino, "to be assaulted in this way by a common geisha!" The sleeve of the girl's kimono was still partly in the Kawachiya box, and Sei with a quick motion of her hand flipped it away. Kino turned regally to glare at the women in the next compartment. The Kawachiya maids, who had been absorbed in the action on the stage, quite suddenly found themselves in the middle of a quarrel. The geisha who had stumbled looked back at them angrily, and she compressed her mouth as though about to explode. But her quick glance told her that these were probably ladies of importance, and, rather than risk unpleasant words, she curled her lip at them, and turned away, sitting down gracefully in front of the old man. The other geisha, taking their cue from her, looked away from Sei and Kino and concentrated on the stage. Their aged customer continued to drink contentedly, unaware both of the stage action and of the little social drama in which his attendants had been involved.

Sei, however, remained irritated. She began signaling the waitress at frequent intervals. As the orders were given, the waitress would nod and say, "Very good, my lady," or "Thank you, worthy

47

lady." By such means did Sei make clear her social position. The geisha in the next compartment wilted, and paid little attention to the stage action. Not only had they displeased their rich old customer and in the process completely failed to tease him out of his bad manners; they had also, and quite unnecessarily, antagonized two formidable matrons, known in the teahouse as important customers. These are things a geisha does not do if she wishes to thrive at her profession.

Kikuji meanwhile, a silent observer, had, rather like the old man in the next compartment, lost all interest in the stage spectacle. He sat at the rear of the box, drinking sake, watching the drunken old fellow in the next compartment, and making no effort whatever to participate in the small feud which had so obviously exhilarated his mother and grandmother. The two ladies fluttered their fans delicately and from time to time made judicial comments on the quality of the acting. O-Toki joined in with relish. They were, he thought gloomily, playing a game. And his mind went back to the day when he had discovered them playing with dolls on the day his son had been born. Games, games. They dressed themselves up and pretended. They were the best actors in the theater.

When the long matinee performance was over, Kikuji's group returned to the Marugame Teahouse, where Kino and Sei changed into the other kimono which they had brought with them on the boat. These were quite different from their afternoon attire, and, if anything, more splendid still. Then, five minutes before curtain time, they walked slowly with their attendants across the street and back into the theater, to occupy the same compartment they had had earlier. Although all boxes were rented for the full day's performance, that of the old man remained empty. Completely disenchanted with both the kabuki plays and the charms of his attendant geisha, he had apparently given up his festive venture and gone home. Left the victors on the social battlefield, Kino and Sei walked proudly in their magnificent kimono, and, followed by their maids wearing matching kimono, they were a striking group. Many eyes turned to watch them as they seated themselves. Kikuji tried to be as different from them as he could, slouching a little, and looking at no one. Yet he knew that, just before the curtain was drawn, many in the theater were looking at Kino and Sei with admiration and curiosity. This was their life, but it meant little to him.

When the play was over, they went back to the teahouse, and boarded the boat once more for the voyage home. It was already past 11 P.M. The women's voices, high with the excitement of the day's events, carried far over the water. The boat moved slowly over the calm surface of the river, a lantern shedding a soft light from its bow. Kikuji sat outside the little cabin of the Yakata boat, staring off into the darkness. Suddenly he was aware of Sei's white face bending over him.

"Kiku-bon, what *is* the matter? You've said nothing all day. And in the theater you sat by yourself and drank. Is that it? Are you a bit tight?"

It was as good an excuse as any. He nodded responsively. But, even though he had consumed a lot of sake, his mind was unusually clear and perceptive. The difficulty was that what he saw, he loathed, himself most of all. A pet squirrel in a cage—

The cost of this one excursion he estimated at about five hundred yen. Ten round trip train tickets to Hokkaido! Kawachiya's, he knew from a recent inspection of Kihei's books, was taking in about five thousand a day. The ladies' grand procession to the theater had cut into the store's profits only slightly. Still, what was its real purpose? Was not this extravagance an outward sign of undeniably great energies being frustrated and wasted? Barred from the male world of business, they made themselves felt in all sorts of other ways. Past the age of child rearing, they were both spoiled and bored. So they occupied themselves with dressing up in high style and impressing their neighbors with their outings. It was the privilege of heiresses to do this. What else was there for them to do, these vigorous, restless and unfulfilled women?

Now that Hiroko was gone, they felt free to indulge themselves. They had refused to share their excursions with any woman brought in from outside the family, as Hiroko had been. For the duration of his marriage they had deprived themselves of their favorite amusements rather than be forced to include his wife in them.

He heard Kino in the cabin yawning and saying, "My. How late it must be." It was long past her bedtime. The boat, under the skillful guidance of the oarsman at the stern, glided into and out of the dark shadows of the Yotsu Bridge and then of the Shinmachi Bridge, slipping under them with the noiseless ease of a dream. He could see

49

the light from his father's room, hundreds of yards distant, reflected on the water. In his mind's eye, Kikuji saw clearly the bowed figure of his father, stolidly closing up the store for the night all by himself, and then carefully checking over the day's accounts in the quiet of his room.

Everybody gets what he looks for somehow, Kikuji reflected. Sei and Kino got their fun by dressing up like court ladies. What sense of reward or justification or pleasure ever came to Kihei from clicking that damned abacus all the time? Was his a kind of pretense too? Did he try to convince himself that he was a man, an industrious, humane executive, and not simply an automaton, stamped with the Kawachiya trademark, an empty box, with none of the feelings, hopes and desires of a person genuinely alive? What purpose could the poor man have in living such a life? If that's what the business world does to a man, I want none of it. The emotional storms of the spoiled women in the living quarters at the rear of the house were bad enough, but, if Kihei was a valid indication, the store at the front produced people without any emotions at all. Both extremes were the drab shadows of life rather than the real thing.

He was recalled from his gloomy thoughts by the squeaking of the oar as the lantern-lit prow of the Yakata boat swept in with dreamlike swiftness beside the Kawachiya dock and stopped amid a swirl of water. He stood up and smiled wryly to himself. The great spring excursion was over.

It was a cool October evening. As the ten o'clock closing time neared, Kikuji tidied up his desk in preparation for leaving. His father, who had just finished counting out a packet of money for Kino and Sei, sat expressionless as his son said goodbye to him. Wasuke bowed his balding head toward him briefly. Hidesuke, his eyes gleaming with curiosity behind his rimless spectacles, said, with the faintest suggestion of a leer, "Have a nice time!"

He felt freer as soon as he came out on the street. He took a deep breath and stood taller than usual filled with satisfaction that, whatever else might be said, he was not retracing his father's dull and meaningless existence. He walked slowly along the West Yokobori River. A lumber merchant along the river had just closed his shop. Under the eaves were piles of lumber, surprisingly white in the dim light. The pungent smell of the newly cut wood came to him

50

strongly in the humid October night. A number of figures were leaving the lumberyard: the workmen just finishing up, and, carrying soap and towel, on their way to the public bath to relax at the end of a hard day's work. They were accustomed to seeing Kikuji, who for the past six months had passed this lumberyard nearly every night on his way to the pleasure quarter at Shinmachi. They greeted him respectfully as they passed and he returned the greeting. Soon he crossed Shinmachi Bridge and after four more blocks, came to the Tominoya Teahouse. Here Kawachiya's entertained customers from the outlying districts when they came to Osaka for business discussions. It was small, but neat and finely constructed. The garden was exquisite, and, like the inn itself, beautifully cared for.

He had come here for the first time this past spring with his father to help entertain some customers. Ikuko, the daughter of the house, although barely twenty, helped her mother so efficiently in taking care of their group that Kikuji felt very much at home. On his second visit, with fifteen customers, he saw that Ikuko was equally attentive. When it was time for him to leave, she had stepped down from the ledge of the entryway onto the concrete floor, along with the serving maids. Picking up his tatami-surfaced slippers, she brushed away a fragment of dirt with the sleeve of her kimono before setting them in front of him to put on. With all these people to tend to, she had been particularly concerned about him. He looked at her speculatively. She was not what would be called a great beauty. But her eyes were lively and darting, her figure graceful and compact. She wore her kimono short, and she walked the corridors briskly, supervising the waitresses and geisha with friendly efficiency. As daughter of the Tominoya family, she was treated with respect by the inn employees. Customers liked her because she gave good service and understood their special needs.

After the incident of the slippers, Kikuji used Tominoya's whenever he needed to entertain customers. No matter how crowded her schedule, Ikuko made a point of always appearing at Kikuji's parties to greet the guests and take care of the menu, selecting the geisha for the entertainment of the guests herself, rather than leaving it to the waitresses. After seeing her many times at these large parties, Kikuji took to dropping in frequently all by himself to have a relaxed supper without customers around.

So his solitary visit this evening was not unexpected. Ikuko, as

51

soon as she stepped into the room where he sat, frowned thought-fully, and said, "If you are going to stop in every night, young Master, I'm going to have to think up some special arrangement to keep the cost down. Otherwise these pleasant visits will become too expensive, and you won't come any more. So suppose I just take care of assigning geisha to you in my own special way? I want you to be —well, thrifty. I hope that's all right."

And with that she whispered something to a waitress, who nodded knowingly and stood up to leave. Ikuko fingered the subdued satin waistband over the rusty vermilion of her intricately patterned kimono, and said with cautious nonchalance, "If you continue to make a habit of coming here, the firm of Kawachiya's will not mind. But the two ladies of the house might not like it. Isn't that right?"

"Oh, my. Even here, in Shinmachi, people talk about my family, do they?"

She regretted having spoken; yet his irritation was not directed at her, but at his father, whose lifelong submissiveness to his mother and grandmother had made them and him notorious and the subject of gossip even in districts outside the Semba. Ever since the spring excursion Kikuji had been obsessed by the riddle of his father's life. Was he smart or stupid—a big man or a fool? Although Kikuji had made no secret to Kihei of his visits to the pleasure quarter, his father showed no sign of annoyance or irritation. Unconcernedly, he kept clicking the abacus, and the business steadily expanded under his direction.

"Good evening, sir."

The sliding door had opened, and an apprentice geisha in a long party kimono with hem trailing came into the room. She was very young, very graceful, and spoke with a Kyoto accent. Kikuji had not seen her before at the teahouse. He turned in puzzlement to Ikuko for explanation. She gave a quick smile. Whatever was happening, she had intended it.

The geisha looked at him tentatively. "I've seen you here often and I learned from Ikuko that you are the young master of Kawachiya's. I have wanted to serve you. But up to now you have patronized only Fukusuke-han and Momoko-han. Please include me also."

She picked up the sake bottle and he held out his cup for her to fill. She poured the wine with a graceful movement of her hands, and he drank it off.

"You down them very fast," she said, laughing. He took her bottle and gave her his cup, which he filled. She accepted it formally, lifting it up to her forehead and bowing. He suddenly realized that this apprentice geisha was still a little shy and nervous, not quite used to the role she was to play. Part of her charm was in this very uncertainty. She wasn't quite sure what to say.

"Where were you born?" asked Kikuji.

The simple question brought back her normal high spirits with a rush.

"I wish I could say that I'm the daughter of an established firm in Nakakyo (if it's Kyoto we're thinking of), or in the Semba (if it's Osaka), or in Nihonbashi (if it's Tokyo). But unfortunately, I'm just a turnip from Saitama. That's why I'm so white and crisp, don't you think?" Kikuji laughed aloud for the first time since he had arrived.

"This Mamechiyo of yours," he said to Ikuko, "though she doesn't talk much, makes remarkably good sense when she does. She is very pleasant—completely unaffected. But of course all the geisha here at Tominoya's are superb."

While he and Ikuko sat chattering, the sliding door opened silently again, and a geisha in a subdued purple kimono appeared in sitting posture at the doorsill. She bowed to them.

"Oh. Here is Kimika. How nice of you to join us," said Ikuko affectionately.

The geisha at the doorsill raised her head, ending a long bow. She was, Kikuji thought, middle-aged: perhaps thirty-four or thirty-five. Of delicate build and plain features, there was about her an indefinable air of perceptiveness and quietude not normally associated with the professional geisha. When Mamechiyo tried to give her a better seat, she said only, "I really feel more at ease where I am, thank you," and kept her seat at the rear. She feared ostentation. Ikuki didn't urge her; changing the subject, she said, "Kimika, could you play something on the samisen so that Mamechiyo can dance?" Kimika nodded, took her seat, tuned the samisen, and held it ready in her lap, waiting. Mamechiyo looked at her, and said modestly, "Now, then, sister, please," and to Kimika's accompaniment danced the "Evening Shower." Since she was still in her apprenticeship, it was not a very perfect dance, but she danced its every gesture with scrupulous care from beginning to end. At the finish, she went gracefully into a seated position on the tatami, placed both her hands on the mat in front of her, and bowed low to Kikuji.

At this moment, the sliding door opened wide.

"Good evening, everyone. Sorry we're late!"

Three additional geisha came in together. Kikuji was worried for an instant, thinking about the service fee he would have to pay for all these geisha. But, looking around he observed that Mamechiyo had departed, leaving only Kimika and the three new geisha. Ikuko during the evening was busily engaged in getting up and sitting down, entertaining the guest. Sometimes a waitress entered inconspicuously, and then, following a whispered conversation, Ikuko would leave the room, but always she came back fairly quickly. After an hour had passed, three new geisha joined the party, and the other ones left as though they had been replaced. Only Kimika stayed on without interruption.

When it was almost midnight, Kikuji felt exhausted. He concealed a yawn and turned to Ikuko. "Tonight was like a coming-out party for all your geisha, wasn't it? We saw them all."

She looked at him fondly. "You had best get on home. It's quite late. But come again soon, eh?"

He walked along the corridor with uncertain steps. He felt the need to relieve himself and stopped off at the lavatory. Returning to the corridor, he stretched his hands toward the wash basin and, from the side, warm water was poured over them. A towel enveloped them. It was Ikuko. She dried his hands thoroughly.

"Tonight I showed you a way of entertaining yourself without spending much money. I borrowed all those geisha for short times from other big parties. I don't want you to waste your money," she said softly. Her voice was completely different from that which she had used earlier. Now, it was warm, rich, domestic: a mature woman's voice. He straightened up and looked down into her face. It seemed older than her twenty years.

The waitresses and some geisha were hovering around the entryway. As Kikuji stepped down and into his wooden clogs on the concrete floor, he heard a shrill voice behind him. It was the proprietress of Tominoya's.

"Oh, sir. We do thank you for visiting us as often as you do, and I hope you'll be back again soon. And, please, if you think of it, convey to the master of the house my warm regards." She paused for only the briefest instant before going on. "Ikuko, my dear. You don't have the young master's collar adjusted properly. Better fix it up! And the line of the sleeve is off, too—" She jabbered on in the tinny, raspy accents of a phonograph playing too fast. Kikuji didn't like fat women. Although his grandmother and mother were of uncertain temper, they were both slim and graceful. The proprietress wore an ostentatiously expensive waistband, which had the effect of making her stomach bulge out even more. Kikuji turned toward the door without looking back. As he left, the runaway phonograph was blaring again. "Ikuko. Ikuko. Why don't you walk the young master home? You really know nothing about correct behavior!" The proprietress's chatter faded as he walked off along the silent midnight street. Since his home was not far away, he normally did not use a cab, preferring the walk. After sauntering slowly for half a block, he heard rapid steps behind him. He half expected, on turning, to see the proprietress. But it was Ikuko.

"Oh, master, what a difficult person you are," she said, panting for breath. "You walked right out and kept on going even though Mother was talking to you. This makes things very hard for me, I hope you realize."

"But why, Ikuko? Why do you let her treat you as she does? You are not a geisha or a waitress. You are the daughter of the Tominoya family. I have never understood why you should have to organize and manage the parties and affairs of the teahouse. Because of that, people tend to think of you less as the daughter of the house than as an efficient head waitress. It isn't right."

She in her turn stared at him. "You don't understand. I am an *adopted* daughter. It isn't the same thing. And so I have a great obligation to this family, don't you see—" Her voice trailed away, and the two stood silent in the midnight street. Kikuji, tired and a little confused by her confession, could think of no suitable response.

Quickly assessing his mood, Ikuko gave a short laugh, and, as though trying to cheer him up, said animatedly, "I hope you didn't mind all my advice about money when we were talking in the hall by the restroom. Maybe I fuss too much about money. I come from a very poor family. That's why they allowed me to be adopted, you see. But I hope I didn't seem to be trying to tell you how to live your life. I didn't mean to. It just slipped out."

"No, no. It was good of you. And you're quite right. I do have to learn how to use my money sensibly." He smiled at her. "Thank you for the low-cost entertainment, Ikuko. You're the very essence of thriftiness."

"Maybe so," she said somberly. "It's a hard discipline to learn, I sometimes think; and one is lucky if he never acquires or needs it. A thrifty person worries too much about the future, and makes a nuisance of herself."

Kikuji looked at her gently, and, as they walked slowly on, moved closer to her. Then he looked ahead and stopped.

"We are already at Shinmachi Bridge. Perhaps we should say goodnight here," he said.

Ikuko moved slowly back from Kikuji and bowed. She understood that beyond Shinmachi Bridge was the Semba District, where all things were controlled by rules. Even in the middle of the night a reliable businessman could not run the risk of being seen walking with a woman from the pleasure quarter. One might whisk her off in a cab to some secret rendezvous but not walk openly with her.

He parted from her at the dim bridge light and crossed the bridge quickly. Walking along the river, he saw Kawachiya's from a distance. To his surprise, there was a light in the store. He hastened his steps. As he approached, Seikichi, one of the clerks, rushed out.

"Oh, sir, I'm glad you've come. Your son, little Hisa-bon, has had some sort of convulsion. The doctor is here—"

Kikuji ran through the yard at the side, the quickest way of getting to the inner room toward the back. There, under the bright electric light, was the two-year-old, stretched out asleep or unconscious on the bedding, wearing a nightdress. As he knelt down, Kikuji could hardly notice any breathing from the pale, exhausted face. Diagonally across from the doctor, were Kino and Sei, looking very concerned. Behind them sat Tome, wringing her hands and licking her lips in her distress, while the doctor held the baby's tiny hand in his, taking its pulse. Observing the child now, Kikuji was struck by how much it had come to look like Sei and Kino. His skin was light and clear, his eyes rounded. In the tiny nightgown he looked exactly like a girl. Perhaps it was for this reason that the two ladies had altered their original hostility toward the child, and nowadays were constantly paying attention to him. All his clothing, all the toys hanging in the crib were for girls. Their affection for the boy seemed cloying and narcissistic, as though they were trying to make him like themselves. Kikuji didn't like it at all, but as yet he lacked any deep feeling for his son, and he refrainvd from stirring up a quarrel. He left the routine care to the child's nurse, and saw fit not to notice that she allowed the ladies to rule the nursery.

While Kikuji stood gazing quietly at the sleeping little boy, the sliding door flew open with a bang. It was Kihei, just returning from an evening with some business associates.

"What has happened to my grandson?" he said in a loud voice. And he pushed abruptly between Kino and Sei to watch Hisajiro's face. The doctor hastily raised his hand to warn the distraught old man not to disturb the child. But Kihei knelt over the small sleeping form and would not move. "Kihei!" said Sei in surprise, "what has got into you?" He didn't seem to hear her. The doctor leaned forward and touched his shoulder.

"My dear sir, there is no cause for worry. The convulsion is over, and the child is resting. We must not wake him just now." He motioned Kihei away, and the old man slowly moved back.

"Ah, Doctor." Tears were in his eyes. "He is all right, then?" His voice trembled uncertainly. The doctor nodded. Kihei muttered his thanks, and bowed his head, trying to control himself. But suddenly he looked up, his face wet still with tears, and with passionate intensity cried out, "You do not see! A boy in the family is *important!* We must take great good care of this little fellow, no matter what! We must, we must!" His urgent appeal resounded through the house. He paused in confusion, as though, having now broken his rule of patient nonparticipation, he was uncertain what to do next.

Soon after the family had privately celebrated Hisajiro's recovery, Kihei took to his bed with a nasty cold. At first, he took only a patent medicine sold at the noodle shop. At fifty-three, he did not know how to deal with illness. Since coming to work at Kawachiya's as a fifteen-year-old apprentice, he had never been confined to bed with any ailment, not even for a few days. Now, he found it very boring to rest all day in bed, looking at the courtyard through the glass panels of the sliding door when he was accustomed to the bustle and liveliness of the store. He belonged there. But he saw the New Year in while still confined to his bed in the master's room, next to Sei's. Since the house had been built in the days of Kihei I, the master bedroom was spacious and fine. The little alcove in which flowers and art objects were traditionally displayed was supported by a twisted post of cherrywood, now polished and gleaming. The adjoining room, belonging to the mistress of the house, was only slightly smaller. When Kihei I had wished to sleep with his wife, he summoned her to his room. But, at least for the twenty-five years of Kihei VI's marriage to Sei, the custom had been modified significantly: now, it was the wife who decided when a nocturnal visit would be appropriate. Normally after dinner Sei would go to Kino's rooms and pass the evening in relaxed fashion, talking or playing cards with the chambermaids. At around ten, she would return to her own room. Kihei, meanwhile, would stay awake. And sometimes on such nights he would hear the faint purr of the door sliding smoothly on its track, followed by the rustle of silks as Sei's body slipped under the covers beside him.

They wasted no time with tender words. He would do what was called for and fulfill her needs. When not fully satisfied, she would let him know it by twisting and turning restlessly, but when the sexual encounter had been a good one, she would move close to his side and sleep. Sei was the one who decided when and how they should do it. Kihei never knew how the sexual act had come to be controlled by the wife and not the husband. Clearly, Kino and Sei thought this mode of marital behavior perfectly natural. He was not unhappy with such an arrangement. A mechanical fulfillment of his marriage vows was about all that Kihei could without hypocrisy muster for Sei.

When he first came to Kawachiya's as an apprentice, his ambition had been to own his own store, no matter how small. Just about the time he had realized, after years of service, the impossibility of achieving his modest ambition, he had been offered an alternative: he could become the adopted son-in-law of the family by marrying

58

Sei, with the understanding that he would, in due time, become Kawachiya Kihei VI. As he lay of an afternoon on the bedding spread on the mats of the sickroom, he recalled with wry amusement the hardheaded Osaka proverb, "If you have three cupfuls of flour, don't become an adopted son-in-law." Certainly there were drawbacks, but there were the obvious advantages too. In the close-knit world of the Semba merchants, becoming the adoptive son-in-law of a flourishing commercial house meant that one had been recognized as an able businessman, capable of taking over the top management of the firm. Becoming the husband of an heiress had been a much less important consideration to him than the accompanying promotion to managerial status.

Kihei's marriage was a business transaction. But he made a businessman's mistake in taking the husband-wife relationship for granted. Too late he understood that he had married into a family where all domestic authority had resided with the wife for three long generations. He was subject to family traditions which he had no inkling of, as well as to the Semba customs with which he had been familiar.

But Kihei accepted his bargain without complaint. Reluctantly, he conceded that the happiness of a normal family life would never be his; but he felt that he could find pleasure in his work, since Semba tradition excluded women from business dealings entirely. Looking back on it now, he realized that, from the third year of his marriage on, Kino and Sei had, by their spendthrift habits, affected the conduct of the firm's business far more than they should have. His predecessor had been completely unable to control Kino, and Kihei himself had never been able to stand up to the two of them, united as they were in all matters. More and more as time went on, he allowed them to regard him as nothing more than a convenient money-providing machine.

He heard the soft scuffle of feet along the corridor outside his room. It was Sei, dressed in her most magnificent kimono. She smiled politely.

"How are you feeling, my dear?" she asked.

"Mmmm. So-so, so-so," he said vaguely. She wasn't interested in his symptoms, even though he speculated on them endlessly. He didn't feel any localized pain, but was strangely weak and listless, so exhausted all the time that he could do nothing but lie flat on his bed. In the evenings, especially, he felt feverish and unwell.

Sei addressed him again. "Kihei, we have a longstanding engagement today to attend the kabuki theater with Mr. and Mrs. Sogawaya. I'm afraid I couldn't refuse without being terribly rude."

She frowned intently, as people sometimes do when reciting from memory. Kihei understood that she had worked hard to invent this excuse for not remaining with him. A sick man often perceives far more than healthy people have time for. He had noticed that since early last night the maids had been fluttering about in the excited anticipation which always preceded one of the carefully planned excursions. And this morning, when Hidesuke came to report to him on the store's recent earnings, he had, just before leaving, smiled vaguely and said in a low voice, "Well, I see the ladies of the house are getting ready for another trip to the theater. They certainly do these things in style! I hope their having their fun at such a time doesn't seem disrespectful to you, sir—"

Kihei stared thoughtfully off into the distance. He realized that one did not talk these things over with one's employees, but he wanted to talk.

"It doesn't matter. The main thing is for me to get well again so that I can go back to the store. I want to leave Kawachiya's well off. I want people after my death to say of me, 'Ah, that Kihei VI! He took over a good business and made it one of the great firms of Osaka. He increased the family holdings by—oh, by such-and-such an amount. He was the best of the adoptive sons-in-law.' Then I will be satisfied. It isn't much of an ambition, but it's mine. That is what I have lived for."

Would Sei, standing in that superb kimono at the doorway, understand if he spoke like that to her? Almost certainly not. Still, she needn't have lied to him. The deviousness of her leave-taking annoyed him. This was no forced social obligation; it was a long-anticipated outing. By force of habit, however, he suppressed his irritation, replying only, "I understand. Sogawaya is an important customer. Do your best to give him a good time."

Feeling a little guilty at leaving him in this way, she hesitated to rush off too quickly.

"I'll leave O-Toki at home today, and she can take care of you. If you're bored, perhaps she can bring Hisa-bon here to play."

She was being unusually considerate, and he realized from that that he must be very sick.

"No, no. We mustn't take any chances with a cold that lasts this long. If he caught it, it would be terrible. I think maybe Mother Kino ought not to visit me either—for the same reason, you understand."

"Yes, of course. Older people are just as susceptible to disease as children are. I'll tell her."

Sei's response was, on the surface, polite and appropriate. But she had detected something surprisingly sarcastic in her husband's suggestion: Kino hadn't come from her safely detached rooms to visit him in more than a month. She had, moreover, warned her that any long-lasting cold was likely to be the beginning of a severe attack of tuberculosis, and had suggested that Sei keep away from Kihei as much as possible. Then she instructed the kitchen maids to separate all his dishes and utensils from those used by the rest of the family and boil them. Kino took no unnecessary chances.

Sei took her farewell of Kihei, closed the sliding door, and then scurried to join Kino, who was waiting impatiently. When she tapped the door panel of Kino's room, there came a hurried, shrill voice asking, "Have you disinfected yourself?"

"But I just looked in to tell him we were leaving, Mother."

"No, no! That makes no difference. Even a minute is enough for a microbe. Go wash your hands thoroughly, like a good girl."

Exasperated though she was by these morbid fears, Sei did not wish Kino's shrill voice to penetrate to the sickroom, so she gave in. She hastily went to the kitchen and had O-Toki pour water over her hands and clean them. Then she hurried to the front entrance. In deference to Kihei's sickness, they had given up the special pleasure of going to the theater by the Yakata boat, and instead left as inconspicuously as possible by taxi.

Kikuji, who knew the ladies' schedule, had been working in one of the storage vaults. Hearing the motor of the departing taxi, he came back to the store. The assistant manager's eyes gleamed as he entered.

"They were looking for you, sir."

Kikuji looked at him. "Oh? I'm sorry to have missed them." No need to let this fellow know any more about the family's troubles than one could help. The man was too curious. Kikuji entered the latticed accounting room and began working. He found it hard to concentrate.

With the beginning of his father's illness, he had given up his visits to the Tominoya Teahouse. Forced by necessity to stay near his father, he was especially irritated at what seemed to him empty-headed preparations by the ladies for their kabuki excursion. They had belittled Kihei's lengthy sickness, saying it was lasting so long because of the doctor's incompetence, and they had delegated O-Toki to take care of the patient rather than run any risks themselves. They were too busy gadding about town: fashion shows featuring new kimono, the Bunraku puppet theater, and, of course, their beloved kabuki plays. Had they no feeling at all for the man who had so faithfully protected their interests all these years?

Kikuji finished one page in the account book, then closed it, and went to Kihei's room. In a low voice he asked, "Are you awake, Father? How do you feel?"

"Ah, Kiku-bon. I feel much better today. Much better. So why don't you go out tonight for a change? Good idea?" A smile flitted across his face. Kikuji thought he had grown extremely gaunt and haggard in the last two months. He had been thin and bony to begin with, and, when he lost weight from illness, he looked emaciated. This ailing creature seemed almost lost in the spacious setting of the master bedroom.

"I ought to stay here, Father. Grandmother and Mother are both out, and won't be home till late. If I went too, you would have no company at all."

"But I want you to go out just because they are out, and not watching. While they are around, what freedom do you have?" said Kihei. "They want to be sure that you are keeping proper accounts until I'm well again. Isn't that so?"

He seemed, even from the limited horizons of his bed, to know exactly what was happening in every corner of the house during his illness.

Kikuji laughed.

"I have been told over and over again by them that I must"—and here he imitated Kino's shrill, nagging voice—"discipline myself, be strong, resourceful, so that I can manage the business in place of my father. It's quite a change. Once, all they wanted was that I should be as idle and wasteful as they were. It is a tribute to you. They are fearful that no one will take care of their spending money as you have done."

After this talk with his father, Kikuji decided on a short visit to the Tominoya Teahouse. When he arrived, Ikuko greeted him as though wearied of waiting for him. Her first words were an inquiry after the health of his father.

"He is not doing at all well," he reported to her.

She suddenly turned to him with a very earnest expression on her face.

"I have a favor to ask of you concerning your father." She hesitated a moment, as though ordering her thoughts. "There is someone who cares very deeply for the worthy master of your house. She wants very much to see him and take care of him if he gets any worse. She prays constantly to the Buddha for the fulfillment of her wish. I thought I ought to tell you."

"She wants—to my father?" Kikuji was dazed. The thing was incredible.

"Do you remember when you were here in October, Mamechiyo, the apprentice geisha, danced for you?" He nodded. "And do you remember the older geisha who played the samisen music for the dance?" He threw up his hands in uncertainty. "Well, that was Kimika. She has been your father's mistress for the past eight years."

Eight years! He thought back rapidly. His grandfather had died one year before. He had just entered business college. It was as though a curtain had opened on the past, revealing a totally new picture of his father to him. Now that he had almost grown accustomed to thinking of his father as an emotionless creature, an empty shell of a man with few redeeming inner qualities, he had to adjust to the fact that this seeming automaton had for eight long years loved and been loved in defiance of the self-serving rules of Sei and Kino. How he had paid them off, those two! There could be no more complete a rejection than this.

He was curious about the woman. Vaguely, he recalled the quiet geisha who had played the samisen that night. But he wanted to know her better. Ikuko summoned one of the waitresses and gave her instructions.

"Tell her that the young master of Kawachiya's is here, and he wants to see her. When you have given her the message, I want you to look around at the other parties going on. See if you can contact some of the girls who are lively, and ask them, if they can, to disappear for a little while and come up here to entertain our honored guest."

Kikuji frowned as the waitress left, and said irritably to Ikuko, "You've got to stop that sort of thing. I'll pay my way like any other customer. I know you mean well, but this borrowing of geisha someone else is paying for is just about the cheapest thing I've ever heard of. I'll pay my way."

Ikuko bowed her head. "Of course. I just didn't want you to spend too much while seeing me. I thought it was a sort of discount—"

"I know, I know. It's all right. Thanks. But no more discounts. I hate a man who won't pay his way. I guess that's my businessman's heredity coming out. No more discounts!" And he tried to pass the matter off by turning the conversation to livelier subjects. As he did so, her troubled gaze studied his every gesture. He found himself looking back deeply into her eyes. They reminded him of the direct and honest eyes of Hiroko. They didn't belong to the pleasure quarter.

At that moment, he heard rapid steps in the corridor. The door slid open, and there was the geisha, Kimika, in a watered green silk party kimono.

At thirty-four or so, she was, Kikuji realized, elderly for a geisha. Her face, though delicate, was too elongated to be completely beautiful. But her whole presence, her way of moving, of speaking, was one of modest dignity and reserve, qualities not conspicuous in her profession.

She bowed to him. "I am Kimika," she said, simply. "Your father has been very kind and good to me for many years, and I— Perhaps I should have introduced myself to you long before now, but secrecy seemed necessary to both of us."

"Ikuko has told me about your relationship with my father. Are you—that is, is there anything that I—?"

"He has taken good care of me," she answered, bowing low. But Kikuji had watched her face as he had awkwardly asked and she politely answered. She was protecting her patron's reputation. The

64

green silk kimono she was wearing did not have the texture of new material. It had lost its sheen from too much laundering, and the fold of the brocaded sash was faintly worn.

She asked timidly about Kihei's condition and Kikuji told her what little the doctor had said.

"But—will he stay long in bed, do you think?" she asked anxiously. He looked at her, frowning. But he was spared an answer by the sudden appearance of the three geisha summoned by Ikuko. The room was filled with their laughter and lively talk. Kikuji found it hard to join in. The gloomy thoughts of his father's illness had followed him here, and now there was an implied responsibility for yet another person's welfare, his father's mistress, whose existence he had never suspected.

Kimika watched him unobtrusively while she played dance music for the three geisha. At ten, he stood up to leave. At the entrance hall sat the fat proprietress, waiting to see him off.

"We are much concerned here for the health of your distinguished father," she said politely. "Please take good care of him. I hope before long he will be up and around, and perhaps visiting us here from time to time."

Kikuji nodded. What she said was polite enough, he supposed. Maybe a shade too cheerful in the saying? She was a nuisance.

He turned abruptly to Kimika. "Would you be able to walk part of the way home with me?" The question took all the women by surprise. They had expected Ikuko would go with him. But Kimika immediately tucked up her kimono for easier walking, and stepped down into her wooden clogs on the concrete exit floor.

After walking a block or so, Kikuji slowed down. Even with his long coat, the wind of January was piercingly cold. Kimika was wearing an open-necked party kimono without even the protection of a shawl. "I shouldn't have let you come," he said. "You'll surely catch cold."

She shook her head. "Not at all. We are used to dressing this way in cold weather. It's nothing."

"Don't take such risks. Someday soon I may have to rely on you to take care of my father in his last illness." He halted, bothered by what might seem an alarmist's exaggeration. "Of course, the doctor has not said that, and no one really knows—"

65

Kimika did not reply. He cast about for words to cheer her up, but could think of nothing. An empty cab came slowly and noisily down the street. He signaled it and, when it stopped, made her get in. When she was seated, he said to her, "I'll arrange to have money sent to you from my account at Tominoya's. You'll be taken care of." He shut the door and signaled the driver. She opened the window, and said to him in a voice made husky by emotion, "Ah, sir, you should not, you should not—" And she bowed her head as the cab drove slowly off.

By July, Kihei had become much worse. Following the rainy season, he had seemed to improve, but, with the heat of summer, the hottest (so the papers said) in twenty years, he lost weight steadily, as though sweating away his life. The doctor was unprepared for this change, since he had been very sure from the beginning of the patient's eventual recovery. The heat seemed deadly and there was little they could do about it. A large block of ice was placed in each corner of the sickroom, but it had little effect. Every two hours Kihei's night kimono, soaked with sweat, was changed.

The summer was a slack season for Kawachiya's, and Kikuji was free to spend time sitting with his father. There wasn't much anyone could do. His father was too weak to carry on a long conversation. Sometimes his son read parts of a magazine article to him. Often, he moved the fan over him. Even a healthy person found this clinging heat unendurable. But Kihei didn't complain. All his life, from fifteen to fifty-three, he hadn't complained. He had lost the habit.

One afternoon while he was sitting by the sick man, his father went into an extended fit of coughing. Kikuji supported him, and rubbed his back, but the coughing became more violent. Kihei's body bent like a lobster, and the newly laundered white sheet was covered with blood. Kikuji shouted to O-Toki, and, when she saw what was happening, she sent for the doctor. He gave the sick man an injection and made frowning comments which, when Kikuji turned them over in his mind, seemed to mean little except to suggest that, whatever happened, the doctor had foreseen it.

Kino and Sei, hearing of the seizure, had come to the door of the sickroom, and were sitting nervously in the corridor by the doorsill as the doctor paid his visit. When he started to leave, Kino caught up with him, and said, "I don't understand how it could be TB. TB is hereditary, and we studied his family carefully before he was married. There was no TB among his relations!"

"No, my lady." The doctor looked very learned. "TB is not hereditary. It is a contagious disease."

Kino was horrified. "Then my daughter has already caught it, don't you suppose?"

"I couldn't say without a thorough examination," the doctor answered. "But right now, I think you should hire a registered nurse and a practical nurse to care for him and keep the risk of others contracting his sickness to a minimum. Yes, indeed."

Kino went flying to the sickroom and motioned to Kikuji to join her in the corridor. When he did so, she said excitedly, "You must keep away from him. And Sei too. This is a contagious disease. Stay away! Hire some nurses! They're paid to run risks."

He looked at his frightened, nearly hysterical grandmother for a long moment. Then he said, "I'll get the nurses. You go to your rooms and avoid getting infected." He watched as she fled down the hall, then turned back into Kihei's room. He shielded the light bulb so that it was as soft as candlelight. Even at night the heat was intense. Kikuji sat, helplessly moving the fan back and forth in slow arcs over his father.

Later on, he called the nursing association and asked them to send a trained nurse in the morning. Next, he called the geisha house and asked for Kimika. When she came to the phone, he told her quietly, "I thought you should know: my father is much worse. If you wish, you can come here tomorrow to act as a practical nurse. It will call for some pretending on your part. There will also be a trained nurse to take care of strictly medical matters. You won't need any special knowledge. A little kindliness at this stage is worth more than medicine, I think."

"Yes, sir. I'll do my best," she replied in a shaky voice.

"I hate to say it, but, since my mother and grandmother will be around, you can't just be yourself. As a practical nurse, you would be most useful and in many ways most natural. Don't you think so?"

"Yes, of course," she answered. "I am grateful to you for thinking of it. I'll be there tomorrow at noon, sir."

When he returned to the sickroom, Kihei was lying on his back, staring up at the dim light.

"Do you feel well enough to hear some news, Father?" he asked. He wanted to cushion the shock of surprise which Kihei was certain to feel on seeing his mistress as a practical nurse.

Kihei grunted.

"I don't want you to be surprised or upset. Kimika will be here tomorrow."

"Ah-h-h-h-h?" Kihei opened his eyes wide, and looked skeptically at his son, as though doubting his own ears.

"She'll be here serving as a practical nurse. I thought it would be the best way for the two of you to see each other."

Kihei was upset. "This is the craziest scheme you could have dreamed up, Kiku-bon. It won't do! The ladies— We don't want trouble. Not at this time."

"Forget the ladies! They don't like sickrooms. They won't be around much. The doctor told us to get a registered nurse and a practical nurse. Kimika will do very well as a practical nurse. It's all settled. There's nothing to worry about. Really! She'll be here tomorrow around noon."

"You really think it will be all right?"

"Of course. We have only O-Toki to worry about. Mother and Grandmother will leave everything to me and the doctor."

The sick man nodded feebly and his face brightened up noticeably. He had a defined future ahead of him once more.

Next morning the registered nurse from the agency came as scheduled early in the morning, and briskly took charge of the patient. Just after lunch, one of the apprentices taking inventory in the store came to him.

"Sir, the woman who is to be the practical nurse for your father is here."

He took a deep breath, rose from his desk, and turned toward the entrance without haste. But then he raised his brows in astonishment and almost began to object. The woman in front of him, dressed in faded summer kimono, and carrying a large bundle of belongings in a cloth knotted together, was the very image of a practical nurse. Gone was the elegant coiffure of the geisha; the woman's natural hair was pulled back in a tight bun at the back of her head. Gone were the mincing gestures of the professional entertainer; in their place was the coarse vigor of a robust country woman. Kikuji controlled an impulse to laugh in delighted surprise, and said for

68

the benefit of others in the store, "You are the practical nurse I called for yesterday?"

"Yes, sir. I hope I'm not late." Trying to be careful even in the way she made a bow, she lowered her head in the unsophisticated manner of a peasant.

"Very well. If you will go through the yard on your left to the family quarters, you can report to the housekeeper, O-Toki, and she will get you started."

Kimika bowed low to him, and then, with country naivete, to all others in the store. Wasuke, the manager, observing this, said to her courteously, "It's good of you to come to help us." But Hidesuke, the assistant manager, simply looked at her impassively through his rimless spectacles. She put her bundle down, secured a new grip on it, and walked out of the store and along the yard to the family area, as Kikuji had directed.

As soon as she was out of his sight, Kikuji went to Kihei's room.

"Father," he whispered. "She'll be here in a minute. She is reporting to O-Toki for instructions."

Kihei's eyes, so lackluster these past few months, gleamed with pleased anticipation. His son gently adjusted the collar of his kimono to cover the emaciated chest on which the contour of the ribs stood out. Looking up, he saw Sei standing in the open doorway, cool as always in her summer silk kimono. Behind her were O-Toki and Kimika. Sei entered the sickroom, sitting at a distance from her husband, and introduced the practical nurse to him.

"This is the master of the house. You are Motohashi—?"

"Motohashi Yoneko, my lady." This was, Kikuji knew, her name prior to entering the geisha profession.

Kihei kept his eyes closed. "Thank you, Sei. You take good care of me. And with these nurses, there will be no danger of your getting the disease, a very important consideration, certainly." He opened his eyes and looked into hers.

She reddened. "I didn't mean that," she said vaguely.

He looked at Kimika. "So this is the practical nurse." She bowed.

"This is not an easy illness to take care of," said Sei, briskly. "The registered nurse will instruct you in your duties, and you are to pay close attention to the master's every wish. O-Toki here will help you out if you need anything."

"Yes, my lady. I don't know much, but I always try hard. Please give me your favor." She bowed to the two ladies. O-Toki, looking at her, had difficulty in figuring her out. Somehow, she struck her as more refined and neater than one would expect a practical nurse to be, despite her worn clothing and country manner.

Sei, who had no desire to linger any longer than formality required, finally left, taking O-Toki with her. Kimika moved immediately to Kihei's side. For a moment she took his withered hand in hers, tears glistening in her eyes. Then, hearing the approach of the registered nurse in the hallway, she hastily dabbed at her eyes with a handkerchief, and folded the sheet over Kihei. The nurse came in briskly, and, after the introduction, picked up a bundle of soiled linen in the corner.

"I'm sorry to have to put you to work so fast, but could you launder these clothes for us?"

Kihei frowned, and Kimika for an instant stared at the armful of laundry. A geisha to wash underwear! Then she smiled and bowed her head. "Of course. Where are the washtubs?" And off she went.

"Kiku-bon, please—towel! Sweating!" croaked Kihei.

The nurse jumped up, but Kikuji was there before her with a towel. It was not, in any case, sweat. Large teardrops were streaking his thin face.

In August, the heat intensified. The price of the ice blocks went up sharply, and in addition O-Toki had to bribe the apprentice at the ice house to get decent pieces. Kikuji could see that Kihei's will to live had become much stronger since Kimika's arrival, but he could also see that he didn't seem to be getting any stronger. The doctor remained noncommittal, giving regular injections of glucose to keep the patient well nourished, but not much else. The long stasis of summer hung over them like a pall.

Kino and Sei had decided to go to Arima Hot Springs in mid-August, announcing that the trip was necessary to cure Hisajiro's heat rash, which had spread all over his body, causing the child to cry hours at a time. "His constant fretting will bother his grandfather if we don't do something about it," said Sei. And so they made their plans to escape from the monotony of Kihei's sickness. They were bored with the heat and illness alike, and needed diversion.

Out of deference to Kikuji and Kihei, they announced that they would limit their stay to three or four days. And off they went, taking a sullen and uncomfortable Hisajiro along with them.

No sooner were they out of the house than the servants relaxed and performed their duties carelessly or not at all. The maids and seamstresses now had ample spare time for gossip. Even the trained nurse seemed unconcerned with her duties, and often lounged around the sewing room, watching curiously as the seamstresses put together kimono for Kino and Sei.

O-Toki was perhaps not the best person to run the household in the ladies' absence. Divorced and past thirty, she did her work with single-minded concentration, never paying much attention to others. The kitchenmaids tried to hide their loafing from O-Toki, but they might as well not have bothered. She had a rare capacity for ignoring others and tending to her own affairs. Kimika found her puzzling and never knew where she stood with her. O-Toki never gave any orders. When Kimika asked for instructions, she was told with the greatest precision and courtesy that she should do what she thought best.

Once the ladies had left, Kihei's desire to be taken care of by his mistress became more and more evident. When the registered nurse began to prepare his meal, he stopped her and sent for Kimika, saying that it was the place of the practical nurse to do such things. In actuality, the menu was so simple that no skilled cookery was called for. A normal supper for Kihei consisted of no more than a small bowl of rice, the white meat of fish, and some apple juice. Still, the nurse was glad to let Kimika take over this task along with many other duties of the sickroom. Kimika, on her side, was a little worried that her zeal in nursing Kihei might give away her real reasons for being there. But Kihei, smiling feebly, and pointing insistently with his thin, wrinkled hand at the chopsticks, insisted that she serve him.

"As long as the two ladies of the house are away, I want to enjoy my freedom!"

So Kimika took out the black lacquered chopsticks, and, holding his hand in hers, helped him to use them, as one helps a small child. Before giving him the broiled fish, she carefully removed each of the small bones. He took it, bit by small bit, into his mouth, savoring it the more because of her nearness. She strained the apple juice

71

through tightly woven cotton cloth so that he could suck it up easily through a straw. And when it was time for tea, she was careful to make a very mild brew so that his illness would not be aggravated by it. By her many tender attentions she tried to repay him as best she could for the many favors of love he had bestowed on her in the old days when he had been in good health. On alternate nights she and the trained nurse used the room next to Kihei's, which Sei had vacated when, realizing the serious nature of her husband's illness, she had moved to Kino's detached rooms. During the evening, Kimika took her bath after all the others had finished, then applied light makeup and put on a clean cotton kimono. She would wear an apron over it as long as the maids and the nurse were still up, but after they had gone to bed, she would remove the apron. Often she passed the hours of the night slowly and steadily fanning Kihei.

During one such evening, he reached over and caressed her hand, by now callused from her hard work as a nurse, and said with a wry smile, "I hate to see you doing all this menial labor. You are used to better things. It is very hard on you." He kissed the palm of her hand.

Kimika leaned close to him and said softly, "Suppose that all through this long illness I had not been able to see you. That, surely, would have been hard on me. But this way, as my reward for doing some laundry and keeping things tidy, I can be with you as much as I wish and I can make sure that you are properly taken care of. I think I am very fortunate."

Kihei sighed, and patted her hand again. "I haven't done enough for you, I'm afraid."

She tried to shrug this off with a slight toss of her head, but against her will her eyes filled with tears. "You have been my lover these eight years, gentle, constant, kind—" She could say no more. She leaned over him and softly embraced his frail body covered by the sheet.

On the fifth day of their stay at the Arima Hot Springs Hotel, Sei and Kino had phoned for more money. Hisajiro was completely cured of his ailment, but they had met in the inn's communal bath a lady who taught the difficult art of singing Japanese classical music, and the two ladies had stayed on to practice under her tutelage. Another three days passed after the money was sent, and still they did not return. Kikuji, remembering their grand manner at the kabuki play, supposed that, whatever else they did, they would dress magnificently and tip extravagantly, if only to attract attention and curiosity.

He lay in his room thinking about his mother and grandmother as the electric fan in the corner hummed and turned back and forth in slow, sedate arcs. Like empty-headed, self-centered children they had fled the boredom of the heat and the sickroom, abandoning husband and provider to the uncertain care (as far as they knew) of two strangers. It was their nature, he supposed, and nothing more could be expected. They were, he sensed, beginning to use him too as though he were nothing more than a piece of business equipment —just as they had used his father and grandfather.

He drank the rest of the cold tea, and looked across the hall to the sickroom. Kihei was awake. No one else was around. He stood up and went in to his father's room.

"When do you think your mother will come back?" Kihei asked.

"It has been a week now since she left, hasn't it?" replied Kikuji. "It really is a little—unfeeling, considering your state of health."

Kihei said nothing, and, as the silence lengthened, Kikuji wondered if his father were about to fall asleep. But then he said, "It is no matter. If they were here, it would make no difference. The longer their vacation, the better. I am very content with things the way they are. Send them more money so they'll stay longer. I have Kimika here."

Kikuji looked at his father for a moment, and then quite deliberately turned his gaze toward the darkened courtyard, trying to speak casually.

"You remind me, speaking of Kimika: last night I sent a large amount of money to her. So don't worry about her. I'll take care of her. She won't suffer."

Kihei breathed so deeply it was almost a sigh. "So! I am greatly relieved. You are very—thoughtful of me. Won't the ladies of the house give you any difficulty, though?"

Kikuji laughed. "Not so long as they stay at Arima Hot Springs singing Japanese classical music! And even when they're here, they see only their mirrors, if you'll excuse me for saying so. The only

73

one who might notice our special concern for Kimika is O-Toki, and, as far as I can see, she simply doesn't care."

Kihei pursed his lips thoughtfully, and nodded.

Suddenly, he gave his son a sharp, urgent look and said, "Kikuji, you have charge of the books now: how much do you think I have increased the value of the family holdings?"

"Uh?" The son stared at his father, mystified.

"I want to know," Kihei said stubbornly. "It may not seem important to you. But to me it's the measure of my whole life. How much have I added to the family wealth?"

"But not now, surely," protested Kikuji. "Not when you're sick! That's no time to fill your mind with business statistics. You must forget—"

He stopped himself. He had been on the verge of saying, "You must forget for once that you are only an adopted husband." He looked into his father's drawn, serious face.

"You really want it?"

"Yes. Yes. The sooner, the better."

"As you wish. I'll get at it tomorrow morning," Kikuji promised. "But right now I have to go downtown to assist with the fireworks display I've been helping to organize."

He went slowly into the business offices and sat down. He was for some reason profoundly shaken by his father's insistence that the meaning of his life could be added up in a business account book. What could possibly be a suitable return for working dutifully thirty-seven years, day in, day out, under the watchful eyes of an unloving wife? He had, thought the son, surrendered his individuality to become an automaton, a trademark for a family business. Kihei VI. And soon there would be an equally meaningless Kihei VII. He shivered at the prospect.

He opened the account book, stared at its pages for a few moments, and closed it.

"Young master—" Kikuji was startled and turned to see Hidesuke at his elbow, carefully resetting his rimless spectacles on his sweaty nose. "I'm sorry. I hope I didn't startle you. How is the master feeling today?"

"Oh, he's—doing all right, I guess."

"Yes." Hidesuke smiled a respectful smile. "He seems to have improved quite a little since that hard-working practical nurse came. Don't you think so?"

Kikuji felt as though the assistant manager had given him a small, deliberate electric shock. He tried to conceal his alarm, saying merely, "Ah, yes. She's very good." He opened the account book again to signify the end of their talk, and, although he found it hard to concentrate, he continued studying the figures for half an hour. Then he asked Hidesuke to take over, and he went downtown to assist with the fireworks display.

After the show was over, he walked back in leisurely fashion, along the road by the Yokobori River. He pushed open the side gate leading into the courtyard. All the apprentices and clerks, he knew, had gone to town to see the fireworks and had remained to enjoy themselves. The yard was unusually silent. From a distance, he heard the pleasant sound of someone splashing water around in the bath: one of the maids, probably, finishing up her late bath. Walking down the courtyard beside the house, he saw that Grandmother's detached rooms were still dark. They had not yet returned.

He went quietly to his room. O-Toki had spread out the bedding on the floor, his nightclothes neatly folded next to the pillow. He stretched himself lazily on the quilt. He was bored. For days he had thought the same thoughts, beginning and ending with his father's illness. And always there was the stifling heat to contend with. He half dozed.

Suddenly, he heard a commotion at the front entryway: a car driving off, the clatter of wooden clogs on cement, women's voices. His mother and grandmother must just have come back. He quickly changed into his sleeping kimono, hooked the unattached corner of the mosquito net, and crawled inside, intending to ignore their arrival until morning. But it was not to be. Soon he heard O-Toki calling him softly through the paper panels of the sliding door. He did not answer. But then the door was thrown open with a great thump and his mother stood in the opening, calling him in a loud voice which he couldn't pretend not to hear.

"Kiku-bon! Wake up! I've something I want to talk to you about right now!"

He rolled slowly over on his back, rubbed his eyes, and asked sleepily, "What on earth is going on?"

As she came in from the lighted hallway, he saw her, as always, cool and immaculate in her Oshima silk kimono, her neck long and graceful.

"Welcome home," he said. "But why so sudden and late?"

"Ah, you weren't expecting us." She smiled in triumph.

"What *is* the matter? Please get it off your mind. What are you fussing about?" asked Kikuji angrily.

"Very well. Come back to your grandmother's rooms where we can talk without disturbing anyone. Right now!"

She pulled at his sleeve in her excitement. He got up, put a loose sash around his kimono, and went with his mother to Kino's rooms. His grandmother sat waiting expectantly for him. He greeted her, and started to ask about Hisajiro's rash, but she interrupted him stormily.

"Ah, to think that you are capable of such hypocrisy! Welcome home indeed!"

Kikuji stared at the two of them. "You've had your vacation in a nice, cool spot while I've been working for you here in town. What more could you want?"

"Oh, we know all about your work. And that of the practical nurse, too," replied Kino with a bitter laugh.

"What is that supposed to mean?" said Kikuji stiffly. "You saw both of the nurses and approved them just before you went off on your vacation."

"Hmf! We saw her coming out of the bath chamber just now. She had applied her makeup not only to her face, but to her neck and shoulders as well, just as professional geisha do. And then she puts on a cotton kimono as good as any I have before she goes into the sickroom. She's no practical nurse, that woman!"

"Oh? I've never paid much attention to these things—" Kikuji stalled desperately, trying to think of a way out of the mess. But there was none. His grandmother only became angrier and more positive.

"I saw her with my own eyes! Just now! When I came in after paying the taxi. I went by the bathroom, and there she was, the hussy, powdering her neck in the geisha fashion, and then sneaking like some woman of the night along the hallway into Kihei's room. What kind of a place are you running here?"

"For goodness sake! Even a practical nurse has a right to a bath after a hard day's work. And if she powders her nose and happens to have a better-than-average kimono to wear after everyone else has gone to bed, what difference does it make? Surely I don't have to buy her a nurse's uniform at the store?" Righteous anger seemed to be his only defense.

Kino rose to her feet and walked around the room in her fury. She loosened the sash of her kimono, and, as she tugged at it, it gave way and whipped through the air, brushing Kikuji's face. An empty purse fell from it on the tatami mat. Three days before Kikuji had filled it so tightly with bills that he could barely snap it shut before giving it to one of the clerks in the office to deliver to the two vacationing women. Was this empty purse the real reason for their sudden return? His grandmother turned and came close to him, her eyes sparkling with anger.

"Don't think you can fool me with back talk, young man! I've been around a long time. I know a kept woman when I see one. As soon as I saw her after her bath, I smelled the skin of a kept woman!"

Had Grandfather too sought solace at the geisha houses, he wondered.

"But this is only your guesswork, based on a bit of makeup that you didn't approve of—"

"Not at all, my dear," said Kino briskly. "We had reports about the nurse before this, but until we saw with our own eyes what was going on, we didn't take it seriously."

A vision of rimless spectacles on a sweaty nose came to Kikuji. Hidesuke had, perhaps, added his own note to the ladies when Kikuji had sent the clerk with the money. It would be like him. He braced himself and said nothing.

Sei dabbed at her eyes with her handkerchief.

"Kikuji, how could you do this to us? To deceive your own mother by helping with a sordid romance! Where is your human decency?"

He looked incredulously at the two women. Then he leaned forward toward Sei, and smiled even as he frowned.

"Human decency. I completely agree with you. It is very important. But the Semba has rules for all things, so don't you worry your

77

heads about what people will think. One of the nicer customs of the Semba provides for an illness like Father's. If a man is sick, his mistress may come to his house to take care of him, not openly as his mistress, but secretly and in disguise to keep the neighbors from talking and to prevent loving wives from grieving." As he talked, his smile became a savage grin. "You must realize, of course, that I am not applying all this to the practical nurse now in our house. But even if she *were* Father's mistress, the custom of centuries would permit her to come in this fashion to nurse her friend."

Kino, still walking around and rubbing her arms, turned to him.

"I can't imagine where you have learned all these filthy things. From some waitress in the Shinmachi, probably—fooling around just as your father did before you. A fine way for an adopted husband to behave! A fine example to his son!" Her loud words went ringing through the house, and Kikuji urged her to speak more quietly.

"I'll do what I please!" she snapped. She saw O-Toki sitting by the door sill.

"O-Toki! Give us your impression of the practical nurse. What did you think of her?"

O-Toki bowed her head and mumbled unintelligibly. Sei's voice rang out. "Speak up, woman! What about her? You were in charge of the sickroom during our absence."

The housekeeper kept staring at the floor in front of her. Finally, she said timidly, "Everything she did seemed all right to me, my lady. She took good care of the master."

Sei stood up, walked over to the maid, and slapped her resoundingly. O-Toki fell on her face. Kikuji grabbed the hem of his mother's kimono from where he sat, and pulled her back from the terrified chambermaid. The two women and the young man all looked at each other, frozen for the moment by the violence of their feelings. Then, there was a hurried padding of feet in the passageway, and Kimika was in the doorway.

"Please! Quickly! The master is very ill!"

Kikuji pushed by and ran to the sickroom. The nurse was giving his father oxygen. The doctor had been called, but was not at home. After a time, Kihei waved his hand and took the oxygen tube out of his mouth. The nurse tried to put it back, but he waved her away. Breathing hard, he turned to his son.

78

"Kiku-bon," he said with difficulty between noisy gasps of air, "women! Take over! You know? Be *bonchi!* Owner! Boss! Master of merchants!" He lay gasping for the right words and the breath to express them. Kikuji leaned down to catch his whisper. "Crack the whip. *Bonchi.* Make it go!"

He lay back, closing his eyes. His mouth was twitching in pain, but he was fully conscious. Kikuji tried to quiet him so that he could inhale the oxygen again, but he continued to mutter unintelligibly. When finally the nurse succeeded in placing the tube in his mouth once more, he was too weak to breathe deeply. Sei and Kino came timidly into the room and sat quietly at a short distance from the sick man. Behind them, Kimika watched nervously. But there was nothing anyone could do. Kihei's breathing grew slower and slower, although the nurse worked frantically at the machine. And then his head fell to one side and the oxygen tube fell out of his mouth. He opened his eyes, looked hazily from face to face, tried to say something, and then suddenly his gaze stared fixedly off into infinity.

Realizing that her husband was dead, Sei burst into loud and unrestrained sobs. Kino gazed thoughtfully at the dead man's face. Kimika placed both hands before her on the floor and bowed her head low. The nurse, with Kimika's help, rearranged the dead man's body so that his head pointed north, and his robe with the family crest on it was spread over the blanket. Kino took Sei by the arm and led her, still weeping uncontrollably, back to the detached rooms. Kikuji continued sitting at his father's pillow. When the incense burned low, he renewed it. Behind him sat Wasuke, the manager, with Hidesuke. Kimika was nowhere to be seen.

Suddenly, at the very edge of his vision, he sensed a quick movement among the trees of the courtyard. Kikuji stood up casually, put on the clogs set out for walking in the garden, and strolled toward the storage vault. At one side of it stood Kimika. From that spot she could look through the bushes and see Kihei with his head lying to the north.

"Kimika! You disappeared so suddenly I didn't have a chance to talk with you."

She bowed her head. Kikuji took a deep breath.

"I have no wish to be unpleasant, and you have been a tremendous help to me. But now that Father is gone, I think it would be best if you left right away."

79

From the dark shadow of the vault where she stood, her cry came out with the sharpness of a needle. "Ah, soon! Master, please, give me just a little time—"

"Look, I understand how you feel. But you know the rules as well as I do. For a man's mistress to be seen after his death at the mourning rites or the funeral would be unthinkable in the Semba—and maybe anywhere else, now that I think of it. I'm sorry, Kimika, but I've done the best I can for you, and that's the way it has to be."

She nodded resignedly. "As you wish, sir."

Kikuji squared his shoulders, trying not to weaken. "If you go through the garden here, you'll come around to the front entrance. I'll have your things brought there."

"I want to see him just once more."

"I'm sorry," said Kikuji stonily. "It would only prolong your distress. Here. This is inadequate payment for all you've done—"

He handed her a purse filled with bills. While they were standing thus indecisively in the shade of the vault, O-Toki came out to them. Ignoring Kimika, she said to Kikuji, "The undertaker is here, sir." He nodded, and she returned to the house. Kimika took a few steps toward the front. He watched her, and then, acting on sudden impulse, called after her.

"Kimika, until the hundred days of mourning are over, I hope you won't attend any of those parties. I'll take care of you."

She stopped, turned, and looked searchingly at him over her shoulder, then finally nodded and walked off through the trees toward the street.

Kihei in his quiet way had made many friends, and the line of mourners in front of Tojiji Temple, where the funeral was to be held, was a long one. Many who came to offer up incense for the repose of the dead man's soul were business associates and longtime customers of Kawachiya's. There were also women from teahouses and restaurants who came quietly and deferentially to pay their last respects. As chief mourner and the one in charge, Kikuji in his crested white silk mourning kimono kept exchanging bows with guests who had made their offerings of incense.

In the main hall, the priest, Keimei, was conducting the funeral. As he chanted the Buddhist sutras, Kino and Sei sat near Kihei's coffin, fingering their red rosaries, designed especially for the ladies.

Behind them sat relatives and the families of various branch managers of the firm who had been trained and promoted to their present positions by Kihei. An unpainted altar was placed at the center of the room, above the steps. The mourners looked hot as they moved slowly through the temple yard into the funeral chamber, offered their incense, and left. It was the third of September, and the heat had unseasonably returned. Kikuji was sweating through the white cloth of his mourning kimono. As he stood at the exit door bowing to the departing mourners, he recollected for the hundredth time his father's final command to him: "Women! Take over! You know?" He knew. It was one of the few times when he had heard his father speak with the full force of his mind. And, up to a point, the message was clear: "Don't do as I have done. Take charge. Of the business. Of the family. Of your life." But those last words? They were hard to interpret. "*Bonchi*. Make it go!"

At this moment someone in a black kimono stopped in front of him. It was Hiroko. She had filled out a little since her departure two years before, and, although her face was set and serious, as the occasion required, her eyes were quick and perceptive, as in the early days of their marriage. He was glad to see her, and would have liked to talk with her. But her father was at her elbow, and the portly old man spoke first.

"Ah, Kikuji-han, terrible, terrible. You'll have your hands full from now on, I'm afraid. Well, I'd like to talk with you, but you see, Hiroko is going—"

She cut in on her father. "Please, Master, take good care of your son. He is a nice boy."

She looked for a moment through the doorway where the funeral was going on: they could see Hisajiro squirming on his nurse's lap. Then she bowed and walked quickly away.

Kikuji was suddenly aware of a small commotion at the temple gate. He went out to watch. The Kawachiya clerks had appeared dressed in yellow kimono with the family crest, carrying black lacquer trays with candies and cakes from a well-known shop in Osaka. The head clerk intoned, "The funeral of the illustrious Kawachiya Kihei IV is concluded. We will now perform the Hungry Ghost Feeding Rites in his name for the repose of his soul." And they passed around their trays to the old women and children who had gathered at the temple in anticipation of the ritual. They were unstinting in offering, because it was popularly believed that the more they gave away, the greater the chance of the dead man's achieving salvation. The eager children crowded around the clerks. "Hey, Uncle. Don't be stingy, now. I can eat lots!" they shouted, and the clerks good-naturedly doled out the cakes until their trays were empty.

As Kikuji watched, he suddenly saw Kimika in the crowd. She caught his glance and, too late, moved behind a telephone pole. She came out into his view again, looking miserable at having been recognized. She had dressed herself inconspicuously, with none of the hallmarks of a geisha. For, although the proprietresses and ladies of the teahouses and restaurants were, by Semba custom, permitted to attend funerals, the geisha and former mistresses were simply not allowed. Kikuji was annoyed. He had told her clearly what he wanted, and she had not done as he asked.

At this point there was a great shout from the children. Kakushichi, the head clerk, had appeared with a new supply of cakes. All the children tried to reach in at once, but the clerk raised his tray high over their heads and shouted, "Only for those who haven't yet had any. No fair loading your pockets. Give the other kids a chance!" One of the old women elbowed the children out of the way, and passed cakes back to others in the rear of the crowd.

"That's the spirit, Grandma, that's the right idea!" shouted Kakushichi. "Pass them around for the peace of a good man's soul!"

"*Namu-amida-butsu, namu-amida-butsu*," chanted the old woman dutifully. Kimika, caught in the crowd next to her, was looking for a way out.

"Hel-lo, there," shouted Kakushichi. "Here's our friend, the practical nurse who took such good care of our master in his last illness. You must take at least three cakes!" And he held them out to her. She hesitated for an instant, then took them and bowed hurriedly. Some members of the funeral party were leaving the temple and Kikuji feared that she would be recognized. But he recollected his duties, and spoke courteously to the guests as he saw them off at the gate. When he turned again to look for Kimika, she had managed to escape.

With the funeral service over, and the line of mourners gone, it was time to bring the coffin out. He adjusted the crease of his white trousers, and went back into the main hall to participate with the

82

rest of the family in a last incense-burning over Kihei's body. Then, under the priest's supervision, the coffin lid was set in place and nailed down at the corners. As the noise of the hammering stopped, Sei dropped her red rosary, threw the sleeves of her kimono over her face and began to wail unrestrainedly. Kino in embarrassment tried to pass her a white linen handkerchief, but she didn't see it. Kikuji looked at her in near-disbelief. She was a hard one to figure out. During Kihei's lifetime, she had treated him, even in marriage, like a hired hand. And now she was putting on a great show of being inconsolable. Was it possible that a love too long taken for granted had now at its completion in death suddenly surfaced in her awareness and understanding? Or was she in her willfulness weeping that death had taken away one of her useful possessions and demanding that it be given back? Kikuji observed her as remotely as he might have watched a total stranger, and had to admit that, at the age of forty-five, she was in her thin summer mourning kimono as cool and elegant as a stand of green bamboo. If only she would stop blubbering.

The coffin bearers were the four heads of families related to the Kawachiyas, assisted by the strong hands of young employees in the firm. Quietly and slowly they proceeded up the paved walkway to the hearse with their burden on their shoulders. After the casket had been carefully deposited in the vehicle, Kikuji, as head of the family climbed into the front seat, beside the driver, holding the funeral tablet. Kino and Hisajiro with his nurse sat in the back with the coffin. Sei, in accordance with compassionate custom, was spared this last trip. But before the departure of the procession, one more ceremony was called for. Sei stood motionless in front of the temple gate. Her hair, done in mourning style with a low chignon tied by a black ribbon, gave her a look almost of majesty. In front of her a heap of straw had been piled. Bending down, she threw a bit of lighted paper into it and the straw blazed up. Then she took what had been her husband's favorite teacup at all his meals, and threw it onto the flames. After a moment it broke into pieces with a dry, hollow "Pock!" which seemed peculiarly final. And, as this little cup, which he had used habitually at meals over the hours and years of their marriage, lay in scattered fragments, so all connection between the living and the dead was now completely severed.

For a few instants after the ritual breaking of the teacup, she

83

gazed sightlessly into the flames, lost in her thoughts. The hearse began to move with a faint squeak. Thus summoned back to the present moment, she stared wildly at the hearse with its cargo of the living and the dead, and suddenly crumpled into a heap on the gravel. O-Toki, always alert, succeeded in supporting her as she fell. Kino uttered a distressed exclamation and started to stand up in the hearse. But, as she did so, she noticed the curious gaze of the people standing on both sides of the road to see them off. Slowly, she sat down again, her back straight and unsupported by the seat rest, her head up, her eyes staring straight ahead of her as the hearse moved slowly past her daughter and on down the road toward Kihei's final destination.

Three

Kikuji was nervous. Carefully, in order not to disarrange his ceremonial black kimono and striped trousers, he sat down on a cushion placed at the center along one wall of the large, tatami-matted banquet hall. Kino and Sei, resplendent in their best kimono, sat on either side of him. They were unusually silent, not being quite accustomed to invading the male privacy of a business dinner. But it was a great occasion and they felt they had a right to be there. Now that the forty-nine days of mourning were completed, Kawachiya's had invited all its major business associates to a party at the famed Kishimatsu-kan Restaurant so that they might participate in the Rite of Accession to the Name. Henceforth, Kikuji would be known as Kawachiya Kihei VII.

From his central vantage point, he surveyed the scene. Sitting on cushions along the walls of either side of the spacious hall were some eighty men, most them gray-haired, experienced in the ways of the world, and about the age of his father. This was, he knew, just as important a day for them as it was for him. They had come to assess the quality of the new master at Kawachiya's. They knew what they had a right to expect. If he did not pass their inspection, Kawachiya's might suffer a downturn in its fortunes. There they sat quietly, the little, red lacquered tables of food before each of them. They had been assigned seating according to their standing in Kawachiya's, those of greatest importance being nearest to Kikuji. There was a saying of the Osaka merchants, "Laggard at parties, sluggard in business." All the guests had arrived a half-hour before the scheduled starting time. Hidesuke sat at the door to greet any latecomer. Wasuke, sitting at the far end of the room, opposite Kikuji, awaited the appropriate moment to begin the ceremony.

At such occasions, Kikuji knew, style was everything, content very little. Like a kabuki actor giving a performance, he would deliver his speech of welcome, the sentiments of which were prescribed by tradition, and he would be judged on his ease of execution, his rhythms, his inflections, his stylized earnestness. It was a question of style: did he have that special quality, indefinable, but instantly recognizable, that it took to be head of a large mercantile organization? He was dealing here with tough-minded merchant princes. Would they find him capable enough to represent their interests? He had rehearsed his performance over and over again. He thought it would do. But small beads of sweat formed on his brow.

Wasuke saw that it was time to start. Sitting at the center of the lower side of the room, he said, "Gentlemen, we are grateful to you for joining us this evening to participate in this Rite of Accession to the Name of Kawachiya Kihei VII. It is a great moment for our organization. I give you our new chief executive." Wasuke bowed, and, still sitting, moved himself backward with his hands. Kikuji slid forward, propelled by his hands, off his cushion. He placed his closed fan on the tatami mat, and, with great deliberation, made a full, low bow. Kino and Sei, behind him and on either side, also placed their hands on the floor and bowed low. He raised his head, looked slowly and regally at the guests to either side of him along the walls, and waited for the silence to define itself.

"Supported by the interlocking net of my business associates, carefully woven for me by my respected and loved predecessor, I am succeeding to the great name of Kawachiya Kihei. I am not yet thirty. I have much to learn. You must be my helpers and teachers as you continue to work with Kawachiya's to make it even greater in the future than it has been in the past, under the skilled guidance of my father. I thank you in advance for your continuing good will." He bowed again, his forehead touching the floor.

For a moment there was utter silence. Then it seemed as though a gentle spring breeze had blown through the room, leaving the guests invigorated. Sanoya Rokuemon, the senior member of the business associates, sitting in the first place at the left side, pushed his lacquer tray aside and placed both hands on the floor in front of his knees.

"Speaking for all my colleagues here assembled, I am greatly moved by your courtesy, your sincerity, your vigor. You may count on us to continue praying for your success and prosperity, just as we always did for your wonderful father, Kihei VI!"

Thereupon, in good Japanese fashion, there were loud cheers and tumultous applause. Everyone seemed elated and happy. A promising start had been made. Kikuji thanked them, and, raising both his hands with palms upward, urged them to enjoy themselves. Sliding doors on both sides of the room opened wide, and geisha carrying sake bottles swarmed in. A formal toast was first given to the new head of the organization, and then the guests served each other and the geisha. Within an hour's time, the hum of conversation had risen to a lively hubbub of conviviality. Although it was already the end of October, the spacious room seemed warm to the guests because of sake consumption, occasional dancing and cavorting about. But nothing was ever unseemly or out of control. Wasuke and Hidesuke (the only members of the main establishment allowed to be present) had seen to that in their careful planning of every minute. One after another, the guests came to Kikuji and offered him their sake cups. When he had taken the cup, the guest would pour it to the brim with sake, and Kikuji would drink it off. Then he passed the guest his own cup, and filled it for him to drink. This friendly custom had only one drawback: it could easily result in the guest of honor forfeiting his dignity by passing out. To prevent such a catastrophe, Kikuji had been in training for five days, and had tasted no sake in that time. Also, just before the party began, he had swallowed down a whole pound of noodles to absorb the liquor which inevitably would follow. He had calculated that eighty cups of sake would come to somewhat more than a gallon, and the thought of comporting himself with distinction before his father's business associates with a gallon of sake in his stomach gave him pause. Fortified with noodles, however, he showed no hesitation in receiving the many cups, and he retained his sobriety.

Sei and Kino, on either side of Kikuji, nibbled without interest at the delicacies on the lacquer trays in front of them. They felt neglected. The guests were not used to seeing wives and mothers present at meetings of this sort, and so, without intending to, seemed almost to ignore them. Meanwhile, Kikuji was the center of all attention: cups were exchanged with him; his every word was listened to with enormous deference. Sei and Kino were accustomed to public attention, and they grew irritated at what seemed to them a calculated discourtesy. It never occurred to them that they should not have come to what was essentially an aspect of the family business, from whose operations they had always been excluded.

Kino trembled so much with suppressed anger that her tinted hair shook at the temples, and she breathed deeply with indignation. The guests noticed nothing, but Kikuji, with an ear trained to catch family nuances, observed the increasingly haughty tone Sei and Kino used in responding to guests who did offer them congratulations. Now that Kihei's death had receded seven weeks into the past, the two of them had reverted to their normal behavior. For two weeks or so, Sei had wept incessantly and uncontrollably as she grieved for her husband. But she thought of him less and less, and soon the burden of grief had been lifted entirely from her shoulders. Kino, more restrainedly, had had a phase of reciting Buddhist sutras every evening. This lasted for only a short time before the sutras were shelved. Now, after forty-nine days of enforced mourning, they craved action.

Sanoya came lurching up to Kikuji to make yet another speech on behalf of the guests. Under his white hair, his face was a deep red from too much sake.

"Kiku-bon!" He clapped him on the shoulder. "Oh. Excuse, excuse. No more Kiku-bon, but Ki-Ki-Ki-Ki-Kihei! Hey? You put on a good speech today. I was proud of you. Very, very, very proud. And from now on you'll have to keep a tight rein on that business, and on yourself, and on the women in Shinmachi, hey? You fellows who inherit your position in business, well, you have a lot to learn, hey? And so, congratulations! I'm very, very, very, very proud, you understand—" And he shoved his sake cup toward Kikuji. From the seemingly empty cup sake flashed up and fell on Sei's best kimono. Now she had a focus for her irritation. She gave a high-pitched exclamation which could be heard all over the room, and then brushed her lap as though trying to send the sake back where it had come from. Then she started to stand up. Kikuji caught her sleeve and whispered to her, "Mother. Do sit down. Don't be rude."

Sanoya, perceiving the accident through the softening haze of alcohol, kept repeating, "Oh, I'm so terribly sorry, so terribly sorry." He pulled out a handkerchief and offered it to Sei. She stared at it, and pulled out her own from her sleeve. She wiped the wet spot with it and, as she was getting up, she threw the wrinkled handkerchief vigorously at Sanoya. As it floated in midair, Kikuji caught it and hoped that Sanoya hadn't noticed the enraged woman's gesture. But on looking at him, he saw from his bewildered expression that he had indeed noticed.

"Sanoya-han, please excuse us. Women get confused sometimes, when they think their garments are in danger. Don't give it a second thought."

But his mother said sharply, "Kiku-bon. Stop talking nonsense when your mother has been made a fool of!" Her eyes flashed at him and at Sanoya. She and Kino swept out of the room.

The banquet hall for the moment was very quiet. Sanoya awkwardly broke the silence. "Well, I—that was all my fault, I'm afraid. I treated the Kawachiya ladies the way I treat my old lady at home. I'm not used to ladies at parties. I'm sorry. This country boy ought to be spanked." And he hit himself on the forehead with his open hand.

"Ouch!" A young geisha at his side laughingly put her fingers to his forehead, and massaged it. "I am more important than any two ladies," she said to him soothingly. "Look."

She held up her hands. On each of her fingers was a ring: a diamond, a ruby, green jade, cat's eye—they were all very colorful, and big.

She did a kind of slow, processional dance, exhibiting her well-decorated hands with every step.

"I heard someone tonight say Haru-Danji, the kabuki actor, is a widow-killer. Well, I'm a young-man-killer. I have as many men as I have rings!"

Suddenly the whole room erupted into laughter. She raised both bejewelled hands to quiet the laughter. "Excuse me. But these are not all. I have more."

Without interrupting her eccentric dance, she loosened the clasps of one of her tabi, and drew it off, showing her foot. There was a small ruby ring on her little toe.

Her audience was ecstatic. They threw flowers, handkerchiefs, coats, anything that came to hand, just as they did when tremendously excited by the performance of a good stage actor. Sei and Kino were forgotten. Kikuji breathed a sigh of relief as the party resumed its pleasurable activities. He looked at the young geisha who, now that the crisis had passed, had concluded her little show, and was off to one side, putting on her tabi again. He thought he had seen her somewhere before, but couldn't tell where. Judging by her unusually high tabi, as well as by the little performance which he had just witnessed, she must be a dancing geisha.

When she finished fastening the clasps of her tabi, she smiled at Kikuji and approached him.

"You must be the new master at Kawachiya's. But just because you are in the tabi business, you must not scorn my tawdry old tabi. Give me time—I'll buy some of yours soon, master. My name is Ponta. Please, may I serve you?"

With breathtaking suddenness, the impudent tomboy was suddenly transformed into the geisha, queenly but submissive.

As he drank, he said, "Your face is somehow familiar. I've seen you somewhere before."

She looked askance at him through lowered eyes. "I think not. I've never been at any of your parties before this one."

But the puzzlement continued in his mind. He had seen her before. But where?

The party which had begun at six, drew to its close at ten. Kikuji went with Wasuke and Hidesuke to the entrance hall of the Kishimatsu-kan. They sat at one side, and as each guest prepared to depart, they bowed to him. Kikuji then thanked him for coming and gave him what he called "a small present for remembering the accession ritual." In each case it was a pair of Kawachiya tabi, carefully packaged in fine wrapping paper. Each of the guests bowed in appreciation, but he noticed that they seemed to carry the gift away in a rather casual, even disdainful fashion.

Sanoya made no secret of his opinion of the gift. On receiving it, he said, without opening it, "Ah. Tabi, I'm told. Very nice. Always useful." And with this pro forma acknowledgment, he tossed his package in his hand and left. Now that he was sober again, he associated in his hungover mood the apparent stinginess of Kawachiya's in the way of present giving with the absurd behavior of those two fantastic old women who had made such a fuss about a little misplaced cup of sake. The boy had given a good speech, to be sure. But, even if he was born to the role, one had to remember that his father had originally been only an apprentice. With such a background, one could hardly expect the boy to take his place among the foremost merchants of Osaka, even if the one speech had had about

90

it a certain authoritativeness. No, thought Sanoya on his way home, the boy was too stingy and limited to make the grade.

On arriving home, he tossed the package in the air for his wife to see.

"The gift from Kawachiya's turned out to be a pair of old tabi they couldn't get rid of any other way."

He laughed and threw it carelessly to the floor. It hit the polished cherrywood post in the corner, and the tissue paper split open; against the white cloth of the tabi, there was the glint of metal.

"Let me see that," he said abruptly. His wife passed it to him and watched in puzzlement as he tore the paper off and studied the footwear.

"Look at those clasps," he said. "What do you make of them?"

"Well, they're big, heavy clasps, certainly. I prefer hook-and-eye clasps for my tabi—so much more convenient." She hesitated an instant. "That *is* brass they're made of, isn't it?"

Her husband smiled reflectively at her. "No, my lady. It's solid gold. He had me fooled, that fellow. How finely Japanese to pass off a most expensive gift as though it were a mere trifle, unworthy of consideration. To do that, one must be to the manner born. I wonder if the other guests will find out the value of their gifts before giving the tabi away to the kitchenmaid? He's sharp, all right. He'll handle the firm well. But I wonder how he'll make out with those two women." He yawned. "Thinking of them makes me tired. Let's go to bed."

One raw afternoon in mid-December, Kikuji performed the hundredth day memorial rite at the grave of his father, and went directly from the cemetery to the Tominoya Teahouse in Shinmachi. Upon arrival, he went to a room reserved for him and changed his clothes. In place of the black mourning kimono, he put on a rather dandified mat silk kimono and short *haori* coat which had been sent ahead earlier by his servant. As he was putting on the finishing touches, the talkative fat proprietress appeared at the door. She gave him an assortment of greetings, connected by giggles which too often degenerated into coarse laughter. She tried to assist him with the final touches to his kimono, and kept chattering all the while. Through the fog of words, he learned that Ikuko, who had gone shopping in Kyoto, would return very soon. When she had finished tying his waistband at the back, he interrupted further aimless remarks from her.

"Please, I usually enjoy the company of two or three geisha. Perhaps you can get them for me? But before they come, I want time to have a talk with Kimika. Could you call her for me?"

"You want Kimika alone, don't you?" she asked with a knowing air which he found almost intolerable.

He nodded. "Certainly."

"Ah, well, since it's from one of the Kawachiya family, you can be sure she'll drop everything and come right over."

After issuing instructions to a waitress, she ushered him into a larger room in which to receive visitors and enjoy himself. She politely offered him a sake cup, and poured for him.

"Now that you're officially head of the firm and have the name of Kihei VII, I know I shouldn't keep calling you Kiku-bon. But you'll always be just Kiku-bon to me. To me it just means 'young master'. And you're still young, and you're certainly master!" She laughed at her joke until saliva came out of the corner of her mouth and trickled down her chin in a tiny rivulet. He suppressed his annoyance.

"I haven't thought much what I want to be called in private. Kawachiya Kihei is my business name, but I'm still not accustomed to being called Kihei. Perhaps just plain Kikuji is most comfortable and suitable."

"Ah, but Kihei is a venerated name, full of weight and dignity, my dear sir," she simpered. "We must use what the gods have given us."

"So it's weight you want, is it? Not the light touch, but weight. That's what everyone seems to expect: gold leaf to freshen up the faded old name!" he said half-ironically to this preposterous old baggage of a woman. He was tired of all the formal acts and ceremonies he had had to engage in since becoming Kihei VII. It was almost as though everyone were trying to encase him in the garb and manners of someone else. He wanted to be fully himself. That was in large part why he had felt such relief on changing out of his mourning kimono. He wanted to mourn no longer; maintaining the appearance of a mourner without the inclination made him feel hypocritical, a prisoner of dead convention.

Certainly, since his father's death, he had had a great many ceremonies to plan and function in. Even today, he had spent most of his time organizing the hundredth day memorial service not, as was customary, for the family at home, but for all his father's business associates at Tojiji Temple. He had reserved the whole temple for the occasion, and, after the service, had had a sumptuous meal presented to the guests, along with presents.

The funeral had been an ending for Kihei VI, but for his son it had been the start of an endless series of rituals and ceremonies. There had to be memorial services for his father one week after his death, two weeks after, and so on up to the forty-ninth day. At that time he had staged his own ceremony of accession to the family name. And now the one hundredth memorial. He wondered what unassuming, self-effacing Kihei VI would have thought of all this activity. And yet there was his last command. Had he not wanted his son to jettison mere modesty and diligence, to "be the boss"? But Kikuji felt sure that, whatever authority consisted of, it was certainly more than putting on a front, a public mask, for the benefit of celebrity hunters and bored newspaper readers.

"You look a little tired, sir," said the proprietress, holding the sake bottle at the ready.

"Mmm, yes," he said shortly. And then, to make up for his discourtesy, he added, "A busy day."

She poured for him, and he drank, shutting his eyes for a moment afterwards, sounding the depths of his weariness, and shutting off further conversation. He drank again. It suddenly occurred to him that he had been drinking very heavily of late.

The sliding door hummed in its track as it opened, and there in the doorway sat Kimika.

"Come right in, my dear," said the proprietress. "The master has been waiting for you. Sit right here." She offered Kimika a cushion. The geisha thanked her, but remained at the door. After an awkward moment of silence, the proprietress rose and left, saying as she did so, "She'll take care of you, I'm sure."

Once the door was closed, Kimika bowed low. "I owe you an apology, Master. I behaved badly at the funeral. I couldn't adjust, somehow. I hope my behavior caused you no trouble and that I may continue to think of you as—in a humble way, of course—as my benefactor." Her voice was low and uncertain. Since she had been summoned unexpectedly, she had not had time to dress with care. Her hair was swept up without any hair oil, and through the chignon at the back was a single ornamental comb. It was obviously a hasty hairdo. No geisha would be caught so unprepared. Clearly, she had taken very seriously Kikuji's request that she not practice her profession for one hundred days following the death of her lover.

"You have not been a geisha these one hundred days."

She had seen him studying her hair, and she reddened. "I was glad to do even such a little thing for him. I have avoided work by using sickness as my excuse."

"It can't have been easy. The geisha office and the various tea-houses must have been calling for you often," he said.

"At the beginning, yes. Now—not so much."

How worn she looked, without her makeup.

"I can't tell you how much I appreciate your long sacrifice of yourself for him. Please accept my heartfelt thanks." He put down his sake cup and bowed to her somberly. "But I have more to ask of you."

"Oh?" She raised her eyes and stared at him with a puzzled expression.

He found it hard to meet her gaze, and stared fixedly at her hand as it rested on her knee.

"I realize that every geisha, as she grows older, wishes to acquire a patron who will take care of her. You had a kindly patron in my father. Now that he is gone— But I have no right to ask this—" He broke off in embarrassment.

"Please say what you have in mind. It is all right."

"I'm not sure that it is all right, but I'll say it, and you can decide." He drank a quick cup of sake. "I hope you will not take another patron, a lover, until a year has passed from the time of my father's death."

She looked at him intently, but said nothing. A long moment of silence followed, while each of them examined thoughts too quick and private for utterance.

"Why do you ask this?" she said finally. "What purpose is to be served?"

"Kimika, I have no right at all to ask it. I know that. I have no wish, after all you've done, to offend you. You see, as I view it, my father's life, except for the eight years he had with you, was a total waste, a desert. Because of you, his life took on color and meaning. You rescued him from utter meaninglessness. For eight years you celebrated each other, and he was a happy man, even if secretly so. And now I want him to rescue you from the monotony of daily living, as before you rescued him. Through me, he gives you this allowance for the coming year. I have thirty-six hundred yen in this purse. Please accept it without protest. I'm not trying to paper everything over with money, believe me. And I know that I may have made you angry. But he wishes me to do this. It is a scant return for those eight years."

He reached desperately for his sake cup. It was empty. She had the bottle poised for him, and poured carefully.

"I am not angry," she said softly. He looked at her now, and there were tears brimming in her eyes.

"You are a worthy son of your father, I think," she said. "Like a kindhearted Prince Genji, you are taking care of this wretched creature, and doing it with a delicacy which Genji could not have surpassed. I shall accept the gift which your father, acting through you, bestows upon me. You are generosity itself. How can I thank you?"

He smiled at her in youthful relief. "I'm so glad you agree to accept it."

She too smiled. "I also have had my eight years of color and meaning. I want no more. And I am getting too old and serious to continue much longer as a geisha. One of my best pupils at the samisen has said she would be glad to take over my name. And why not? With thirty-six hundred yen I can start a small business in Shikoku, where I come from, and live very happily for the rest of my life. For one thousand yen, I can buy a fine house in Shikoku. Your gift—your father's gift—rescues me from a life of meaningless routine!"

With the weight of her future off his mind, he felt relaxed.

"I'm so glad. Who knows? Maybe in the future you'll meet some suitable man and settle down comfortably." On finishing this thought, he wished he had never expressed it. Something about the way she was looking at him reminded him that she was at least ten years older than he, and in need of no youthful advice. He laughed. "Anyway, please take it lightheartedly. And then live lightheartedly." He pushed the packet toward her. She looked deeply into his eyes for an instant, then picked up the purse, and, opening the collar of her kimono, placed it next to her skin.

"And now let me play you something on the samisen."

"Fine! How about 'Cherry Blossom in the Night'?"

Kimika clapped her hands for a waitress, and, hearing a voice in the corridor, asked for a samisen.

Ikuko brought the instrument in.

"Oh, my goodness, Miss. You shouldn't be doing that," said Kimika. "I thought it was a waitress outside."

"It's all right," said Ikuko. "There are those who think I act less like a daughter than a waitress." Her glance flicked over Kikuji. He searched in his memory for the exact statement he had made, but could recall only its general sense.

"Oh my. I must learn not to go around analyzing people any more. It gets me in trouble," he said with a smile.

"It's all a question of who says it," she replied. "From some people, criticism passes me right by; but when people who know me well say such things, I am bound to pay close attention. Isn't it so with you, Kimika?"

"Indeed, yes, Miss. The weight a word has on us depends on the worth of the speaker."

Kikuji raised both arms and balanced them up and down against each other, like the pans of a scale. "And how do you weigh the worth of a man, Ikuko?" he asked.

"Me?" She looked at him with strangely intense eyes. "First off, I want to be sure he has a backbone and will stand up for what he believes in."

"Ah, but Ikuko, if one's going to make money, a backbone can be a nuisance. We moneymakers must be very flexible, backbone and all!" he said, laughing.

She looked at him in complete seriousness. "Always you make a joke of what I say," she said.

Kimika intervened hastily. "Ah, Miss Ikuko, you mustn't take the men too seriously. Their jokes sometimes seem harsh to a woman's ear."

As Kimika tried to cheer Ikuko up, three geisha appeared at the door. Soon they were dancing while Kimika played the samisen for them. Ikuko left to take care of her various tasks.

When, after eleven o'clock, Kikuji was about to leave, the proprietress came into the room. "Master, I have something I wish to talk with you about. Could you spare me a little time before you leave?"

Kikuji was mystified. "What's the matter?"

"Maybe if—" The proprietress looked blandly at Kimika and Ikuko. "If we were alone, don't you know—"

Kimika hastily took her departure, thanking Kikuji once more.

"You too, Ikuko."

"But—?" Ikuko hesitated, looking upset.

"I wish to speak with the master *alone*."

Ikuko left with obvious reluctance.

When they were alone, the proprietress became very formal, thanking him for his patronage and that of three generations of his family. Then she bowed very slowly and elaborately. Kikuji's puzzlement grew with each instant. What was the woman up to? She straightened up and looked at him with a kind of placid insistence.

"Now that you have just completed the hundredth day memorial service, I thought it might be a good time to speak my mind to you, Master."

"Yes. What about?"

"About my daughter, Ikuko."

He stared at her. "Ikuko?"

"That's right, Master. About Ikuko." She moved closer. "For a long time I have hoped that you would be fond enough of her to want to take care of her. But you were young then, and hemmed in by family restrictions, so I hesitated to mention it to you. But now you are the master, and you can do as you please. So I thought I would put it to you. Won't you take care of her from now on?"

He looked at her in stunned disbelief. Each wrinkle at the sides of her eyes seemed to conceal craftiness and ignorant greed in its folds. Poor Ikuko, with such a mother!

"As you know, she is my daughter, and no mere geisha or waitress. She is a charming and sensitive girl as surely you have observed by now. I've only pretended not to notice what has been going on." When he did not reply, she continued more aggressively. Suddenly Kikuji stood up, terminating the interview. The proprietress was startled. He smiled icily at her.

"Madam, everything you have said from start to finish seems to

97

me to have been, shall we say, most unpleasing. You waited for my father's death before speaking? With the greatest eagerness, no doubt. And what is it that you pretended not to notice, I should like to know. Ikuko walked with me to the Shinmachi Bridge sometimes, but should that constitute an event which you must pretend not to notice? You must think me an absolute fool, a spoiled rich brat ready to be fleeced."

He strode toward the door, then turned and said to her, "Henceforward, I shall not set foot in this place."

He slid the door open with a bang. Ikuko was standing in the hall, tears of exasperation in her eyes.

"Kiku-bon! This was her idea, not mine." She stood in front of him, as though to prevent his departure. "Surely you know that?"

"Ikuko, I am sorry, but I don't wish to be bothered with any such nonsensical stuff again. With your permission, I'm leaving." He tried to squeeze by her, but she clung to his shoulder. Thus encumbered, he walked to the bend in the corridor, and, in his confusion, bumped into someone coming in the opposite direction.

"Hey! Hey! Watch out! This outfit's not yet paid for," came a lively young voice. "Oops! The master of Kawachiya's. How nice to collide with you."

It was Ponta, the dancing geisha whose vigorous action at his Rite of Accession party had kept Sei's bad temper from depressing the guests. Her face was flushed and she was in a pleasant state of tipsy exhilaration. Behind her was an old fellow in his sixties prancing about with elephantine steps, followed by five or six lively geisha. The deep lines of authority in his aged face were softened by the sake he had drunk. Kikuji suddenly recalled who he was as he looked at his stylish kimono with its matching *haori* jacket. It was the old fellow who had turned his back on the kabuki play in the box in front of the Kawachiya group. And the young geisha who had at that occasion inadvertently struck Sei's face with her long sleeve was Ponta. How could he have forgotten?

"Eh, Ponta, you clumsy foot. Pay a penalty for breaking in on these two busy people," the old man said, laughing, and giving Ikuko, who still looked distraught, a quizzical look.

"A penalty for indiscretion! I'll pay up!" Ponta stretched her hands out close to Kikuji's face. "How much, how much?"

Ikuko responded at once from behind Kikuji, "Since this penalty will be a big one, I'll defer sentencing and let you pay later." The dancers with the old man passed on. Kikuji walked quickly to the entryway, stepped into his clogs and went out, but he heard the hollow scuffle of Ikuko's clogs on the pavement behind him.

"Wait, please," she said.

He turned around sternly.

"One must know how to end things tidily. Let's not make a scene here in the street."

Then he turned around once more and walked off.

As time went on, Kino and Sei observed that Kikuji was less and less frequently at home of an evening. Since he never neglected the family business, they did not at first complain. But one day, having made sure of Kino's assent, Sei decided to speak up.

"Kiku-bon, we see very little of you, these days," she began.

"Yes."

"I hope you are not—doing things you should not do."

"Like what?"

Kino, who had been listening carefully while watching Kikuji's face, intervened.

"Like squandering your money and your health on some shady lady of the Shinmachi District. That's what! We don't want her in our home."

"Is that what you think of me?" he asked, more from genuine curiosity than irritation.

"You didn't play fair with that 'practical nurse.' I can't trust you in matters of this sort."

He laughed. "Grandmother, I once tried to bring a very nice girl of good family into this house as my wife, and failed. How could a woman of lesser pedigree ever be allowed into our sacred halls?"

"Ah, you're exactly right, Kiku-bon. Just so!" And Kino moved closer to him with a very serious expression in her eyes.

"I have something of the utmost importance to talk to you about." She paused and looked about her indecisively. Then she leaned forward, and said in a low, confidential tone, "I have been consulting a very learned man, a fortune teller, concerning the destiny of our family. He has informed me—you mustn't tell this to anyone else—that the spirit of a divine fox has selected this house for its earthly habitation. Handled properly, this is a great honor.

But we must rise to it. My seer says that we must build a shrine in our inner courtyard here, just outside my rooms, for the fox goddess to reside in. Otherwise, she might affect our fortunes for the worse. So we'd best do it right away. Now, isn't that great news?" Kino fairly trembled with excitement. "I also asked about Hiroko, and my seer told me that she was not congenial to the goddess, and so she lived under a curse from the moment she entered our house."

Kikuji had stared open mouthed at his grandmother throughout most of this speech. What would these two idle, energetic minds think of next? He shook his head.

"I really can't possibly—"

"Kiku-bon!" His mother lunged forward and put her hand over his mouth. "Don't say it. She hears! One careless word, and you are accursed!" Nervously, she looked around the garden, half-expecting the fox goddess to appear in a rage to reprimand her skeptical son.

Kino, terribly pale, bowed her head and intoned, "Pray, goddess, spare us thy curse. He knew not whereof he spoke." And she clapped her hands piously as she faced the garden.

At first Kikuji had thought that, just possibly, this was some wild scheme intended to deflect him from getting married again or even bringing in a mistress. But he realized as he watched them that the two women were fearful believers of their superstitious tale.

"You really are serious about this, aren't you?" he said.

Sei answered him in a rapid, hissing whisper. "Stop saying such impious words, Kiku-bon. The goddess fills our house. She is everywhere. We must make her welcome."

And Kino urgently added, "Please say nothing more! I have arranged for a carpenter to come tomorrow to build a shrine for our fox goddess. You must not object!"

He did not object. They had to keep busy with *something*, of course. But, seeing that his skeptical expression did not change, the ladies fled his disbelief, rushing away so fast that they bumped into each other in the hall.

Next day the family contractor came early with three carpenters, and set to work in the garden to build a shrine. On his way to the restroom, Kikuji saw them placing a large sacred straw festoon around the site before beginning to work with their materials. He put on garden clogs and walked over to the place where the workmen were busy. Suddenly, through the bushes he saw the faces of his

100

mother and grandmother. They glared at him silently, like two possessed spirits warning away an unbeliever. Their black eyes stared with an intensity almost hypnotic. Confronted with such fanatic resolve, Kikuji made a quick retreat, leaving the ladies in possession of the field. From the security of the walkway, he looked toward them: they had forgotten his existence and were carefully working with the straw festoon around the site of their shrine. He smiled wryly. They were enshrining the spirit which lived within themselves. In the fox goddess they had immortalized and made sacred their every whim. Surely Kihei, his father, would have enjoyed this latest escapade of the ladies of the house.

Five days later the intricacies of the little shrine were complete. It occupied the corner of the garden diagonally across from Kino's detached rooms. At the front of the eight-foot-square shrine were two stone images of the fox goddess. A cypress fence painted bright vermilion surrounded the shrine. Inevitably, Kino and Sei held a magnificent opening ceremony, at which the shrine was dedicated to the Sacred Bright Goddess of Umechiyo.

Facing a newly painted torii gate, the sorcerer who had inspired the ladies to their act of religious devotion was chanting prayers, making in the process many violent, agonized gestures. Kino with childlike humility offered to him a basketful of fried tofu, a delicacy especially favored by the fox goddess, and in return received a blessing from the priest. Sei followed, holding three-year-old Hisajiro, seeking a blessing for herself and her grandson. The sorcerer was busily pacing about, shaking white paper cuttings used as emblems of purity at Shinto shrines. Frequently he would move his arms in a sweeping angular motion, the long sleeves of his ceremonial kimono flowing gracefully, as he chanted in a quavering falsetto voice calculated to please the ears of the immortals. But it scared Hisajiro, who broke into shrieks and sobs louder than the priest's chanting. All the apprentices, clerks, and maidservants were present, wearing identical uniforms. Wasuke and Hidesuke led the single-file procession through the red torii gate. Each celebrant dutifully picked up a piece of fried tofu and placed it before the statue of the fox goddess, offering up a little prayer.

Noticing that Kikuji alone of all those present had not joined in the ritual, the sorcerer-priest sang in ever more frenzied fashion, until finally, unmistakably, they could hear the long-drawn-out syllables, "Kiiii-Ku-bon!" He smiled. The fox goddess, like her two most assiduous worshippers, wouldn't take no for an answer. Sei, standing beside him, urged him in a low, intense voice to bow his head before the shrine. Though it was a cool February day, her forehead was beaded with sweat. To keep her happy, he rose, went through the torii gate, picked up a piece of the fried tofu and deposited it at the foot of one of the statues. The tofu left his fingers oily and warm, and as he looked at them, glistening and sticky, ready to soil anything they touched, he felt they were utterly characteristic of the cheap vulgarity of Sei and Kino's religion.

He recalled their delight in the doll ceremony on the day of Hisajiro's birth: that regression to childishness had had its base in superstition. With two such tenacious and willful women in the house, it was clearly impossible for him to bring in another. They would destroy her just as they had Hiroko. Still, now that he thought about it, silently studying his sticky fingers in front of the stone fox goddess, maybe he could work out a truce, a detente, whereby he went his way and they theirs. They could have their fox goddess along with the inviolability of their house. He on his side would be completely free to do as he pleased outside the confines of the tradition-haunted family mansion. He felt suddenly cheerful, and he clasped his oily hands together to give the fox goddess her due.

Since meeting her at his final visit to Tominoya's, Kikuji had been seeing Ponta nearly every day at the Kinryu Teahouse, a small, well-run establishment situated in the same neighborhood as Tominoya's, but on a different street, so that there was little chance of accidentally meeting people he desired to forget.

In his early meetings with her, he behaved as any other fashionable young man would have done: he requested four or five geisha along with Ponta, and with their help had fine sociable evenings, with singing, dancing, joking, and everyone chattering delightedly at once. They were pleasant occasions, yet soon he found that more and more he preferred being with her alone.

One late afternoon in the spring, he quit work early and walked to Kinryu's. The waitress telephoned the geisha house to ask for Ponta after escorting him to his room, but was told she had gone to the public bath, and would be a few minutes late. To pass the time she brought Kikuji a bottle of sake and poured for him. A strange, lingering silence enveloped the teahouse at this early hour. He was sure that he was the only customer. The waitress apparently liked Ponta, and was telling him an amusing story about her, when the sliding door opened, and the subject of her anecdote appeared.

"I'm sorry to keep you waiting. In addition to washing myself, I decided to wash all my rings, and that took time."

She sat knee to knee with Kikuji. There were five rings on her scrubbed fingers: a diamond, jade, and ruby on the right hand, and an emerald and opal on the left. He guessed that they were worth, altogether, around five hundred yen. He knew what the three-carat diamond had cost, because he had given it to her himself a week ago.

"Why don't you wear just the ring I bought for you? Or at least one at a time. Wearing them all at once makes you look like one of the newly rich who don't know what to do with money. It would be in good taste to wear mine alone," Kikuji suggested.

"That would make you happy, but it would make my other ring-givers unhappy. These rings are from my five main admirers."

"There are more than five, then?"

Ponta laughed musically. "Of course! Look here." She opened her silk brocade purse and Kikuji saw inside a jumble of seven or eight rings mixed with coins.

"Why do you carry them around with you like that?" he asked.

"It's quite necessary, really. If one of my lesser admirers calls me, I put on his ring right away."

"At my name-accession party you had rings even on your toes. Do you still?"

"You can't walk far with rings on your toes. That was my little act, invented on the spur of the moment, to make your guests forget a little unpleasantness which had taken place—as you may remember. I like inventing little acts." She spoke carelessly, as though the recollected performance were a trifle of no importance. He studied her profile without seeming to do so. Her long neck was exquisitely graceful, even queenly. She was conscious of this asset herself, for whenever she wished to make an emphatic response, she would raise her chin high, showing off the sculpturesque beauty of her

103

throat and neck to full effect. But in this as in all else, her chief charm was spontaneity: she was remarkably self-aware, and yet, as often with young people just past their teens, nothing that she did seemed calculated or contrived.

"I still think it's better to wear one only," he said.

She tilted her head and looked at him roguishly. "Mmm? Really?" And she raised her hands upward toward the light and moved her fingers rapidly so that the precious stones shone brilliantly. "But these are so pretty!" She went on weaving her hands in graceful patterns over her head.

Kikuji leaned forward. "Ponta, I will arrange it so that you will agree to wear only the one ring."

Her hands, still extended, stopped waving. She looked sharply at him and lowered her arms. Kikuji was offering to be her sole patron henceforward. She realized that the proper thing to do now was to put him off and consult with her mother and her more experienced friends. She raised her eyes to his for a long look.

"Thank you," she said at last. "Allow me to accept your offer. I think we are well suited to each other."

He realized that as she had been speaking, she had been removing four of her five rings. Only Kikuji's diamond ring remained. She placed her hand with the ring gently in his.

"Is that all right?" she asked softly.

But at that instant, there was a tap at the door. It slid open slightly, revealing one of the waitresses, who with some embarrassment said, "Excuse me, Ponta, but there is a telephone call from your office. They want you to participate in a party later this evening. Is that all right?"

She shook her head. "I'm sure I can count on you to decline courteously for me."

"But, you see, it's from Toyoshima's. They're very anxious to have you join them." The waitress was trying to coax her because it was one of the five best teahouses.

Ponta started again to refuse, but Kikuji interrupted.

"I'll speak to the proprietress of the geisha house. Will you ask her to stop over here for a short time?"

They remained quietly at Kinryu's from early evening until ten. The lady in charge of the geisha house talked with Kikuji for a time, and departed after wishing them well. Shortly after ten, they left together for Kyoto.

Whenever Kawachiya's wined and dined a customer in the Kyoto area, they used the Kyotomi Teahouse, overlooking the Kamo River. The waitress at Kinryu's had called and made a reservation for Kikuji and Ponta, and they were expected. The proprietress came out to greet them as their car ground to a stop. They were escorted up to a spacious room. A charcoal brazier glowed in the center. Although the sliding panels of the windows were open, the Kamo River below them and Mount Daimonji across the stream were hidden in the moonless dark. The faint, delicate music of the river waters flowing slowly by in the April night came to their ears. There was a spring chill in the air.

Ponta sat down at the dressing table and removed the heavy stylized makeup worn by geisha while entertaining. Without it, she looked younger, simpler and more natural. After taking a hot bath, they dressed in their night kimono, and sat lazily on the cushions around the low table, eating a midnight snack, and washing it down with sake. They were in no hurry.

"Tell me about the old fellow who took you with him to see the kabuki play at the Nakazu Theater," Kikuji asked. "That was where I first saw you. He was the same one who was snaking around with you and some other geisha in the corridor at Tominoya's the last time I was there."

"Yes, I remember." She smiled. "Well, first of all, he's fun. He's the owner of a big fish processing house on Utsubo Street. He has made his money, and so he turned the business over to his son. Now he can have a good time from morning till night and on to morning again."

"He's quite a character."

She giggled. "He says it's more healthy to attend teahouses than temples. He's already past sixty. He entertains us rather than our entertaining him. He's a very young old man."

"And you are one of his favorites?"

"Oh, part of his team, you might say. The other geisha are the main dishes. I'm a side dish—a salad, maybe! He likes me around because I'm noisy and make jokes. So he pays to have me along. But the other geisha are senior to me, and they do most of the work of keeping him happy."

"They didn't do much of a job of it at the Nakazu Theater," said Kikuji. "He was in a terrible mood."

She nodded. "Yes, he gets that way sometimes. And when he does, he can be very stubborn. But he usually snaps out of it fast. After we left the theater that afternoon, for instance, he cheered up and made it up to us for missing the rest of the kabuki play by buying each of us a ring."

"Just the thing for you."

"Yes, that's what I thought. Here it is." She opened her purse and selected a ring with a green emerald on it. He looked at it and handed it back.

"How does it rank among your rings? One of the important ones?" Kikuji asked.

She tilted her head slightly and looked at him, smiling. She gave a slight shrug.

"Yes, I think so. He's my referee."

"Your—?"

"Yes. He's on the sidelines because he's old, but he likes me because I'm young, and he watches me play my game. That's what he says. He buys me rings and he keeps after me to find myself a good man."

He smiled gently, moved closer to her and took her hand in his. "Ponta, how old are you?"

"I . . ." She closed her lips firmly, then laughed. "Oh, all right! I guess I can tell you. I say I'm nineteen but I'm really just seventeen. I wanted to seem mature." She laughed. "Gentlemen don't want to get mixed up with children. They can't take the young ones seriously, you know."

"Not at all," said Kikuji, teasingly. "Some old goats find young children enormously attractive."

"Ah, how disgusting!" She broke into a long series of giggles. Finally she smothered them and became suddenly serious. "No, even if I am a geisha, and even if geisha usually end up with some old grandfather for a patron, I don't want an old man. I want someone who's young and capable of making money, and capable in other ways too, as an old man is not. See what I mean? I want you." She said this very pertly and matter-of-factly. Her manner fascinated Kikuji. In part, it stemmed from the utter directness and simplicity of the very young. But superimposed on this essential innocence was the sophisticated behavior of the experienced geisha. He had inquired of knowledgeable persons in Shinmachi, and he knew that Ponta had never yet had a special patron. Whence this cool self-awareness, this poise which he had always associated with skilled practitioners in the art of the geisha?

"Tell me about yourself, Ponta," he suggested to her in an effort to glean an answer to the riddle.

"Where shall I start?"

"Where all stories start: at the beginning."

"Well, I was born in the Shinkaichi District of Kobe. When I was still small, my mother brought me with her to Osaka. The Horie District."

"The Horie District? Then your mother too was a geisha?"

"Of course! I am second-generation geisha. Mother taught me all I know. My dances and my wisecracks are practically hereditary."

In a way she was right, he realized. The easy confidence which enabled her to hold her head high, arch her neck so beautifully, and act with such serene spontaneity must have resulted from the mother's careful cultivation of all the daughter's aptitudes. Her charming oval face at this precise minute expressed a serene receptivity and an engaging impulsiveness. From this very contradiction came that sureness of touch, that expertness in social dealing so delightful in someone so youthful. Delightful, and yet a little disturbing, somehow.

He looked at the bedding spread out on the floor. She caught his glance, and dimmed the light. She was about to slip under the heavy quilt when she stopped suddenly and began to work with the pillow. Hers like his, was a round oblong, but, unlike his, it was cradled on a small, padded, boxlike structure, concave at the top, to hold the pillow. The slight elevation helped a lady to preserve her hairdo through the night hours. Untying the pillow, Ponta lifted it, and carefully placed her purse in the concavity of the box. Then she tied the pillow down once more. How efficient. How sensible. But mightn't one have expected that, embarking on her first affair, her first serious affair, certainly, she would have been a little more ner-

107

vous, timid, uncertain? Was it a measure of her trust in him that she was not? Or was she, a second-generation geisha, simply being the skillful practitioner of her art?

She moved in under the covers, and, after a second's hesitation, moved over to where he was waiting for her. He turned and caught her in his arms. The intense heat of her body all along the length of his, through the single layers of their light kimono, was like an electric shock to him. The beauty of Hiroko, the wife he had sent away, came suddenly to him with a sensual immediacy. He clasped Ponta to him, gently smoothing her hair under his chin as she lay with her head on his chest, listening to the thumping of his heart.

It was, perhaps, the unfamiliar sound of the river waters coming through the windows which wakened Kikuji: he lay wide awake as the white paper panels of the door emerged with ever-increasing distinctness from the darkness. The first rays of the sun rising above the mountains fell on the quilt, welcome after the chill of the night.

Careful not to wake Ponta, he lit a cigarette, in the process jarring the pitcher of water near the bed so that the tatami mat was wet. He tried to soak it up with the sleeve of his cotton kimono. When the one was wet, he switched to the other, and, as he did so, felt Ponta's warm breath on his ear. His fussing with the water pitcher had awakened her.

"Stop worrying about it," she said, yawning and leaning against his back. Her arms encircled his neck. "There are nicer ways of greeting a fine spring morning."

He laughed. "It's already broad daylight and time to be up and doing." He held her a moment longer, his finger tracing a sensuous path down her spine until she cried out. He threw the quilt back and stood up. In the process, he knocked over Ponta's box-pillow, and rings, jarred loose from her purse, were scattered over the floor. She gave a little shriek.

"No, no, no. All my possessions kicked over the floor of an inn. Help me!"

Frantically, she gathered her rings together again, put them in her pocket, and then helped him tie the sash of his kimono behind him. Ponta had arranged to have her daytime clothes delivered to her by the ladies' attendant from the geisha house in Osaka. It was a long trip for anyone to make in the early morning. Kikuji gave her a five-yen note to use as tip. It was a few minutes after seven when the messenger arrived. Ponta asked the maid to tell him to wait at the entryway while she finished her breakfast. At last she went downstairs. Kikuji rested his elbow on the windowsill and sat comfortably smoking as he looked out over the river toward the mountains. It occurred to him that Ponta would take a long time getting dressed with the aid of the assistant from the geisha house. The hushed beauty of the spring morning made him restless. He decided to go for a walk by the river. He descended the steep, narrow stairway, and, as he was passing the entryway, he saw through a partly closed door, Ponta talking to her attendant. She had given him his tip and he was thanking her. Just as Kikuji was about to pass out of hearing, he heard her say, "I have only the five-yen bill, and my tip is two yen, fifty sen. Do you have change?"

The geisha house attendant, a little annoyed, took out his purse and slowly studied its contents, finally extracting two dirty one-yen notes. "I do not have fifty sen," he said flatly.

"It doesn't matter," she replied smoothly. "We can skip the fifty sen. Now, shall we go to the other room so that you can help me get into my new outfit?"

Kikuji quickly turned and walked through the rear door into the garden adjacent to the river.

The water in the river was low. A breeze blew the surface into small wavelets which glinted and sparkled in the morning sun. Downstream, some workmen were rinsing fabric. He was tired. He sat down on a large rock in the dry river bed, squinting a little at the brilliance of the ripples in the river's central channel. The whole atmosphere was strangely quiet. He could not hear the voices of the workmen washing the large sections of dyed cloth, and, aside from an occasional birdcall, there was little else to hear.

Ponta, he thought, was an enigma. That, to be sure, was a main part of her attractiveness. Yet he had been perplexed by her methodical action the night before, when, as a preliminary to her first romantic venture, she had carefully tied up her rings under her pillow. And this morning she had extracted change from the tip of a poor servant. If she's that crazy about money, how much will she extract from me before she's through? He tossed a pebble up and down in his hand and finally threw it over the water. In his talk with the lady in charge of Ponta's geisha house in Osaka last night he had already made arrangements to pay off the indenture entered into when she was sold to the geisha house. Ponta would have her freedom to do as she wished. And what she wished was to set up her own small, select geisha house. She had seen, she said, too many fine geisha decline into abandoned mistresses, and that was not for her. Maybe in cheating the geisha house servant and in hiding her rings she just had not yet adjusted to the idea of his continuing financial support. But he was inclined to think that she would keep right on saving every ring and every coin, building her wall of security stronger and stronger, as one might do with all these smooth river pebbles. He picked up some and scaled them along the surface. The water was too shallow for good skipping.

Another two months passed, however, before he allowed the ceremony of independence to be celebrated. She had wanted it earlier, before ugly rumors about her changed situation had a chance to circulate; but he had held out for June fifteenth. It was the day when all the merchant houses in the Semba, as well as in adjoining Shimanouchi, changed into their summer wardrobe. On June fifteenth, the whole town suddenly blossomed out in cool linen kimono, and the result was a summery sense of exhilaration. He thought it a good day for giving Ponta her freedom.

Acknowledging his love of ritual, she secured permission for him to be present at the ceremony marking the end of her indentured service. In the reception room of the geisha establishment, she sat at two in the afternoon in her violet, full-dress kimono, with the organization's seal on the back, while her mistress with great formality placed a small, red lacquered table before her. She held a congratulatory cup of sake in her hands, and bowed to the youthful geisha. "Henceforward, you are freed of all obligations, financial and social, to this house. May you prosper as an outstanding member of your profession." She offered the cup to Ponta, who replied, "If I succeed in my profession, it will be the result of your advice and training. I thank you for your encouragement." She received the cup, held it high to her forehead, and returned it immediately. The next step in the ritual alarmed Kikuji and he later told Ponta he thought it at very least untidy. After drinking one sip, her mistress took a quantity of the sake into her mouth, held it, puffed her cheeks, and blew the sake as a kind of mist onto Ponta's carefully arranged hair. Then she took a tortoise-shell comb from her pocket and combed the hair in front, which had been dampened by the spray of sake, so that it stood out impressively. Finally, in compliance with custom, she wrapped the comb in paper and chanted, "A crane, ten thousand years, a turtle, ten thousand years. May your future be filled with happiness!" And she handed the comb to Ponta. The aroma of sake filled the room.

"But why on earth did she have to spew all that liquor all over your hair?" protested Kikuji later on, when they were alone.

"Why do they break champagne on a battleship?" lightly retorted Ponta. "Because that's the way it was done the last time."

An hour later, Kikuji held a reception at the Yonedaya Restaurant in Shinmachi for all the teahouse proprietresses and senior geisha with whom Ponta had associated. In his white linen kimono he sat in front of the ornamental post of the little alcove where a scroll and a flower arrangement were exhibited. The geisha, who had come not as entertainers, but as guests, were relaxed and ready for festivity. Kikuji was paying for their time for that whole day and the following night; in addition, he had made it clear that, should they be called by other patrons, they were free to go if they wished. So they were enjoying this little vacation from the regular routine.

Ponta was walking continually among them, pouring sake and chatting. As she did so, she took a count. There were twenty-three guests Kikuji was paying for: six teahouse proprietresses and seventeen geisha. Each geisha cost him eleven yen, twenty sen. Seventeen times that came to a total of one hundred ninety yen, forty sen. Add to that a twenty-yen present to the house mistresses and fifteen yen for each of the geisha, and the amount came to two hundred seventy-five yen. And the party itself brought the total to the staggering sum of one thousand yen. One could buy a house for that. Ponta felt a little dizzy thinking about it.

Kikuji was busy talking and drinking with the mistress of her geisha house and with the mistress of Kinryu Teahouse. As he drank, his pale complexion became flushed. Smiling sociably at the ladies, he absent-mindedly raised his right hand to finger the lapel of his *haori* coat. His deep-chested laugh contrasted strangely, Ponta thought, with the feminine delicacy of those graceful hands. As she watched him amiably exchanging pleasantries with the elderly women, it suddenly occurred to her that he looked far older in his whole manner, behavior, and attitude than his twenty-eight years.

He was to be sure, Kawachiya's master, young, a good spender, handsome. And yet—if he were old in spirit, what did these things matter?

"Ponta. Come out of it. This is your party!" It was Kikuha, a fine dancer and her friend, who urged her gayly. "I have an idea: let us dance together."

Ponta picked up a dancing fan and went with Kikuha to the next adjoining room, closing the sliding doors behind them. When the opening notes of the music sounded on the samisen, the doors opened smoothly to either side. Ponta held the starting pose with her fan gracefully extended. Half-seeing, half-sensing Kikuha's movements, she timed her own gestures so that the two dancers flowed together in one complex harmony. Although smaller than Kikuha, she danced with a formal precision very appropriate to the song, "The Green of the Pines." Throughout the dance, she had been aware that Kikuji's eyes had been very intently upon her. At the end of the dance, Kikuha shook her finger at Kikuji in mock reproach.

"I might as well have stayed home in bed for all the impression I made. When the main dish is served, who pays much attention to the salad?" Then she smiled and bowed to him. "But in all seriousness, thank you for this delightful celebration. I look for your favor as future events may require."

Following her example, the other geisha and teahouse mistresses began to express their thanks in preparation for departure. Kikuji then signaled the waitress, who brought in on a large Shunkei lacquered tray presents for all. There were two piles of packages. One, Ponta decided, clearly contained the now-famous present of Kawachiya tabi. Kikuji's generosity astounded her so much that she hardly knew what she was doing. But she controlled her motions, and politely handed each of the guests a package of tabi along with a small envelope, thanking her for having joined in the celebration. The guests accepted the gifts without undue excitement, and slowly departed. When the last one had gone out of the door, she turned excitedly to Kikuji.

"Those tabi which you gave: did they have gold clasps?"

Kikuji looked at her with a puzzled expression. "No. Not one gold clasp in the lot. Why?"

"I just thought— I mean, I know you gave gold clasps before, and so I—" She waved her hands vaguely to complete her thought.

"But that was my name-accession ceremony, Ponta. That was big business and lots of family tradition. This party was to celebrate your receiving your independence as a geisha." He leaned toward her affectionately. "Surely you can see that these two ceremonies are of quite different magnitude?"

"Then—the tabi you gave are just like the ones I'm wearing now?"

"Just plain old tabi, that's all."

"I see." Earlier in the evening she had been exasperated by his heavy spending for the party. Now she was embarrassed because his farewell presents to her friends seemed inadequate.

"I don't think your friends will be unhappy," said Kikuji softly, as though reading her mind, "The small envelope contained enough money to enable them to buy dozens of tabi. And, in actuality, the tabi I gave as gifts are not just plain old tabi. You can't buy footwear like that anywhere in town. It's a new line I worked up. Look." He stretched out from his sitting position on the tatami mat and put his foot on an armrest so that she might study it. At first she thought it an ordinary tabi.

"Look carefully at the lining," instructed Kikuji. "It is made of silk organdy for coolness and comfort in summer. So you can see, all your friends will be in the forefront of fashion, wearing my new product before it has become popular. Am I exonerated from the charge of stinginess?"

He rolled over and seized her hands. Laughing, she fell beside him. He gave her a long, lingering kiss. Then, while her head was nestled against his chest, he tried to work out a catchy commercial slogan for advertising the new line of tabi: "For feet that deserve the finest: Kawachiya's silk-lined tabi." He went on thinking about slogans as they lay in each other's arms. He had been working on his new line for the past several months and was proud of its quality. Soon, however, thoughts of anything but Ponta were erased from his mind. They remained at Yonedaya's for the night.

When he reached his home the next morning at around eight, he stopped and stared at it in surprise. The whole front facade of the house had been cleaned and hosed down with a thoroughness duplicated only at his wedding, his father's funeral, and various occasions when Sei and Kino were in a fury about something. When they were angry, they rode herd on the employees of the house and everything was cleaned to the point of utter exhaustion. Each individual piece of wood in the lattice work had been painstakingly scrubbed by hand. Warily, Kikuji entered the front door.

"Welcome home, sir. Let me take care of your footwear." Ceremonious as always, Hidesuke picked up his clogs and deposited them in the courtyard. Looking around, it seemed to Kikuji that all the clerks and apprentices were nervous and apprehensive.

"Are there—any important customers waiting for me inside?" he asked casually.

"No, sir. Nothing at all unusual." Hidesuke's ever-attentive eyes gleamed more brightly than usual. Was it curiosity? or anticipation? Something peculiar was going on, and Kikuji walked on into the living quarters, regretting that he had shown the assistant manager his awareness of the tension.

Beyond the curtain shielding the family area, everything was quieter than usual. The maids were not chattering sociably as they cleaned the house; Hisajiro's nurse, Tome, could not be heard singing, laughing, and scolding her charge. As he was about to enter the room of the master, formerly his father's, now his, he heard a low chanting from the next room, which contained the Buddhist altar. The large door panel slid silently open, and there, standing in the opening was his mother, head high, eyes severe. Whatever the trouble, he knew at once, here was the storm center. Behind her, his grandmother sat with head bowed before the altar. Candles burned just in front of the black lacquer of the altarpiece.

"How good of you to say prayers for Father," he said respectfully.

"We have been attending to our family obligations," replied Sei icily. "Whereas you, I assume, have just spent the night at the Shinmachi Pleasure Quarter."

"You make it sound so nasty," he replied with a smile. "I do my work, and do it well. Then I take time off and enjoy myself."

"At Shinmachi."

"At Shinmachi."

"Very well!" She flexed her eyebrows severely even as Kikuji, watching her, was admiring her statuesque beauty. "Your grandmother and I wish to have a talk with you about all—all—this!" She

114

made a disparaging gesture with her hands. "We have been waiting for you for quite some time." She stepped aside to allow him to enter.

"Oh, my. Another wrestling match," he thought. He could not but admire their tactical skill in choosing the appropriate time for battle. He hadn't had much sleep last night, and his thoughts at this early hour were curiously disembodied. But the whole household was clearly ready for the fight, and it had to be made, even though he felt a little as though he had been ambushed. The monotonous sound of his grandmother's shrill, aged voice reciting the sutra continued without pause after he entered the room.

"Mother? Mother! Kiku-bon has come back," said Sei finally.

Kino stopped her prayer and turned slowly around to look at him. How formidable she seemed, even now, even at his age.

"Well, Kiku-bon. I'm told you had quite a spree last night."

"You—were told—?" Even as he asked, he decided that Hidesuke's love of spying out other people's business had again overcome better judgement.

"Oh, everybody knows about it. It's all over town. That's what you wanted, isn't it? Otherwise, why would you be so—so—" Here she shook with indignation. "So flashy, and gaudy, and wasteful in throwing away your money on—on—on *creatures!*"

"I am not an automaton. I will enjoy my life," he said quietly, thinking of his father.

"Very well, but there's no need to make a public spectacle of yourself. Don't forget Hisajiro! Do you want people to make fun of him because his father misbehaves in public?"

"Maybe we should get clear on just what it is that you have heard. From the buildup, I'm not at all sure that your conception of what I've been doing is accurate."

Kino tossed her head impatiently. "Don't give me that legalistic nonsense, young man. I know what I'm talking about! You had a party announcing the independence of the geisha you have decided to take under your protection."

"That is correct," admitted Kikuji. "I can't apologize, and I intend to go right on seeing the young lady you speak of."

"Seeing her? Pah! That isn't the half of it!" shouted the old lady at him. "Have you no shame? Have you no regard for appearances?"

"Appearances. Always in this family we come back to the subject

115

of appearances," said Kikuji somberly. "If it's the proper appearance you're after, I guess I could get married again."

"Married!" shrieked Sei. "Who said anything about getting married again?"

"You *have* a son," said Kino. "Why on earth would you get married again? Don't you remember what a mess your last wife was?"

He snorted a mirthless laugh. "You don't have to worry. I'm not likely to forget anytime soon what a fiasco my marriage was. I would never consider bringing in another wife to face what Hiroko had to face. Surely you understand that my first marriage fell apart because the two of you could not stand to see someone unrelated coming into the family on roughly equal terms with you. You treated my wife as though she were the lowliest servant. No woman from the outside could ever survive as my wife in this house! You're fully aware of that, aren't you?" he said, almost as though he were reading their minds.

His mother stared at him in confusion, but Kino looked at him calmly, pursing her lips. "Well, if you want to be crude about it, I guess it comes approximately to that. No need to beat around the bush. But we're not talking about your getting married, Kiku-bon. We're talking about this nasty, clandestine adventure you're embarked on."

Suddenly he realized her dilemma. Much as she wanted to scold him and reestablish her dominance over him, she feared that, if she did so, he would simply go the path of Kihei VI, and engage in secret amours of which they would be ignorant, a situation which would inevitably make them seem ridiculous in their own eyes and in the eyes of the world. So she hesitated. He in turn waited calmly. The battle was not going too badly, all things considered.

Hidesuke suddenly interrupted the discussion by opening the hallway door and announcing a phone call for his employer. At the same time he carefully inspected the faces of the three, trying, Kikuji thought, to satisfy that enormous curiosity which was like a gnawing appetite to the man. When he returned, the women had recovered their composure. Kino, he could see, had made up her mind as to how best to proceed.

"Kiku-bon, sit down, and let us talk this matter over rationally," she began. "You probably know that when one of the masters in the Semba has taken a mistress, it is the custom for the woman to pay a

116

courtesy call on the members of the family." She smiled a peculiar smile which Kikuji found hard to interpret. She was up to something. Probably it was a good idea to make his relationship with Ponta an acknowledged and accepted fact. But he couldn't quite believe that that was all these two women wanted. Their motives were always veiled in secrecy. But he felt that he couldn't refuse to present Ponta to them.

From then on, for a number of weeks, both Sei and Kino appeared to him strangely elated, just as they had been before making their kabuki play excursion. Usually, at about this time of year they would go off to Arima Hot Springs or Kinosaki for an early summer vacation, but they gave no indication of making any such trip this year. For the most part, they remained inside the house, emerging only occasionally to supervise the watering of the plants in the garden. When Kikuji expressed surprise that they had not taken their early summer trip as usual, Sei said with considerateness which was foreign to her usual way, "It doesn't matter. You have to stay here and work all these hot days. The least we can do is to keep you company."

He had quite deliberately procrastinated about setting a time for Ponta's visit. But his mother and grandmother didn't press him. The more he delayed, the more he felt uneasy about it, and the more pleased and gentle they became. It was almost as though they were as glad as he to hold off on the ceremony. But, whereas he was glad to postpone the inevitable visit simply because he dreaded it, they were in no hurry because their anticipation of the event was a major part of their pleasure in it, and, even before it took place, they felt a little sadness at the thought of this fine affair being finished and done with, as it would have to be, sooner or later. Much better, then, later! And they gloated over Kikuji's nervousness.

Kikuji threw the switch on the electric fan, and its busy hum declined to silence. The clock on the wall of his accounting room showed that it was past five. O-Toki came in and told him that the water for the bath was now hot. He quickly took a bath, and began getting dressed. Kino unexpectedly peeped in just as he was about ready.

"Ah, going out, are you?" she said with an arch smile. "Well, have your fun!"

117

It was always Kino, he realized, whose comments tended to strike him as faintly obscene.

He walked as usual across the Shinmachi Bridge. But then he went in a direction slightly different from his usual path, and came to a halt in Echigocho before a small, tidy house with a neat little sign by the door identifying the house as "Koharumoto." This was the geisha house he had obtained for Ponta to preside over. It was the first time he had visited her place, and he did so only at her repeated request. Echigocho had a great many fashionable geisha houses in it. He had felt a little absurd in his role of master of a geisha establishment. It wasn't his idea of a good business investment. But Ponta was worth it.

When he opened the scrubbed and polished lattice door, a bell rang above his head. Ponta, looking cool and fresh, came out in her cotton summer kimono.

"I've been waiting for you ever since you called me at noon," she said excitedly. "You came to look the place over the day you bought it. Now, I hope you'll stay here to relax and enjoy yourself. Come on in."

Before taking him up the stairs, she took him around to the side to study the staircase. Each step marked the height of a series of boxes or drawers. The whole space under the stairs was filled with these drawers. Ponta was very proud of her box stairway. Although she knew they were traditional in Osaka, she had never lived in a house in which she had access to such a storage space.

In the small room on the second floor to which she took him, there was a tray of tidbits set out for his use. The window was open and faced a small garden; the bamboo blind was rolled up for maximum air circulation on this hot evening. She spread out a freshly laundered summer kimono.

"You must have a hot bath and change to a summer kimono."

"No, no," he said, laughing. "I bathed before leaving home, and I'm quite cool and comfortable."

"Ah. How typical of men!" Ponta replied. "When you visit your own special Ponta, you are too lazy to take a bath." She scowled at him, then broke into a laugh. "But I know the way to a man's heart. How about some beer?" She clapped her hands and the maid brought some beer up to the landing, where she left it. Ponta had instructed her for the sake of privacy to leave all that she brought on the landing halfway up. Ponta went down to get it.

"Where is everyone this evening?" Kikuji asked.

"Oh, they're around," she said vaguely. There were two geisha working for her in addition to the maid. She had wanted four, but Kikuji thought it too many for a start. On this evening she had seen to it that both of them were off on parties.

"Now that you know the way, you'll come here often?"

"No, Ponta. It's better to spend our evenings at Kinryu or one of the other teahouses."

"Oh? But you called me. I thought—"

"Well, you see, I wanted to discuss something with you which just didn't seem to fit in with teahouses," he said.

"Ah! What terrible thing is it that you can't tell a geisha at a teahouse? Stock quotations? A murder plot?"

Although a little anxious, she was determined to maintain a light mood. She picked up a fan and gently moved the air around him as he drank his glass of beer. He looked at her and laughed.

"Nothing so dire. It's just that my mother and grandmother want you to pay a formal visit to them, in acknowledgement of your status as my mistress."

"Oh, my." Ponta was surprised and for a moment she stopped fanning, and stared at him with the beginning of a frown on her smooth brow.

"It's one of the customs of the Semba, I'm afraid, and, if they want it, we must go through with it. I thought you might like it," he said sympathetically.

She twirled the fan and tilted her head. "I would like very much to meet the ladies of the house and bid for their approval. I had thought you were going to ask something difficult of me. But this is no trouble."

It was his turn to look perplexed. "You don't know, my dear! This is one of those incredible Semba rituals: everything must be done just so. You can't just visit and be natural and easy. It is a performance, a fencing match, don't you see?"

"I know your Semba and its hidebound ways. Don't worry!" She laughed again.

"Ponta, it's no laughing matter. If they can, they'll make a fool of

119

you, and then spread the story of it all over town. They would do just about anything to discredit you. And I hate to think how they would react if they were to realize that you were the geisha who slapped my mother in the face with your kimono sleeve at the kabuki play."

"With all due respect to you, they sound like rather terrible people. They can't possibly recognize the impudent geisha in the theater when they meet modest little me. They saw me at your name-accession celebration, just as you did. And you didn't remember me, nor did they. For much of the evening I sat diagonally across from your mother. Anyway, I'll be all right." She fanned him once more. "My family has some experience in these matters. My mother was once a mistress to a gentleman of the Semba. So I know some of the procedure, and I can easily find out everything I need to know from my friends. I'm not helpless."

And indeed, as he looked at her, it was hard to believe that she was only seventeen years old. She seemed completely confident, and at ease.

He leaned over and kissed her lightly. "I know you're up to it, my darling, but it seems such a rotten hurdle to set up for us just at the beginning of our life together. Still, you had best see them, and know."

He stretched out lazily on the tatami floor covering. Quickly Ponta raised his head and cushioned it on her lap. He reached with his arms and touched the soft firmness of her thigh.

"You're not angry?" he asked. She shook her head, and, looking down at him drew her chin in toward her neck so that her marvelous throat suddenly rippled into folds. They were both silent, waiting, studying little details about each other. His longing for her became intense, and he reached gently for her shoulder, trying to pull her down beside him. As she bent over him, her starched collar was loosened, and he could see her natural skin, below the line of the makeup. He loosened the sash of her kimono and brought her nakedness into view. It was a deep twilight outside, and the room was almost dark. Slowly, voluptuously, he put his arms around her, stroked her, drew her to him. . . .

Afterward, he felt more drowsy than usual. Ponta had given herself to him with a passion which was unusual for her. And the quiet, almost deserted house had had a poetic, even aphrodisiac effect upon him. For once, he had lost himself completely in the act. As he rested, Ponta slowly rose, adjusted her kimono in the darkness and went quietly downstairs. Soon she returned with a small bucket of ice. Dipping a towel in the icy water, she sponged off Kikuji's chest, stomach, and thighs. She said nothing as she massaged him quietly and expertly with the cold cloth.

"Are you sure you can manage? The visit to my house?"

"Of course. It's better to be open about these things," she answered.

"When?"

"Why not the day after tomorrow? That's the first of the month, which is always a lucky time."

"You're sure?"

"Stop *worrying*, Master. Trust me. All my training has been to fit me for complex social interrelationships." It was a plain statement of fact. He bowed to her judgement.

To most of the others in the store, it seemed a pleasant day like any other. The clerks and apprentices did their chores as usual. Hidesuke figured endlessly and needlessly over the account book. But Wasuke, perhaps aware of the impending visit, criticized the appearance of the entryway and dispatched several apprentices to go over it again. Kikuji couldn't sit still. He wished now that he had not trusted her so easily to get through this visit. In some ways she was still inexperienced. Surely she had never had much experience with people like Sei and Kino. Like an idiot, he had wanted to be bighearted and give her freedom to do it her way. But what was her way? Kino and Sei this morning had brought in the hairdresser, and were studying their wardrobes with an intensity reserved for the greatest ceremonial performances. What could Ponta do against that? In accordance with prescribed custom, the two women had spent whole afternoons readying a present for his mistress. How would she react? She was too informal, as the young always are. But it was too late now. In five minutes she was scheduled to be here. The pendulum of the old clock swung with a loud tick back and forth, and the minute hand edged closer to ten o'clock.

"Welcome! Welcome!" It was the voice of the clerk, Kakushichi, addressing someone who had just come into the store. The customer was silhouetted against the light. She closed her parasol. It was

Ponta. Her white summer kimono had an arrow pattern, and over it she was wearing a black silk half-coat, with a crest on the back, and woven straw slippers. Kikuji gritted his teeth in his exasperation: it was all wrong. She shouldn't be wearing the half-coat, as though she were a highborn lady of leisure. And those very expensive straw slippers. She should be wearing humble wooden clogs.

Ponta didn't even look at him, which was, perhaps, just as well. After closing her parasol, she asked the clerk, "Please, is it all right if I use this corner to leave some of my things in?" When he assented, she took off her half-coat, and removed the elegant straw slippers, replacing them with solid wooden footwear. She placed both coat and slippers in her bag. She rearranged the folds of her white kimono so that the collar no longer revealed her neck and a little of her shoulders in the latest fashion, but was furled modestly around her throat. Looking in a pocket mirror, she smoothed out her tightly curled hair locks, then, turning to Kakushichi, said quietly, "I am from Koharumoto in the Echigo District. Please, would you inform the ladies that I am here?"

The clerk, never having seen her before, said politely, "Yes, Ma'am. May I have your—"

Hidesuke hurriedly interrupted. "Kakushichi, just go and tell the ladies they have a visitor."

Immediately after the clerk had hurried off, O-Toki appeared, and led Ponta to the garden at the left side of the house, and then along stepping stones to the parlor, open on this warm day to the summer breezes. O-Toki motioned her in and, saying, "Please wait here," went off in search of the ladies of the house. Ponta sat on the entrance step leading to the parlor and waited. The hemp palm in the corner of the garden looked a translucent green in the sunlight filtering through its branches.

"Thank you for waiting." Behind O-Toki were the two ladies, both wearing freshly sewn, elaborate summer kimono. When they had seated themselves on cushions which O-Toki placed on the tatami mat, Ponta, from the step of the entryway, bowed low to the two women above her on the level of the parlor.

"Thank you for coming. Please come in. Have a cushion." Sei said all this with a completely impassive look on her face. Kino looked the geisha over as she entered and as O-Toki offered her a cushion. Ponta accepted the cushion from the chambermaid, but, instead of sitting on it, folded it in half and placed it beside her. In accordance with Semba etiquette for such occasions, she sat humbly on the tatami mat before the ladies. Kino's opinion of her rose markedly: the young lady certainly knew the rules.

Kino asked O-Toki to summon Kikuji. Then she took out the tobacco pouch from her sash, and with her slender finger packed the grains of tobacco into her long-stemmed pipe.

"Oh, my lady, let me take care of that." Ponta's knee slid toward Kino; she took the pipe, held it lightly in her mouth, lit it, took out a snow-white handkerchief, wiped the mouthpiece carefully, and returned it to Kino. During this operation, Kino and Sei stared at her with no trace of a smile, but Ponta realized that their hostility had nothing to do with the mix-up at the kabuki play. They had not recognized her as the offending geisha. Her offense was the greater one of having lured the son of the house away from their control.

O-Toki returned looking harried, to report that the master couldn't come just now because of business problems which he had to take care of.

Kino was nettled. "Business problems? Hah!"

Sei said reasonably, "It doesn't matter, Mother. The young lady came to see us, not Kiku-bon. He sees her all the time anyway."

"Maybe so, maybe so," muttered Kino.

Thinking this as much encouragement as she was likely to get, Ponta began the session by introducing herself. "I am Ponta of Koharumoto. Lowly as I am, I am honored beyond words to be received by the illustrious ladies, the representatives of the great Kawachiya name and tradition. I am deeply aware of my unworthiness to be associated with your house, and pray to be made worthy." She spoke slowly and carefully, pronouncing each word and syllable for maximum effect.

"How old are you?" asked Kino bluntly.

"Twenty-two, my lady." Ponta added five years, to be on the safe side.

"And your health: how is it?"

"Thanks be to the Buddha, I'm as strong as a horse. I've never been laid up, not even for three days, not even with a cold."

"My, my. You're fortunate to be so healthy. Strong as a horse! Well." Kino paused for an instant, then, in a different tone, asked, "When did you start?"

"I beg your pardon, my lady?" said Ponta, wrinkling her brow in momentary puzzlement.

"Oh, come now. You know what I mean. Your menstruation: when did it start? Twelve? Thirteen? Fourteen?" Kino looked at her, stone faced.

Ponta thought she had been ready for anything, but her eyes widened in astonishment at this question.

At last, in a quiet voice, she said, "Oh—perhaps, at twelve."

"Ah. You are most precocious in every way." Kino kept staring at her woodenly, but Ponta from the corner of her eye realized that Sei had been unable to repress a peculiar smile.

Kino leaned forward, a stern expression on her face. "One thing you must understand. There is a little boy called Hisajiro in our house. He is four years old."

Ponta wondered where this subject led. She said nothing.

"He is our heir. Do you understand?"

Suddenly the light dawned on Ponta. They were telling her that she was not to bear Kikuji a child. Was there anything they did not try to control? She felt as humiliated as though she had been slapped by these two formal, insensitive women.

"Yes, my lady," she said, "I understand completely."

Kino continued as though nothing untoward had occurred. "Where are you from?" she asked, resuming her grim catechism.

"I was born in Shinkaichi in Kobe," Ponta replied quietly, trying to keep her composure.

"What are your parents doing?"

"My father died when I was small; and Mother—just three years ago."

"Your mother was also from a pleasure quarter?"

"I am a second-generation geisha," replied Ponta calmly.

Kino looked her over moodily. Ponta restrained an impulse to scowl back at her, and instead, smiled radiantly and easily.

"How much allowance are you getting?" The question was rude and unexpected. She masked her shock and irritation and said without hesitation, "Praise God, I receive an ample stipend: one hundred yen a month." She thought it wise to subtract fifty yen from what Kikuji actually gave her.

"One hundred yen? Very well. Just take good care of our son and we may increase your allowance in time."

We? Now they were paying her salary!

Kino signaled to O-Toki, who waited at the door with a long wooden box in her hands. Sei took the box from her and turned to Ponta.

"Thank you for coming to see us on this hot day. Here is a small testimony of our favor." She placed the box on the tatami mat, as a person of high social status does when giving a tip to a laborer. It was all part of the Semba ceremony for acknowledging a son's mistress, Ponta knew. She took out tissue paper from her pocket and smoothed it on her knee. Thanking them for the gift, she put the tissue paper in her left hand, and received the present on it.

"You are very skillful in understanding and carrying out our Semba rituals," said Kino unsmilingly. Then Ponta bowed to the two women, and they left. O-Toki was about to see her out through the garden when the sliding panel to the next room opened with a loud snap, and Kikuji was by her side.

"Oh, Ponta! What an ordeal! How tired you look," he said. "I heard the whole thing through the panel here."

For an instant she looked at him with a troubled expression, and was on the verge of saying, "Is that too a Semba custom?" Instead, she bowed to him, saying in formal tones, "Excuse my presence here today." She rose and followed O-Toki out the garden before Kikuji could stop her.

Hastily, he hurried to the front and saw Ponta walking some sixty yards ahead. Her parasol was in her right hand, the present in her left. Even from a distance the movement of her hips under the sheer silk kimono aroused him. He caught up with her and lingered about ten feet behind, wary of eyes from neighborhood houses. She must have known he was there. But she was so angry she refused to acknowledge his presence. On reaching the Shinmachi Bridge, he called to her.

"Wait for me! What's the matter? Still upset?"

She looked at him as he came up to her. "What difficult people your relatives are!" she said angrily.

"I tried to warn you. You're annoyed because I didn't join you in the interview. But what good would I have done?"

"And instead, you eavesdropped behind the sliding door. A fine thing!"

125

"When women fight, a man is no help," he said. "Anyway, you didn't need my help. You were magnificent! Even Kino admitted it."

She put down her parasol on the wall of the bridge.

"They made me feel so—so dirty, and so unhappy," she said. "I'd like to throw their present into the river, sight unseen!"

"Why not?" he urged. "Throw it away!"

"All right! I will! What airs they put on! Like court ladies in the old days!"

She stripped the wooden box of its ribbons and wrapping paper, and leaned it on the railing of the bridge.

"I'm going to throw it into the river. You don't object?"

"Let's get it over with," he said excitedly.

"All right. Here goes! One, two—"

But she hesitated, and rested the box on the bridge railing.

"Maybe I'll look in and just see what the pattern is before throwing it? It would be a shame to waste it entirely."

She loosened the string and pried open the lid. Inside she could see a thick, brocade silk of the most expensive sort.

"Mmmm. Not bad," she whispered, and then, as in a trance, put the lid back and retied the string.

He stared impatiently at her. "What's the matter? Aren't you going to toss it in?"

"Ah, you don't understand," she replied. "I expected stuff as shabby as the treatment they accorded me this afternoon. But those two always do what is technically correct, and they have given me superb silks along with vicious talk. Let me throw the talk overboard. I'll keep the silks!"

"Ponta! Throw them away!" he urged. "I'll buy you better."

She looked at him appraisingly. "Do you mean it?" she asked. And she thought about it for a moment. Then she shook her head, and smiled, and said, "No, I don't think I could do anything so wasteful. I'll keep my present." She adjusted the wrapping around the box, and put it into his hands. "Oh! I'm so hot! And thirsty!" She fluttered her side sleeve back and forth like a fan. "Let's get something cold to drink."

Kikuji looked at her affectionately. "There's a nice little shop at Yotsuhashi. Shall we go there?"

She looked into his eyes, then shook herself as though waking from a dream.

126

"I can't stand it. That's your woman-seducing look, isn't it? All soulful, and soft, and doleful, and sweet. I love you. Let's go!" Opening her parasol, she walked on ahead. They found the little place in Yotsuhashi. A reed shade kept the sun off the verandah where the tables were set. They ordered glasses of iced tea, and Ponta thirstily swallowed the contents of her glass in one sustained gulp.

"Oh, that was so good! When one's mistress visits one's relatives, she isn't even allowed a cup of tea. The customs of the Semba make me thirsty." And she moved her tongue in her mouth to sound as though she were a cat lapping up milk.

He laughed. "Take your *haori* coat off, if you're so hot," he said. "Why did you wear it to begin with? You took it right off as soon as you arrived."

She looked at him with a faint suggestion of a smile. "I had you worried, didn't I? I knew that such a visit was to be made without the half-coat. But I wore it and the straw slippers, and changed them at the last minute, just to show them that I was completely in control of all the conventions which they value so much. That's why I used the corner of the store to deposit my belongings." She giggled. "How worried you looked. But, you know, I thought I gave them tit for tat."

"You were wonderful," Kikuji said. "Who taught you all that kind of thing?"

She smiled reflectively. "In my profession you pick up a lot of information on how to behave without even thinking about it. It's second nature. My mother trained me well. And, when I knew I would be seeing your relatives, I talked with my friends among the senior geisha. They are enormously wise and helpful."

"Tell me, who was your mother's Semba patron?" he asked.

"Oh, come now. I don't know the details," she said, evading his question. Kikuji didn't much care about her mother anyway. He paid the bill.

She put her hand on his sleeve. "We're very close to my house," she said. "Come with me and stay for a while."

"But it's not yet noon, my love," he protested "I have to go back to my store and make money to support you. Especially now that my grandmother thinks you might rate a raise sometime soon. But tonight we'll really do it. I'll see you at six at Kinryu." Then he went close to her and whispered, "You are wonderful this morning, my darling. I love you." He gave her back her present, and backed away, saying, "Till six. Till six!"

As he turned away, she looked at the nape of his neck: he had just had a haircut, and the skin now below the hairline was freshly shaved. The sweeping, simple lines of his kimono accentuated his slim gracefulness. She sighed, and called to the proprietor of the little shop, "What time is it?"

"A little after eleven, Ma'am," he said.

A long, long time to six o'clock, she thought.

During the early phases of that night's festivity, as Ponta's geisha friends were walking about the room trailing their party kimono, Kikuji was conscious of a new sound. It was a soft, rustling sound, a cool sound. He realized that it came not from the crinkling of the kimono, but from the tabi brushing softly against the straw of the tatami mats.

"You're wearing my new brand of tabi, aren't you?" he asked Shimekichi.

"We're all wearing them," she answered. "These are the ones you gave us the night of Ponta's independence party."

"How do they feel?"

"Oh, my. They are so cool, well ventilated and comfortable. The feet stay dry, and so there is no possibility of athlete's foot."

He laughed. "You are as good as a housewife's testimonial on the radio. Just keep talking that way. It's good for my business."

When the waitress appeared carefully bringing trays of food, he noticed that she too was wearing the silk organdy tabi. He was delighted. The things were becoming popular. Ponta had been watching him. Now she began to imitate him. She put her hand to her mouth, removed an imaginary cigarette, inflated her cheeks, and pompously exhaled. She folded her arms and leaned back judicially and snorted a little through her nose as she addressed the waitress.

"Ahhhhh. You don't say so. Them there tabi is goooooood tabi, right? We put our heart and souls into those tabi. What you're walking on so comfortably is our heart and soul. That's why it makes a peculiar, squishy sound, don't you know! Yes, yes, yes!" Kikuji and the geisha broke into laughter. The waitress, engaged in placing

128

dishes on the table, looked from one to the other in puzzlement. She smiled uncertainly at them.

"I guess it's a little funny for an older woman like me to be wearing such stylish summer tabi. My boss said they were cool. I just copied her," she explained with plodding earnestness.

Ponta nodded, rubbed her hands together, and totted up a bill on an imaginary abacus, as a store manager might do.

"Oh, thank you, Ma'am, for patronizing us. You must buy more of our tabitabitabi," she said, bowing low to the astonished waitress, who, shaking her head in bewilderment and muttering under her breath as she departed, made clear that she thought they had all lost their minds.

Kikuji laughed along with the others, and yet he felt in addition a delight which they could not share. He had delayed Ponta's independence festivity until June fifteenth, the official beginning of summer in Osaka, partly in order to introduce his new line. Originally, the silk-lined tabi had been thought up merely as a rather special gift for guests at the party. But then his business instincts had taken over, and the party became an opportunity to introduce a new line of merchandise. And it had paid off, for if the geisha of Osaka and the teahouse waitresses were wearing them, it wouldn't be long before everyone in town would be buying them. The example of the geisha was bound to be far more effective than any advertising campaign could be. He was greatly excited, and half wished to leave the party and go back to his office to make plans for the deluge of orders which would soon come his way.

Not realizing that Kikuji's thoughts were far away from the party, the geisha chattered on animatedly. At formal parties, they had to follow a prescribed social behavior. They couldn't eat even if food were offered them. But this was like having a party of their own, even though Kikuji was paying for it. They ate freely, and they talked in relaxed fashion, knowing they were among friends.

"Ponta. What a lovely ring you're wearing," said one, sure that it must have come from Kikuji. It was a jade stone about the size of a soybean. Ponta had not worn it on her visit to Sei and Kino, but as soon as she arrived home, she put it back on. It was her favorite.

"He bought it for me at Tenshodo's."

"Tenshodo's! Then he must have paid a fortune for it."

"Of course he did." Ponta put the ring back on, and raised her hand toward the light to show it off.

Kikuji frowned in pretended boredom. "Are we finished with the ring? If so, I have an idea. How about going to Yonedaya's for a firefly hunt? Would you like to?"

There was an immediate hubbub of approval. "Just the thing!" "We'd love it!" "Let's go before the fireflies get sleepy!" Two of the six excused themselves because of other appointments; the others joined Kikuji in the short walk to Yonedaya's. In the garden behind the teahouse was a thatch-roofed hut. It was surrounded by skillfully shaped bushes and little hills. The group walked to it from the main building on stepping stones. They had the place to themselves. Kikuji turned off the light in the room, and blew out the torch in the stone lantern. It was pitch dark. A servant with a flashlight brought out the container of fireflies which Kikuji had ordered that morning from Uji, where they flourished. After turning off his flashlight, the servant unscrewed the lid. The fireflies streamed out. When the cold, greenish light in their bodies was turned on, they left behind them little threads of luminescence in the darkness. Everyone was given a paper fan for guiding the fireflies, and a basket with a lid in which to capture them. The fireflies flashed erratically among the trees in the garden and the women, barefoot, chased after them.

"I'll cheer you on," shouted Kikuji. "Pretend that you are at the Uji Firefly Hunting Festival!"

When the women flapped their fans vigorously, the fireflies were aroused and flew madly about. It looked as though a fire had broken into pieces. Kikuji wove his way among the darting fireflies and the women running here and there. Dazzled from staring at the shining insects, the women often stumbled over the garden shrubs and stones. Ponta at one point almost fell into the pond. They shrieked with laughter and anticipation. Kikuji bumped into now one and now another, and, when he did, he gave them hugs and held them until they went off after more fireflies. He could not distinguish whose soft body had fallen into his arms. Whichever amiable presence came his way he kissed and stroked and sent on its way. In the sweaty, hot night they pursued the greenish lights in delighted abandon, and Kikuji pursued them, enamored of the unknown breasts and soft shoulders and rounded hips which he touched. He felt in the darkness a strange ecstasy.

At around two in the morning the night became cooler. Kikuji, Ponta, and their four geisha friends cleaned their feet, took a hot bath, and had a light snack. Kikuji suddenly wanted to sleep with all of them together. He felt a little lightheaded, not so much from drink as from relief that Ponta's worrisome visit to his mother and grandmother was over. And he was happy that his business was thriving. He had no worries. He felt great love for all the girls with him.

When he broached this newest project, Ponta made a face. Shimekichi said playfully, "Oh, wouldn't that be fun! Do you snore?" The others went along willingly, not noticing Ponta's stiffness. They didn't particularly look forward to going back to their houses in the small hours of the morning. And Kikuji was paying. They were excited at the prospect. The maid brought in the starched sheets and the linen-covered summer blankets. Each received a box-pillow with red tassles on it. They stretched out like tired children at the end of a busy day. Kikuji and Ponta were at the center, and two were at the sides, two more at the head and foot. There was hardly room for walking. Mosquito punk burned in the four corners of the room.

Within minutes most of them were sound asleep. Ponta remained wide awake. She raised her head and gazed into the darkness. The lights in the hallway were out, but there was now a little moonlight, and, once her eyes were accustomed to the darkness she could see the little alcove of the room where kimono were piled in untidy heaps. Kikuji lay sideways, away from her, facing Shimekichi, who was hard to see. Ponta knew that Shimekichi alone of her friends had been casting provocative glances at Kikuji when she thought no one was looking. And Ponta felt sure that she had sought out Kikuji's embrace more often than the others during the firefly hunt. She was in her way an attractive woman. Ponta slowly stretched her arm over Kikuji and moved it down between him and Shimekichi. It was just possible that—but no, they were widely separated. She began to withdraw her hand. But suddenly it was seized in a vise-like grip. Kikuji turned quickly and silently, bringing his body close against hers. She kept silent, holding her breath. Sleepers on both sides of them had been disturbed. They moved around a little, but then were quiet, and soon their even breathing showed that they were still deeply asleep. His breath was hot on her neck.

"Oh! Lecher!" she hissed into his ear. "If you wanted it, why didn't you take a room for just the two of us?"

"Mmm. This is nice," he whispered. "While they snore around us, we alone are alive. Let's play just like this in each other's arms. All right?"

And without waiting for an answer, he kissed her ear lobe and his fingers began to wander.

Four

December at Kawachiya's was always a frantically busy month. In preparation for holiday sales, tabi were produced at a tremendous rate. Kikuji often pitched in with the clerks and apprentices, wearing heavy work clothes and an apron. Like them, he tied pairs of tabi together with strong paper ribbon, slipped in the Kawachiya circular trademark, blew open a paper bag, and pushed the finished product inside. It was monotonous work, but it had to be done carefully, and he felt that his own example set the standard for the others in the store.

His mother and grandmother were equally busy in the rear of the house, producing kimono for the family to wear during the holidays. The seamstresses' room was the center of their activity. They went there many times each day to supervise the sewing. The six seamstresses worked long hours trying to meet the demand for their skills. They made kimono with the family crest on the back for Kino and Sei to use on formal occasions. These called for a number of underkimono with harmonizing colors. Kikuji too received a splendid kimono for the holiday season. Even little Hisajiro got one. In addition, each employee was given a kimono as a present for the new year, and so there were endless fittings and measurements. And, profiting from the domestic example, Kikuji visited Ponta's seamstress and ordered three kimono for his mistress: a black, crested one for the formal visits of New Year's Day, and two more colorful ones for the next two days of the holiday week.

The seasonal activity in the store had kept him so busy that he had little free time. For ten days, he hadn't seen Ponta. Now that December twentieth was past, however, the pace at the level of the wholesaler slowed down a little, and one evening he was able to leave his work and go to Shinmachi once more.

Ponta was pacing impatiently when he came in and, on seeing him, ran to greet him. She yanked off his scarf and tugged impatiently at his overcoat before throwing her arms around him and hugging him.

"What a difficult man you are to love," she said. "For thirteen long winter days we haven't seen each other."

She led him to a cushion and began rearranging the charcoal in the brazier, all the while complaining moodily. "I wanted to call you, but I knew I'd be scolded if I did. A woman who pesters a man with phone calls loses his respect and affection, they say. But I *was* worried."

Kikuji watched her as, faintly pouting, she busied herself, poking at the charcoal with iron tongs. What a variety of moods! He smiled fondly.

"What a terrible man you are," she said, catching his smile. "You laugh because I'm angry. Anyway, I want you to stay with me tonight."

"I wish I could, Ponta. But I must go back in a few hours. When the men in the store are working long into the night, I can't very well stay here with you."

"Then, maybe after dinner—?" Her eyes pleaded, finishing the sentence.

Kikuji held her hands in his over the charcoal brazier.

"I'd like that," he said quietly. "I've missed you very much, you know."

The door slid open and the waitress placed a sake bottle and the various dinner dishes inside the doorsill, saying, "Miss Ponta, perhaps you would like to take care of the serving?"

Ponta nodded, and, following the waitress's departure, turned to Kikuji.

"I've tried on all three of the kimono you gave me as New Year's presents. They are all so beautiful. I am the envy of Shinmachi. Not many of the girls living around here can change to completely new outfits on each of three holidays. I hardly know myself, I'm so dressed up. And all this even though it's only our first New Year together."

134

"I'm doing it right just because it *is* the first time," he answered. "In business we take extra special care with the first delivery of goods to a customer, you see."

"Ah, I see, of course," she said, tossing her head, "I'm the first load of goods in your lady collecting. Is that it?"

"You're a very special model, my dear, and I am investing heavily in you. A very special model!"

When his loud laugh stopped, he realized that the house was unnaturally quiet, and it depressed him.

"Where *is* everybody tonight?" he asked.

"They're all at their stores this time of year," she said lightly, "keeping their workmen company so that they won't get lonesome. Your Semba merchant is a busy fellow around holiday season, making money all over the place."

He laughed. "Let's call Shimekichi, Mamechiyo, and any others you like and let them earn some money."

"Very good. You will improve my standing with my colleagues."

She summoned the waitress and gave her a list of names to call. Then, while waiting, Kikuji took a hot bath. Ponta, her underkimono tucked up and the sleeves tied up with a sash, scrubbed his back. Kikuji changed into a silk robe, and, when he returned to the room, found that the four geisha, Shimekichi, Mamechiyo, Kimishige, and Komako were there. He greeted them.

"It's good to see you again. Let's have a pleasant evening together, shall we?"

Mamechiyo jumped up. "I'll do my latest, very fancy dance, if you like."

But Kikuji vetoed the idea. "Let's just eat together and chat quietly. If a merchant celebrates before good business comes his way, he is likely to look a little silly. Let us wait to see what sort of luck the new year brings us. Then will be the time to dance and cavort around. Tonight, let's just be quiet and comfortable. Now, what would you like to eat?"

Mamechiyo hesitated, but Shimekichi laughed and said, "I know what I want. First, sliced raw fish, and not just any old fish, but blowfish. I haven't eaten it in a long time. And then, how about blowfish fricassee? That will make it a New Year's party to remember in my dreams."

The meal was quiet and relaxed and they lingered over it with pleasant talk.

"I think maybe I want to sing," announced Shimekichi dreamily.

"How about playing 'Singing Turns'?" joined in Mamechiyo. Kikuji looked at her questioningly, so she continued, "Each singer sings one of the old Japanese classical ballads to samisen accompaniment. She sings as many stanzas as she can remember, but if she doesn't sing them all, she must pay a penalty."

"Three cups of sake: that's the penalty," urged Shimekichi.

"Good. I'm first," announced Kikuji. And he sang the traditional favorite, "Waiting for You." Komako, the shyest of Ponta's four friends, came next with the New Year's song, "The Best in Japan," and then Ponta sang "The Garden of the Palace." Kikuji was pleased to observe that she had improved greatly with her singing in the short time since achieving her independence. He had given her money to take lessons from a famous singer, and the results obviously were well worth it. She must have practiced hard.

"Very operatic, very operatic," heckled Shimekichi. Ponta was faintly annoyed, and turned her head to one side, drawing in her chin in a way which fascinated her lover. Was it her youthful impulsiveness he found so enchanting? In her was compounded in exquisite proportions the complex simplicity of youth: an unsparing keenness of perception, self-assertiveness, an intuitive talent for friendliness mixed with a truly incredible greediness and just a hint of the shrew to come once the glittering chrysalis of youth had become tattered and outworn. For now, her lighthearted and even irreverent approach to life was just what he needed.

After several hours the four geisha diplomatically prepared to leave, saying that they had another party to attend. As they rose to leave, Kikuji said cryptically, "But, surely, you have forgotten something?"

For a moment they stared in puzzlement at each other.

"Ah. Of course!" said Shimekichi. "Our little account books." She brought out hers, and the other geisha did likewise. It was in these that the patron signed to indicate the hours of the geisha's time which he had used up and would pay for. Kikuji was thoroughly familiar with the system of points on which payment was based: each point listed stood for two hours of the geisha's time. But what he was suggesting now, as the girls very well understood, was that he would enter into their books a New Year's bonus. The bonus points amassed by a geisha served as a practical measure of her popularity and of her professional excellence. They knew, of course, that Kikuji had no responsibility for them and had invited them tonight simply because he knew they were bored and unoccupied. They showed that Kikuji's offer struck them as a grand gesture of generosity. He meant it to be.

He asked for an ink stone, and then began writing into each notebook with his brush the number of points allotted to each of the girls. He entered three points for Mamechiyo in tribute to her graceful dancing and lively conversation; Komako and Kimishige received only two points because, although generally good performers, they were a little too shy; to Shimekichi, in remembrance of her delightful coquettishness on the night of the fireflies, he accorded five points.

"You must promise me not to look in your little account books until you get home. And under no circumstances must you look in each other's records to compare," he said, handing the notebooks back to them. They agreed and left in a flurry of thanks and farewells.

As soon as the door was shut, Ponta said, shaking her head apprehensively, "I don't know what you're thinking of, giving them a bonus. Just having them here was quite enough."

"It's no matter. It will keep them happy."

"Possibly so—assuming that you gave them all the same number of points. Even so, it seems a great waste."

"Oh, Ponta. Don't be so stingy. Money is meant to be used, and I'm making plenty these days." He rose, came over to her, bent down and kissed her neck just under the hairline. "Come," he said softly. He opened the sliding panel to the next room and revealed red silk bedding spread out on the tatami mats with two pillows at the head.

At first she was in a sulky mood, but, after he indicated that he would have to leave soon, she clung to him passionately. She had come to him totally inexperienced in sexual matters. He had been her patient instructor. But tonight it seemed to him that he could feel a difference in the contours of her body. She was more soft and supple; the thinness of late adolescence was lost in the rich curves of maturity. Her skin, next to his, was as smooth and silky as a New

Year's rice cake. He massaged her gently, and she twisted skittishly. But by degrees she learned to like it and snuggled closer to him. How young she was, and trusting—

Kikuji got out of bed and went to the restroom, where he took off his robe and, straddling the porcelain trench of the toilet, squatted down to relieve himself. As he did so, his eye came level with a small aperture. Through it he could see beyond the trees of the courtyard into a window of the adjoining wing. There in the lounge of the ladies' room sat the four geisha busily studying the entries which he had so fatuously made in their books. He smiled ruefully to himself. "Ponta was right. There'll be some hurt feelings there, I'm afraid," he thought.

His mind was brought abruptly back to his own situation by the sudden thump of the sliding panel opening. There stood Ponta staring down at him.

"What on earth—?" he began.

"Ah, look at my lover now," laughed Ponta. "The most accomplished dandy looks pretty pathetic straddling a toilet. Such a pose. Like a monkey in a zoo!" And without a trace of self-consciousness at the impropriety, she shut the door with a bang and he heard her bare feet scuffling on the floor as she ran back to their room. When he returned, she greeted him with a crescendo of laughter.

"I'm just not used to all the things a man's body can do," she said, trying to control her laughter. Kikuji bore her amusement with an embarrassed patience. What a child this mistress of his was at times despite all her wit and perceptiveness. What would she think of next? He soon found out.

He saw her again on New Year's Day. After participating in the ceremonial meal with his mother, grandmother, and son, he went off to make his New Year's visits to his customers and friends, accompanied by his servant. He finished the calls just after noon, let the apprentice return home, and hurried to Yonedaya's Teahouse in Shinmachi, where Ponta was waiting for him. She was wearing the black, crested kimono which he had had made for her. The train stretched magnificently behind her; on her elaborate coiffeur she wore an ear of rice for good luck and a pigeon-shaped ornament. As he crossed the threshold she placed her hands before her on the floor and bowed low, wishing him a happy new year and then going on with the traditional formula, "My humble thanks to you for everything you have done for me during the past year. May your favor continue in the year to come." Then she removed the one-eyed pigeon from her hair, took a brush from her pocket, dipped it in red ink, and gave the pigeon a second red eye.

In response to his questioning look, she said, "The pigeon gets his second eye. And that he deserves only rarely. The tradition is that, if you meet a man you love on New Year's Day, you may put two eyes on the bird."

She moved closer to Kikuji to show him the pigeon. Her heavy black silk kimono had a soft lustre to it. The first underkimono, of an avocado green, showed at the hem and sleeves, and the second, also visible at Ponta's wrists, was of a brilliant red satin. She saw what he was looking at.

"Tomorrow I'll astonish everyone for miles around with the beauty of the new mauve kimono you gave me, and then, on the next day I'll appear in the blue one, and all traffic will stop in the streets."

From across the hall, came the sound of the samisen accompanying a singer.

"The merchants are back with you again, aren't they?"

"And about time, too," she said crisply. "For a month before the New Year holidays the place was like a tomb while they stayed at their offices. Now school is out and they are relaxing here, telling their geisha friends their lofty schemes for the whole of the coming year."

He looked at her curiously. "What lofty scheme for the coming year do you have, Ponta?"

"Well—" She kept her eyes modestly down in a manner not customary with her. "I do have a small ambition, if you would consent to hear it."

"Please."

"Would you let me participate in the Tenth Day Festival to Ebisu? I've watched the procession of the palanquins every year since I was a small child. Any geisha in Osaka would give a year of her life to go bouncing along in a finely decorated float carried by four strapping apprentices. It would be such fun!"

Kikuji thought for a moment, then pursed his lips, nodding.

"It's a fine idea. Merchants have a special interest in the fat god of luck, Ebisu. Let's splurge on it! It will do both our reputations good. I'll send you in a magnificent palanquin to bring back a huge

139

supply of good luck for Kawachiya's. But there isn't much time, is there? The festival comes next week."

"On January tenth." She hesitated an instant. "I should mention that, besides the expense of decorating the palanquin, I—well, I hate to bring it up—but I'll need a new kimono for the procession."

"Of course, of course. Let's get it made right away. Nothing but the best, you understand? No one must criticize us for skimping on costs. We'll knock their eyes out with our display. And you will be at the center of it. But—is there enough time for us to get everything ready, do you think? You should have mentioned this much earlier, my dear."

"You had already given me three beautiful sets of kimono for the new year. I didn't want to ask for more," she answered.

"Ah, but this is good for both of us. Each palanquin will be sponsored by one of the local businesses, and each will carry, enthroned in state, the geisha nearest to a certain merchant's heart. So this is a legitimate business expense: an investment in beauty—and good public relations besides. We'll deck you out in all the magnificence that money can buy. But we must work fast."

The Tenth Day Festival for Ebisu dawned cold and overcast. There were snow flurries in the morning, but by afternoon the snow had stopped and the weather warmed a little. Kikuji went to Yonedaya's Teahouse a little after four and was ushered to a room on the second floor overlooking the street. The procession was due to start at five. He slid open the window slightly and looked down. It was already nearly dark, and street lights lit the scene dimly. The crowd milled around restlessly, sampling the wares of a few street vendors. Across the way the lights from the neighboring teahouse shone cheerfully through the twilight, although the paper-panelled windows were still closed. He turned back into the room and downed several cups of hot sake in an effort to get warm. Just then a waitress called from downstairs, "The procession has begun to move. It will be here in a few minutes." He stood up quickly and slid the window wide open just as the panels of the teahouse opposite opened to reveal to his gaze the gloomy features of the elderly merchant who, while with Ponta and several other geisha months before, had turned his back on the kabuki play. He was now leaning against an armrest, drinking sake which an elderly geisha poured constantly into his cup. A festival clown was doing tricks in the bustling room,

140

but the old fellow paid no attention. For an instant, his eye caught Kikuji's, but he turned away and held out his cup for more sake. At crucial moments this old man kept reappearing. Kikuji felt almost haunted by him: as though he were a prophetic vision of himself grown old and loveless. Well, the oldsters just had to pay more, he supposed, and even then they could not expect to gain the attentions of the most lively and attractive geisha. Like Ponta.

From a distance he heard the chanting of the palanquin bearers as they yelled in unison to keep the proper marching rhythm. Then, tall lanterns, each bearing the name of a geisha, danced in the darkness. Spectators on both sides of the street shouted their applause. Festival clowns danced beside the procession of ten palanquins.

Ponta's was third in the line passing by. She sat, elevated on two thick, flat cushions of red silk. The palanquin was in effect a tiny, square house, big enough only for one person, covered by a curved roof decorated with silken streamers, and open to the view on three sides. It was built on a framework of bamboo poles, lacquered black, and four bearers held the frame as they marched through the crowd. As they came abreast of Yonedaya's, they shouted their marching chant as loud as they could, *"Hoekago, Hoi! Hoekago, Hoi! Hoi! Hoi! Hoi!"* and heaved the palanquin with Ponta in it as high as their arms could reach. She held a strap suspended from the roof at one side. The bearers, still keeping the palanquin elevated above their heads, turned in a slow circle to show Ponta off to the crowd. The spectators clapped their hands and shouted their appreciation. Kikuji's heart swelled with pride. She wore a set of three kimono; the black, crested outer one had been slipped off the left shoulder so that the flowered red and white pattern of the underkimono was exhibited on her shoulder and arm after the manner of kabuki actors. Her glistening black hair was swept up in towering formal fashion, with tortoise-shell ornaments and combs decorated with cherry blossoms. Three festival clowns, attached to her float with garlanded ropes, performed gymnastic stunts as they moved along. But Kikuji thought all eyes, like his own, were on his mistress. As the bearers tossed the palanquin frame up and down for the spectators' enjoyment, he worried about her safety: just to stay in that open-sided contraption, much less to stay in with dignity, seemed a major feat. Gradually, the bearers lowered the framework to shoulder level, and proceeded on their way a little less exuberantly. Kikuji managed to throw an envelope with a bonus in it to the man in charge of the bearers. The man caught it, and once more, on his signal, the departing palanquin was raised high up in salute to Kikuji.

He had not had much sake, but he felt intoxicated with the liveliness of the festival and the admiration directed at Ponta. What was money for, if one could not spend it on the woman one loved? He would keep her beautiful with his money, and, in making her happy, feel an enormous satisfaction himself. And, if he played the patron not only to her but from time to time to her friends and followers as well, his reputation as connoisseur and man of discrimination would be even greater. Sei and Kino were spendthrifts on themselves; his father, Kihei, had never spent anything if he could avoid it. It wasn't the women's large spending which offended him; it was their fakery, their lack of genuineness. He would be genuine, like Kihei, but willing to invest in his particular vision of beauty and love as well. It was as good an objective in life as any he could think of for a businessman. It meant that he would have to work even harder because he intended to spend very freely. Work, earn, spend, enjoy. Why not, why not? He was intoxicated with his thoughts and wondered that a decision so sensible could be arrived at so easily. Ponta in her palanquin had seemed to him an image of beauty with impact enough to alter his rather meaningless life.

Yells from the crowd brought him back to the festival. The last of the palanquins had stopped in front of the teahouse across the street. In it sat a gaunt and forlorn-looking geisha. The bearers circled in the street, and they swung the float up and down recklessly. The old merchant passed an envelope to the festival clown standing beside him, who threw it to the bearers. The aged fellow gave a long sigh and drank more sake. Kikuji wondered vaguely what his life style had been and how it had paid off. The last palanquin disappeared down the street, taking with it the clowns and the tall lanterns which had brightened the scene. The spectators closed in behind, shouting cheerfully in the cold winter air.

It was mid-March, and, as they walked, the warm breeze of the daytime still remained, caressing their cheeks. Ponta had wanted to walk home with him from Kinryu's, and, although it was past ten, they sauntered slowly along the river. He glanced at her. She was absorbed in her thoughts. The moon etched their shadows on the deserted road behind them. The willows below the street lights on the river bank were budding new leaves and extending down fine new threads. They walked on in silence. Something, surely, was different from usual, he thought.

"You're very quiet today," he ventured.

She turned her head and looked full into his face.

"I'm having a baby," she said simply.

Kikuji almost stopped, then resumed his slow walk. The possibility of their having a child had, of course, occurred to him, but her quiet and direct statement had caught him off guard. Without sorting out his feelings he said, noncommittally, "Do you want to have it?"

Ponta stopped walking, and turned to him with a look of strain. "Would there be any difficulty if I did? Would you be upset?"

"No, not at all."

They resumed their slow walking.

"I would like us to have a child, sometime," he said flicking his toothpick into the river. The moonlight caught the tiny ripples it made.

"Really?"

"Really. Of course, you would have to give up your career as a geisha. A geisha with a baby is—incongruous."

"I don't understand." Her voice trembled slightly. "Lots of geisha attached to a patron have babies."

"I'll find a nice, quiet place for you to settle in and have the baby."

"—And be one hundred percent your mistress, and nothing else?"

"But what's wrong with that? In either case I'm taking care of you. Isn't that what's important?" He frowned at her in perplexity. What *was* the matter? How difficult women could be sometimes.

She kicked the earth hard with her wooden clog.

"What is important is that I should go on doing what I love to do and what I do best. I am a professional dancing geisha. I am good at my profession and I regard its practice as an art. I want to continue with it. I want to have my baby. I see no difficulty except in your mind." He could see tears glistening in her eyes. "I cannot take pride in introducing myself by saying, 'I am someone's mistress.' When I say, 'I am a geisha,' I am confident and happy and sure of myself. Don't you see?"

Hastily, Kikuji beat a retreat. "Now, now. Don't get yourself all upset. We'll work something out."

"You bought me my independence, I thought. What is independent about a kept woman, pray? She is nothing but a sexual convenience. I cannot, Master, really, I cannot—be—just a mistress."

No one was around. He took the weeping girl in his arms and comforted her.

"What terrible things you say," he said tenderly. "Don't make yourself miserable in this way."

"You didn't know it," she said, sniffling, "but I was already pregnant when I rode the palanquin on the Tenth Day Festival."

"Good heavens! What a chance you took. Why didn't you tell me?" he exclaimed.

"If I had, you wouldn't have let me ride in the procession. And I wanted to be in it. I am a skilled geisha, even when pregnant, and I showed my professionalism very well then, I thought."

"I never thought the career of a geisha was that important," he admitted.

"As long as I have my looks and my ability, I can look forward to catering to the most select clients. And—who knows?—sometime I might need another patron. A geisha can shop around, but a deserted mistress can't."

She looked at him with the open urgency of a child trying to convince a sympathetic but obtuse adult.

"I give up, Ponta. You can continue being a geisha if you want it that much."

She started to throw her arms around him, but he lightly dodged, laughing at her.

"The whole town may be watching. But I'm glad you want to, again." Then he became serious once more. "But you must promise me that after you reach the fifth month, you will stop working until after the child is born. And the child must be raised in a foster home until he is of school age. I won't have the child squealing in a geisha house. Is that agreed?"

He walked briskly ahead while she lingered behind. Suddenly she ran to catch up with him.

"All right, all right. If you will help me, we can work it out that way," she said, soberly.

"You're sure?"

"Yes. As long as you help me."

They were at the bridge. On the other side was the Semba District. Ponta prepared to leave. Suddenly she recalled Kino's thinly veiled threat to her: "We already have an heir." Involuntarily, she shuddered.

"What's the matter?" asked Kikuji.

"Nothing, Master. Just a chill," she replied. "Have a good sleep, and come soon to see me."

She turned away cheerfully and walked briskly off.

When five months pregnant, Ponta took leave of her geisha activities, and began to prepare for the birth of her child. In order to celebrate this progress toward birth in customary Japanese fashion, Kikuji asked the proprietress of Kinryu's to obtain a white cotton maternity sash used by women to support the baby in the last months of pregnancy. Normally, he knew, the sash would have been provided by the mother-in-law, but nowadays he acted on the set principle that the less Sei and Kino knew of his doings, the better, and he was particularly anxious not to have them passing harsh judgement on Ponta's pregnancy. For that reason he stopped by at Ponta's establishment early one evening accompanied by an apprentice from Kinryu's.

A middle-aged maid whom he didn't recall having seen before came rushing out, and began to simper familiarly at him.

"Well, if it isn't Master Kikuji. Coming to rest himself at the end of a long, hard day."

He stared coldly at her for an instant, then, with a jerk of his head motioned to the parcel the apprentice had in his hands. In frightened haste the presumptuous maid took the package. Just then Ponta appeared and knelt gracefully at the raised edge of the entryway while he removed his clogs on the concrete below. Kikuji looked at her fondly. In her striped silk kimono and half-coat and her superbly upswept hairdo, she certainly didn't conform to any stereotype of a woman in an advanced state of pregnancy.

"Happy fifth month (and sixth, seventh, eighth and ninth) of pregnancy!" he said smiling.

145

She laughed. "Ah, you are so exact. It was very considerate of you."

Upstairs, in her room, she unwrapped the maternity sash. As she opened it, some yen notes fluttered from it.

"A little extra so that you can get the baby all that he'll be needing."

"I already have some of the proper equipment." She gestured toward the alcove where there were a pile of diapers, a number of tiny shirts, and several small blankets.

"At that rate, by the time the baby arrives, you'll have enough for a whole nurseryful! And besides, you don't know whether it's a boy or girl."

"Yellow will do for either," she replied. "I want to be very well prepared. I have other things besides the clothes and blankets."

He sipped at his cup of sake. "Like what?" he inquired.

"Like this."

She pushed back the table on which Kikuji had been leaning, tapped the edge of one of the tatami mats lightly, and, hooking a hairpin under it, lifted the corner. As she raised the mat, Kikuji saw that underneath, on a sheet of newspaper, she had spread out row after row of dusty bills: five-yen notes, ten-yen notes, one hundred-yen notes.

She lowered the mat again.

"See how economical I am," she said, smiling. "Don't you approve?"

"But it seems so—unnecessary," he protested.

"No, no! All my friends in this profession waste their money, but not me. I save everything. Everybody has his own way of doing things and enjoying himself. This is mine."

"But why not put it in the bank?"

"That would spoil the pleasure. Here, under the tatami, they warm me at night when I sleep, and make me feel good when I think of them."

"Don't I give you enough money?"

She looked at him, puzzled. "Of course you do. Most of these bills came from you. That's another reason for putting them just under my sleeping place."

She replaced the tatami mat and, after ordering more sake, talked entertainingly of the parties at the various teahouses. She knew every absurd detail and with gestures and voice made vivid caricatures of the persons involved.

"Who tells you all these things?" he asked. "You can't be present at every party."

"No, but the geisha from my house get around, and then, of course, they talk with their friends in the profession. And every night when they come home I talk with them to find out what the latest news is. Maybe sometimes they exaggerate a little, just to keep me happy."

"You really enjoy these parties very much, don't you?"

"Of course. It's my profession and I love it."

"Then why— Oh, never mind."

"Why did I decide to have a child, you were going to ask."

"That's right."

"I have to think about the future. A geisha is finished by the time she's thirty."

"Here at twenty you're thinking of your old age."

"From the time that I first remember her, my mother was over thirty," Ponta replied. "A second-generation geisha should learn from the trials of the first, don't you think? This child may support me when I'm old."

"As a third-generation geisha?" he asked.

"Perhaps. Or as a soldier or scholar—or just plain butcher, maybe. Who can tell?"

He smiled reflectively. "Of course. Who can tell?" He drew her hand, clasped in his, to his mouth and kissed it. "And now"—he emptied the second sake bottle into his cup and drained it—"I must go."

"But not so soon."

"I came especially because I wanted to share your fifth month with you."

"But don't leave me alone tonight." She toyed with the sleeve of his half-coat. "Stay a while."

He looked at her bulging waistline. "It wouldn't be good for you," he said softly. "I don't want to crowd our son or daughter."

Again he kissed her upturned palm, and stood up. Kikuji did not like to sleep with pregnant women. It had been so with Hiroko. He would rather do it outside than run the risk of hurting a child by the thrustings of his desire. He quickly took his leave, and walked to the street on which the trolleys ran. Then, after an instant's hesitation, he crossed it, and walked in the direction of Yonedaya's Teahouse. Upon arrival, he asked the proprietress to send for Shimekichi, Mamechiyo, and two or three other geisha. He drank sake as he waited for them. Mamechiyo arrived first.

"You are so quick," he said, as she hurried in.

"A party at Tominoya's had been canceled, and I wasn't doing anything." Then she bit her lip. She recalled that Kikuji had stopped visiting Tominoya's suddenly because of some difficulty concerning Ikuko, the daughter. She should never have brought up the name of the offending teahouse. She said so, and apologized.

"It's all right," he replied easily, emptying the sake bottle into his cup. "How is everyone there?"

"Everyone? Well—you knew that Ikuko left Tominoya's to become a geisha?"

He stared hard at her. "No. No, I didn't know that. When did she leave?"

"It must be about six months ago. She registered at the Soemoncho Geisha House."

Kikuji frowned and shook his head in puzzlement.

"Oh, but it's true, sir," insisted Mamechiyo. "Ikuko's a quiet girl, but she has backbone, and, when she kept having trouble with the proprietress, she gave up her position as adopted daughter of the house. It was a big sacrifice, but the old lady was very hard to get along with, I think. Still, I never expected her to become a geisha. Her geisha name is Ikuyo—"

The sliding door opened and Shimekichi, Komako, and Kimishige burst in on the two of them. Kikuji greeted them.

"Just the same people as were at the year-end party. Good. We'll pick up from there," he said in a loud voice.

"Ah, yes, sir. But the best of us, Ponta, is busy with other matters tonight. I have heard about the baby. Please accept our congratulations," said Shimekichi, who, having seniority, spoke for the whole group.

Kimishige, normally the quiet one, added breathlessly, "Oh, isn't Ponta the lucky one, though? She was the star of the Tenth Day Festival procession through your efforts, and now she is to have a baby. She has everything a geisha could want. While the rest of us,

148

well—" She shrugged her shoulders suddenly and made an odd face to hide her sentimental gloom. Shimekichi laughed gently at her. "One is born with a special attractiveness to the menfolk. A special genius for love, that's what it is. And if it's one's fate not to possess that talent, you've just got to make the best of what you have, that's all. It's the same with everybody, I guess."

Then, realizing that she had been a shade more serious than she had intended, she threw her head back and said, "But let's have a lively time tonight. No more philosophizing!"

After drinking several bottles of sake with Ponta, walking briskly through the cold to Yonedaya's, and downing several more bottles there, Kikuji found his head whirling.

He stared heavily at the tatami mats. "That's right," he said, frowning with the elaborate seriousness of the drunk aspiring to sobriety, "no more philosophizing. No more status quo. Let's change everything. Beginning with this room."

The geisha looked at each other in uncertainty.

"What do you mean, sir?" ventured Shimekichi.

"Let's stack the room!" Kikuji shouted.

"Stack it?"

"Yes, yes. Haven't you ever stacked somebody's room? It's fine fun. We did it in school. You take out every bit of furniture and stack it in a big pile in the yard or garden or street or wherever and however. We can start with the tatami mats." And he began to tug at one corner of a mat.

"The proprietress will have a fit," whispered Mamechiyo to Shimekichi.

"Not if he pays for the inconvenience and any damage. And, of course, he will, twice over," replied Shimekichi. "Anyway, let's try it. It might be fun at that."

To Kikuji she said, "Perhaps I ought to inform the waitress, so that no one will be upset?"

But he would allow no delays. "We want them upset. We're upsetting the established order, and stacking it in the garden!" He had tucked up the hem of his kimono and tied a towel around his head. The geisha followed suit, and soon everyone was pulling and tugging at tables, tatami mats, flower vases, charcoal braziers, and cushions.

"A special bonus to the hardest-working mover!" shouted Kikuji. To make way for the larger objects, the geisha unhooked the sliding doors and tried to carry them out to the garden. But they were unskilled at such work, and repeatedly banged the wall with the wooden frames, and several times broke windows. The chief waitress of the teahouse came rushing up to investigate the sudden commotion. Reassured by the geisha as much as by her own awareness of Kikuji's impeccable credit, she reluctantly retreated to let the game take its course. First came the tatami mats. When he raised the first one with difficulty, he looked underneath it, but found only a few dusty sheets of torn newspaper.

"What did you expect?" asked Shimekichi.

"Oh, I don't know. Hidden money, maybe," he replied. "All geisha hide their money under the tatami mats, I know. Or, maybe not money. Maybe some erotic 'spring pictures,' such as they hide under the pillow of a bride to inspire her as to correct etiquette in the give-and-take of nocturnal wrestling. But there aren't even any spring pictures. What kind of a teahouse *is* this?" He snickered drunkenly, half-amused at his own absurd expectations, half-sympathizing with the women, who were laughing at his outrageous chatter.

Mamechiyo produced a broom from somewhere, and began to brush off the dusty tatami mats before carrying them outside to the garden. As she brushed, she began to sway to the rhythm of her sweeping, and soon was gyrating her hips in elaborate bumps and grinds like an Egyptian belly dancer. The other geisha stopped moving furniture, and gathered around her, urging her on to further experiment. Kikuji joined in the laughter and applause. As he watched Mamechiyo in her frenzied dance, the image of Ikuko came suddenly to mind, leaving him detached, quiet, and far removed from stacking the established order. It occurred to him for the first time that he might not have been fair to her at their separation. Surely she hadn't had any notion of what that impossible fat proprietress had been trying to do. He ought to have believed her. She had always been scrupulously honest with him. Now she had broken with her adoptive mother, probably in part because the old chatterbox had tried to ensnare him into a permanent relationship with her. He had not thought of her in months; yet now his mind was strangely overwhelmed with pity for the girl.

He realized suddenly that all the noise of laughter and applause had ceased, and the geisha were turned to look at him and beyond him. Wheeling around, he found himself face to face with the proprietress of Yonedaya's. She looked at him mildly through her gold-rimmed spectacles, smiling in a way that was both gentle and alert. "What a novel idea, my dear sir. You are helping to clean up my teahouse, I see."

"I felt the need for change." It didn't sound very convincing to him, now that he was sober. But what else could he say? He wasn't about to apologize for foolish behavior to a teahouse proprietress.

"Yes, yes. That's very understandable, sir." Bowing her head respectfully, she was, he could see, darting her eyes here and there, trying to estimate the extent of damage to the room. "Very understandable." Hah.

"Madam, since it's change we're after, and since some of your funiture is somewhat the worse for wear after our parlor revolution, you really ought to change all the tatami mats and fixtures. Please do so, and send me the bill."

It was as though he had been reading her mind. Her head bowed appreciatively up and down and she went off clucking contentedly about the fine quality of the customers who frequented her special, very refined establishment.

The Dotombori River flowed directly below the window of the second-story room to which he had been escorted. He had been sitting for well over half an hour at this unfamiliar teahouse in Soemoncho, waiting for them to bring him some word of Ikuko. His tension seemed to have infected the waitress. She wiped the table interminably after pouring him sake, then went out to see how the search for Ikuko was progressing. He sipped the hot sake moodily. The waitress opened the sliding panel, and knelt deferentially in the hallway.

"I am so sorry, sir. We have requested the party for whom the young lady is working tonight to allow her to come here instead. It will take a little time—"

Kikuji waved a deprecating hand. "Don't worry about me. I came without any advance notice, and I'm willing to wait. The view of the river will keep me company until she arrives."

151

He heard the soft thump of the sliding door closing behind him as he stood up and walked to the window. The wavelets reflected the lights of the restaurants on the opposite bank. Soemoncho, he reflected, had a different sort of mood from that of Shinmachi, the oldest quarter of Osaka. He was accustomed to the heavy roofs of the Shinmachi looming over the low facades of the houses protected from the street by their characteristic lattice fences. While he loved the traditions enshrined in these old houses, he had to admit that they were often gloomy and oppressive. The weight of tradition is sometimes a treasure, sometimes merely a burden. Soemoncho was much newer; the houses were more airy and spacious, gleaming with the prosperity funneled into it from nearby Shinsaibashi, the commercial center of modern Osaka. As he leaned on the window-sill, the laughter and singing of a party at another teahouse, down-river, came to his ears.

He heard a familiar voice in the corridor, and the sliding door opened. She bowed deeply from her sitting position, her hands on the floor.

"Good evening, sir. It has been a long time." She avoided looking into his eyes. She wore a lavender party kimono, and her face was covered with the thick white makeup required of professional geisha. But the sharply chiseled lines of her nose and mouth marked her still with the individualizing quality of a quiet, persistent intelligence. How different she was from Ponta. Without speaking, she picked up the sake bottle and poured for him.

"I hadn't dreamed of your becoming a geisha. It took me completely by surprise," he said.

"How did you hear about it?" she asked, her eyes downcast.

"From Mamechiyo, on Tuesday at Yonedaya's."

Her expression softened and she looked at him with the ghost of a smile in her eyes. "You came to see me, then, as soon as you knew."

"Why did you leave Tominoya's?"

"You know why," she said in a subdued voice. "My adoptive mother and I did not agree about most things, and—" Her voice trailed off into silence.

"Was I the cause of the trouble?"

"No, there were many problems. But she did keep trying to find a patron for me from among her 'better customers,' as she put it. And

152

she made a fool of herself and of me by her ridiculous meddling with you. I was happy with everything the way it was."

"I see," he said meditatively, sipping at his drink. "Did you want to become a geisha?"

"Well, last spring when I left Tominoya's and went home, things were rather crowded. I'm the oldest of seven daughters. I couldn't stay there long."

"You had no savings?"

"No. Madam was generous enough in many ways, but I was her adoptive daughter, and you don't pay your daughter wages."

Kikuji frowned thoughtfully. "But—did you especially want to be a geisha? I mean, is it your line? Weren't there other jobs available?"

She looked at him with a faint smile. "You think I'm too serious-minded for the life of a geisha, is that it?" She leaned forward earnestly. "When I was in Shinmachi, the girls used to say a geisha has an identity. I wanted to have an identity, and I have a certain professional pride in establishing and maintaining that identity. Does that make sense?"

He shook his head, puzzled. "Maybe," he said.

"As a geisha, I belong to a certain house, I have my special talents which are recognized and called for. Society makes room for me. Too many women's jobs in our country call for a cringing nonperson. Whatever I do, I want to be respected for doing well. Do you see?"

He smiled, looking into her eyes, and nodded. "Of course I do," he said softly. "It is just like you. You are so beautifully organized in your life. When you see a problem, you set to work and solve it."

"Just like that," she replied with a laugh. "Wouldn't it be nice if it were that simple." She saw him looking at his watch. "I regret that I have an appointment at nine. But I can stay a little longer with you."

She clapped her hands for the waitress. As she began to order, Kikuji said, "Let's have cold beer tonight. It's just too hot for sake."

He loosened his collar. Under the reddish silk of the outer kimono, she saw the celadon green of the underkimono.

"You are as particular about your clothes as ever, I see," she said.

"I like to dress well at night. In my business, even the boss wears work clothes during the daytime so that he can lend a hand when

153

there's need. At night I like to be a fashion plate. It's a trait I inherit from my mother, I think." He laughed.

"And you always go to Shinmachi at night?"

"I grew up watching Shinmachi just across the river. My affection for it seems to be getting steadily deeper these days."

"Naturally so, I should think. You started visiting there when you were twenty-three or twenty-four, and it has been five or six years since then."

The conversation drifted on effortlessly. Kikuji felt completely relaxed. Ikuko was not as pretty or as entertaining as Ponta, but, with her alone in this way, he felt completely natural and comfortable. Ponta was exhilarating and competitive; Ikuko was restful, and better at drawing out his thoughts.

The waitress tapped on the sliding panel to remind Ikuko that she was expected at another party. The two of them looked at each other without moving.

"Go ahead," said Kikuji. "I'll come again soon."

"Stay a while," she said on sudden impulse. "I'll be back in an hour."

He nodded, and she left hurriedly. He moved over to the window, and sat on the broad sill while drinking his beer and staring at the river flickering with lights reflected from the restaurants on the opposite shore. A boat with a big lantern on its bow worked its way upstream. When close to the teahouse, the young oarsman put down his oar with a clatter, and stood high in the stern to look into Kikuji's room. Kikuji waved at him, beer bottle in hand. The boat veered quickly and came directly under the window.

"Oh, for a bottle of cold, cold beer," yelled the venturesome youth.

Kikuji laughed, and dropped the bottle neatly into the young fellow's hands. The oarsman raised it high.

"I toast you and your generosity and the generosity of your mistress! May this be a good night for you!" And he drank his beer while drifting downstream again, then picked up his oar and proceeded on his way.

Kikuji looked at his watch, yawned, waited.

One hour later, Ikuko returned, breathing rapidly as a result of her haste.

"You needn't have hurried that much," he said.

"I didn't want you to be bored." She poured some sake for him and a little for herself. "One can't be a geisha without drinking, and now I find I like it—fortunately."

She leaned toward him, holding out the sake cup. Her skin between her shoulders, revealed by the low collar of her party kimono, was wet with beads of sweat. Kikuji too felt damp and uncomfortable.

"Let's get out of here," he said suddenly.

"Where to?" she asked, putting on her clogs at the entryway.

"To someplace that's cool," he replied. "Taxi!"

They drove through the center of the city and got out of the cab at Chausuyama Hill in Tennoji Park. Silently they walked along the dark, wooded path, picking their steps with care. Ikuko climbed the stone steps leading to the museum, balancing easily on her wooden clogs. He followed. The trees loomed overhead from both sides of the path. Here and there he could see whitish shapes on the ground, the last vestiges, he supposed, of late-blooming cherry blossoms.

"How quiet it is," Kikuji said to the dark form of Ikuko ahead of him. "I wish I could keep walking slowly into the unknown, following after you all the night long until at last we would see the dawn breaking through the trees—"

She stopped, half-turned. He came up to her, leaned down, kissed the back of her neck, smelling the special fragrance of her skin.

"Kiku-bon," she whispered, using the name he had had when she had first met him six years ago.

Gently, he turned her around to face him.

"Let us go back to where the cab left us. There was an inn to one side of the park entrance. We'll spend the night there."

They turned and, arm in arm, retraced their steps.

From the second floor of their inn on Chausuyama hillside, Kikuji, who had risen for a drink of water, looked out over the center of Osaka. At some distance from the inn was a branch of the Dotombori, and the garish neon lights of midtown were mirrored in its waters.

"What are you looking at? Is something the matter?" said Ikuko, straightening the sheets and blanket.

155

"I was just—admiring the beautiful lights. I've never seen Osaka from here before."

But his mind was not on the lights. He was thinking instead of that strange and intricate moment when he had bent over her exposed neck in the darkness and inhaled the fragrance of her skin. Before that instant Ikuko had been for him a good friend, protective, serious, a trifle too domestic in her instincts. After it, he had been borne along will-lessly on a tide of passion. He had made no decision: it had been made for him by the subtle chemistry of sex. And now, after this utterly unique experience, he felt contentedly used up, fulfilled as he had never before dreamed of being. Her body was a rich and still unknown continent which he yearned to explore in endless detail. The sheen and texture of her skin, the musk of her breath—everything about her was intoxicating, even to think about. He yawned slowly and noisily, with a sense of luxurious repletion.

He went to Kino's detached rooms in response to a formal invitation. It was just afternoon tea, but they had been practicing the tea ceremony of late, and he supposed they wanted someone to practice upon. It came at an inconvenient time. He had been trying, with Wasuke and Hidesuke, to straighten out the books at the end of June. For once, what with all the bills from teahouses, tailors, restaurants, and jewellers, it wasn't easy. When Kikuji had read off some of the larger figures, Wasuke, embarrassed for his master, became confused in working the abacus, and had to start over. Hidesuke, however, remained efficiently unmoved, and through his rimless glasses those piercing eyes took in everything: Wasuke's embarrassment, the master's rising irritation, and the significance of the large sums that had been spent. With easy precision, the assistant manager calculated the figures needed. This would have been their third and last session at this monotonous task, and Kikuji wanted to be finished. But O-Toki had tapped on the office door and announced quietly, "The ladies sent me to ask how soon they may expect you."

It was five after three when he opened the sliding panel to Kino's room. He and Kino were to serve as guests, while Sei was hostess. Kikuji took off his heavy work apron and sat down next to Kino.

156

There were times when the tea ceremony with its silent attention to the minutest details of ritual was very restful, but this apparently was not to be one of them, for as Sei went through the motions of ceremonial cleaning with a red silk cloth she said to him, "You must be exhausted with making out the month-end bill settlements."

"I'm used to it by now," he replied shortly, placing a small cake on his napkin.

Kino carefully took the first sip, as the first guest is expected to do, and then said, "It seems that you've got good, high gross sales, but you've also a very heavy demand for payments." He said nothing. He received the tea bowl from Kino in the prescribed manner and had one sip. Oh, these restful tea ceremonies. That damned spy, Hidesuke! How else would the women know about his business in this detailed fashion?

"A good business must not rest satisfied with just making a profit," he said pontifically. "It must reinvest to make the profit a continuing thing."

"Reinvest. In teahouses?" said Kino, flashing her eyes at him with a hard smile.

Kikuji restrained himself. After a pause, he said evenly, "You are always interested, I see, in my relationships with other women. Sometimes I think you want to evaluate them in terms of profit and loss. It isn't that simple, unfortunately. Ultimately, each of us has only himself to invest. And who can say what the return will be? Sometimes I gain most in understanding and memory from a devastating loss. But with all respect I don't think I should stand before you, account book in hand, and justify the intimate details of my private life. Do you?"

"Ah, you talk a lot of philosophic nonsense," snarled Kino. "I'm trying to tell you: don't let those women make a fool of you and take your money away from you!"

"I'll chance it," he answered quietly. "I'll risk spending myself and my money, provided I always have a chance to grow and understand myself and my world. I know that sounds pompous and unreal to the two of you. But you would, if you could, coop me up in this houseful of dead traditions to play safe and meaningless games as you are always doing. If I did that, I would lose all character, all identity and meaning. I must do it my way."

157

"Kiku-bon, that's what *you* say," shouted Kino. "It doesn't sound pompous and unreal to me! It sounds stupid! It sounds ungrateful! You forget one thing: you succeeded to the directorship of Kawachiya's because your mother and I consented to it!"

She waited for a reply, but he remained silent, debating in his own mind whether or not he ought not just storm out and get away from this dreary family row. Only Sei and Kino would have set this confrontation up in the context of the tea ceremony, he reflected bitterly.

Kino continued more gently. "I'm told you're paying a big bill to Minoya's Teahouse in Soemoncho. Are you supporting a new mistress there? Or are you just diverting yourself while Ponta is pregnant?"

Astonished as he was, Kikuji showed no emotion, and slowly took his second ceremonial drink of tea. His mother and grandmother eagerly watched his hands, trying to detect any trembling or convulsive movement which might give him away. He slowly and correctly finished his tea in a third drink, and then, having rotated the cup properly, turned it over, as the tea ritual required, to study the name of the maker. Having gone through all the prescribed forms, he set the dish down and turned to them again.

"This is certainly an odd way to learn that I am to become a father again," he said, with a suggestion of a laugh in his voice. "Where did you pick up this fine bit of scandal?"

There was no way for them to know. It was simply a sharp guess. And it was none of their business. The strictest taboo observed by the geisha community was that prohibiting any gossip whatever concerning liaisons between patron and geisha. Ponta had not been seen outside her quarters since the fifth month. And Kikuji himself had been delivering her monthly stipend to her. There simply was no way for them to know. How greedily they pursued his imagined sins in the great outer world of which they knew no more than two children!

His mother sought to make peace between him and Kino.

"Very well, then. We're delighted to learn that there is no truth to the rumor. Much as we love you, my dear, it would be a great nuisance to find ourselves stuck with an unwanted baby as a result of all your wasteful habits. We have to keep the family in mind."

158

He opened his mouth to reply, then relaxed, smiled, admired the tea bowl in his hands for a few seconds more, and excused himself to return to the office. The tea ceremony had served its purpose.

Next day he waited with scarcely concealed impatience for the evening so that he might visit Ikuko, whom he hadn't seen during the last few busy days. His tea ceremony confrontation with Sei and Kino had accentuated to him the need for defining clearly the meaning and extent of this new relationship which had sprung into life so suddenly. Ikuko had clearly been thinking along the same lines, so much so that she seemed almost to be reading his mind. When he apologized for not having stopped by sooner because of the press of business, she simply nodded, and said, "Of course. I realize that you have many responsibilities. Soon, your mother and grandmother will have heard of your visits to me, so we must, I suppose, make some decisions soon."

"You know of my mother and grandmother, do you?" he asked in surprise.

"Shinmachi is near the Semba District, and your family is well known around there," she answered delicately. "Particularly the ladies of the house: your mother and grandmother. I worry that they may learn of my existence in your life and be displeased."

He laughed. "They know of your existence by now, you may be sure."

"If I were in the position of your mother and grandmother," Ikuko went on firmly, "I would be upset at your free spending in the Soemoncho District. I would say, 'Who is this evil woman who is tempting our heir to spend his hard-earned money?' And they would be right to ask."

Kikuji frowned. "They have already asked," he growled.

"Ah? So!" she exclaimed. "Then—I know you are in a gloomy frame of mind just now and need other things from me than dull advice—but you must arrange matters so that you don't spend so much on me from now on."

"Ikuko. I won't cheapen us by looking for ways to cut costs," Kikuji protested. "If I become your patron, I would want to do it in a way that would allow you to live in dignity and comfort. I've seen these loathsome fellows who, for their own comfort, stash their mistresses away in some seedy, out-of-the-way place you wouldn't want even a beggar to live in— I can't do that."

She looked into his eyes for a moment, then down at her hands in her lap. "Let me quit the geisha profession entirely."

"Would you allow me to keep you and provide for you—as my mistress?"

She smiled. "Yes. Unlike Ponta, I am not really a geisha through and through."

"We have never mentioned Ponta before. You—know about her."

"And the baby."

"You don't mind?"

She hesitated for the briefest instant. "I am willing to share you."

"Then this next month I'll find a place for you to stay. And I'll assist you in settling up when you leave your geisha group."

"A small, quiet place is all I need," she said. "Nothing expensive, please."

She looked at him happily, then suddenly placed her hands in front of her on the tatami mat and bowed her head in a long, lingering bow. When she straightened up, she said in a low voice, "There is one other favor I would like to ask of you, if I dare—"

He smiled. "Just one?" he teased. "Are you thinking of a party to celebrate your leaving the geisha house?"

"No, no. Not that," she insisted. But she said nothing further.

"What, then?"

She looked at him nervously. "Once I settle down as your mistress, I would like your permission to wear the *marumage* hair style."

Kikuji didn't quite know what to say. The request had taken him by surprise into an area of feminine custom in which he felt incompetent to judge. Since the *marumage* style was reserved for legal wives, it seemed to him inappropriate for a mistress to wear it. Ikuko would be sailing under false colors, and there might be awkwardness resulting—

"It is important to me just now," she explained, "for two reasons. In the first place, it will tell people I am not a geisha." She stopped.

"And in the second place?"

"In the second place, I shall feel that I am to serve you with the love and care of a wife—but only until you marry again."

Kikuji postponed the decision. "Let me think about it," he said.

In late July he bought her geisha contract. Recalling Ponta's example when she became independent, he suggested that she have a huge retirement party. But she arranged everything much more modestly. Ponta had been setting herself up as an independent geisha, and her farewell party had served to publicize her new enterprise. Ikuko, however, was leaving the profession and giving back the geisha name she had used. She was finished with the life of the geisha. Even so, she discovered a need to say farewell to her friends, and her modestly planned party was much larger than she had initially thought it would be. Three days after the party, she moved to a small house in the fashionable Unagidani District of Osaka. Most of the houses on the street were occupied by women who, like herself, were the mistresses of wealthy businessmen.

Visiting her in her new home, Kikuji soon realized, was an experience utterly different from his sessions with Ponta in her geisha establishment. As he walked down the gravel-covered alley and turned in at the latticed doorway, he felt as though he were going home. The mood was domestic. He experienced a sensuous pleasure as his eyes adjusted to the half-darkness of the downstairs rooms so that he could distinguish the forms and shapes of objects. One late afternoon when he came to see her, she answered the door and escorted him into the rooms. He stretched out in front of the electric fan and wiggled his toes luxuriously as he looked at her *marumage* hair style. She had begun to wear her hair in that fashion soon after moving in, and he had said nothing to prevent it.

"If you keep on wearing your hair *marumage* style all the time, you'll get as bald on the top of your head as some of the old grandmothers I know," he said, teasingly.

"Do you like it?" she said with a shy coquettishness that never failed to excite him.

He kissed her hand. "You are beautiful."

"I give you my promise: when you take a bride—a respectable bride of good family—I will give up my married hairdo, and, if you wish, bow out of your life."

161

"Have no fear," he laughed, observing her closely. "There is very little likelihood of my ever getting married again."

"Eh, how serious we are," she said, laughing. "Now that that's settled, would you like a bath?"

She went off to prepare the bath water, first covering her hair with a cloth, so that the steam would not mar it. He looked after her thoughtfully. Unlike Ponta who, baby or no baby, would always have a life of her own, Ikuko seemed to be merging her existence inextricably with his. The *marumage* hairdo was a way of announcing to him that, although he was completely free, she was married, and would have it no other way. He scratched his chin reflectively. On the day after her farewell party she had visited his mother and grandmother. There had been no *marumage* hair style in evidence then, of course. In fact, she had seen fit to present herself to the ladies of the house wearing an astonishingly unfashionable, conservative outfit. Her hair had been pulled tightly into a knot at the back of her head, and was decorated only by one slim tortoise-shell comb. She had been calm and composed on being presented to Sei and Kino, and they for their part had contented themselves with routine exchanges while they studied her carefully. After receiving the customary present of silk cloth, she had bowed to the givers and astonished them by asking if she might pay her respects at their domestic shrine to the fox goddess.

"But how do you know about our shrine?" asked Kino suspiciously.

"The master, when relaxing at the teahouse, often talked about the respected ladies of the house and of his home, filled with the traditions of past ages. And so I know about your shrine. I ask to visit it only so that I may respect and honor those traditions and values which you and he participate in."

It was an impressive speech, and his mother and grandmother clearly liked it. Had Ponta said it, she would have been lightheartedly making fun of them and their shrine. But not so Ikuko. She meant it. This essentially serious and devoted attitude toward all of life and toward him especially was one of her most remarkable characteristics. Kino, in any event, her suspicions for the moment quieted, led her to the shrine, where she prepared a sacrifice and said a prayer before leaving.

After her departure, Kino turned to him, head wagging assertively, and delivered her judgement, "Ah, that one. Why couldn't you have picked her first? I'll bet she pinches and saves wherever she can. She'll be a good influence on you. God knows you could use one." And she went off mumbling about thrift and simplicity.

He slowed the electric fan and lay on his back, hands clasped behind his head. The splashing of the bath water sounded from the bathroom. It was quite true, of course, that Ikuko was frugal. She had hired a seventeen-year-old farm girl from her home town of Yamashina to serve as her maid because the wages there were less than in Osaka. But the thrift extended to a spare, devoted attitude toward her whole world. Perhaps this was the very stuff of maturity. It occurred to him that she shared this quality of quiet dedication with Hiroko, his first wife. Even in appearance she looked somewhat like Hiroko. Ponta, with her full face, big, round eyes, and carefully trained sidelocks, was by far the most beautiful of the three, just as she was the youngest and most childlike.

The door to the bathroom opened, and Ikuko came out, wiping her wet hands, to announce that it was ready. It was a good bath. Ikuko scrubbed his back, and, when he had dried off, helped him arrange the freshly laundered, heavily starched cotton summer kimono so that it was comfortable. He came out of the bathroom yawning luxuriously and feeling very domesticated. Ikuko added to that effect by serving up a superb supper: sliced raw prawns, chilled custard, broiled sweet fish, steamed clams, and sauteed eggplant. Her portion, he noticed, was much smaller than his, and, when he commented on the discrepancy, she laughed and said that such fancy food would upset her work-a-day stomach, used as it was only to sturdy, working-woman's meals. Then she served him beer, reserving for herself just enough to keep him company as he drank.

"How is Ponta doing these days?" she asked suddenly. "It must be hard for her, approaching her full term in all this hot weather."

"I stopped by to see her several days ago. There she was, chattering away over that huge stomach like some kind of bird, just as lively and curious and happy as ever. But I know she'll be glad when the nine-month wait is over, and she can see her child."

"I realize that Shinmachi and Soemoncho are far apart, but sooner or later she is going to hear about me," said Ikuko, "And I think you should prepare for it. I think it would be very unfortunate for her to hear some careless gossip about us before the baby is born."

"You've finished worrying about me, so now you're going to worry about her," he said, laughing. "You're a born worrier. Well, you can stop it for the time being. I've already asked the proprietresses of Kinryu's and Yonedaya's to see to it that all mouths in the area are closed about a certain topic. I too want Ponta to be easy in her mind just now."

With approaching darkness, the mosquitoes began to fly in, so they went upstairs. As they went into the hall, Kikuji heard the country maid singing in the kitchen. He climbed the steep, almost ladderlike, staircase with care. Ikuko spread the bedding. They crawled in under the mosquito netting, conscious of the pleasant smell of camphor from their kimono. He wriggled quickly out of his night clothes, and opened hers to his roving hands. Diligently and with ever-renewed surprise, he explored each hill and valley of his soft continent of love, stopping only now and then to stroke her hair, her ear, her cheek, while her hands were equally busy with him, moving constantly around and over and under and into. With Ponta, it had been a delightful game. With Ikuko, he lost all awareness of self, and was absorbed, mind and body, into her richness.

Five

After he turned the corner at Echigocho, he was in a residential district with small, well-kept, fashionable houses. Although it was already early September, the summer heat persisted. From time to time a servant appeared in front of one of the houses to hose down the dry dust. But it made no difference as far as Kikuji could see. It was a parched, hot day.

He came to Ponta's house and turned in. He had planned his monthly visit to his customers so that it would take him near her place. As he entered, he heard her voice from the downstairs room as she practiced classic Japanese songs. Without announcing himself at the entryway, he took off his clogs and walked quietly into the room where she was singing. From the corner of her eye, she saw him, but continued her practice, tapping her finger lightly to the rhythm and humming the tune of the samisen accompaniment. With her light-colored summer kimono, her meticulously powdered face and neck, her frowning concentration on the book in her hand, she did not look at all like an expectant mother, and yet he knew she was approaching her term and would be having the child very soon.

When she had finished, he said, "Do you think it suitable to sing so strenuously just now?" She didn't reply. "I mean, that kind of sustained singing involves the whole body—"

"You keep saying nothing is good for my condition: not eating, not sleeping with you, and now, not even singing," she answered. She turned an inquiring eye on him. "But what have you been doing while I have been occupied in growing the arms, legs, head, and

165

mind of our child inside me? Have you been trying the wares of some other lady? I must abstain. Can you?"

He knelt beside her and ruffled her hair affectionately.

"Don't be this way, Crazyhead," he said softly. "I'm only concerned about your health. It was the same when Hiroko was pregnant. From the fifth month on, I—refrained."

"Oh, I do so want it to be the truth," she said, looking at him earnestly. "But these days I see so little of you. You bring me my money for the month and then leave right away."

"You worry too much," he replied, stroking her hair and the delicate line of her chin.

She leaned her head on his shoulder, turning herself heavily toward him. "Just me! Promise?"

Kikuji continued stroking her hair, looking down at her head as he fondled it.

"Promise."

She brightened up and called to her maid to prepare dinner. But Kikuji interrupted. "Never mind all that, my dear. A glass of beer will be enough for me. I've just finished my rounds with customers, and must get back in an hour or so."

"But it's already evening. Can't the business wait?"

"I'm afraid not. We've invited a group of retailers to a party at Kinryu's tonight, so I've got to get back and make sure everything's in readiness."

She gave up the argument. "Well, have some beer." She poured the cold beer into a large glass.

He took an envelope out of his pocket and handed it to her. "Here's some extra money to pay for the expenses of the delivery. It should be soon now."

"Thank you. It will be soon." She tried to take his hand and place it on her stomach. "Just feel here. The baby is moving!"

But somehow Kikuji's hand slipped out of hers, and he reached instead for his beer glass.

"I can sense it very well, even without touching," he said with a smile. "It must be almost at its full growth by now, don't you think?"

He drank three glasses of beer continuously to keep his hand occupied.

Suddenly Ponta's face was distorted and she turned quickly away from him. "You really don't want the baby at all, do you?"

"Oh, come, now," he protested vaguely.

"I knew from the very beginning you didn't care about it much. But I didn't think you would remain so—so uninvolved. A child is—is—important!"

And she broke into great sobs, her shoulders trembling convulsively. Kikuji tried to comfort her, feeling that the situation was getting out of his control.

"You're letting your imaginings run away with you. If I hadn't wanted it, I would long ago have suggested an abortion. If you want it, I want it. So dry your tears and stop getting upset. It isn't good for you."

He handed her a handkerchief, and, while she dried her eyes and blew her nose, he went on talking. "I've made arrangements with the proprietress at Kinryu's. Please tell your maid to call there as soon as labor pains begin. Kinryu's will let me know immediately. All right?"

Ponta looked at him shamefacedly and smiled timidly. "I'm sorry. I got upset all of a sudden."

She reached for his hand and placed it firmly on her stomach. He felt the mysterious movement of small bones and muscles within.

Upon returning to the store, he jotted down a few notes concerning the business conferences he had had during the afternoon, asked Hidesuke to supervise the wrapping of gifts for the guests to be entertained at Kinryu's, and then went into the living quarters to take a bath. Just as O-Toki, the chambermaid, was about to scrub his back the door of the bathroom slid open with a great crash, and his grandmother, still wearing her tabi, walked in on the wet floor.

"Kiku-bon!" she screamed.

In his surprise, he stood up and turned toward her.

"Grandmother. You'll get your kimono wet."

She scooped up hot water in the wooden washbasin and dashed it into his face.

"What on earth! You must be out of—" He caught himself and didn't finish the sentence.

"Out of my mind, you want to say, don't you, you disobedient boy! You're the one who's out of his mind!" And she threw another basinful of hot water into his face.

"Grandmother!" Kikuji tried to grab her, but his foot slipped on a bar of soap and he fell to one knee. Kino stepped outside the wet bathchamber and stood in the anteroom, staring grimly at her wet, naked grandson.

"You've been using your equipment well," she spat out. "Ponta just had a baby!"

"What?" He had only left Ponta two hours ago.

"Are you still trying to fake it? It won't work! We had a phone call from the maid. She asked for help because the midwife didn't answer the phone."

"So what did you do?" Kikuji asked anxiously.

Kino smiled coldly at him.

"Why don't you at least dry yourself off? And besides, even if I am your grandmother, the least you could do is to wrap a towel around yourself and not stand there naked and wet and ridiculous!"

He put a towel in front of himself.

"Is everything all right over there?"

"How should I know? I told her the master was taking a bath and that when he was finished I would give him the message. I told her that until then she'd have to manage by herself. And then I hung up!"

"My God, how unfeeling you are."

"Unfeeling? Hah. I call a spade a spade. You're bathing, phone rings, I answer, and I tell her what's what. No more fakery around here!" she spat out. Then she gave the sliding door a great push and it crashed shut once more.

O-Toki sat impassively on a stool in the corner of the bathroom, listening to the exchange between the two. Following the grandmother's stormy departure, she assisted him in dressing. As she finished tying his sash, Kino reappeared in a fresh, dry kimono. Sei was with her, looking pale and upset. But Kino by now had recovered her composure. She held out a packet wrapped in purple cloth.

"Inside there are two envelopes, one containing fifty thousand yen, the other ten thousand," she said.

Kikuji took the parcel, frowning in puzzlement at his grandmother.

"Why two? What's this all about?" he asked.

"You should know very well. When a Semba master fathers a child by a woman not his wife, it is the custom that he give the mother fifty thousand yen if it's a boy and ten thousand if it's a girl for its upkeep. By giving this money, you end your responsibility for the child without saying so in so many words, since words on such a subject could be embarrassing. Now do you understand?"

Kikuji felt the blood pulsing in his forehead; he clenched his teeth tightly together to prevent any attempt at an angry reply. A tiger must be handled, not reasoned with.

Kino by this time had relaxed completely. With a slight smile she said, "That one has such a healthy body. By the time you get there she'll have given birth with all the ease of a dog or cat. So hurry up and go. See if it's going to cost us fifty thousand or ten thousand. I hope it's a girl."

He got out of the cab a few blocks from Ponta's house, and walked slowly the remaining distance in an effort to recapture some semblance of calmness. As he started opening the latticed door, he heard the tiny, urgent cry of the newborn child. It was an unsentimental, demanding sound, saying to his unwilling ears, "I am here in response to your act. Care for me!" He wished he had not heard it. In the kitchen he saw the maid and midwife filling a basin with hot water. He learned from them that, as Kino had in her ugly way prophecied, the delivery was over and had gone smoothly.

He went upstairs without being announced. Through the open door, he saw Ponta lying with her eyes closed. On a small quilt beside her lay the baby, wrapped in yellow clothing, indistinguishable in its wrinkled solemnity from all other newborn infants he had seen. Kikuji sat quietly on a cushion beside Ponta.

"Are you awake?" he said softly. She opened her eyes in surprise. "Tell me, is it a boy or girl?" he continued.

She smiled in weary contentment. "A boy."

He looked again at the baby, and now could see in the way he cried, making his face all mouth, that he moved and acted as only boy babies did. His hair was thick and dark, not yet quite dry. Before seeing him, Kikuji hadn't thought much about the baby, but now, faced with the fact of its individuality, ever evolving, he felt

169

the responsibility like a great weight. Assuredly, the only sensible course was to put it out for immediate adoption. But how would Ponta feel?

He turned back to her, holding her hand.

"How fortunate we are that there were no complications."

Her eyes filled with tears, and she said indistinctly, "Thank you for coming so quickly. I—didn't know what you would do."

He looked at her somberly for a moment without saying anything.

"I'll always take care of you," he said in a low voice. He opened the purple cloth and took out the thicker of the two envelopes. "Here. This is for the boy baby."

"Oh? What is it?" Ponta was puzzled and looked over the envelope tied with red and white ribbon. On it, highly stylized brush strokes in a woman's handwriting labeled the contents, "Fifty Thousand Yen." She was completely mystified, and turned to him for explanation.

"Well, the fact is that on this sum anyone could live well without working," he began cautiously. He hesitated. "Don't you understand the meaning of this gift?"

"Is it a congratulation to me for having a boy?"

"N-n-n-no," he said slowly, "not that. The fact is that the custom of the Semba requires that, when a baby is born to a Semba master and the mother is—not a member of the family, then he must discharge his obligation to the child by giving fifty thousand yen if it is a boy and ten thousand if it's a girl."

She stared at him, horrified incredulity all over her face.

"What sort of talk is this?" she said. " 'Discharge his obligation'? Do you mean to say that with this envelope you are in effect cutting off all ties with your own baby, disowning it?"

Lying quietly on her back, she pointed one listless finger at the envelope, making no effort to pick it up.

"Well, you see, with that sum the child will be well off all his life. He'll need no more—"

She turned her head on the box-pillow and stared coldly at him. "You Semba people bury all inconveniences in piles of money. Not only geisha and mistresses, but even helpless newborn babies!"

She brushed the envelope off her bedding, and, turning away from him, pulled the heavy quilt over her face.

He sat for a moment looking in unhappy frustration at the recumbent form under the quilt. The he stood up and went to the window, where he lit a cigarette and stared out over the city, trying to organize his thoughts. Although he had resented Kino's crudeness in trying to dictate his affairs, he had long been of the opinion that Ponta's baby could be nothing but an embarrassment, and would, therefore, have to be put out for adoption. But how could he persuade Ponta of that necessity? She had trusted and loved him. And he wanted her to continue to do so. She was quite different from Ikuko; he needed them both. He went back to Ponta, resumed his seat on the cushion once more, then folded back the quilt from her face.

"I am sorry if my suggestions seem harsh or unnatural, my dear. I want to do what's best for both of us, don't you see? I thought that we had already agreed on sending the child away to foster parents anyway. Don't you remember? I said I didn't want him raised in the environment of the geisha district— Nothing has changed except that I've added this money for his education, that's all."

But, if he had hoped to change her mood, he failed miserably.

"That's not true!" she flashed out. "Sending him away from the geisha district is one thing, and severing the tie between father and son quite another. This is blood money, and it says, 'I wash my hands of this baby, and he can sink or swim as luck will have it from now on without any help from me, his father.' This sin will haunt you all the rest of your life."

"Oh, come now, Ponta! Think of it this way: my father died at a relatively early age, and for all we know I might not last beyond tomorrow. Then what would happen to this little one? That fifty thousand would make quite a difference. Think it over for the child's sake, Ponta!"

"It isn't the money I hate. It's your easy rejection of your own son," she replied weakly.

"Well, but think about it for a bit."

She fell silent, then gave a long, dispirited sigh.

"I am very tired," she said.

He leaned over, clasped her shoulder and kissed her. Perhaps as a result of the recent delivery, her lips were surprisingly hot. As he kissed her, he placed the envelope with the money back at her side once more.

171

"I'm sorry, Ponta," he breathed as he hovered over her face.

She opened her eyes and looked at him quickly, then closed them in exhaustion. Suddenly the small form at her side moved convulsively and screamed.

Kikuji looked at the child curiously. "What lungpower he has," he said. "He scared me!"

With a slight smile he played tentatively with the tiny fist, tightly closed.

"Let's send him away soon, then, as we agreed. All right?"

Ponta nodded slightly. She thought bitterly, "If it had to come to this, I'm glad he's a boy. A girl would have been worth only one-fifth as much!"

She turned to Kikuji. "Give him a good name at least."

"A name?" He cocked his head and thought, but no name would come.

"Give him one of the syllables of your own name, Kikuji," she suggested.

"Oh, but I couldn't do that. The elements of my name were received from my ancestors, and can be given only to members of the family."

"Even in naming a baby you Semba people have a custom of distinguishing between the main family and the outsiders," Ponta exclaimed sarcastically from the depths of her fatigue. It wasn't fair, she felt. She was in no condition to fight back. She resigned herself to the inevitable.

"Well, whatever you like. But give your son a name."

"Let me see, let me see—" After a moment's thought, he leaned forward. "How will this be? We'll take the 'ta' of Ponta, and add a syllable to make Taro." Ponta frowned. "You don't like it?"

"Taro seems too simple. Can't you think of a name which is a little different from the common run?"

"Eh, it's a good, healthy name for a good, healthy boy," he answered, trying to be jovial. "Let's leave it at that."

Kikuji took out his watch from his sash. It was after seven.

"Well, now that I know you and the baby are all right, I must leave. I still have that party for the retailers which I'm obligated to attend at Kinryu's tonight. Remember?"

"Oh, not tonight? Surely you can be excused tonight?" she cried.

"I'm afraid not, my dear," he said gently. "The world goes on, you know. Wasuke and Hidesuke are doing the honors until I get there. I'm thirty minutes overdue right now."

"I'm so sorry," she replied. "Had I known, I would have had the baby thirty minutes earlier."

"Ponta, Ponta," he said softly, stroking her hair. "Now, get some sleep and rest."

He stood up abruptly and opened the sliding door. Just outside stood the middle-aged maid, holding a tray with a beer bottle and a glass. She looked flustered at his sudden appearance. He realized that she had been busily listening to his whole conversation with Ponta. He turned angrily and shouted back to the figure lying in the center of the room, "Ponta, for God's sake, get yourself a maid who's deaf. This one likes to listen!"

Then he slammed the door shut and left.

He walked rapidly along Echigocho for a few blocks. At the corner where he turned toward Shinmachidori, he saw four or five children playing. He stopped nearby and watched them. They were perhaps around the age of ten or twelve. They wore kimono which, although subjected to hard wear, were made of expensive materials. All five of them, three boys and two girls, were bright-eyed, handsome children, the sons and daughters of unknown fathers and geisha mothers. They had been playing in mud puddles and were quite dirty. A geisha passed by on her way to an engagement. The oldest of the boys held out a stick and with it pulled up the hem of her immaculate kimono. She screamed and hurried away, scolding him. The children broke out in a roar of laughter. How precocious they seemed. By fending for themselves on city streets these children, bright by heredity, seemed somehow to have become blighted with adult cynicism and boredom. All children of geisha shared that special beauty, refined and sharpened by the light of intelligence shining through it, and all of them—lighthearted analysts of human frailty—had a special, unchildlike quality about them. His child, disowned or not, would never join this legion of strays on the city streets.

He could see at a glance that the party at Kinryu's was going along very well without him. As soon as he was seated by the open doorway, he made his greeting speech with great formality and ease. It was what they had a right to expect of the master of Kawachiya's.

"Please accept my apologies for being so tardy. Urgent family matters kept me from you, but now I am free to enjoy your company, as I have wanted to do these many months. Because of your skilled efforts, Kawachiya's tabi have sold handsomely right through the time of the August Bon Festival. Your constant support has been greatly appreciated, and tonight we can relax together after our labors." He placed his hands before him on the floor and bowed till his forehead touched the mat.

Someone in the center of the group shouted, "Kiku-bon, old fellow! Enough of all this hocus-pocus formality. Come on over here and have a drink with us!" It was Sanoya Rakuemon, largest tabi retailer in Osaka. The merchants had seated themselves informally, but the most influential ones sat near Sanoya. The lesser retailers could be taken care of by Wasuke and Hidesuke. Kikuji set himself to keep the most important group happy. Sanoya emptied the cup given him by Kikuji. Although over sixty, he drank with the greedy impetuousness of a young man. As he returned the cup, he gave Kikuji a great wink and said, "Master of Kawachiya's, you are a rare bird among businessmen, young as you are. Unlike the other young bloods trying one minute to make good in business and the next to make it in bed with all the pretty girls they can find, you have your fun and somehow manage never to forget the business. That's an art: to have fun and keep a cool head about you for balancing the books, by God! I think maybe the ladies inspire you in your business ventures, by God! I'll bet one of them suggested that silk organdy summer tabi which has sold out completely two summers in a row. If so, you'd better make her a partner. That way you get business ideas while you're prowling around under the blankets, hey?"

Kikuji laughed. "It wouldn't have sold without your skill in making it a popular item. I make a good product, but you alone know, all of you here, how to make the public enthusiastic about it."

Sanoya snickered drunkenly. "You're a cool, cool type," he said. "All your business advisers are pretty women, by God!"

Kikuji circulated among the guests, exchanging cups with them as he went. As he met each retailer, he recalled his exact trade volume over the past year, and handled him accordingly. It was almost as though the various figures in his account books had come alive to cavort around the banquet room. The sake cleared his mind and he was enjoying himself.

Suddenly he felt a great impulse to laugh. Just an hour ago he had been embroiled in a serious difficulty with Ponta about the child. But as soon as he had crossed the threshold at Kinryu's he had been able without appreciable effort to put that trouble behind him and perform competently in a totally different situation. Without this flexibility, what kind of a businessman would he be? Or, for that matter, what kind of a lover? Some time ago, Ikuko had said rather mournfully, "Kiku-bon is the sort of person who, drunk as he may be inside the teahouse, sobers up and faces the world the minute he steps outside. It is a rare talent." Perhaps, even though she didn't approve of his constant drinking, she was right in so defining his adaptability. Hence his love of variety.

As he reflected on this estimate of himself, he continued making his rounds of the guests. He had hired fifteen geisha for the party. When he came back to Sanoya, he found Mamechiyo and Shimekichi playing the hand game of paper–scissors–rock with him. He squeezed in next to Mamechiyo to watch. She turned to him when the others were talking to each other, and said in a whisper, "Master, congratulations. I hear you have had a son!" He raised an eyebrow and laughed. "A geisha who talks of babies at a party is not going to find herself much in demand," he said in joking reprimand. She flipped her sleeve over her mouth, bowed contritely, and said, "Sorry. Let's start talking all over from the beginning." He nodded lightly, and played the hand game with Sanoya.

Shortly after ten, Kikuji saw his guests off. As he returned to the banquet chamber, breathing a sigh of relief now that the party was over, he met Hidesuke, who said deferentially, "The dowager lady of the house has just called to say that she wants you to come directly home and not stop at Miss Ikuko's in Unagidani. She has some emergency she wishes to discuss."

Kikuji restrained an impulse to groan, and replied calmly, "Thank you. I had intended going straight home tonight in any case."

When the cab stopped, Hidesuke got out first and pulled out his key to open the door. But it opened from inside. O-Toki stood there, waiting for them. She was still dressed in her daytime working clothes, and Kikuji guessed that she had been on watch for him at the door for a long time. The ladies of the house must, he guessed, be in a very bad mood to stay awake two hours past their usual ten o'clock hour for retiring. Managing the manager was no easy task for them.

His mother's room was brightly lit. He entered on somewhat unsteady feet. The panels to the adjoining room had been opened, and he saw five-year-old Hisajiro sleeping soundly there. He wondered if this was a new device of the ladies to supervise the youngster. Always before his son had slept in his own room, away from them. Kino and Sei sat sternly waiting for Kikuji to speak. They ignored his greeting.

"What was the baby, boy or girl?" asked Kino abruptly.

"I'm sorry to report it's the fifty-thousand-yen one and not the cheaper brand. Maybe we'll have better luck next time."

"Next time?" said Kino, her eyes flashing in outrage.

He threw the package of ten thousand yen on the floor beside her. She picked it up without looking at it, and tapped it mechanically against her knee.

"You have made clear to Ponta that you are severing all ties with the child and have no responsibility for it henceforward?" she asked grimly.

"I have acted according to the custom of the Semba, and that should be enough to satisfy you," he replied with a cold ironic smile.

"When does he go to the foster home?"

"Not before his neck is strong enough to support his head."

"What's his name?"

"Taro of Momotaro," said Kikuji, laughing. The two women stared at him sternly, and he gave up on his joke.

"Who gets his navel cord?" asked Kino eagerly.

"What?" He looked at her incredulously. "You ask the most amazing questions! Who gets his navel cord? At the moment, it's his, possession being one criterion of ownership."

Kino ignored his irrelevancies.

"You must get her promise that she will give you the navel cord in return for the fifty thousand yen. It will come off in a week or so. It is customary to wrap it in paper with the names of both parents

176

written on the outside, along with the child's name and the date of birth. Unless you get it now, you'll have trouble concerning paternity later on.

"This is incredible!" he said in exasperated tones.

"You must get the promise of that navel cord tomorrow; do you understand?"

There was no way of answering this onslaught of old wives' logic. He stood abruptly and shut the door to the room where Hisajiro was sleeping. Then he turned to the two women and looked at them angrily.

"I've had all I can take of this nonsense. She has borne me a child, and in return I have paid her a fee and disclaimed all further responsibility for my own son. She asked me to suggest a good name for the child, and I gave her one as common as water in a ditch. And now you want me to go and apply yet another of your irrational 'customs'. I must demand the child's navel cord for some remote legal reason. Well, by God, I won't. She is a geisha and completely outside our family, but she is an admirable human being. I will not engage in cruel and unkind acts with her just to keep you happy."

He felt himself shaking with rage and hatred at these two self-centered, self-indulgent women whose capacity for sympathy and love had atrophied from long disuse. Ponta was worth ten of them. Kino at sixty-five and Sei at forty-seven had led their lives so carefully protected by their wealth and position that they had never even cut their fingers. How ignorant they were of life: little girls playing at dolls! Only this time Ponta was one of the dolls they were trying to manipulate.

More quietly, he continued talking. "I have tried to conform to family traditions to the extent of my ability. It's easier and better that way. I'm no romantic rebel, and I dislike disagreements with you, Mother and Grandmother. Because of your attitudes, I will not bring a second wife into this house, or any other woman, for that matter. And I have tried to settle the future of my second son so that there will be no future claims or difficulty. If it makes you any happier, and I am sure it does, I shall remain a bachelor and an expert moneymaker for the rest of my days. But you must understand this: I will spend as I please. I'm a big boy now. Do not, if you value your peace of mind, meddle in my private affairs any more."

177

He spoke calmly and even politely, but in increasingly emphatic tones. When he had finished, he walked out, closed the door behind him, and went up the corridor to his room. He heard Kino calling him back, and he ignored her. On reaching his room, he locked the door behind him, turned out the light, and stretched out fully clothed on the bedding which O-Toki had spread on the floor.

During the next three months, there was an uneasy truce. Kino waited with ominous patience, never once mentioning the navel cord. Whenever he saw Ponta, Kikuji thought of bringing the matter up casually, but he could not. He was already ashamed of having paid money to disown his son and he hadn't the heart to upset his mistress again. He realized, nevertheless, that he could not ignore the problem; Sei and Kino would never rest, despite all that he had said to them, until everything concerning the child was settled to their satisfaction. And Kikuji himself didn't want to leave the baby's status in doubt, so that future claims might be made against the father. By paying the fifty thousand yen, he had bought his freedom from responsibility. The baby would not be named in the official family register, and would be listed as an illegitimate child of Okamura Miyo, Ponta's real name.

Since it had been decided that the baby would be sent to a foster home as soon as he could hold up his head, Kikuji on his visits to Ponta always paid close attention to the baby's neck. Seeing her lover so intent on disposing of the child, Ponta made arrangements to send him to a foster home one hundred days after his birth.

On the appointed day, Kikuji left his place of business shortly before four in order to meet the foster parents at Ponta's house. They were already there when he arrived: a sturdy farmer and his wife from Kishiwada. Ponta had already told them something of the baby's brief history. When introduced to Kikuji, they greeted him with awkward formality. He knew that Ponta had selected them from among other applicants only after long study of their background. They seemed diligent and honest. They would teach his son good habits.

"I assume that you have been told what you need to know about the baby. I hope you will take good care of him."

He pulled out his wallet and gave them one thousand yen. He realized that they had already received a considerable fee from the money he had given Ponta, but he wanted to make sure that they would feel it worth their while to bring the child up well.

The wife thanked him for the gift. "We'll care for him as one of our own, sir. And every month there will be a report on his progress for Miss Ponta to study."

She picked up the sleeping child and wrapped him carefully in a blanket without waking him. Ponta started instinctively to stand and take the baby again, and then slowly sat down. The foster parents, Mr. and Mrs. Oda, seemed accustomed to this sort of situation. They moved briskly and without wasting time in needless civilities. The wife took the baby and the husband gathered together the layette and the bottles.

"Leave the navel cord here," said Kikuji, as though it had just occurred to him.

"Pardon me, sir? The navel cord?" The couple looked at each other, puzzled.

Ponta, eyes narrowed, said, "I have it. What do you want with it?"

"Give it to me."

"But why?"

Kikuji looked at her impassively. "I need it to keep everything straight in the future."

She stared hard at him, her face pale and severe. "So you will go this far to make sure that your son never ever bothers you in the future."

"Perhaps we should discuss this matter fully when we are alone," he said quietly, and by a look and nod he dismissed the Odas, who stood awkwardly at the door and were glad of a chance to leave.

After seeing them off, Ponta turned back to him.

"The ladies of your house still have you under their thumb, I see. The way you accept their nasty orders is completely beyond my comprehension." And beneath her hostile stare her mouth twisted into a smile without warmth or good nature. He recognized the look: it was the sneer he had thought the special facial gesture of his mother and grandmother. But now he understood: this was the look by which women universally informed their men that they had failed in their pretension of exercising disinterested masculine authority. It was the look of trust betrayed, of knowledge judging fallibility. Sei and Kino hadn't needed to remind him to do their bid-

179

ding; the fixed sneer on their faces over the past three months had been quite a sufficient reminder. Only a woman could do it, and all of them knew how, instinctively.

Kikuji remained impassive despite her look. "What difference does it make to you? A baby's navel cord is of no consequence. If they want it, let them have it."

Without looking away from him, she opened a drawer, drew out a white paper package and threw it down before Kikuji. He picked it up and opened it. In Ponta's childish calligraphy was written, "Okamura Taro: born fifteenth year of Taisho, September first. Father: Kawachi Kikuji (Business Name: Kawachi Kihei); Mother: Okamura Miyo." Inside the paper was the dried and shrivelled navel cord. Kikuji folded it up again and put the package in his pocket.

"By the way, when will you start working again?" asked Kikuji as a way of changing her mood.

She stared at him for an instant longer, and then turned away without replying.

"You could easily put it off till next year if you wanted to," he continued.

Suddenly Ponta's severe posture crumpled. She sat heavily on the tatami mat and began to weep.

Kikuji looked on in exasperation. Women's tears. Their final weapon. He stood up and walked out without saying anything. He had no wish to be harsh, but the best thing was to let her cry it out. In the morning, things would seem brighter. That's what mornings were for: an end to storms, a beginning again of life's routines.

On the street, he signaled a cab, climbed in, and looked at his watch. Sanoya had invited him to a party in the Soemoncho District at 6:30. It was now 5:30. He gave the driver Ikuko's address in Unagidani. Upon arriving at the small alleyway, he asked the cab driver to wait, and proceeded on the narrow stone walk to the latticed front door. The countrified young maid answered the door and called his name to her mistress in a shrill, nasal voice more appropriate to the barnyard than to a lady's house. Ikuko with a surprised expression came hurrying to the door. She was, of course, wearing her prized *marumage* hairdo, but, since she hadn't been expecting him, she had her kimono tucked up, her apron on, and had been cleaning house.

"I'm sorry you see me this way," she said, smiling. "It was such a fine day I decided to do the laundry, and have just finished hanging the clothes on the line."

Kikuji sat casually, leaning against the decorative post of the alcove. "I can't stay long. I'm on my way to a party Sanoya and Ichikawaya are giving for me in return for the party I gave them."

She looked disappointed. "But maybe after the party?" Her voice sank to a whisper. "Come by later."

He moved over to her side and clasped her to him. His cold hands moved smoothly into the lapel openings of her kimono and he touched the soft warmth of her breast. Ikuko seemed about to lower her head to his lap. But just then the taxi driver yelled outside. He was getting impatient. With a sigh, Kikuji withdrew his hands and looked at his watch.

"Gracious. It's almost seven. I must hurry!" he said, jumping up.

As Ikuko saw him off at the front door, she asked reservedly, "When will you come back?"

With strangely gentle eyes, he answered, "Expect me soon after ten." Reluctantly, he walked out to the waiting cab.

He arrived at exactly the right time, but Sanoya and Ichikawaya were already amusing themselves with five young and attractive geisha. When he saw Kikuji, Sanoya skipped the usual greeting, and, turning to the guests, said, "This is the resourceful young master of Kawachiya's who is to be our guest of honor this evening." His fat, red face was wreathed in smiles as he led Kikuji to his place. Each geisha greeted him courteously. They were from Soemoncho and new to Kikuji. He had known only one geisha in that district. But the oldest of them said, with a gleam of recognition, "I have never met you, but you are famous in our quarter as the man who invaded Soemoncho and in two months took Ikuko away from us."

Ichikawaya, who had been about to drink, suspended his cup in midair and then lowered it, leaning forward curiously. "What is all this?" he said. "I have long known about Ponta of Shinmachi, but I hadn't heard a word about the one from Soemoncho." He looked at Kikuji and grinned the obscene, meaningless grin of an old man. "You are very energetic day *and* night, aren't you?" He laughed thinly and raised his cup once more.

Sanoya joined in. "Yes, indeed. Kawachiya acquires bed companions the way we buy plants at a sidewalk sale."

181

"Ah, what weeds we are, then," laughed one of the geisha. "Valued no more than an old pot of cactus or geraniums!"

The party became very lively. Now and then out of the genial hubbub of conversation there emerged a song; occasionally there was a dance, skillfully performed by the geisha, clownishly imitated by the guests.

Sanoya, his face flaming red from too much sake, looked around in perplexity. "Where under the sun is O-Fuku? I haven't seen her at all this evening. See if you can find her," he said to one of the geisha.

As she was about to obey, the door slid smoothly open to reveal a tall, even statuesque woman with a hauntingly beautiful face and white skin. She put her dimpled, soft hands by the doorsill, sat down slowly, and bowed her head low.

"Thank you for deigning to patronize our establishment, honored sirs."

Each movement was unhurried and perfected before the next one. Sanoya introduced her to Kikuji. As head waitress of the teahouse, she bowed to him and spoke the formal phrases of introduction unhurriedly in a rich, throaty voice he found exciting.

Sanoya obviously regarded O-Fuku as his special discovery.

"She's head waitress here, Kiku-bon. Tell her what you want and it will be served to you fast and in good style. Also, she knows how to drink, this girl. A fine drinking companion. Watch. Watch how she drinks."

The old man handed her a cup. Unhurriedly in a soft, flowing motion, the cup went to her full lower lip where, with no perceptible tilting, the contents were transferred from cup to mouth. She seemed to inhale the sake. Sanoya filled cup after cup for her to demonstrate her special talent. She continued to be quiet, alert, and completely sober despite the huge amount which she consumed.

Kikuji studied her with interest while engaged in persiflage with one of the geisha. In anyone less sure of herself, the loose knot of her sash would have seemed negligent. Completely comfortable with her customers, she attended to their wants with the ease of long practice. Where other waitresses fussed anxiously over their guests, O-Fuku in her sureness could afford to be more remote, conferring favors instead of services. Always she moved slowly, quietly, with an almost catlike grace. Kikuji, like Sanoya, was fascinated. She was a find for the connoisseur. And yet, when the occasion demanded, she would rise and pick up trays of dishes or pour drinks. He could see her worth in the eyes of the geisha, who normally were highly critical of waitresses who took over any of their functions. They bowed to her with real deference.

When Kikuji had the opportunity of exchanging drinks with her, he somehow became excited so that his hand shook. The sake spilled on the mat. Sanoya and Ichikawaya laughed at his mistake.

"There's many a marksman whose aim is blurred by good liquor," said Sanoya. "How much do you have to drink to be drunk, O-Fuku?"

"Ah, sir," she smiled mysteriously at him. "It all depends on how you drink. There is the miser-type drinker, who never wants to let go of what he has drunk, and sooner or later he has a bad attack of oblivion or at least the staggers. But there is the free, generous soul like me, and that fellow gets rid of it at one end as fast as he swallows it down at the other. He drinks the way the whale swallows sea water: for the sheer pleasure of spouting it out. That's your true, sociable drinker, don't you think?"

She smiled at Sanoya. "You, I would guess, are a whale-type drinker, not a miser."

"Right, right," shouted the old fellow standing up and moving toward the door, "And off I go to spout!"

At that moment a young waitress came in and whispered briefly to O-Fuku. She moved quietly to Kikuji and whispered that he had a phone call from Unagidani. He went to the phone in the hall a little unsteadily.

"I'm sorry to bother you," said Ikuko in a weak voice. "But I have been waiting—"

"It's all right. I'll be there in a little while. Just wait. Your calling like this is a little awkward."

"I know but—this neighborhood is rather unsafe for two women at night, and I thought if you weren't coming, I would lock up—"

"No. Keep the door open and wait."

He hung up and returned to the banquet room. As he resumed his place, Sanoya turned to him and said, "Kawachiya, old boy, it's already quite late. Why don't we sleep all together here tonight? O-Fuku, you join us too."

Kikuji was completely baffled. As guest of honor, he could not possibly leave at this juncture without offense. Even wispy old Ichikawaya was anxious to stay on for the night. The geisha cheered the decision delightedly, knowing that their pay would continue while they had a good night's sleep.

Under O-Fuku's supervision, the maids spread bedding in a large room adjoining the banquet hall. The beds were spread in two rows, one with five, the other with four beds. Then they brought in a pile of cotton sleeping kimono. When she saw this, the oldest geisha, who had earlier revealed Kikuji's affair with Ikuko to Sanoya and Ichikawaya, said, "Since all of us must change, let's make a contest of it."

"What sort of contest?" asked O-Fuku.

"Let's give a prize to the girl who can strip the quickest. We'll all line up here in front of the room alcove, and start at a signal."

"Well," said one of the younger geisha, "if I have to hurry at this time of night with all those knots and sashes, somebody had better make it worth my while."

Kikuji, stimulated by drink and his urges first for Ikuko and now for O-Fuku, was wildly excited by the suggestion. "I'll donate the prize. Ten yen to the quickest to be barest. Line up!"

The young ones who, before the contest had been announced, had already begun to loosen some of the knots of their many sashes, looked at each other, realized that they could not very well say no at this juncture, and so retied the knots and took their places before the alcove.

"You too, you too," said Kikuji, gently pushing O-Fuku in the direction of the alcove. She looked at him with a slight smile and an air of puzzlement, but allowed herself to be guided to the end of the line of five geisha.

Kikuji raised his hands excitedly. "Everybody ready? One, two, three, go!"

A geisha is not a package which comes apart easily. The women went to work on the knots in their sashes immediately. There were many: the outer, decorative sash, then the stiff waistband, the ribbonlike undersash, and the hip cord. Each was under the other. The room was filled with the rustling, scratchy noise of silk on silk. The young women were clearly quicker in taking off the heavy sash and undersash. O-Fuku, moving without apparent hurry, was the slowest. But, while the others were still tugging and pulling at the various knots, suddenly the clothing slipped from O-Fuku's shoulders all at once, and, except for the white half slip around her hips, she stood naked to the admiration of the men. A half-smile played over her face.

"I'm the winner," she said calmly, and then ran laughing out of the room. The men scratched their heads. "I thought she was way behind the others," said Sanoya. In a few minutes she came back clothed in one of the night kimono to receive her prize from Kikuji.

"Thank you for this prize," she said, taking the ten-yen note. "Now I have some spending money. But it's nearly two in the morning. Let's go to bed."

Kikuji, without any effort on his part, found that his bed was next to O-Fuku's. The sight of her lush white body had aroused his lust and the awareness that she was lying beside him did nothing to allay it. Quietly in the dark he reached out to touch her arm. Her skin was delightfully smooth: it was, he thought, flowing and graceful, like her whole personality.

He moved closer and closer until he could feel her lying alongside him. There was no resistance. It would be difficult in this crowded room, but she might be willing. Tentatively he threw an arm over her. So far, so good.

Suddenly, he was aware that she had moved, and her white face hovered in the dark over his. "I want to enjoy the wonderful aftereffects of drinking this superb sake, my good sir. As for you, have a good sleep now, sir." Somehow, he found his extended arm back in his own bed once more, and, when he looked again in O-Fuku's direction, he found that she had turned her back to him. He listened in the dark for a moment to the snoring of Sanoya and Ichikawaya, trying to digest the fact that, for the first time in his life, he had been refused by a woman.

He turned on his side, and as he did so felt the crumpling of paper at his waist. He remembered that he had moved the package containing the navel cord into the sash of his sleeping kimono. This served to take his wakeful thoughts to Ponta and Ikuko. He recalled with humiliation Ponta's appearance as she had scolded him. And he writhed, thinking now of Ikuko, whom he had been so ready to abandon temporarily, waiting patiently for him far into the night, only to digest the bitter realization that he wasn't coming at all. But as he faded away into a drunken sleep, it was the lush image of the naked waitress that remained with him.

On January second, Kikuji was up before dawn. He was dressed as an artisan: red headband and a short red and white work coat. His employees bustled all around him in the yard, following the last-minute instructions of Wasuke and Hidesuke. Three wagons piled high with tabi which the workers were to pull were brightly decorated with the red and white colors of the firm, matching the workcoats of the Kawachiya employees.

At last everyone was in his place. Kikuji climbed onto a rickshaw just behind the loaded wagons. Hidesuke surveyed the silent procession with a critical eye.

"Is everyone ready?" he bawled out. "Kakushichi, you may pick up the shafts of the wagon. Watch my fan, all of you!"

He went to the head of the procession, turned to face the marchers, swung open his fan and gestured with it for them to begin singing. They began to move in orderly steps, singing as they went:

> *Yoi, yoi, to makasho!*
> What a splendid commotion we make,
> Greeting good customers
> With New Year's first fine goods!

The three wagons, pulled by clerks and apprentices, moved creakily over the city streets. They proceeded along the West Yokobori River to the foot of the Shinmachi Bridge, and then turned east in order to reach Sanoya Rokuemon's store. Hearing the singing, Sanoya and his employees came out in front of the store. The procession rolled to a stop. The singing continued to its end, and an impressive silence followed.

Kikuji slowly stepped from his rickshaw, and made the formal pronouncement: "We, from the House of Kawachiya, have come to wish our friends of the House of Sanoya a prosperous new year, and, to add to that prosperity, we are here in friendship to make our first delivery of the year."

Sanoya immediately responded in a loud voice: "Our thanks for your good wishes, our appreciation of your first delivery of the year. Please come into our store for refreshments."

186

He then wrote out a receipt for one hundred pairs of tabi and, giving it to Kikuji, urged him and his numerous followers to enter his house to sample the New Year's sake.

Resplendent in his black, crested kimono, the old merchant sat in front of a gold screen happily dispensing refreshments. But they could not stay long, and, after a very short interval, Kikuji gave the signal, and the procession re-formed and moved on to the house of the next customer.

Kikuji remembered when he was a very small boy watching his father leave on one of these New Year's expeditions. He had yearned to go with him, and, from that time on, he had always loved this procession of the first delivery of the new year. His father had told him that it had taken place every year for hundreds of years.

At each place they were given sake and sweets, so that the employees became steadily livelier as the wagons grew lighter. Even Hidesuke achieved a semblance of amiability as he stalked along, singing and waving his red fan to keep the rhythm.

It was already past twelve by the time they returned home. Hastily, Kikuji changed the work coat for the formal, crested half-coat required for full-dress occasions, and went to the main parlor. In front of the alcove containing the flower arrangement and decorative scroll sat Kino and Sei, with Hisajiro, proudly wearing his formal kimono for the first time. When Kikuji entered, Sei moved over to make room for him. He sat down with an expression of amiability and well-being on his face. But suddenly his features hardened. Among all the managers of branch stores and their employees who filled the two connecting rooms waiting to pay their respects, he spotted Ponta and Ikuko. They sat far apart, and both of them looked acutely uncomfortable. He guessed that they had come early to make the ritual visit, but, since he had been late in returning, they had waited, and had been overtaken by the large group of employees from the various branches. They tried to make themselves inconspicuous toward the rear of the room, but Kikuji could see that they were the object of great curiosity and attention on the part of all the men there. Seeing the boss's mistresses, both at the same time, was something to be talked about for a long time to come. So they studied first one, and then the other, comparing their faces, their figures, and making guesses about how passionate they might be. A few, like Hidesuke, simply kept their eyes averted in an expression of refined distaste. Ponta, dressed proudly with formal hairdo and powdered to the neck so that she could go to work immediately after the reception, reciprocated the men's interest, and turned her shapely nose casually right and left, bouncing their curiosity back at them. Ikuko, foregoing the pleasure of her *marumage* style, was wearing her hair in western fashion so that it covered her ears. She did not look at the audience, but kept her head down as though wishing neither to see nor be seen. Once she looked up and found herself staring directly into Ponta's eyes. She gently averted her gaze. Ponta continued to stare at her.

Slowly, the branch employees came up to Kikuji, bowed, made formal speeches of well-wishing for the new year, sipped ceremonial sake, and departed. At last it appeared that all had gone through the line and left. Ponta rose and walked from her place in the rear of the room to the cushions in front of Kikuji and his family, and sat down. But Kino quickly raised her hand and said, "Wait just a minute! One of our craftsmen has not gone through the reception line yet." She pointed toward the corner. There was a wretched, thin fellow sitting half-asleep from too much sake. Ponta looked at him, then at Kino, and finally at Kikuji. Then she rose and stepped aside. An apprentice escorted the thin man up to Kikuji, so that he could present an inarticulate good wish for the New Year, sip a cup of ceremonial sake, and stagger off.

When he had left, Kino called to Ikuko in the rear, "Thank you for waiting so patiently, Ikuko." Ponta shot a furious look at her rival. With eyes downcast, Ikuko came forward, sat in front of Kikuji, and without much expression spoke the ritual greeting, first to him, and then to the ladies. Kikuji responded routinely with the standard phrases, but not so Kino. She smiled amiably and said, "Thank you, my dear. A happy new year to you. You have a full-time job in keeping our son happy. Please keep at it, with our blessing."

Ikuko's eyes widened, and involuntarily, she looked at Ponta standing nearby, deathly pale. Kino presumably was mocking her, since she was not Kikuji's full-time mistress, but an independent geisha.

"That's such a nice kimono," continued Kino. "Is it a New Year's present from my grandson?"

"Yes, my lady."

188

There seemed nothing more to say, so Ikuko bowed before them preparing to take her leave. As she did so, Sei leaned forward and thrust an envelope between the lapels of her kimono. The action was so unexpected that Ikuko jumped in surprise. It was, she realized, the New Year's bonus, presented to her not cordially as a well-meant gift placed properly in her hands by Sei, but with mechanical arrogance, as one might with no feeling whatever dole out feed to a horse. She looked down. The narrow envelope protruded from the front of her kimono like a price tag. She glanced at Kikuji. He watched her with expressionless, cold eyes, lazily leaning on the armrest. Meekly, she took her leave, the envelope still sticking out of her kimono where Sei had placed it.

Ponta, when her turn came at last, sat in front of Hisajiro, a position from which she could give her greetings impersonally to all three of the adults. Kikuji was amused at her tactic, but it obviously displeased the ladies. Unconcernedly, Ponta talked to Hisajiro.

"My, how you've grown, little Master. Hap-py New Year!" she said, giving the whole speech a deliberately childish intonation. But Hisajiro, who had been sitting still too long, and who, with a child's intuition had divined the irritation of his mother and grandmother, burst into tears in a fury of noncooperation. Dismayed, Ponta stretched out her hands to comfort him, but he only redoubled the strength of his wailing. Ponta's careful stratagem was being wrecked on the hard rock of childish intransigence. Kino was quick to seize the advantage.

"He is comfortable only with the members of his own family." And she picked him up and placed him on her lap. Sullenly, he put his thumb in his mouth and stared resentfully out of the corner of his eyes at the strange woman who had tried to make friends with him.

"Yes, of course," replied Ponta briskly. "It's so much better for a child to be raised by his own mother, isn't it? A foster parent is no substitute."

Kikuji, finding the situation becoming increasingly dangerous, snapped suddenly at Hisajiro, "Stop that sniffling! Only girls do that. You're not a girl. You're a boy, and six years old." Hisajiro's eyes grew large in horrified surprise at the rebuke, and he screamed.

In this completely unfestive atmosphere, Ponta rose to take her leave. Sei leaned forward again to thrust a bonus envelope into her

189

collar. As she did so, however, Ponta wheeled with flashing eyes and faced her, smiling strangely. She took the envelope from her hands, thanked her demurely and departed with her head held high. Kikuji looked after her, half in admiration, half in vexation.

Late that afternoon, he took an early bath and put on his most festive clothes. The kimono was of fine Oshima silk. The covering half-coat, lined with light silk, had a hand-painted scene of a mountain landscape on the lining. Kikuji, as he finished dressing, felt a sensuous exhilaration in wearing these clothes of a texture lighter than any dragonfly's wing. He escaped from the somber family home, and headed toward Ponta's house. As he turned the corner at Echigocho, he saw children in holiday clothes playing together quietly in the alley. He recognized them as the rather precocious children of geisha whom he had seen before near Ponta's house. And now, as then, he slowed down as he watched them. It occurred to him that, if he visited Ponta, she might bring up the subject of Taro's being kept in a foster home, and the mere thought of yet another argument on that subject depressed him. Half a block ahead he saw Ponta's latticed front door. He turned abruptly and hailed a taxi. He would visit Ikuko instead. His pulse quickened as he thought of her. To the uninformed observer, Ikuko would seem reserved, serious, and hardworking; but at night, in bed, she was transformed into an eager experimentalist in the art of love. As a violinist coaxes beauty from his instrument, so Ikuko played upon their bodies, coaxing great delights from them. She was an artist in love. Ponta, on the other hand, looked tremendously seductive and amorous in daylight, but at night she was still ignorant and unawakened, too young, perhaps, to know the meaning of real passion. Only by sleeping with a woman could one know her real essence, Kikuji thought.

It was pleasant comparing the two women. Suddenly both of them faded from his mind, and the image of the bare-breasted O-Fuku remained, looking to him for all the world like a statuesque figure of Venus. It was she he wanted this gloomy winter's evening, far more than either Ponta or Ikuko. He hadn't seen her since Sanoya's party. Her rejection of his advances that evening had not put him off much. If anything, it made her seem an even rarer prize.

190

But, attracted as he was, it was quite possible that he was trespassing on Sanoya's property. It wouldn't do unintentionally to steal the old man's special friend. There was only one way to find out: he instructed the cab driver to drive to the Hamayu Teahouse, where O-Fuku worked. He would call Sanoya and invite him over. It would seem a gracious return for the big show Sanoya had put on for him at the time of the New Year's first delivery procession.

On entering the teahouse, he was immediately greeted by O-Fuku. In the same unhurried, almost remote, manner which had so intrigued him the first time he saw her, she welcomed him to the establishment, and took him to a pleasant room. As she adjusted the charcoal in the brazier, she asked, "Will there be anyone else joining you this evening, sir?"

"Perhaps you could call Sanoya and ask him to come on over for a drink with me?"

"Right away, sir." She stood up and moved toward the door.

"Are you still angry with me about the other night?" he asked suddenly. She paused a moment, and looked at him calmly.

"I'm sorry, sir. But I don't understand what you mean."

"Come, now. Don't put on an act of innocence. You snubbed me —as I have never been snubbed before, I might add."

She continued looking at him quietly, with a faintly puzzled expression.

In the face of such self-possession, he became a little confused. "You were lying next to me. I reached for you. You said, 'I want to enjoy the effects of this good sake I've had. You have a nice sleep.' That's exactly what you said. A complete snub."

Her white face reddened slightly. But with no change in her expression, she bowed her head slightly and said, "Please wait for a moment while I go and call Mr. Sanoya." And Kikuji, feeling like a fool, was left alone to recover his self-possession. A short time later, she came upstairs and into his room with a bottle of sake.

"I am sorry to report that Mr. Sanoya is off visiting relatives. I left a message for him to come over if he returns soon."

"Thank you, O-Fuku. Can you find any geisha at the spur of the moment, do you think?"

"I inquired just now at the geisha headquarters. It is their busiest time of year, and all their people are engaged. I'm very sorry."

191

"Not at all," Kikuji responded. "It's my own fault for not having made advance preparations. But it doesn't matter."

O-Fuku suddenly clapped her hands together. "Oh, I have an idea, sir, but I don't know if it will please you. There is a very capable jester I am acquainted with, a male geisha, you might call him. I don't know if you have ever dealt with such jesters before now, but they are generally very highly skilled people, and can often sing, dance, and talk far better than many geisha. They must, of course, be more skillful than the ladies are, because they lack their—their physical attractiveness for the gentlemen."

"Ah. Then they are not—"

"No, no, sir. Not at all! The one I have in mind is a humorous philosopher of sorts."

"Fine. I could use a humorous philosopher of sorts. I am out of sorts this evening."

"Good. I'll go get him. I think you will enjoy his line."

Kikuji sat for some time moodily drinking sake and listening to the parties in the other rooms. After thirty minutes had passed, there was a tap at the door and it slid open to reveal a sharp-featured person of indeterminate age.

"Good evening, sir," he said with a pleasant smile. "Allow me to introduce my ignoble self to your sensitive perceptions. You have before you the earthly compound which goes by the name of Ogiya Tsuruhachi. I am reputed to be scatterbrained, and, having been busy scattering my brains for the inspection of lesser-minded individuals, it has never been my good fortune to meet you. Let us amend that defect now and henceforward. My routines, you may wish to know, are adaptable to all tastes. Some like slapstick."

Here he hit himself on the head with his fan, and the hollow noise from the light blow reverberated through the teahouse. His deep-set, large eyes, which gave his face a melancholy appearance, twinkled in delight at Kikuji's puzzlement. He nudged him and said confidentially, "It's the scattered brains as does it. A regular drum, this unschooled skull. But it's appropriate to call attention to the symbolism of my humble fan at this New Year season. As its ribs spread out in all directions, so may your ventures in business, in love, in experience, range out in every direction. Eh, well. My other talents, you would ask? Oh, so many that to enumerate them would weary

192

anyone less involved than I myself. Perhaps I can just show you some of my skills as they may seem appropriate?" And he picked up the sake bottle and poured it with intricate movements which seemed to turn the routine into an art.

Kikuji could see that his underkimono, visible in his sleeves, was threadbare, but expensive.

"You have the look of a ladies' man, I think," he ventured.

The jester cocked his head and smiled slowly. "I have dallied here and there, sir."

"And what do you think of the ladies when all is said and done?"

"With the ladies, sir, nothing is ever all said and done. But if I had to put in one word what I think of the ladies, the word would be, I am sure, expensive!"

Kikuji laughed. "And they have reduced you to being a jester?"

"Not a bit, sir. I am not reduced to being a jester. All life is a jest, and through my calling I appreciate it more than most."

"You talk so strangely."

"Help me to change, sir. My ideas are strange? My mode of elocution? Tell me, that I may improve."

"I mean, your voice is all scratchy and gravelly, like a strangled duck."

"Ah, yes. Although I have not recently talked with a strangled duck, it is true that I understand what you refer to. You see, there are people, and I am one of them, who talk *all* the time. This can be very hard on the mind, if you think about what you are saying, but I never do. It is also hard on the vocal cords. I hold the record for continuous talk in the city of Osaka: four full days and nights, sworn to by three drunks I paid to listen to my every word!"

"But—" Kikuji's businessman's attitude showed clearly. "Why do you do such foolish things?"

"Ah, sir," the jester smiled sociably, "I won't say again that life is a jest. Maybe it is not so with you. But perhaps I might say that I adapt my levels of humor to the minds of those I meet: slapstick and pratfalls for the yokels, aphorisms with mayonnaise for the sophisticates. And sometimes it is necessary to injure one's vocal cords in the interest of earning a living. I do as ordered: peevish talk, foolish talk, unreasonable talk, reasonable talk. Anything!"

"All things to all people?"

193

"Approximately so, sir."

"Even a first-class female geisha hasn't that range of ability," said Kikuji.

"Neither have I, sir, most of the time. It is an ideal, not an achieved reality. One keeps trying."

"True. One keeps trying," repeated Kikuji. "And when in the course of time I have used up all my money and have run through all the many varieties of women, perhaps then I too may become a jester."

"Ah, but, sir, the greatest jester is he who is successful in love. Your genius with women is a man who stimulates others to heroic endeavor and philosophic musing. He is the honor student in the subject whom we admire from afar. A man like myself, sir, is, much as I regret to say so, a hangdog failure in the subject of womanizing. Once the money is gone, never a kiss, never a liquid look filled to the brim with lasciviousness. And it isn't only money, either. Remember not to get bald, sir, if you would prosper in the pilgrimage toward love."

And he massaged his shiny pate.

O-Fuku entered with more sake.

"What do you think, sir?" she asked as she served. "Isn't Tsuruhachi an interesting and unusual person?"

"He reminds me of the one-man band which occasionally you see on the street: one man bangs the drum, blows the clarinet, strums the guitar, rings the bells," laughed Kikuji. Tsuruhachi raised his glass to him in appreciation.

Kikuji offered O-Fuku his cup and filled it for her, watching her smooth, easy way of sitting, moving, drinking. She poured for him. They exchanged cups many times. But before the talk had progressed very far, one of the waitresses came to raise problems concerning some guests, and O-Fuku excused herself to take care of her busy house. Tsuruhachi took over the serving. He had observed the close attention which Kikuji had given O-Fuku.

"A remarkable girl, that. Without her, this place would have to close its doors. She takes charge of absolutely everything."

"How long has she been here?"

"Five or six years. With that easy efficiency of hers she became head waitress in a very short time. And, be it ever to her credit, she is very good at fending off overly affectionate men."

"Is that so? How interesting," Kikuji replied.

"Yes. It's a skill other waitresses and geisha could use to good advantage. If she had been more yielding, she could have had a rich patron before this."

"I thought maybe Sanoya was—interested in her."

"No, sir. I know Mr. Sanoya well. He often has me as one of his entertainers. But, although he likes O-Fuku, he has never wanted to crawl into her bed."

"I'm amazed. Anyone that sure of herself usually has a patron behind her to give her security."

"Usually so, sir, I admit. But not in this case. Not yet." And he looked at Kikuji with a speculative expression.

Kikuji studied the bottom of his empty cup for a moment to conceal his pleasure at hearing that O-Fuku was not already spoken for. He looked up cheerfully.

"Tsuruhachi, sing me a song. Any song you like."

The jester asked the waitress for a broad-necked samisen, which, as he explained, had a mellow, low register of sounds well suited to his voice. Skillfully and with subtle feeling, he sang the familiar "Sanju Sangendo." Kikuji was greatly moved by the performance, and thought over the jesting conversation he had had with Tsuruhachi. By suffering through all experiences with women in love, might one become a kind of model for others in the difficult art of living? Tsuruhachi's words seemed to be a commentary and prophecy on his own many-sided lusts.

Six

The boats darted forward with leisurely grace from the mooring place at the Seta River inlet, and moved closer and closer first to the arched pedestrian bridge and then to the flat railroad bridge beyond which lay the main body of Lake Biwa. They could see several boats at a distance which, in the windless calm, looked as though they had been pasted on the watery blue background. Kikuji called over to Sanoya, who was drowsing against the gunwale of his boat in the warm sunlight. The old man waved carelessly to show that he was in good spirits. Two geisha and the jester, Tsuruhachi, kept a watchful eye on their patron for the day's outing. Kikuji's boat, with O-Fuku and a young geisha, moved beside Sanoya's, separated from it by a little distance. On the mirrorlike surface, the two boats by their movement carved wedges which spread out and intersected in the wake behind them. The giggles of the women seemed oddly lost in the immensity of the scene; beyond this, one could hear only the slow rhythmic creaking of the oars, and an occasional cry of a bird wheeling in the sky.

After proceeding out into the open lake a goodly distance, the boatmen put down their oars and threw their nets from the stern. Sanoya and Kikuji drank cold beer and leaned against the sides of their boats watching the boatmen as they flexed their muscular arms for the throw. Suddenly, Sanoya's boatman began hauling in the net with long, rapid pulls on the rope. The quiet surface of the lake was suddenly thrashed into a boiling foam beside the boat. Many small fish jumped and splashed frantically as their confinement closed inexorably around them. The women screamed, fearful that the fish would splash water on their new silk kimono. With careless skill the boatman drew the fish into the boat without getting anyone wet. He speedily cleaned the fish and threw them into a pot of hot oil. Within seconds they were fried to a crisp golden brown.

"Most of the fish are just *funa*," said Kikuji, "But there are also some *ayu* mixed in with them, and they're hard to come by in Osaka restaurants."

"Hard to come by, and delicious," agreed Sanoya.

"And expensive," said the practical-minded young geisha in Kikuji's boat.

One of the geisha in Sanoya's boat poked around in the hot oil with her chopsticks and drew out the first morsel, which she bit into. "Whee!" she shouted. "I drew *ayu!* Tastes very fancy-fine!"

"I'll bet. I'll bet," said Kikuji's young geisha morosely. She turned impatiently to the boatman. "Hey, Mister! Aren't you going to find me some *ayu* in that net of yours?" The old fellow bowed hastily and nervously and began looking through his catch.

"Leave it to me," said Tsuruhachi, stripping to the waist and pulling another net into Sanoya's boat. "Lots of *ayu* coming up. But there is a catch, young people. The *ayu* may be said to take his name from our verb *ai*, which means 'to meet,' 'to love.' And so, if any two people draw *ayu* from the oil at the same time, they are divinely ordained by the sign of this unfortunate fish to meet this night and to love long, long, long until the dawn sends them off to sleep. So sayeth Love Doctor Tsuruhachi to all his feverish patients!" He extended his arms in a sweeping gesture to include all the people in the two boats.

The geisha scoffed at him lightheartedly. "Listen to old Lecherous Looney, here. *Ayu* is his prescription for an aphrodisiac. With that face, he should try it himself!"

"I'll try it," laughed white-haired Sanoya. "I'll try anything!"

"Oh, my," said one of his geisha, laughing and patting him affectionately on the arm. "Up to now you've given us only money— which we have found very satisfying, Master."

"Well, at our love doctor's advice, I too will fish for *ayu*," said Kikuji laughing, "in hope of putting my evening to its best use."

The geisha who had drawn the first *ayu* stopped eating, dropped her chopsticks, and clasped her hands prayerfully as she turned with a beaming smile toward Kikuji in the boat beside hers.

197

"Assuredly, I would cooperate in giving you your medicine," she said, arching her brows and rolling her eyes in an almost alarming caricature of passion.

"Keep that up, and you'll fall into the water!" shouted another.

"Is that the way the *ayu* makes you behave?" laughed the young geisha in Kikuji's boat. "I think I'll take plainer fare!"

O-Fuku, wearing a faint smile which seemed never to change, busied herself in frying the fish caught by Kikuji's boatman. Now and again, observing that one of the guests had finished his drink, she would stretch her hand over the side of the boat to the beer bottles tied there in an underwater basket, pick one, open it, and serve it. She did everything with her usual, unhurried grace. Kikuji wondered if her mind were on something far removed from this lake picnic. It was almost as though she didn't quite hear them.

The boatmen picked up their oars, and rowed slowly back toward the Seta River inlet. When they passed other fishing boats, the pleasure seekers were stared at with undisguised amusement and curiosity by the fishermen. As the two boats approached the railroad bridge, Kikuji asked the boatmen to stop directly underneath. He had seen a train approaching in the distance. In the shadow of the bridge, they looked down into the dark green depths, and despite the movement of waves on the surface brought on by the afternoon breeze, they could sometimes see the pebbles on the bottom. The boatman profited from his break by lighting a cigarette, but the wind tore at the ash so that it burned too rapidly for pleasure. He threw the cigarette into the water; the paper uncurled and shreds of tobacco descended from it. Everyone in the two boats was quiet, enjoying the breeze.

Above them suddenly was a muffled rumbling as the hurtling mass of the train moved over their heads. Kikuji stared up at it intently. As it vanished, he heard a woman's voice at his ear.

"Here. It's done to perfection. Please eat it." The young geisha held out a dish of tempura to him.

He picked up a fish with chopsticks while she continued to hold the plate. When his teeth crunched down on a mouthful, he recognized the very delicate flavor.

"Oh! It's *ayu* that I—" And he stopped, seeing O-Fuku starting to signal with her chopsticks, and then smiling with embarrassment.

"Well, what do you know," said the young geisha loudly. "Both

Kawachiya's master and Sister O-Fuku have tasted *ayu* at the same time!"

"It's a plot, it's a plot!" said one of Sanoya's geisha. Tsuruhachi pounded the side of the boat, making a hollow, drumlike noise.

"We professional prophets never go wrong," he said. "They *must* go to bed with each other. All nature says they must. Including little fried fishes!"

Kikuji raised his beer in salute to the prophet. "Keep on prophecying such a pleasant future for me and I shall die a very happy man."

"Yes," said Tsuruhachi. "A happy man. With many children of all shapes and sizes standing at his bedside as he gasps his last."

Kikuji glanced at O-Fuku. With her faint, abstracted smile, she placed some fresh fish in the cooking oil and removed those that were done. Was she indifferent? Frigid? Or just good at hiding her feelings? He wished he could tell.

Slowly, delicately, the boats glided toward the shore. Their prows slowly parted the reeds, and there was a coarse, scraping sound as the keels slid over the sand at the bottom. The women with their kimono tucked up to their knees climbed into the shallow water and waded ashore, chattering, Kikuji thought, like birds at sunset. He leaned back and yawned, making no effort to get out. Sanoya was likewise half-asleep. Under the protecting shade of his fan, Kikuji closed his eyes to see again O-Fuku's white legs as she climbed over the edge of the boat into the water. From there, he moved to the recollection of her sudden nakedness at the teahouse contest. How tempting she was to visualize. If only Tsuruhachi's prophetic utterance were true. Then he could stroke those legs and that smooth skin tonight. He had been trying now for six months. It was very frustrating.

Always on his visits she had managed as the evening grew late to convey to him with perfect courtesy that it was time to leave. Somehow her calm assumption that he would of course leave at the appropriate moment had the effect of shattering all his spur-of-the-moment schemes. Calm efficiency applied to intimate relationships, he reflected, has a way of making them much less intimate. If she had been a geisha, his way would have been clear: he would simply have paid off the debt she had contracted on becoming a member of the profession. But head waitresses could not be bought and sold in

199

this way. Or if she had been a little less mature and experienced, he might have pleaded his cause in lovelorn fashion. But the thought of being refused again, however adroitly, however sympathetically, was simply not to be endured. Her first refusal was indelibly branded on his mind and made her the more attractive, her desirability being somehow proportionate to her remoteness. He felt that her first, unfavorable decision would have to be appealed and reversed. His self-esteem was at stake.

For these reasons he had devised the overnight excursion to Lake Biwa with Sanoya. How else could he approach her? Sanoya, now dozing on the boat, would have been amused had he known how much trouble Kikuji had gone to to make this elaborate picnic serve his needs.

The rumbling sound of another train sweeping across the bridge brought him back from his sleepy state. He removed his fan from his face and looked at the passengers being conveyed doll-like on their busy errands to the next town or to the four corners of the earth. The high-pitched voices of the women came to his ear; they were returning to the boats. O-Fuku and the young geisha climbed into Sanoya's boat; Tsuruhachi and the other two geisha joined Kikuji. As their boats proceeded they said little. It had been a strenuous day, and they were enjoying a pleasant lassitude. Sunset colors had tinged the slopes of Mt. Hiei. Other looming shapes were fast receding into brief evening silhouette. Tsuruhachi led the way up the hill to the inn. It was almost dark when they got there.

Kikuji, last in the procession, noticed that O-Fuku was walking unsteadily. He caught up with her and took her arm. "What's the matter? Seasick from the huge waves of Lake Biwa?" he asked with a smile.

She answered him with a weak seriousness which made him wonder if she were not indeed quite unwell. "Yes. I grew up in the mountains, you see, and I'm not at all used to water."

"Or sake?"

"I am used to sake," she replied with a quick smile. "But maybe not on water."

When they came to the inn, she went off with the geisha for the evening bath. When he next saw her, she was wearing the cotton evening kimono, which pleasantly revealed the whiteness of her skin, now a little pink from the bath, around her neck and shoulders. Whatever her indisposition, she was eating a good supper. Sanoya, sitting in the place of honor near the alcove, was being attentively served by Tsuruhachi and a geisha. His face was red and glistening after his bath.

"Tsuruhachi. Let's have a time of it tonight!" he shouted. "Everyone's half-asleep here. Go and find some of the local geisha, hey?" Tsuruhachi glanced quickly at the geisha in the room, and replied, "It has been a strenuous day and the ladies who have come with us should now be allowed to rest. I'll inquire about replacements."

In response to his efforts, five local geisha soon appeared at their room. All were young and good-looking, but their kimono were not fashionable or expensive. The Osaka geisha looked at their country cousins with calm disdain. As a result the new arrivals lost all spontaneity and performed nervously and even awkwardly. The party was becoming strained and unpleasant. To save the situation, Tsuruhachi suddenly picked up his fan and hit himself on the head, each time producing a tremendous noise of reverberating hollowness, and, with this introduction, launched into the telling and acting of an elaborately comic tale filled with erotic suggestiveness. After the manner of the celebrated storyteller, Haru Danji, the sad-eyed jester acted the role of the dashing libertine. His subtle exaggerations of gesture and tone soon had his audience delightedly enjoying his every flick of eyebrow or wrist. Their inhibitions dissolved in laughter, the geisha relaxed, and the party recovered its liveliness.

Kikuji asked that the local geisha dance for them, and, after Tsuruhachi started tuning the strings of the samisen, they lined up before the sliding doors of the next room and began their performance. Once they started, Kikuji lost interest. He could see that they were still learning the basic steps, and, although he kept beating the rhythm, his mind was on other matters. The inn projected out from the forested hillside. Beneath it the waves of the huge, dark lake slapped with timeless regularity on the beach. The lights on the opposite shore sparkled like the fluorescence of some rare sea animal. As those lights receded into the distance, so his hopes for a memorable night with O-Fuku were glimmering more and more faintly. Why *would* such an amiable girl be so damnably stubborn? She wasn't especially beautiful and she was older than either Ikuko or Ponta. She ought to be infinitely grateful for his attentions instead of constantly sending him on his way. And yet he persisted. Why? He looked at her. She was exchanging cups with Sanoya; he poured for her, and those slim, shapely hands carried the cup serenely to her lower lip, where she seemed in her own special way to inhale the contents. Sanoya kept filling her cup, and she kept accepting the drinks quietly and without haste. Kikuji smiled as he watched Sanoya's tireless celebrating. When did the old man sleep? The local geisha by now were looking as worn out as the women they had brought with them from Osaka. Sanoya was about to order more sake, but Kikuji stood up laughing and said to him, "You can keep partying forever, but the rest of us mere mortals are in danger of collapsing." He turned to the geisha, thanked them, and dismissed them. The local ones in sleepy relief set off for their homes, while the ladies from Osaka sought out their rooms. He walked with the local girls to the entryway.

"You have been very helpful tonight. I shall send special tips for each of you in addition to the regular fee," he said.

"Excuse me, sir," came O-Fuku's voice at his ear, "but here are the little remembrances you asked for." She handed him five small envelopes. He thanked her and gave one to each of the departing geisha. They bowed energetically, and left.

"I'm sorry to be so obtrusive," said O-Fuku. "But I know these local geisha. They much prefer an immediate tip in cash to one received later on when the whole bill is settled. They appreciate it more. Those five have opened their envelopes already and are counting their tips as they walk home. I hope I did not act too forwardly." She bowed, and departed. He looked after her. At the bend in the hall, she staggered, threw open a sliding panel, and half fell into a room. The door slid shut behind her. Kikuji watched intently from the entryway. The panel was shut tight. There was no noise from within. He walked quietly to the door and opened it. The room was dark. He found the light switch and turned it on. It was a storeroom. Two large rows of bedding were carefully stacked up in it. In the dim light he saw O-Fuku lying, face down, behind one of the piles. He quickly switched off the light, shut the door, and moved slowly in the dark until he was near the sleeping woman. He stretched out beside her, supporting his head on one elbow; with his other he stroked her hair and face. She gave a comfortable sigh, and he leaned forward to kiss her lightly on the lips. A faint tang of sake came to his mouth. He pulled a heavy quilt over and folded it, placing it under her head as a makeshift pillow. The strangeness of the scene filled him with excitement: the musty smell of the bedding, the straw scent of the tatami mats, the taste of sake from her lips, the faint murmuring of Tsuruhachi's voice somewhere down the hall were part of a strange erotic fantasy in which he was involved. He loosened his cotton kimono and moved closer to O-Fuku. There was no resistance. She opened herself to his advances, though still remaining essentially passive and quiet. After a time, he roused himself from his half-tranced state. He could feel himself wet with their intermingled perspiration. He slid to one side, resting her head in his arm. She moved slightly and turned to him in the dark.

"Did that mean something?" she asked in her low, throaty voice. "Was it just another conquest? Or did you mean it?"

He said nothing, but leaned down to kiss her tenderly. Suddenly she coiled around him with her whole body, embracing him, hugging him, drawing him closer, as though the dam of her inhibitions had suddenly burst in a flood of passion.

One afternoon several months after the Lake Biwa excursion, Kikuji took O-Fuku, along with Tsuruhachi and two youthful geisha, to a performance featuring the great Narikomaya, in the most famous of the kabuki epics, *The Forty-seven Ronin*. Kikuji was inattentive to the stage action, in which the virtuous prostitute, O-Karu, was timidly climbing from her second-story room down to the hero, Yuranosuke, who occupied the time by looking up her skirts and making bawdy observations. Kikuji was in no mood for comedy. His eye swept over the side walls of the theater, the boxes of which were draped with the crested curtains of various teahouses. To one side of his own spacious compartment was the walkway jutting out from the stage and ending at a curtained entrance on the left. It was along this passageway that the major actors often entered, freezing now and again into dramatic and unforgettable poses. It was natural that, with this favorite play of the kabuki repertoire, performed by the greatest of living actors, the hall should be filled to capacity. Still, he could not give himself to the play. His own thoughts meandered ceaselessly through his mind. Allowing them to wander as they would, he felt that they might lead him to some insight, some meaning he would never otherwise grasp. And if they did not, he could always watch the play. These samurai! It was wonderful the way the girls always tended to lie down and die for the love of a samurai. Reflectively, he drank the sake Tsuruhachi poured for him. He reached for O-Fuku's hand. She was deeply involved in the play and paid no attention as he entwined his fingers with hers. He gave it up in suppressed irritation, returning her hand to her lap. She threw a quick, appraising glance at him before returning to her rapt concentration on the stage.

For almost four months now, ever since the Lake Biwa picnic, he had been seeing her regularly. But it was different from his relationships with Ponta and Ikuko. With them, the sexual surrender had been complete, trusting, and undemanding. He had reciprocated it fully. But with O-Fuku, there was, he sometimes thought, submission without surrender. The path to complete and absolute trust, which he required if he were to be fully content with his mistresses, was blocked by some stubbornness, some unexplored area of her personality. It was very exasperating. He looked at her: she was sitting very straight, leaning a little forward in her anticipation and excitement as she watched the stage. The lighting in the area of his box was dim, and she had a dark shadow on her cheek. It was almost, he thought, a visible mark of the undefined difference which somehow kept her apart from him, even when they were most together. How essentially mysterious she was—and how fascinating the mystery!

Always when he called to take her out, she seemed genuinely pleased to go, and yet she always directed him to teahouses outside of Osaka. She never felt quite free in that crowded old city, she said. But why not? He had asked himself this question many times, but never had come to an answer that made sense. Was he, he wondered, feeding in someone else's leftover dish? He gritted his teeth at the thought. If so, she had enough passion for more than one lover. In bed she was never still, and played upon his body as though it would yield her music. But then, after climax had been achieved, she became once more calm, efficient, and amiably distant. It was maddening. So it had been in the accidental tryst that they had experienced in the bedding storeroom at the Lake Biwa inn. While he was still panting from his exertions and holding her tenderly, she had risen quietly, adjusted her kimono, and said, "Please excuse me now. I must go." And he was left lying on the floor in the dark.

In his desire to win her full acquiescence, he had been even more lavish in his spending than usual. For every excursion they undertook together he had new clothes made for her: underkimono, kimono, hair ornament, and footwear. In addition he had given her ample spending money. All these gifts she accepted politely and calmly. She never, like Ponta, showed any special pleasure in the possession of a fine gem or a splendid robe; nor did she, after the manner of Ikuko, radiate a deep and tender gratitude. She merely smiled politely, and put the gifts on, wearing them as though she had always worn such gems, such clothes.

His thoughts were interrupted as the curtain closed on the scene and the house lights went on. Waitresses were weaving dexterously among the boxes with their red lacquered towers of food trays. Their own waitress, after placing the trays they had ordered before them, tinkered with the charcoal in the brazier, using metal tongs to move it about. Then she put a full sake bottle on the grate to warm it. As the members of Kikuji's party began to sample the dishes, a stage hand walked across the huge stage, drawing behind him a huge red curtain on which was written in large white characters, TO NARIKOMAYA, FROM THE CORNER SUSHI STORE.

"Oh, I like the advertising curtains," said one of the geisha to Tsuruhachi.

"The Corner Sushi Store hopes that you do," he replied. "Look at the audience. They like it too."

As the people in the theater ate, they kept their eyes on the curtain, and a loud commentary on the characters displayed filled the hall. A green curtain followed the pink, containing a compliment to another of the main actors from a local bakery. Beneath the inscription were colored drawings of muffins. This second curtain brought forth scattered applause, a few loud, raucous comments on the quality of the muffins, and jeering laughter.

The third curtain was an eye-catching vermillion. In its center was the large dyed crest of the actor, Narikomaya, and on it in gold characters was inscribed, KAWACHIYA TABI. As the curtain rippled, the golden characters danced before the audience. The self-appointed commentator from the cheap seats in the back of the hall yelled, "If you like tabi with hooks of gold, that's the place for you. I get mine from peddlers on the street!" Kikuji, acting on sudden impulse as he gauged the audience reaction to the sumptuous and expensive

205

curtain, sent Tsuruhachi backstage with a tip. His curtain had been removed, but was drawn out once more by the stolid old stagehand who had pocketed the tip. The audience was surprised by the repetition. "Don't smother me in that damned rag. I'll buy your tabi!" came the commentator's drunken cry from the rear of the house. The audience burst into laughter.

Tsuruhachi returned and took his seat. Turning to Kikuji, he said, "The repetition of your ad was very effective, I think."

Kikuji laughed. "It's the only means of advertising our wares that we have. They laughed at the repetition, but they'll remember the product. Even the old drunk in the back. This is a new way of merchandizing. My father and his father before him relied on the good report of satisfied customers to bring him new business. But I think we need to publicize our wares a little, and make the public conscious of our reputation and product. Anyway, it is something of an honor to be allowed to advertise at intermission. They selected only established firms and tasteful designs. There was a long list of applicants."

The house lights were dimmed and the great curtain opened once more on the scene of epic vengeance. But Kikuji had other things on his mind. After the play he was giving a party to a group of bankers at Hamayu Teahouse. Idly, he went over some of the planning for the party. As he did so, his glance fell on O-Fuku, and he was amazed at what he saw. During the earlier acts, she had been calmly attentive to the play. But now she leaned way forward, her face expressing an intensity which he had only observed in her when they had been in bed together. Her hands were at her sash, clasping and unclasping nervously. Quietly, he slid from his cushion and moved so that he was directly behind her. Instantly, he could see that the young actor playing Rikiya, the warrior son of the hero, was looking at O-Fuku whenever his role permitted. He was a handsome young fellow; each time he glanced at O-Fuku, she drank in his gaze and seemed almost to tremble with emotion. It appeared so obvious to Kikuji that he could not understand why everyone else in the theater was not watching these two lovers speaking to each other in passionate looks over a distance of fifty feet.

Suddenly in the dim light of the auditorium Kikuji moved beside O-Fuku, and threw his arm around her under her shoulder so that his hand was resting over her breast. Tsuruhachi and the two geisha pretended not to notice this surprising development. O-Fuku gently tried to disengage herself, but refrained from any decisive gesture or sound for fear of attracting attention. Kikuji, smiling now with the enjoyment of a directed defiance, kept his grasp tight and glanced at the stage. The handsome young actor who played Rikiya had seen what was going on by now, and he gazed steadily at the dimly lit box, watching O-Fuku being embraced publicly by the business-man. It was his turn to declaim: he began forcefully enough, but then stumbled over the words, stopped, and repeated himself. Kikuji enjoyed the actor's confusion immensely, and out of the corner of his eye looked at O-Fuku. Tears glistened in her eyes, and for the first time he saw her distraught and uncertain. He knew now that the little drama in which he had been both actor and spectator would never have taken place had not O-Fuku and the spirited young actor been lovers who had slept in each other's arms many times. Now he understood how she had managed to be so calm and analytical following a strenuous night with him. She had all the while been comparing his lovemaking with the ardors of that flashy adolescent on the stage.

But, angry as he was, he would never give her the satisfaction of asking questions or taking any notice of her duplicity. It would not do to cast her off just now. It would look as though the actor fellow had cut him out, an impression that his own self-respect could never allow. How trivial and even disgusting had been the cause of that mysteriousness which had fascinated him so much.

The play over, Kikuji went to Hamayu Teahouse. He had an hour to wait before guests would begin to arrive for the party. The geisha who had accompanied him to the play had returned to their head-quarters to freshen up for the evening's entertainment. Accompanied by Tsuruhachi, he went to a small room upstairs, took off his *haori* coat, and stretched out to rest. He closed his eyes, but couldn't sleep. The incident at the theater haunted him. There were steps outside the room. He opened his eyes to see O-Fuku at the door. Her hands and arms were still wet, as though she had been washing something. She came in and sat beside him.

"They have built a new bathtub in this inn. Would you like to be the first to try it?"

He made no response.

"The fragrant oils from a new cedar tub are supposed to protect a man from having strokes, you know—"

"Strokes?" he exploded. "Do I look so antique that you think I might have a stroke? Is that what you think?"

He glared angrily at her, but she put both her hands on his shoulders.

"Please. Don't be irritated at my hurried words. I was just trying to tell you: the proprietress here has had a new cedar tub made in a great rush because one of the imperial princes is coming here tomorrow on a secret visit. Wouldn't you enjoy taking the first bath?"

Gently, she turned him toward her, and looked into his severe eyes. "You were always one for a fine escapade, Master," she said softly. "Wouldn't it be a feat to sneak in and take to yourself the special virtues of the cedar tub bath meant for a prince? Doesn't that take your fancy?"

He smiled suddenly. "As a matter of fact, it does. In the prince's bath I shall absorb the life-giving fragrance of the cedar, and leave behind, perhaps, a few farts as a substitute to perfume the royal waters. By all means, let's do it. But, O-Fuku, the proprietress. If she finds out, won't she be—" He hesitated, and put two fingers up to his forehead to suggest the horns of an angry demon.

"Don't worry about her. She's out now. The bath is at the end of the second floor. No one is there now, and I will stand guard until you are finished." She went off immediately to make final preparations. Tsuruhachi went with Kikuji to help him undress.

As he entered the bathroom, a delicious smell of new cedar greeted him. He sank deep into the hot water; it seemed to him that the cedar fragrance blended into the water and permeated his body. The effect was enormously exhilarating. In two months this special fragrance would evaporate completely, and the tub would be just another tub. He hadn't expected to enjoy himself so much. Could it be that O-Fuku had set up this little surprise to make him forget her theatrical lover? To be sure, it was a pleasant way to wash away all anger and humiliation.

Returning to his room, he found Hidesuke there, ready to take charge of tonight's party. Kikuji was still having his bottle of after-bath beer when the key people from the Bank of Yamaguchi arrived.

He had had no financial difficulties as yet. But a panic had swept the country and investment capital was hard to come by. It seemed only good sense to entertain the people who made the loans. They would remember him in their sober moments as a solid citizen. Many companies in Osaka had done their banking with Bank Fifteen, and it was this institution which had precipitated the financial crisis by going bankrupt. Kawachiya's, however, had placed its main deposits with the Bank of Yamaguchi, and the rest with Sumimoto and Mitsubishi. These institutions had remained untouched in the chaos which followed the bankruptcy of Bank Fifteen. On such small strokes of luck are the fortunes of great commercial houses based. Had not Mr. Ueno just been starting as manager at the Bank of Yamaguchi, and had he not aggressively courted Kawachiya's so that Kikuji felt obliged to transfer the company's funds to his bank, the firm would have been ruined.

Mr. Ueno, president of the Yamaguchi Bank, accompanied by four or five branch managers, was the first guest to arrive. Kikuji knew him and his associates well. To keep them amused he had hired not only the two beautiful young geisha who had been with him at the play, but also two older ones skilled in music and dancing. Tsuruhachi also was on hand, watching over the guests and skillfully varying the tempo and mood of the entertainment. When it was time for dinner, O-Fuku in her fashionable blue silk kimono came in, bowed to the bank president, and sat down beside him. By her slow, assured entrance and the graceful way she sank down beside the guest of honor she created a small sensation. People talked better and ate more freely after she had come, as though they had absorbed some of her friendly assurance simply from watching her. Kikuji watched her too. He could not forget the unsavory episode at the theater, but it no longer made him angry with her. The woman was a work of art, not, like Ponta, because she was always striving for effect, but precisely because she seemed never to be acting or pretending, and was always calm and natural in her own profound womanliness. It was a great talent she possessed. Even Mr. Ueno, who normally did not drink and was therefore a difficult man to entertain, found her irresistible, and accepted cup after cup of sake from her. His subordinates, observing O-Fuku's mellowing influence on the old man, themselves relaxed and began to joke with the geisha. Tsuruhachi, noticing that the young men were enjoying the geisha, decided that no more of his acts were necessary, and he sat watchfully and at times half-asleep in the corner.

Slowly and inevitably, the relaxed party percolated toward noisy incoherence. Mr. Ueno, quite drunk by this time, was grinning foolishly at one of the geisha. Kikuji, glad to see that his efforts at entertaining were not needed, gave way to a mood of overpowering depression. He caught Hidesuke's eye and signalled him with a jerk of his head to carry on. Then he rose and left, pretending to go to the men's room. Instead, he returned to the small room where he had rested earlier and lay down, using an armrest as a pillow. Just to be alone was a great relief. But the door slid open quietly, and O-Fuku was there. Her breath smelled of sake, but she seemed quite sober. She quickly sat beside him, offering him a glass of water.

"Are you exhausted by all your activities, Master?" she asked.

He shook his head.

"Sick, then? Too much sake?"

The casual question touched his nerves. He would have liked to have said in tones of despair, "You are the cause of my illness." But he resisted this impulse with an effort. She was quite composed and calm. Why should he show himself to be upset? Surely he had interpreted correctly the young actor's eyes and their effect on O-Fuku? Or was she so calm and unconcerned because accustomed to making eyes at all the actors whenever she had the chance? He couldn't understand. She made no effort to explain. She was natural as usual, and it was a damned nuisance.

She reached into the closet and pulled out a pillow for him. She tried to place it under his head. "Take a good rest now, and you'll feel better," she said.

Impatiently, he pushed the pillow away, and, looking sternly at her, said emphatically, "I do not need it!"

For an instant she looked at him, a slight frown forming on her smooth forehead. Then she bowed slowly and gracefully, as she did everything, apologized for intruding, and was gone. Looking at the shut door, he weighed his deprivation and found it overwhelming. He hated himself for needing her. The lively noise from his party in the banquet chamber was intolerable to him in his present mood. Hidesuke would have to make excuses for him in his absence. He stood up and walked downstairs. At the foot of the stairs stood Tsuruhachi, looking distressed and uncomfortable.

"Where are you headed, Master?" he asked.

"Home."

"But—you can't. Your guests—"

"Amuse them. Get them drunk. Do what you want. I'm leaving."

And off he went, Tsuruhachi following close behind. Across the Dotombori Bridge hastened the ill-assorted pair, master and clown. On the far side, they found themselves in an atmosphere contrasting raucously with the staid, austere quality of the Soemoncho District which they had just left. Near-darkness was replaced by the steely insistence of neon lights. Noisy crowds of night people promenaded before the brightly lit restaurants and night clubs. Kikuji heard snatches of music coming theough the doors of the various establishments. This was unfamiliar territory. Distraught by the glare and hubbub, he turned abruptly into a cafe, the Polka Dot, whose sign indicated that it was "the largest in Osaka."

The noise was worse than that outside. The customers were singing in unison the words of a cheap popular song. As Kikuji took a table, to be joined instantly by Tsuruhachi, and more slowly by a number of hostesses appraising his worth, he was puzzled by his behavior. Heretofore, he had always hated these palatial establishments where noise passed for conviviality and drunkenness for wit. Yet here he was, fleeing the intimacy and refinement of the teahouses for the brawling camaraderie of a cheap nightclub. As he drank his beer, he watched Tsuruhachi, who was beginning to try out some of his little "acts." As the hostesses snickered, he rolled his eyes at them without changing his deadpan expression. One of the girls patted him on the head.

"Ah, you are wonderful. Better than a professional comic!"

He twisted his neck and looked sidelong at her. "Witness my triumph," he said with a theatrical sigh. "I *am* a professional comic, my dear."

"Oh? Oh!" she said, adjusting to the information. "And do you make funny faces for a living?"

"I am a professional jester, Madam." Tsuruhachi drew himself up solemnly, and nodded his head peckishly, like a schoolmaster at a recalcitrant student. But the lady continued to look puzzled, if co-operative. "I see the funny side of things. For a price. And sometimes, when there is not any funny side, I invent one. As now. For a price. Humor always has a price. Boredom is free to all takers. To avoid it we must have paid jesters."

"Yes. Yes, indeed," said the hostess vaguely. "Imagine. A jester. I suppose it is some Chinese tradition or other—?"

Tsuruhachi's ever-changing features produced a fatherly smile.

"Bless you, my dear. You know only the world of Osaka's largest cabaret. No, a jester is not a Chinese tradition. He entertains people like this worthy gentleman here, but not in beerhalls. In teahouses, usually. I sing, I dance, I make people live in the present moment. I am what you might call a male geisha."

The hostess exploded with laughter. "You? A geisha? With that face?" And she laughed till the tears ran down her cheeks, spoiling her makeup. The other girls gathered around Kikuji's table joined in the laughter except for one clear-featured young woman who looked inquiringly at the others.

"What's the matter?" asked Kikuji. "Do you find him a nuisance?"

She gave him a cool glance and shook her head.

"Oh, don't mind her, sir," said the hostess. "Hisako won't talk unless it's about the only subject which interests her. She's a bit of a nut."

Tsuruhachi scowled judicially and pulled a long imaginary beard. "The only subject which interests her? A condundrum! But surely we can solve it? What most women find uniquely interesting is the little item men keep buttoned up in their pants. Have I hit the target, most noble lady?" He smiled and bowed ceremonially to her. She looked at him coolly, smiling with the faint amusement of the absent-minded.

Tsuruhachi stared at her with a desolate expression, and said mournfully, "Well, well. We cannot always be right. There are the normal, man-directed women, and there are the few others who prove the rule. They do not mind men in moderation. But their interests lie otherwheres, in other beds. I have guessed wrong."

"Hisako's tastes are, well, expensive," suggested the hostess.

"Animal, vegetable, or mineral?" asked Tsuruhachi.

"Jewelry, perhaps?" suggested Kikuji. "All the ladies die for a diamond."

Hisako shook her head slightly. Kikuji was annoyed.

"Oh, come now. What is your addiction? Opium? Perverted sex? Shoplifting? Do tell us so that we can stop this damnable guessing."

She looked him over calmly and then said the one word, "Horses."

"I don't understand."

"All I like is horses."

Tsuruhachi turned his palms up in shrugging amazement. "There was this lady in Greece whose taste was for bulls only, and she had the most unusual son. But horses! I should think that a harmonious union would be quite a gymnastic feat."

"Horse racing, idiot!" she said with an easy smile.

"How very strange," Kikuji said. "You're addicted to gambling, then. Is that it?"

"Addicted? Well, yes, I guess it comes to that," she replied, looking at him thoughtfully. "Just horses, though. Not cards. It's no way to get rich. What are you addicted to?"

Kikuji laughed. "My addiction is more expensive than yours. But horse racing would be no substitute for me, I'm afraid."

"Ah. The ladies," she said softly.

"The ladies."

"Mine is a more uncomplicated pleasure. You win or you lose and the thing is finished forever . . ." Her beautiful eyes looked off into a distance far beyond the confines of Osaka's largest cabaret.

He was about to respond when he heard a man's voice behind him calling his name in liquor-blurred accents. He turned and saw before him an old classmate from his days at business college, Kishida Hiroyuki. He was leaning against the back of the booth across the aisle, his suit disheveled, a full beer glass in his hand. Kikuji greeted him cordially.

Kishida frowned with the elaborate judiciousness of the heavily intoxicated. "It has been a long time. You never come to the annual alumni dinners. We talked about you though. We decided that the masters of the Semba have no time to spare for us salaried types. It's all right, all right. Don't apologize. Never apologize, I always say." He drank deeply from his beer mug and sat down beside Kikuji. Leering brightly, he said in a loud stage whisper, "How's the hunting in the Semba? Have you been spending your dividends on women? I've heard a thing or two."

213

Kikuji smiled pleasantly at him, disregarding Hisako's curious look. "Come off it, Hiroyuki. I'm sure your life has been more interesting than mine."

Kishida put down his beer mug and inspected Kikuji. "You haven't changed a bit," he said with a touch of bitterness. "Hardly shopworn at all, even if you are in your mid-thirties. Those fine clothes, the thick walls of the Semba, the weekly spree at the teahouses—these things protect a fellow from the wear and tear of real living. Coming into this place, too. You must feel as out of place as a dinosaur in a public bath." He fingered his company badge on his coat lapel. "No stamp of conformity like this on you."

Kikuji quietly filled his beer glass. "We haven't seen each other for such a long time. Let's skip the argument and drink to old times."

"No, I can't do that. Seeing you here suddenly gives me all sorts of ideas. Here we are sitting side by side. But in actuality there is a chasm a mile wide between your world and mine. You are an aristocrat, and by now your nerves have become more attuned to rare sensations than those of us lesser people."

Kikuji looked at his onetime classmate in amazement. "Hiroyuki, what are you talking about? The Semba is a merchants' town. We work for a living too. Certainly we are not aristocrats."

But his drunken friend shook his head morosely. "Don't give me that! Merchant aristocrats, that's what you are. Your fathers and your grandfathers have piled up money century after century. And they dug those four canals to cut off the Semba from the rest of the dirty world. Just as the feudal lords separated themselves from common humanity with their huge stone walls and their moats. And as the samurai once in a while venture out among the common people for diversion, so you occasionally leave your castle to see the ladies. And when you're really feeling decadent, you stop in at a beer hall like this place—which is all I can afford."

The visual image of his home and store in all its spacious solidity came to Kikuji. He felt vaguely uneasy hearing Kishida's accusations. Ever since he could remember, this dark, imposing structure had been his security, the center from which his world radiated. The customs which his mother and grandmother lived by still, despite many transient rebellions, bound him. Perhaps his world was larger and more substantial than theirs only because he was a man who could, as Kishida said, venture every so often out of the feudal fortress in search of life and meaning. He had accepted the rules of the game as prescribed by the Semba over the centuries. They must seem very strange rules to the outer world, and to people in that outer world he must sometimes seem not the capable manager of a tradition-dignified business, but a self-indulgent parasite, a pampered anachronism from an earlier age, even (in Kishida's words) a dinosaur in a public bath! He fingered his drink reflectively. What could he do? Everyone sooner or later accepts a set of rules for the game of living, and conducts himself accordingly in the hope that the rules are good ones and the game worth the winning. The indictment of poor drunken Kishida must be dismissed—tentatively—for lack of evidence. But—poor Kishida.

He emerged from his reverie to realize that his former classmate was becoming raucous.

"Kawachiya! We're still here. Stop being rude, like a feudal lord. Can't you spare a word or two for us ordinary mortals?" And he suddenly grabbed Kikuji by his collar. Tsuruhachi, however, ever on the alert, smoothly moved in between them.

"No, no, gentlemen. Only country bumpkins bang each other around in public. We of Osaka talk things through quietly, quietly . . ."

The hostess joined Tsuruhachi in restraining Kishida. In drunken fury he struggled for a moment and a beer bottle broke with an explosive noise on the floor. Kikuji's former classmate rose, stood for a moment staring down at the group in rage and puzzlement, and then walked uncertainly off, muttering darkly to himself.

Kikuji sat for a few minutes stunned and distressed by the utterly unexpected encounter. Beer had spilled on him and now he felt it soaking through his lined kimono and wetting his skin. What had he expected when he entered this sordid place? He could not think straight. His sense of guilt on perceiving the logic of Kishida's attack prevented him from recognizing the self-pity and spite motivating it. Tsuruhachi bent down and dabbed at his kimono with his handkerchief, trying to remove the beer before it damaged the material.

"Really, Master, you must take care of the company you keep. Maybe he was your old classmate, but I don't think you should mix with just anyone in a place like this."

215

Kikuji watched Hisako. She sat listening without concern either for Tsuruhachi's words or for Kikuji's discomfiture. Even when the altercation with Kishida had been at its most violent, she had been an unmoved observer. Sensing his stare, her eyes slowly focused on his.

"More beer?" she asked, lazily reaching for a bottle on the table. "In the glass this time instead of a shower bath?"

"Let's go together," he said. "You will teach me."

Her eyebrow flexed upward. "I don't understand."

"Your addiction. I am—interested. Let's go to the races together."

Something flashed over her face quickly and was gone: a look, perhaps, of contempt? He could not tell. She shrugged and nodded.

"Very well. I leave at one from Temma Keihan station. Meet me there."

"The place was rather beautiful in its way," he said. "There was a pond inside the oval of the track, and the horses were mirrored in it as they ran. It was a fine day: cool, clouds scudding overhead in a light breeze, just the way I like it in September. But no one paid attention to the weather. They were all studying their racing charts, working at their calculations, staring gloomily at the horses as they lined up for a race. They didn't seem to be having a good time at all."

He was with Ponta at Yonedaya's Teahouse.

"Even the girl you were with? She too was bored?" asked Ponta.

"No, no. Not bored. Withdrawn and rather savage before the race; totally depressed afterward. She had promised to show me why the horses were such fun. She said her father, a chronic follower of the race track, never won because he made his bets by intuition. She makes hers by careful arithmetic. But still she lost every bet that afternoon, and I suppose she was embarrassed. Maybe she thought me a jinx. Maybe I *am*, come to think of it. Who can tell?"

"But you won."

"I was just trying it out. There was a frisky little horse there with a fine arch to its neck. It was prancing around, and I thought that nothing with that much spirit could possibly lose. So I went to bet on it, and finally, when I found that I had to bet on first, second, or third place, picked third. And the horse came in third, but only after the front-runner broke his leg fifty yards from the finish line."

"It sounds horrible," said Ponta.

"Hisako had bet on the front-runner. When she saw I had won by betting that horse would come in third, all she could think of to say was, 'What a cautious merchant you are. How could anyone bet on a horse placing third?' "

"But—" Ponta hesitated to finish her sentence.

"Why did I go with her? Is that it?"

"Horse racing isn't your sort of thing. And this Hisako is apparently only a cheap cabaret entertainer. Isn't that so? How could you expect to have a good time?"

He looked at her cautiously. What she meant was, why didn't you put yourself in my hands if you wanted a good time. He thought about it: why hadn't he? And why had he found this distant and quite indifferent cabaret hostess attractive? Partly, he supposed, it was her mysteriousness. She was totally outside his experience. He had never before met a woman so completely uninterested in him. It was a challenge he could not resist. But the whole afternoon at the race track hadn't altered her indifference. If anything, she now felt a little contempt for him because of his ignorance of all that she valued.

"I was curious about the horses. I had never seen a race before."

He recalled Hisako's comment in the taxi on the ride home. She had been completely silent and morose. Suddenly she said, "You must break free of your addiction to these sex machines, these kimono-clad dummies you like to bed down with once you're drunk enough. You should seek out the company of more natural beauty, by God." And he, completely puzzled, had said nothing, but after an instant had held her hand. She briskly, and with a half-laugh of impatience, snatched it from him.

"Not me! Not me," she had said sharply. "I meant the natural beauty of animals, of horses, of course."

"Of course," he had said, frowning in puzzlement.

After that, was there any real reason for a continuing interest in her? But there it was: one could not deny irrational impulses. They were exactly the ones which swept away all before them.

Ponta poured him a drink. "I can't understand people like your new friend."

He laughed. "She said her father died from one leg of a horse."

Ponta's eyes widened. "What does that mean?"

"He had only five yen and a bet was priced at twenty. So he got three others to buy one leg each at five yen apiece and so made up the full price of the bet. The horse won at tremendous odds. And her father had a stroke that night as he tried to celebrate his win from one leg of a horse."

Ponta gave a small snort of disapproval. She looked at him thoughtfully in silence, chin high, her fine youthful figure accentuated by the lines of the kimono.

"But your horse racer is just a passing fancy. There is another woman you love, isn't there? In Soemoncho? Right?"

"You mustn't feel threatened," he replied. "You were busy expanding your establishment, and I didn't wish to interfere. That's why I've stayed away now and then."

" 'Now and then'? Even when you did come to see me, you were far away in mind." Her eyes filled with tears. She concealed them as best she could. "You needn't worry. Kept women must not show jealousy of their rivals, I know. Excuse me for having mentioned the competition." And she poured him another drink.

Esthetically, she was the best of all. She did everything with youthful vigor. She wore a gown with the natural grace of a fashion model. Her conversation was superb in wit, good humor, and sheer high spirits. And she was reliable. Tonight, when he was in need of someone to ease his mind, she seemed to understand without trying. But in some areas, she could not follow him. The world of real passion was and would remain a closed book to her, he felt. In bed she was always rather virginal and unresponsive. It was a pity. Otherwise, she was a perfect companion.

"Where did you have supper tonight?" she asked.

"I took her to the Shibado Restaurant. Right after, though, she said she had to get back to the Polka Dot Cabaret. I walked her there, and left."

"And, with nothing else to do, you came to see me," she said mildly with a timid smile.

"No, my dear. I've missed you, and I felt a great need to see you."

She looked into his eyes for an instant, and then smiled warmly. "I'm glad," she said.

But it wasn't quite true. As he had walked Hisako toward the cabaret, they had passed the Nakaza Theater. On glancing casually toward the stage door, he had glimpsed for an instant in the crowd

218

the back of a woman who in her stance and manner looked exactly like O-Fuku. He had slowed down uncertainly, but Hisako, puzzled, had asked if something was wrong, and they had continued on their way. He became more and more certain that the opulent figure dressed in white revealed by the dim light of the stage door was O-Fuku, waiting for her lover, the youthful actor, Jusho. And it was his pain at the discovery that made him seek out Ponta for comfort.

He noticed suddenly that she was once again wearing many rings. "Surely you're not back at your old habit of wearing all your wealth on your hand?"

She flashed her right hand at him. "They're my best friends, these rings. Excluding you, of course. Don't begrudge me my fun! It's better than collecting lovers, isn't it?"

Chastened, he said nothing. Much as he admired her, he realized that she was the most expensive of his mistresses. Besides a monthly stipend of two hundred yen, he gave her an eighty-yen clothing allowance, and fifty yen for her rings, plus another fifty for cosmetics. The total came to three hundred and eighty yen. It made her the richest of the independent geisha in Shinmachi. At this time he knew that one could buy a small teahouse for no more than one thousand yen. Nevertheless, expensive though she was, she was openly budgeted for just like other employees of Kawachiya's. He had used none of the secrecy which had made his father's life so dreary. And his mother and grandmother, as long as no mistress received more than they, took good care to see that the monthly salary was paid. They had heard somewhere that once the head of the Nomura Bank had paid the enormous sum of one thousand yen to buy up the contract of an apprentice geisha in Gion. The news of this great expenditure spread through the city like wildfire, and, as a result, many new accounts were opened at the Nomura Bank by people who assumed that anyone spending such an amount to buy freedom for an apprentice geisha must have a business which could easily afford such expenditure. Only so could the thrifty middle classes have confidence in a firm. Hence, if Kikuji at the end of the month were tied down with business, the two women would make sure that a head clerk carried the monthly salary to the houses of Kikuji's women. It was a point of honor not to be late. Ponta, especially, as a geisha often dealing with prominent merchants in the district, had to be comfortably provided for at all times.

219

He looked at her appreciatively, and laughed.

"What's the matter?" she asked.

"Nothing. Just that you're beautiful, and I have shared in making you so."

He reached for her hand, and kissed each of her rings before moving up her arm.

She looked immaculate. If she had to attend four parties a night, she changed her whole outfit for each. Her kimono tonight was crisp and new, its colored silk lining showing delicately at the hem of the skirt.

"The night is young," said Ponta. "I'll get some more geisha and we'll have a party."

"Later," replied Kikuji. Slowly, he pulled her down beside him. The lining of the kimono became clearly visible as it opened and revealed her legs.

"No, no!" she hissed. "Not in this outfit. It's my best. Why can't you wait?"

But with quiet insistence he parted her clothing and pushed his way toward her. As he progressed on his sensual pilgrimage toward orgasm, his eyes were closed, and he had a sudden vision of the horses running fiercely around the race track, their slim, beautiful legs skittering over the ground with the lightness of waterbugs moving over a pond. The lead horse with its shining flanks somehow reminded him of Hisako. Other horses reminded him of O-Fuku, Ponta, or Ikuko. To be clasped, to be held, so warm, so deep, so tight— He shuddered convulsively in Ponta's embrace, and in savoring of his sudden release lost consciousness for several seconds. He opened his eyes, met Ponta's, smiled sleepily at her, and pillowed his head on her shoulder.

Pleasantly relaxed, after leaving Ponta he sauntered lazily along the street looking with aimless benevolence into the various shop windows. Before Tenguya's, a store specializing in expensive footwear, he lingered. In the showcase was a pair of clogs carved out of paulownia wood. As he looked, the manager came out.

"That, sir," he said, pointing at the paulownia clogs, "is a pair carved from the very center of the tree trunk. Observe the straight grain, the closeness of the growth rings. A whole fragrant tree crashed down so that those clogs could be made. And for comfort, there is nothing like paulownia wood. It is soft and yielding to the foot, and yet it lasts forever. Men of sensitivity will wear no other footwear."

Kikuji frowned. "I don't need a sales talk, thank you."

The manager bowed and smiled all in the same motion. "Naturally, sir. And here is our special deerhide strap. It just came in today. Soft, supple to the touch. Paulownia wood and a deerhide strap. Nothing like it, sir. Or almost nothing."

"If you can fix me up right away, I'll take them," Kikuji said. He looked restlessly at his watch. Yet he knew there was no real hurry. His business was at the slack season. Hisako wouldn't care when he got to the Polka Dot or even if he got there. And his visit with O-Fuku had been set up by Tsuruhachi. He had plenty of time. And in the afterglow of his intercourse with Ponta, he felt an almost voluptuous ease and comfort. Still, a buyer should not be too easy on the man doing the selling— And the remembrance of that white kimono glimpsed all too quickly at the stage door contended unexpectedly with his feeling of satiety and well-being.

With a flourish the shoe shop manager presented him with the paulownia clogs, complete with deerhide strap. "You will want to take these to bed with you, sir," he said. And then he presented the bill.

Kikuji tried them on. They were soft and flexible, like an old shoe, but solid and supportive, like a new one. They made him feel rich and comfortable. He kept them on, and walked on through the crowd of shoppers. Kikuji fancied himself a connoisseur. He loved the feeling of expensive silks against his body, and he delighted in the soft, yielding support of these new paulownia clogs. Good footwear, like expensive fabric, was to be cherished.

His women, he knew, reacted according to their natures to his sense of the luxurious. Ponta, for example, had no interest in any clothing beyond her own new kimono. She would toss the most expensive and delicately made clogs around with incredible carelessness. If Kikuji complained, she looked at him blankly and apologized without understanding his attitude. Ikuko, in accordance with her careful nature, respected his footwear as she respected all his possessions, and, if he left them, helter-skelter, at the entryway, she would brush the straps lightly with her handkerchief, and put them on the shelf. On rainy days she worked even more carefully, and wiped away the mud adhering to the soles of the clogs. And O-Fuku, when she adjusted his clogs for him to step into as he left Hamayu, would always manage to inspect them closely to determine the maker's name. By such inspections she determined the worth of each guest. The head waitress of a first-class teahouse could do no less.

He shook his head impatiently. Not long ago he had seen his various mistresses as racehorses running against each other. Now he was comparing their esthetic reactions to footwear. What on earth was the matter with him? But he knew the answer, although he would not admit it. The white kimono at the stage door would not let him rest.

He came to the Polka Dot Cabaret, started to pass, and then thought better of it. The red door opened quickly as he approached it, and a boy ushered him to a booth in the corner of the large, dimly lit interior. Hisako came sauntering toward him with long, lazy strides which seemed at once unfeminine and hugely provocative. Her pleated green dress swung delicately as she walked. He was used to the graceful motions which the ankle-length kimono imposed on its wearers. Hisako's long legs, which she crossed as she sat down, disturbed and excited him. He recalled that when he had last seen her she had lost nearly all her money betting. Yet the dress was clearly a new one.

"You're all dressed up," he said. "What happened?"

"I hit a winner yesterday," she said with an odd snicker. "With the odds at ten to one, I made three hundred yen!" Usually so cool and distant, even at times bored, she now chattered animatedly, leaning excitedly over the table toward him, her eyes sparkling.

"So now maybe you're even," he suggested. "Why don't you quit while you can?"

She looked at him with a faint frown. "There's the businessman talking again. Protect your investment, caution, caution! I'm not built like that. I'll bet till I have recovered everything my father lost. It's what I owe my family."

"But surely, Hisako, there's more to life than horse racing? Isn't there anything else you want to do?"

"Of course there is," she replied firmly. "I want to be the number one hostess in this cabaret."

"And that's all?"

"That's all."

"And how does one become number one?"

"Oh, you have to be popular with the customers, wear classy dresses, and give service so good the customers remember you. It's not easy."

He smiled. "Not if you like horses more than men, maybe. What is your rank now?"

She hesitated. "Number ten."

"With your looks and style? We must correct that. Now!"

He signaled a waiter and asked for the manager. A short, fat man in a white coat and a bow tie appeared, solicitously ducking his head and rubbing his hands together.

"Is there something wrong, sir? If so, we will correct it."

"No, I'm just curious. How much does your number one girl earn?"

The manager looked at him sharply.

"I'm not after trade secrets," added Kikuji. "I'm just very curious about your way of life here."

The manager pursed his lips thoughtfully. "I don't suppose it would do any harm to tell such a thing to a gentleman like yourself. Well, then, my number one hostess takes in just about one hundred yen each month. She is very good at her work."

"I'm sure. Now, I would like to pay you one hundred yen a month to make my friend Hisako here your number one hostess. Can that be done?"

The fat man puffed his cheeks and exhaled sharply. "Oh, anything can be done, anything at all—if it's paid for. And you will do all this for her by yourself?" The manager could hardly believe his ears.

"Exactly so. Here is the first installment, and the rest will be sent you regularly." He held out a hundred-yen bill. The cabaret official took the money, but remained at the booth, frowning and chewing his lip.

"It isn't quite that easy, sir. The hostess's main patron usually comes and names her each month. Without that the other girls would think themselves cheated, I think."

"Very well. I'll come when I can. And when I can't, I'll take care

223

of all the details." The manager bowed low to Kikuji, and, without giving Hisako more than a quick glance, hastened away to make the appropriate arrangements.

Hisako sat opposite him with a bored, vague expression on her face, pulling deeply on her cigarette from time to time.

"Aren't you glad you're number one hostess now?" said Kikuji, enjoying his manipulation.

"I'd rather win at odds," she responded, tapping her cigarette to remove the ash. "You deal always in certainties. That's not much fun."

She did not bother to thank him. How different she was from the other women he had been benefactor to over the years. They had been grateful, each in her own way. But Hisako simply did not care. She had wanted to *win* the number one spot; instead, she had been given it. If he had rigged a horse race so that she had won a bet, she would have been angry with him. Perhaps she was so now. But he could not stay to find out. He was expected at the Hamayu Teahouse. She accompanied him through the noisy cabaret to the door, her pleated skirt swinging to her step as a kimono never would. As he left, she waved her hand slightly and turned away.

Tsuruhachi awaited him and helped him change for the party.

"This is no big thing, Tsuruhachi," he explained. "Just O-Fuku and a few young geisha. No company manners. I want to relax."

He told the jester about Hisako and the arrangement he had made to make her the number one hostess. Tsuruhachi snickered appreciatively. "How pleasant to dip into the cabaret world, and with the help of the universal fixer, money, change things around to suit yourself. I'll be delighted to deliver your number one hostess money any time you can't go. It will make me feel like a god, altering the affairs of mortals. And, if I may say so, she is a very meaty little morsel of a mortal, that one!" And he laughed his curiously thin, high-pitched neigh of a laugh.

When the three youthful geisha arrived, Kikuji greeted them courteously. "I wanted your company tonight. You mustn't put yourselves out to entertain me. Let's just enjoy ourselves freely." Tsuruhachi performed a few of his stunts, but the geisha were not called upon to sing or dance. They talked with each other and with Kikuji, and enjoyed the relaxed quality of the evening. When

O-Fuku showed up, they thanked her for inviting them to this very special evening where they were guests and not performers. While they chatted quietly with her, Kikuji talked almost compulsively about the Polka Dot Cafe to Tsuruhachi.

"I'm infinitely more at home in the atmosphere of a teahouse. But in that cabaret I experience a world utterly new to me: a rather sordid world, really, where the inhabitants all seem to me to have no homes, no tradition. Perhaps it's the fascination of evil, and I'm becoming a decadent." He laughed. "But I doubt it."

O-Fuku listened half to him, half to the prattling of the geisha. When his cup was empty, she poured sake for him. The geisha were arguing about drama. One of them suddenly slammed her cup down on the table and shouted angrily, "What do you two know about it? The way you rave about Narikomaya, I'll bet you would lick the dirt he walks on!"

The other two laughed at her and one of them answered, "We'd be glad to lick the ground he walked on. But first we think your favorite actor, Jusho, should kiss the footprint of his master. Everything he knows comes from Narikomaya. And he could stand a few more lessons in acting techniques even now, I think."

Jusho's advocate was red with anger. "I shouldn't talk with ignorant people about the theater. If you haven't been conscious of the flowering of Jusho's talent as an insightful and moving actor this past six months, it's because you've been chattering with each other and not watching the stage. Such people shouldn't be allowed in the theater. They spoil it for serious spectators."

"Oh, these serious spectators," laughed her opponent. "Did they hold an election for serious spectators only, to make Jusho the number one actor? I don't understand these serious spectators. They seem to prefer a pretty young boy to the mature man of genius."

Jusho's defender turned her round face beseechingly to Kikuji. He could see that in her irritation she was near tears. "I need your counsel in this argument, Master. They are two against one!"

Kikuji looked benignly at her and smiled. "I'm not much of a judge in these matters, I'm afraid. You had better ask O-Fuku. She loves the theater."

"Of course, of course," said the geisha. "Say you agree with me, O-Fuku, dear!"

O-Fuku calmly poured Kikuji a cup of sake. "There's a lot to what you say, I suppose. Jusho is talented and, like any young man, he is still on his way up and hasn't reached his full capacity. Of course, he doesn't come from a long line of actors, and he has no patron backing him. He cannot at present be compared with the greatness of Narikomaya."

"You seem to be saying yes to both sides," said Kikuji.

"No, no, Master. She sees the charm and liveliness of Jusho," said the geisha, beaming now that her position had received unexpected support. She turned to O-Fuku and gushed, "When he speaks, he is so passionate. And he is so well formed. And his eyes. Oh, those eyes!"

O-Fuku's own eyes were downcast as she busied herself with the sake bottle. "Indeed, yes," she agreed. "He does have nice eyes."

"Tsuruhachi," said Kikuji. "I am tired." He made a quick, inconspicuous gesture toward the geisha.

"All right, girls, all right!" intoned Tsuruhachi in his nasal twang. "It's time to close up shop now. Master has had a very busy day, and he wants to rest. So you're free to go on to your next party if you have one scheduled. We don't need you here any more."

The girls were distressed at the early end to their evening, but they courteously spoke their farewells, bowed, and departed. Tsuruhachi moved behind Kikuji and prepared to make him comfortable.

"You too, Tsuruhachi, if you please," said his master.

"But of course." The jester bowed to Kikuji, looked sidelong at O-Fuku, and stepped into the hall, closing the sliding panel behind him.

The room which had before seemed small and intimate now seemed enormous. Kikuji and O-Fuku sat without speaking. Kikuji stared at her. She kept her eyes on the table as she cleaned up. She seemed perfectly calm. It was as though nothing out of the ordinary had occurred. She was incredible.

When finally he spoke, his voice sounded strangely hoarse to his ears. "O-Fuku, you have been seeing Jusho." It was a flat statement, and she did not immediately reply. "Have you not?" he added, glaring.

"Yes," she replied calmly as she continued putting the sake cups on her tray and wiping the table dry. "Yes. I've seen him."

Her complete calmness flustered him. He had expected at very least a blush, a stammer, some sign of guilt. There was nothing.

226

He offered his sake cup to her. She took it and filled it to the brim. In her usual graceful fashion, she took it to her mouth without spilling a drop, inhaled it in the way peculiar to her, and put it down on the table without a tremor. She drank the way she bedded a man: no anticipation, one great instant of fulfillment, and no remembrance. When she finished, she was finished. And yet, under that never-failing calmness was a great reservoir of passion which never diminished. What a contradictory person she was.

"When did it start with him?"

"About—last spring."

The excursion on Lake Biwa had taken place in July. She had been sleeping with that young actor for three or four months before taking on Kikuji.

"Do you love him?" He hated himself for asking. By doing so he sacrificed the advantages of his social status and wealth. Almost, he was acknowledging Jusho as a rival on equal terms with himself! But he had to know.

"He is very—how shall I say?—very sweet sometimes. He is very young, and he makes me feel almost maternal in a way." She smiled thoughtfully.

"Do you—meet with him often?" Again he hated himself for asking.

"Not very often. Once in a while. And always after midnight." She said it clearly, matter-of-factly, and Kikuji's cheeks burned.

Long-established tradition said that the rich patron gets the time from early evening until ten o'clock with the geisha, and the good-looking customer gets the hours between ten and midnight. After that, the youthful lover has his opportunity. O-Fuku had been referring to this hierarchy of customers. The young lover does not pay; rather, he makes up for his poverty by doing exactly what the lady requires, whether a massage, sympathy, or sexual acrobatics. This was common knowledge in Kikuji's world. Saying, as O-Fuku had done, "Always after midnight," was a modest enough disclaimer. What it suggested delicately was that, whatever the adjustments she had to make to survive in the world of geisha and servant maids, O-Fuku still maintained a jealous guard over the small vestige of her individuality which allowed her any freedom of choice. Her calm assertion of this freedom, he suddenly understood, was an act of ultimate desperation. She was appealing to his magnanimity.

227

And, looking into himself, he found that he hadn't any. Not in this instance.

"O-Fuku!"

The word lingered on the night air. She remained quiet and motionless, patiently awaiting the next word. But he had none. In his misery he found nothing adequate to say. But something must be said if silence was not to make of itself an impenetrable barrier.

"O-Fuku—if I were to buy you your own home? Would you be my mistress? Mine alone? Could we do that?"

O-Fuku's gaze, until now safely downcast, caught his in startled directness. He plunged on.

"Let us forget Jusho and what he represents in your life. In terms of physical capability, I don't think I need apologize to Jusho. I am just afraid that, to you, his childish love represents freedom, while mine means that you are caught, caged, and restricted. And that shouldn't be."

He fanned himself distractedly, then drank some sake. "It is so hard for me to put it into words. I am tired of being merely a parlor patron. I want to settle down with you. Let me buy you a house. Be my mistress. Let me love you!"

She had been looking at him intently, and, now that he had finished saying what he had to say, she continued looking at him in silence. But suddenly her alert posture changed; her shoulders sagged, and she looked quietly at her hands in her lap.

"It would be no good," she said softly. "I am a good head waitress. Sometimes I think I'm the best of my kind in Osaka. Certainly I'm in the best teahouse in Osaka. From my vantage point, I see the whole human comedy. I know intimately the private lives of many of the most important men in the country. And from this I have learned that the most dangerous thing of all is to give yourself really and fully to anyone. If you give yourself, they take it, and you are no longer free. Only a little, tiny bit of me is free, but, oh, Master, how I treasure that little tiny bit! Jusho could never claim me, but you can buy me without thinking twice about it. Don't you see?"

It was Hisako's race track all over again. He had made her number one at the Polka Dot Cafe, and she hated him for it. The bet was rigged. He moved to get up, but she put out her hand and held him.

"Please, no. Don't go in this angry mood. You are unlike any other gentleman I've ever known. You have made no demands on me beyond the most terrible demand of all: that I love you to the exclusion of all other people and things. And why should I lie to you when you of all people I most respect and love? I *can't* exclude everything but you. I would be bored and so would you."

She helped herself to sake. "I think you are a connoisseur. A collector of rareties. You collect perfections as they appear in a variety of women. I am honored to figure in your collection. Let me continue to be the perfect head waitress. I shall take care of Kawachiya's customers. And when you desire, I shall be meekly grateful that I may solace the owner of Kawachiya's, taking in my arms a man whom I love beyond all others. Let me be, as you might say, your nurse, to speed you back on your way to vigorous living and contentment."

She held his wrist, and, guided by her touch, he moved to her, putting his head in her lap, looking up at her. "You seem old and wise beyond your years tonight," he said dreamily.

She smiled down at him. "A mistress-nurse, such as the old shoguns had in their youth?"

He smiled agreement. "Just so. Sleep with me tonight."

She looked at him. He thought he saw a faint tightening of her eyebrow, the merest suspicion of reluctance.

"Jusho expects you after midnight?" he asked quietly.

She looked at him sharply with a half-smile. "No more of that, sir. Let us go."

In the dim, luxurious atmosphere of their inn room, they prepared for the night. O-Fuku, fresh from the bath, had loosened the knot at the back of her head, and long strands of lustrous black hair tumbled down over her collar band. She was combing it, and the comb, as it ran through her hair, made a faint rustling sound. Kikuji sat behind her drinking beer after his bath. With each stroke of the comb came the smooth, almost melodious sound of the hair. She uttered a surprised exclamation, and arched herself backward as he pulled gently. When she began to fall, he caught her easily in his other arm and gently lowered her to the tatami mat. He buried his hands in her hair, and said, "In just this way does a woman swallow up a man!" He wound his arms in the hairs close to her head and

229

brought her mouth to his. They held each other tightly. At a slight pause in their savage lovemaking, he said, "Is it like this with Jusho?"

"He is a child," she said, gasping for breath. "He has just experienced for the first time the beauty of the body and is wide-eyed in discovering the wonder of it all. But you—well, you are no child."

Her hair was wet with her perspiration. Kikuji, quiet by her side at last, was also bathed in sweat. He stared up at the finely grained cedarwood ceiling.

"You look exhausted," she said.

He nodded. Never with Ponta or Ikuko had he felt so competely used up. As he studied the ceiling, he became aware of a faint wailing sound in the distance. As it continued, he realized that it was a fire siren. Since it was far away, he felt no worry. Gradually he began to fall asleep. But the other inhabitants of the inn, disturbed by the siren, were beginning to move around, slam doors, and pad about the corridor. He reluctantly got up, and walked to the verandah at the end of the hall. Far to the south, he could see the light of the flames against the night sky. He turned to the inn's errand boy standing beside him.

"Do you know where it is?"

"Near the Semba District, I think, sir."

Kikuji turned and rushed back into the hallway to a phone. Hastily he gave the number of Kawachiya's. An apprentice answered. As he stammered nervously in response to his master's sharp question, Hidesuke took over the phone.

"The fire is in Junkeicho, Master, near Sanoya's place!"

"All right. Now, listen. I want you to get our volunteer firemen together and take them over to the fire as fast as you can."

"They are all awake and getting on their firefighting clothes now. I'll have them there in no time."

"By the look of that fire, you had better," said Kikuji. "I'll meet you there. Bring my outfit."

He hung up the phone and found O-Fuku at his elbow with his street clothes. He dressed hastily. O-Fuku had called a taxi and it was waiting for him when he went out the front door. She gave the driver directions.

"This gentleman must get to a merchant's fire call in the Semba area. Go as fast as you can."

She threw an envelope containing a tip to the driver, and signaled goodbye to her lover. He waved gratefully to her as the car moved away. How efficient she was. He glanced at his watch. It was a little before one o'clock. How would she spend the rest of the night?

At the south end of Shinsai Bridge, an excited young apprentice from Kawachiya's stood holding his fire lantern high. As soon as he recognized Kikuji he came running up to the car with a spare fire-fighting outfit. Kikuji climbed into the trousers, stuffing his expensive kimono in quickly. Then he put on the *happi* coat with the firm's crest on the back, and, guided by the apprentice, joined his employees. Their massed fire lanterns blazoned forth the company crest in a way that made Kikuji's heart swell with pride. He greeted Hidesuke quickly, and with the group at his heels began trotting across the bridge. A crowd of spectators had gathered to watch the fire.

"Excuse us, please! Fire call to a merchant in distress! Let us through, please!"

They held their lanterns high and kept close together, making an impressive spectacle. The crowd parted genially. A few lively watchers shouted at them.

"Come on, Kawachiya's! Get in there and fight!"

"Put it out and buy up the goods before the competition gets here!"

It was almost like a sporting event. They knew that when fires broke out the merchants hurried to each other's aid, and they waited to cheer the first company of firefighters and to make fun of the last.

From the eaves of Sanoya's store the flames were curling and darting with a great crackling roar. The main part of the house had not yet begun to burn, although smoke was coming from the roof. The regular firemen had arrived and were connecting their hoses. Kikuji's men went into the store by the side entrance, where there were as yet no flames, and began passing out the goods stored inside. Occasionally the wind would drive a gust of smoke into their faces, and they would cough and laugh. But they never stopped passing out the bales of material from the store. Hidesuke, his glasses gone in the excitement, was directing the operation. Kikuji watched alertly, waiting for any new development in the fire. Flames were still hissing from the signboard and eaves of the building. The professional firemen at last got their hoses connected and their pumps going; water spurted in great streams through the windows at the front of the store. Kikuji looked at the pile of goods his men had rescued, and, judging by his own store, figured that they must have saved a major portion of Sanoya's capital. And they were not yet finished. As the firemen sprayed the front, they moved slightly toward the rear, and continued the process of evacuating all the moveables from the house.

The workers from other companies now began to arrive, and, finding Kawachiya's men busily engaged in emptying the burning house, they joined in. The firemen were on the roof by now, and the blaze seemed less bright. Suddenly, Kikuji heard a militant chant:

> *Wa Sho! Wa Sho!*
> Fire call, fire call!
> *Wa Sho! Wa Sho!*
> Fire call!
> Safe and sound!

And, before he had time to react, he found himself almost knocked off his feet by a group of enthusiastic volunteer firemen. They were from Someichi's Clothiers. The people they had jostled jeered at them angrily.

"The fire is all over, brother! You slept through it! No need to knock me over! A half-hour ago you might have done some good! Go on home and sleep!"

Someichi's men were crestfallen. They walked slowly toward the piles of merchandise saved by the other volunteers, and attempted to be of use sorting the goods.

As the fierce crackle of burning wood declined in intensity, Hidesuke, grimy and weary, came to his employer to report. "We did a good job, Hidesuke," said Kikuji exuberantly. "We were here first, and we saved the larger portion of Sanoya's goods!"

Hidesuke wiped the sweat from his face with the sleeve of his *happi* coat. "Yes, indeed," he replied. "Thanks to your calling me so promptly on the phone."

Kikuji clapped him on the shoulder. "No, no. You had the men already out of bed and ready by the time I called."

232

The assistant manager smiled vaguely. "I try to be ready for anything, of course."

Water splashed off the roof and soaked them. Hidesuke held a lantern, long since extinguished by the water. As they stood watching the last remnants of the fire being put out, an apprentice ran up to Kawachiya's master to say that he had located Mr. Sanoya. He led him around toward the ruined storefront. In the street was a large crowd of clerks and apprentices who had come, just as the men from Kawachiya's had, in response to the fire call of a merchant in distress. But Kawachiya's had arrived first, and with their lanterns and their orderly ranks had made a fine appearance. Kikuji bowed as he recognized the wife of Someichi, the clothing merchant. She was passing out food to the hungry fire callers. Other merchants' wives, assisted by their maids, were circulating about with baskets of food. He frowned. Where was Sei? She and O-Toki ought to be here.

Slowly, he walked toward the ceramics store next to the still-smouldering building. Sanoya was sitting on a cushion in the room adjoining the entrance. He was in conversation with several merchants, discussing the fire and thanking them for having come so promptly to his aid. He wore a short *haori* coat over his night kimono. Kikuji recalled the image of the spry, lively fellow who had dominated so many of his parties, and saw scant resemblance in the huddled figure sitting before the alcove, mumbling repetitiously about the shock of the catastrophe he had experienced. His eye brightened in friendly recognition when he saw Kikuji.

"My good friend!" he said.

"I came to see how you are making out," replied Kikuji. "How fortunate that no one in your family was hurt."

But Sanoya refused to take refuge in polite conversation. He bowed before the younger man until his forehead touched the tatami mat.

"But for your quick and disciplined employees, I would by now have had nothing left. They saved most of my merchandise. I shall never forget what you have done for me. Never!"

"I am glad to have been of use, certainly, but you would have done the same for me, I know. And I am embarrassed to admit that my men got here sooner than I did. I should have been leading them

to the spot, but I was not at home when the alarm came. It was—
unavoidable. But I met them here."

"No, no. No apologies. They came running in like soldiers on
dress parade, but faster. I never saw anything so beautiful! They
swung in and went to work without wasting a minute. They must
sleep at home with their firefighting uniforms right beside their
beds." Sanoya looked at him long and soberly. "And you, Mr. Kawachiya, are a great *bonchi*, a master among merchants. Always you
are ready. Always you know what to do. You break away even from
the soft arms of a lady, and put on a firefighting outfit over your
good clothes just to help out a friend. And even with such impedi-
ments, you are the first to get here. A *bonchi*, a master of merchants!" And again Sanoya bowed.

He had spoken in a low voice so that no one else heard. Kikuji
realized that his expensive dark blue kimono of matted silk, which
showed under his firefighting jacket, was enough for the sharp-eyed
old merchant to form his conclusions on.

As he returned to the street, he saw O-Toki with three of the
housemaids carrying a large basket. He went up to them as they
were setting the basket down. "Where have you been? Why were
you so slow getting here?"

"I'm sorry, Master, but the lady of the house ordered us to make
something very special, so that those eating it would remember
Kawachiya's," O-Toki replied.

Kikuji shook his head angrily. "In an emergency, all that counts is
speed! The men who came on fire call would have been glad to have
had something simple and filling, rice balls and pickled plum, even.
But you had to do the fancy thing—" He paused an instant, then
asked, "Where's my mother?"

"She said she wasn't feeling well, sir, and went back to bed."

By a great effort he managed not to show his anger. Even in an
extreme emergency she kept on playing games! The world of reality
was simply too dirty for her to touch. Still, he tried to conceal his irritation at his mother from O-Toki.

"I am glad she is taking care of herself. Please present the food to
the Sanoya family with courtesy and respect, and then help them
dole it out to the fire callers."

The fire, which had seemed almost out, suddenly spurted up in a
great tongue of flame. For a few moments it illuminated the crowd

in the street, and, among the many faces, he glimpsed O-Fuku's. He had thought that quite possibly after he had driven off to the fire, she might go to Jusho. But she was here, looking tense and worried. He was ashamed of his suspicions. She had not yet seen him. He slipped behind her in the darkness and confusion, and slid his arms under hers through the kimono's armholes, and reaching around from either side touched her breasts. They were round and firm but moist with perspiration. As he did so, he whispered in her ear.

"O-Fuku, let's do it once more, while our skins still smell of fire smoke."

She nodded, trembling slightly in his arms. Looking around quickly to make sure that he had not been observed, he pressed his cupped hands once more to her breasts and then quickly drew out his arms. The fire was not extinguished; he would never be missed. Quietly the two of them slipped away.

Back at the inn, Kikuji took off the slightly singed *happi* coat. He had not had time to put on underclothes when the fire was discovered, so, when he took off his kimono he stood before her in a state of naked excitement. In an instant her clothing was in a heap, and she knelt, embracing him around the thighs. He closed his eyes in near-intoxication, and sank down beside her. Their hands roved in passionate exploration, above, below, between, in, with the speed and lightness of quicksilver. Everywhere from each other they inhaled the dense, musky smell of smoke. With gasps and small moans, they struggled their dark way into oneness; their bodies tensed in ecstatic expectation, and then after climax, relaxed into the profound quietude of utterly sated appetite. Kikuji emerged, finally, from the sexual trance, and moved to one side of her. He began tracing his way down her smooth side with one finger.

"O-Fuku."

No answer.

"O-Fuku!"

"Mmh?"

"No more Jusho! All right?"

"Mmmh-hmh."

Seven

Kikuji stood at the rear entrance to the house and looked out over the river. It was a brisk, sparkling fall day such as he loved. He heard Wasuke and Hidesuke coming, and with a sigh straightened up, grasped his clipboard, and walked to one of the five storage vaults in the yard. Tomorrow was the beginning of the annual fall sale. In the old days, the sale had occurred on the day of the merchants' festival of thanksgiving to Ebisu, their patron deity; but, since the accession of the present emperor in 1926, it had expanded to five days: two before and two after the festival day. Thrifty Osaka denizens bought all the clothing they needed for the year at the festival, for the merchants on this special occasion lowered their prices far below cost. Kikuji tried to feel public spirited as he contemplated his losses after each occurrence of this yearly event.

Hidesuke opened the heavy door of the nearest storehouse, and they prepared to inventory the merchandise.

"You wish to proceed as in former years, I suppose," said Wasuke, "that is, any slightly soiled tabi, and any which seem in any way shopworn should be placed in the pile of irregular merchandise?"

Kikuji smiled slightly. "Let's be generous in our estimates and make it a good festival. We'll get back the 30 percent mark-off by winning the good will of our customers. I'm sure the god Ebisu would regard it as good business."

Wasuke laughed a thin, old man's laugh. "Ebisu should see the way some of these customers at a sale grab for their bargains."

After accumulating a large pile of tabi for the sale, they divided it into two heaps.

"Is this enough for your friend, Mr. Sanoya?" asked Hidesuke, pointing to the smaller heap.

236

"I think so," replied Kikuji.

Through the doorway he saw his grandmother shuffling toward him across the sunlit yard. He continued with his work as though he had not noticed her, and walked inside the vault. She called to him, and he came out immediately.

"Grandmother. What brings you here to our place of work?" Surprised by the old lady's unusual visit, Hidesuke and Wasuke busied themselves with tidying up bales of merchandise in the vault.

At the sunny entrance, Kino squinted in, trying to adjust her eyes to the darkness of the interior. She tucked up the long skirt of her kimono and crossed the threshold, looking sharply into every corner.

"Grandmother! This is no place for you. You'll soil your kimono," said Kikuji.

"No matter!" snapped the old lady. She waved toward the two piles of tabi. "You're still helping out old Sanoya, aren't you?"

"Of course."

"Why do you say, 'Of course'? What's so 'of course' about it? He is imposing on you!"

"Sanoya himself at first refused my offer of assistance. He too said he would be imposing on me. I told him that I was investing in his reputation, and that, once he got on his feet again, he could pay me back. He is a good risk. Also, he is a good friend."

"I don't know why you bother," she replied.

"He depends on me. A lot of workers depend on him. Someday he will pay me back. It is good business to help out an old associate in trouble. Besides, when I came to his aid at the fire call, I took on this responsibility. We saved most of his goods, but his warehouse of reserve supplies was destroyed. He is worth saving."

"You've been saving him for the last three months! Maybe they did that sort of thing in the old days, but not in this day and age. Just because you put out his fire, you don't have to rebuild his whole business."

"I'm sorry, Grandmother, but I must abide by a tradition which I respect. If I hadn't wanted to help him through to a complete business recovery, I should never have bothered to join with him and my other associates in our fire call arrangement. It is understood to be insurance against loss, and I must help him."

She stared at him.

"You are a fool," she said softly. "Soon every bankrupt ne'er-do-well will be burning up his rubbish and making you pay to build him up for a second start."

"But I have to trust my friends. If my home and business were to burn up, I would hope for their support. The chance to help doesn't come often, and, when it does, it should be given completely, even lavishly, without thought of saving a little here or a little there. Grudging help is worse than none." He hesitated for an instant, then added, "That is why I was upset when Mother went back to bed instead of coming to the fire call with O-Toki to pass out food to the firefighters. Courtesy at a time of crisis is hard to achieve, I know, but it is worth trying for."

"This would be all very well if it were Sumitomo or Mitsubishi that had burned down. But it's only old Sanoya. We're a family of merchants two hundred fifty years old. Stop acting like everyone's servant!"

Her eyes flashed. She looked like some old hawk about to pounce.

"And with all your fine talk about helping an associate, what did you really go to the fire for? I'll tell you: you went to pick up a prostitute and slink off with her like any cheap workman with a case of hot pants."

So this was it. This was what she had come to say.

He turned to Wasuke and Hidesuke and gave them a quick sign to leave. After they had gone, the silence prolonged itself. A tiny window behind Kino let in enough light to silhouette her thin outline so that she looked like a huge, black shadow puppet.

Kikuji busied himself, pretending to inventory some of the bales.

"Well?" she croaked hoarsely. "Aren't you going to say anything? You didn't come home after the fire and you left Sanoya's place with a common prostitute. It's all over town, of course. The priest came recently to perform a ceremony at our household shrine, and he had heard it from someone else. Everybody knows that the Kawachiya heir is prowling around like a dog in heat. Was she a good one? Did she teach you some new tricks? Where did you go: to an inn or just behind the barn in some alleyway?"

"Grandmother, please. Your imagination is far worse than anything I could have done."

"Who *was* that woman?" said Kino.

It was the inn, of course. Everyone had been wakened by the fire, and they had seen him drive off toward the Semba District. And later on he must have been a fairly memorable sight as, still dressed in his smudged and smoky firefighter's outfit, he climbed out of the cab in front of the inn with O-Fuku. It had been indiscreet to return in that fashion. But it was too late to change matters now. How much did they know about O-Fuku?

"She is a friend of Sanoya's and she's present at most of his parties. She's a pleasant person, and, after the fire, we went off together to have a drink and relax."

"Relax. Hah!"

"Oh, come, now, Grandmother. Anyone who can think of the horrors you dream up is not going to be much bothered when her grandson spends a night with a lady."

Kino looked at him speculatively. "Then this one is not—still another mistress to be added to your payroll? But even that I could stand better than your taking up with cheap prostitutes. That is undignified."

He frowned. "You know—Sanoya knows—I'm not stingy. My women will be provided for. They will either have their own houses, as Ponta and Ikuko do, or they will meet me at the right places. I can't stand a stingy patron, and I won't live like one. I think, though, that you should realize that I am already past the age of thirty, and I need no instruction from you in arranging my private life."

There was a rustling of silk and Sei, dressed immaculately in a celadon green kimono, appeared, holding Hisajiro by the hand. The boy looked at his father warily, and clung to his mother's skirt. As she moved to enter the dark storage vault, the child whimpered and pulled at Sei's kimono, as though afraid of the darkness.

Kikuji knelt down beside Hisajiro with a smile. "Come on, Hisabon. Let's bounce around on that big pile of tabi there. I'll swing you over to it."

He raised the child playfully, but immediately Sei broke into protests, and Hisajiro moaned in terror. Kikuji set him down.

"Don't do that again," said Sei, hard-eyed. "You hardly ever pay attention to him, and, when you do, you frighten him to death. Suppose your father had treated you like that."

Looking at his son, now barely visible behind his grandmother, Kikuji wondered how he himself had ever survived the upbringing of Kino and Sei. Surely, they must have hated him when he was born for the sin of being a boy. And then they must have tried, just as they were trying now with Hisajiro, to turn him into a dependent household pet. But his resentment of Kino and Sei was balanced by his awareness that he wasn't much of a father. Occasionally he would try to play with his son, but it was merely another chore to be done and gave him no pleasure. He recalled bitterly the little scene of a week before when he had suggested that he and his son play at samurai and bandits, but Hisajiro had held the stick his father had given him slackly in his hand, looking at Kikuji in fear and puzzlement.

"Don't you want to play samurai with your daddy, Hisa-bon?" he asked.

"I—I don't like sticks. They might hurt somebody," the child said, watching his father cautiously. He brightened suddenly. "Maybe we could fold colored papers and make cranes or turtles, the way Grandma does. The ones she makes are so pretty."

Kikuji had given up then, and, looking at his child hiding from the dark and his own father behind his grandmother's skirts, he felt hugely depressed now.

"But what are you two talking about in this dingy storehouse?" asked Sei. "Couldn't it wait until you were comfortably seated in the living room?"

Kino moved over to her with the grotesque smile she reserved for her gossip sessions, and said in a low, throaty whisper, "I've been telling him what I think of his latest escapade."

"What's an escapade?" asked Hisajiro.

"Hush, child!" said Kino. Then, resuming her hoarse whisper, she said to Sei, "I'll tell you later."

Kikuji looked at them with rising impatience. "Yes. Very well. You two can talk about it to your heart's content, but in the house. I am very busy trying to organize tomorrow's sale."

He turned back to his work, and Kino, with a slight shrug of her shoulders, led the way back to the main house with Sei and Hisajiro.

It was already past midnight when he arrived in front of her house in Unagidani. As he walked up the paving stones to the threshold, the door opened and Ikuko stood before him. She must have heard the cab and rushed to be ready. Her hair was still in the *marumage* style of married women, and her kimono was pleasantly simple. She looked at him closely as he came into the entryway.

"You look exhausted," she said. "Come upstairs and rest."

She hurried ahead of him to set everything in order for his sudden visit. Five minutes later, he was stretched out on soft bedding, clothed in a loose night kimono. Ikuko sat quietly beside him as he puffed reflectively on a cigarette.

"The autumn sale keeps you very busy," she suggested.

He laughed, and began reciting in the singsong accents of the street huckster.

> Shop and save, shop and save,
> On the festival day of Ebisu!
> Stop and see, stop and see,
> The value of what we now give you—
> —Cheap!

"I've heard apprentices shouting that so many times today, I think that on my deathbed I shall sit up and chant it."

She smiled, but stared at him uneasily. "No talk of deathbeds. Bad luck." Then she smiled down at him. "Besides, you love every moment of it."

"After my store had settled into the routine of the sale, I walked down the street, mixing with the crowds of shoppers. Bargain hunters are wonderful people. They go along like prospectors for gold, clutching their treasures close to them, and looking here, there, and everywhere for more. You should've seen Sanoya's people! They had red and white banners up around the building to conceal the fire damage. The goods they had on sale at their tables along the street were mostly from Kawachiya's. It made me feel just fine to see it!"

"Are you set for tomorrow's continuation of the sale?"

He looked at her cautiously.

"I'm not sure." The liveliness went out of his eyes. "I haven't been back to the store since noon."

"Oh?"

"You know—" he began, thoughtfully.

"Yes?" she prompted.

"I was just remembering something Tsuruhachi said to me once:

that through loving we become wiser, more compassionate, more interesting people—"

There was a pause, ended once again by that therapeutic encouragement to confidence: "Yes?"

"—And others, seeing how much we are loved and followed after, feel admiration and respect for us, as one must feel for people who have successfully learned not only how to earn a living, but how to live most intensely and fully—" Again he paused, not knowing how to continue.

"I suppose so," she said, leaning toward him and placing a cigarette between his lips. "I suppose that may be one of the reasons successful men collect mistresses as others collect stamps."

She was very matter-of-fact; there was no rebuke in her voice.

"I have never concealed from you that you were not my only mistress, Ikuko," he replied.

"Of course not. I am not complaining. I was just trying to follow your explanation; the more love, the more richly are one's human traits developed, isn't that it? You have me and Miss Ponta and Miss O-Fuku, and each one of us, in giving you our love, must also give you special problems to deal with."

His eyes widened in surprise. "How long have you known about O-Fuku?"

"For the last six months."

"And you've said nothing to me about her? All those nights when I left you early, and thought you wanted me to go home and get rested for a hard day's work ahead—all those nights, you *knew* I was going to O-Fuku's place?"

Ikuko nodded.

"But why didn't you speak up about it?"

"You know the rules which govern our behavior."

"Rules! It's incredible!"

"The rules tell us what will work. They are the distillation of the experience of many wise women over the ages who have had to deal with the same recurrent problems," she replied slowly and quietly.

His mouth twitched with irritation. He leaned closer to her. "Only two hours ago, I was thumping it into the fourth mistress! I'm glad you don't mind!"

His eyes took on a cruel glint; she closed hers as though refusing to see and to listen, but she remained motionless with her head resting on the box-pillow.

"Let me tell you about her," he said savagely. "Her name's Hisako. She's a hostess at the Polka Dot Cabaret. Maybe not a very good one, although I'm paying to have her rated number one. She wears short and expensive western-style dresses, has nice legs, and is crazy about horse-racing. Imagine that. My latest acquisition is a compulsive gambler! I've known her for some time, but we met today by chance while I was walking around the streets. She says it's the only way to do things: by chance. She hates a sure thing. You would love to meet her, you are so much alike!"

He laughed harshly and watched Ikuko's face for some expression of distaste. There was nothing. He plunged on, harsher still.

"With your ideas of thrift and propriety, Ikuko, you won't believe this, but I promised to buy her a whole damned race horse today. Imagine that, if you can!"

He rattled on at great length, like a radio advertisement in praise of a soap or a patent medicine, and watched Ikuko's reaction. But there was none. Her face in the dim light was like a Noh mask.

"Anyway, she is very lively in bed, and I'm quite used up by now."

As though she had been waiting for the words, she said, "You must be very tired. Go to sleep. Things will look better in the morning."

She stood up to unfold the blanket, and, as she did so, her skirt lifted to reveal a white underskirt lined with red silk.

"Ikuko. What is going on?"

She looked blankly at him. "What do you mean?"

"The red and white underskirt you're wearing! Is it—? Does it—?"

Her face reddened, and she lowered her eyes. "I had a feeling that you would come tonight, and I wore it so that you might know. You have the right."

Clumsily, he stretched out his hand and touched the underskirt, warm and flexible from the heat of her thigh.

"I should have noticed. You had to hang out a flag to tell me! How far along is it?"

"Only three months. No one would ever have noticed. But I

wanted you to know and so I made for myself this special kind of petticoat that a woman of the quarter wears when she wants to tell her patron she is having a child."

That, of course, was the point: it announced not only that she was pregnant, but that she intended to carry the child till birth and provide for it afterward. The patron, once he had started the process, had really very little to say about the matter.

"You—you—wish to keep the child?" he asked gruffly.

"Yes."

"Once it is born, you won't see much of it."

"Yes, of course. It will be sent to a foster home. It will have no legal claim on you as father," she replied.

"You know all this, and can accept it so easily."

"Not easily, Master. I have learned to accept—many things. It is better to abide by traditions than be destroyed by them. No woman can rebel and survive."

"You have thought of rebelling, then?"

"I accept life as it is," she said quietly. "All my life I have lived in Osaka. Its traditions are binding upon me."

He looked at her commiseratingly, "How old-fashioned you are."

"I guess so." She laughed softly. "I must live according to my nature."

She lit another cigarette for him, and then lay down quietly beside him on the bedding. He half closed his eyes as he smoked.

"Ikuko—" He started and stopped, unable to formulate his thoughts in words.

"Yes?" The insistent monosyllable hovered delicately in the darkness and silence of the room. It was her best weapon, he realized; a concentration of purpose, softened and feminized by deference. Suddenly, he was overwhelmed with pity for this resourceful woman who never complained, never scolded, always sought out understanding, even when there was little to be had. How many nights before this had she waited, dressed in her red and white underskirt, for him to come, only to realize in the small hours of the morning, that yet another night had passed without the familiar step on the walk, the hand on the door? And to this patient, faithful creature he had bragged insultingly of his most recent conquest. Ikuko, at least, was true to him. But he had parceled his affections out, and could give her only one-quarter of his attention. Surely such loyalty merited a better return? Did this multifaceted love of his enlarge his spirit, making him a wiser, more understanding person, as Tsuruhachi had suggested? Or would it bankrupt him utterly, leaving behind the shell of a hardened, conscienceless cynic? Feeling the warmth of her body as she lay quietly beside him, he felt confused and entangled.

"Ikuko," he said once again. With an effort he continued, "I've treated you badly."

She turned to him with a look of surprised concern in her eyes. "No, Master. I do not think so. All of us must grow into understanding of each other. And you have many women to understand. I am more fortunate. I have only one person I must study to understand and love."

She smiled gently and corrected herself. "No. Not one. Two now." And she touched her belly possessively.

There was a long silence. She heard the soft noise of the cigarette being snubbed against the glass ashtray. Suddenly he was leaning over her, gently kissing her cheeks, her neck, her hands.

"You are so good. I have not been behaving well. And you erase it all by pretending that it didn't happen. I almost lost my self-respect tonight, Ikuko. You've brought it back to me. You must keep it for me."

It was a long time before they slept.

After lunch on the third day of the New Year's Festival, he drove to Yonedaya's to see Ponta. He had to see all four of his ladies before the end of the day, and, while he looked forward to the visits, he tried to keep in mind his tight schedule. She greeted him at the doorsill, placing her hands before her on the mat, and touching her forehead to the floor. In her formal, crested kimono with its white collar she looked graceful and serene. He gazed at her for a moment, and then told her how beautiful she looked. She bowed her head in acknowledgement without saying anything. He was puzzled. Silence from Ponta was unnatural. When he took his seat on the cushion, she poured him sake, still without speaking. She didn't seem angry; indeed, she seemed to be suppressing a smile.

"What are you doing, my dear?" he said in feigned annoyance. "Have you made a resolution not to talk in the new year? That could cause a few problems. Let me see, now—"

He tried out a few signs with his fingers, as though using the alphabet of the deaf and dumb. She put the sleeve of her kimono over her mouth to conceal her laugh, but remained silent.

"No more of this. I like my women to be talkative. Say something!"

He grabbed the sleeve of the kimono which she held over her mouth and pulled on it. She gave a little shriek and lowered the sleeve, looking at it critically for any damage. Something was glittering in her mouth. She saw his stare and, too late, closed her mouth.

"Ponta, you have a diamond in your front tooth."

She reddened, smiled, and lowered her eyes.

"You didn't have it yesterday when you made your New Year's call on my mother and grandmother?"

She laughed aloud. "What would they have thought, to see me flaunting your wealth in that fashion? I have two caps for this tooth: the one, plain; the other—well, sparkling. Like a headlight in a Roll's Royce. They'll see me coming!"

She pulled out the tooth with the diamond embedded in it and showed it to him.

He stared at it for a moment. "My God. What will you do next?"

"Oh, you don't like it!" she wailed.

"It makes you look like a—a—one of those western Christmas trees!" (He had been on the verge of saying, "It makes you look like a prostitute!") "Displaying wealth like that is—well, it's not refined!"

"But when I wear a diamond in my ring, in my sash ornament, in my hairpin, you think it's refined enough. I have a very good dentist. He said it would start a new fashion."

"Well, I don't know. Maybe you can wear it when you're with me, but not in public and not at other parties. Will that do?"

"But how can I start a new fashion if nobody sees it? The reason I have all these rings and things is to show them off." She frowned, then arched her eyebrows as she looked at him with a faint smile. "But, of course. Whatever you say."

There was a cheerful commotion in the hallway, and five geisha came in to wish them a happy new year. After each had presented her greeting, Ponta opened her mouth and cleared her throat to respond, but, before she had uttered a sound, she caught Kikuji's glare, and she shut her mouth quickly. But not quickly enough. One of the geisha had caught a glimpse of her treasure.

"Hey, hey, hey! She's got a mouthful of diamonds. Open up! Open up! Let us see!" she shouted exuberantly.

Ponta kept her mouth shut tight and looked forlornly at Kikuji. Then, as she saw him shrug his shoulders, her worried expression turned into laughter, and she opened her mouth wide for their inspection.

"Oh, how wonderful!"

"Was it all your own idea, Ponta?"

"How lucky you are! We work hard and can't even get a ring!"

"How beautiful! You look just like an advertising poster!"

"If I had a diamond, that's what I would do with it!"

Kikuji sat off to the side drinking cold sake while they chattered. Suddenly they realized that he was not joining their conversation, and they excused themselves politely and left. Ponta looked at him speculatively.

"Are you angry?" she asked.

He shrugged indifferently. "It wouldn't do much good if I were."

"But please don't be angry with me," she pleaded. "I need a little diversion now and then. You only visit me once every eight days—it isn't much, is it? Can't I have more of your time?"

"But, Ponta, you know how it is with business responsibilities." He made a vague gesture with his cigarette.

She looked at him coldly. "Do you visit Ikuko every eight days too?"

"Oh, come now! Let's not bicker."

"And now you've added O-Fuku to your timetable, I hear. Every eight days for her too?" She spoke very politely, with a courteous smile on her face. But, despite conforming superficially to the etiquette which required geisha not to show jealousy, her eyes were wild with torment.

He was surprised. He hadn't told her anything about O-Fuku. "I have my work to do, you know. I can take time off only if I've carefully planned it."

She nodded, not looking directly at him. "I'm sure you do what's best."

For a moment he had thought that she was going to inspect the details of his timetable: one evening for Ponta, then Ikuko two days

247

later, O-Fuku two days after that, and, finally, Hisako. But as yet she had not heard of Hisako. He stole a glance at his watch, and she caught the look.

"And now—you are going to visit Ikuko and O-Fuku with your New Year's greetings?"

He nodded. Her wan expression upset him.

But suddenly a timid smile flooded over her face, and she looked into his eyes.

"Anyway, you came to see me first!" she said.

It was nearly three when Kikuji arrived at the Hamayu Teahouse. O-Fuku had the room warm and comfortable. He noticed that the charcoal pieces were covered in their own white ashes. She must have been waiting for him a long time. When he was seated, she placed herself in front of the table, bowed, and gave him the formal New Year's greeting: "Thank you for the favor you have shown me in the past; I hope I shall deserve it also in the year to come." Then she placed before him the traditional tray with its three red lacquered cups for the spiced New Year's wine. Ponta and Ikuko had had a chance to participate in New Year's greetings with him before this: as acknowledged mistresses, they had visited his mother's house on the second day of the new year and presented their good wishes. O-Fuku, however, still secretly his mistress, had had no chance before this to wish him well at the New Year. So she was treating him more formally than Ponta had, or Ikuko would. Again, he felt oppressed and wretched as he considered her feelings. First Ponta, now O-Fuku. What a mess he was making of their lives. But O-Fuku seemed placid and unhurried. Nothing was bothering her.

"Drink some of the New Year's sake," she suggested. "It's the very best I could find."

As the afternoon light waned, they sat toasting each other in the large ceremonial New Year's cups. Someone in the hall turned on the lights, and Kikuji could see O-Fuku more distinctly. He had offered her many drinks. Her capacity seemed endless. She sat straight and easy, with no sign of intoxication except, perhaps, the pink flush on the marble-smooth, almost translucent skin of her neck and shoulders. If Ponta was a lotus flower, O-Fuku was the sculptured masterpiece of a great artist. How different they were, and how much he loved those differences.

"Someday, O-Fuku, you're going to let me buy you a house so that you can settle down somewhere." He was not urging; it was a plain statement of fact.

She pursed her lips and looked questioningly at him. "If we made it official and you bought me a house, then I would have to present myself in a formal visit to your mother and grandmother, wouldn't I?"

"Yes, but that would be soon done with—"

"No," she replied calmly. "I would find it impossible. Perhaps I am just not docile enough to be a good mistress to you. Let's just keep it as it is."

"But you should have something. Suppose I take out an insurance policy on my life and make you the beneficiary?"

She gave him a stare of amused horror. "But that would be gruesome!"

"For your own protection, I should do it."

She put her hand gently on his, as though to restrain him. "Please. I have my faults, but greed is not one of them. Imagine pawing through the ashes of one's patron in the hope of getting lots of money. Let's leave that to storybook villains." She threw her head back and laughed, exposing the red flush of her throat and shoulders. He moved beside her, and placed his forefinger on her neck and pressed. When he removed it, there was a white impression from his finger, but the surrounding redness swiftly moved in to efface the white shadow of the finger. He looked into her eyes.

"I think, perhaps, you must now go on to your next lady," she said calmly.

When he reached Hisako's apartment, it was already past eight o'clock. He ran up the stairs to the second floor and knocked at the door of her room, but there was no response. When he was sure that she would not answer and was probably not at home, he opened his wallet, took out a key, and unlocked the door. The light was still on. There was not even a vase of flowers around to mark the New Year's holiday. A number of dirty dishes were on the table, marked with the crests of various takeout restaurants. He had moved her into this clean and new apartment several months ago. It had two rooms and a kitchen, but she had no interest in fixing it up. He opened the window in the larger of the rooms, and sat down beside it at a small

249

desk. Its surface was covered with a film of what he assumed, from texture and fragrance, to be face powder. A torn piece of letter paper had been dropped on the desk. On it, written in red lipstick, was the message, "The appointment was for six o'clock. I'm hungry." He recalled that he had once seen her coloring a betting slip on a horse which had lost with red lipstick. He had never seen her write with anything else. Just now, it seemed to express her anger vividly as she waited for him.

She was the most mercurial person he had ever met. Part of her charm was that her moods were rapid, flowing, and inexplicable, like quicksilver. She didn't, in any conventional sense, think. She felt. What felt good, she did. That night in the Polka Dot Cabaret, when he had offered to buy a horse, she had suddenly said, "You do that, and I'll do whatever you say: receive a monthly stipend or move to a better apartment, if you want. But only if you agree to two conditions: first off, you mustn't file me away the way you do the rest of your geisha friends. I'm your girl friend. You love me. That's the first condition."

"Yes," he had replied, smiling.

"And the second condition is almost as important: I can't go around cleaning house all the time. My thing is horses. I don't have time for houses. So get me a small apartment, if that's what you want for me, and don't fuss if I don't do flower arrangements and all that stuff. All right?"

"All right," he said gravely.

Handling her had been easier than he had expected. Her not being a geisha had helped: thorough as the Semba community was in watching over its members, it would hardly concern itself with girls working in places like the Polka Dot. He didn't need to worry about his relationship with her becoming known in some awkward fashion, and so he didn't worry about what others would think if his mode of setting her up in life was much less conventional than in the case of Ponta, Ikuko, and (if she would only let him take the appropriate steps) O-Fuku. And she wasn't as expensive as Ponta: those rings and diamonds had cost him more than any horse would. She had wanted him to be with her when she bought the horse, but he told her to pick whatever animal she liked. He was fascinated with her young, flowing, unpredictable body; he couldn't possibly share her wild race horse fever, even if she found it to be a defect in his makeup. Jewelry or a horse: it made no difference to him.

Nearly an hour had passed, and she had not returned. In the smaller room, he saw, through an opening of the sliding doors, a red velvet dress and a fur piece hanging. These were his latest presents to her; he guessed that, if she had been going to the Polka Dot, she would have worn them. In one corner of the room, he saw a large piece of paper. Picking it up, he found it was a racing sheet. She had marked it up in great detail with red pencil. She appeared to have studied the record of one four-year-old Arabian horse by the name of Wine Red. Kikuji tried pronouncing the name and decided he liked it. It sounded a bit raucous and impetuous: just the sort of name for Hisako's horse. Maybe it couldn't run very well: who cared? He took out the red lipstick from her desk and scribbled next to the horse's name, "Go ahead and buy it. Take a chance." Then he rose, walked out into the hall, and carefully locked the door behind him.

When at half-past nine he reached Ikuko's house, his eye was caught by the whiteness of the paper streamers attached to the New Year's pine branches outside her door. Over the wooden gate hung a sacred straw garland. In the alcove of the room upstairs, a young pine and peonies were arranged in a large and skillful bouquet. At the center of the room was a slender table holding ceremonial rice cakes. The house was spotless and perfect in its holiday adornment. To go from Hisako to Ikuko was like going from the raw, unpredictable emotions of youth to the wise forms and order of art. Ikuko received him in her formal, three-crested kimono. Already six months pregnant, she had covered her waist with a rather wide, stiff waistband. Her freshly done *marumage* hairdo was shiny and black with not a strand out of place. Such ordered perfection, he thought, is an ideal not often achieved, not even in Japan.

After the formal New Year's greetings were done with, she said, "I must apologize to you for not visiting your family yesterday, as I should have done. In my condition, I thought it not a very good idea."

He laughed. "Of course not. My mother and grandmother would have had a fit had they discovered there was to be another son."

251

He kept trying to look at her face and not her stomach. Pregnant women did not attract him. Once Sanoya had remarked to him that he thought there was nothing more beautiful on this earth than a pregnant woman, and that he, Sanoya, felt such a huge emotion on seeing a woman well along that he guessed it must be a violently sexual desire on his part. But he couldn't be sure: he was so old, maybe he was just feeling fatherly. Kikuji had no uncertainty about his reaction: he just wished the baby would get born and out of the way. With her usual skill in reading his reactions, Ikuko moved a table in front of her so that her shape was hidden. On it were the ceremonial red lacquer sake cups and wine.

"Just a little, for form's sake," he requested. "I've had my share."

"Ah. And are the other ladies—in good spirits?" she asked with modest circumspection.

"How like you!" he replied, his eyes shining. "You concern yourself about them for my sake. But, yes, to answer your question, they're fine: all dressed up in their new outfits."

He studied Ikuko's greenish black kimono.

"Ikuko, I like your kimono very much, of course, but—" He hesitated for an instant. "Why not wear something a little more lively and colorful? You are still a beautiful young woman. That kimono would be better on a matriarch of fifty."

She reddened. As she poured him some sake, he thought he saw that her hand was trembling slightly.

"I thought, since I was in this condition this year— Besides—" she hesitated and did not go on.

"Besides? Yes? What else?"

"Oh, Master." She looked at him and he was alarmed to see that her eyes were full of tears. "This is my unlucky year, you see. I'm thirty-three!"

He was puzzled. "What of it?"

"But everyone says that to have a baby in one's unlucky year is tempting fate. Oh, don't you see? I'm frightened, Master!"

She brought her handkerchief up to her eyes. He moved to her side and took her hand in his.

"Ah, Ikuko, you mustn't be such a fool," he said gently. "You, who are so orderly and sensible and good. You must rise above these peasant superstitions."

"I wish I could," she said gloomily, dabbing at her eyes with her

252

handkerchief. "But it's no laughing matter." She turned her tear-stained face earnestly toward him. "You must help me, Master."

"Of course, my dear. I'll do whatever you need. But I do hope you'll not get too upset—"

"Since having a baby in the unlucky year is so risky, please give me the exorcizing ceremony of the seven-colored hip sash to ward off evil. It must be done on the day of the beginning of spring to be effective. Will you do it for me?"

He laughed, and hugged her. "Of course. Anything for my little peasant with her superstitions. Stop worrying about it."

She smiled wanly and thanked him.

"I don't know much about this particular ceremony, so you will have to instruct me," he said. "You say it should be performed on March twenty-first?"

"Yes. When all new life is about to spring up. The multicolored sash symbolizes all the joys of youth and nature, and its brilliance is unpleasant to the dark spirits of the night. I must give one to all my friends. The flashier it is, the better they'll like it." Her vigorous speech was quite unlike her normally quiet, calm manner. She seemed almost feverish. But she paused for a moment, and twisted the handkerchief in her lap.

"I'm sorry about the expense. Especially now that we seem to be in a terrible business depression."

"I'm not worried about the expense," he chided. "I'm worried about the effect this superstition is having on your health and your peace of mind."

She looked at him again with that desolate smile on her face. "It's not superstition. Without the protective sash, I am helpless. At night, in the darkness, I feel the evil forces circling all around me, and then flowing into me, and through me—and into our baby, and through him— That was the way I went to sleep last night. I wished you were here. I dreamt terrible dreams. I am so frightened." She spoke in a low, almost inaudible voice, and fixed her eyes on the empty space before her, while her lips trembled convulsively.

Kikuji looked at her apprehensively. She needed help. The exorcism she asked for would do no harm. Always before she had faintly annoyed him by trying to make him save his money; he was glad to spend something on her, even if he disapproved of the superstitious attitude she was taking.

253

He turned the matter over to Tsuruhachi, who enjoyed organizing events of that sort. The clown was much interested.

"In these days of depression, all of us have demons which need to be exorcized. Business activity is depressed, our wallets are depressed, and our spirits are very depressed. Still, Ikuko has a much more old-fashioned kind of demon bothering her than this ultramodern demon of depression most of us are acquainted with. But I'll set up a fine affair with your backing. Nowadays, nobody spends money on anything except necessities. Ikuko's multicolored sash party will be a gala event. We will cure her, and end the depression at the same time. There's nothing I like more than reviving our fine old traditions." The reedy singsong of his voice almost disappeared in a greater resonance as he spoke of the congenial task which he contemplated. But the expressionless deadpan of his ugly face never changed. He went rushing off to various well-known speciality stores in Kyoto to order the necessary materials.

On the first day of spring, Kikuji finished his work quickly and went to Ikuko's house in the early afternoon. On opening the latticed front door, he found a colorful scene inside: multicolored sashes were everywhere, some spread out on the tatami mats, some folded and ready to be wrapped, and a pile of white boxes tied with ribbons to show that some had been completely packaged. Tsuruhachi, supervising the activities of several assistants, saw his boss and hurried toward him holding a bolt of cloth. As he came abreast of him, he opened his hand and out shot a multicolored sash directly across Kikuji's line of vision.

"Welcome to rainbow land, Master. Sorry we are so confused, but it was a rush order, and they had to hunt up some special vegetable dye hard to come by nowadays. So they didn't deliver our rainbows till early this morning. I'll go on wrapping them up, if you don't mind—" and he sat down to resume his task.

"They're—very pretty," Kikuji said vaguely, looking at the welter of colored cloths.

"It should scare any demon not colorblind," said Tsuruhachi. "It scares me when I look at more than one at a time. The ladies will love them. Just wait and see."

"My God. You have them hanging from the rafters. How many did you order?" Kikuji asked.

"I ordered a hundred of them, just as though I were buying a bunch of cheap giveaway hand towels. No sense in stinting when we're dealing with demons."

"But are there really that many people to receive the sashes? Ikuko is not very sociable, you know. I doubt that she has a hundred friends."

"Yes. Well, her friends are the proprietresses of teahouses. But I plan to give sashes to all the maids and waitresses she has been associated with. Once we've finished boxing our amulets, I shall lead my two assistants around town, delivering rainbows, a cheerful task completely congenial to my calling."

"How efficient you are."

"I try, sir, I try. And you will complete my plans for a fine defeat of Miss Ikuko's demon if you will present yourself at the Minoya Teahouse at five this evening." Tsuruhachi tossed another neatly tied box onto the growing pile.

Kikuji stepped carefully over sashes, tissue paper, and boxes on his way to Ikuko's inner chamber. He found her there when he slid the door open. She had put on her kimono and was tying the multi-colored sash around her middle. She was in her eighth month, and the stiff new material did not at first conform to her swollen shape very well. She examined herself disconsolately in the mirror, and saw his image reflected in it. She wheeled around, surprised.

"Please excuse me for not coming out to welcome you," she said. "There has been so much activity in that outer room with people coming and going all the time that I have pretty much stopped paying attention to it . . ." She was flustered by his sudden appearance. As a result of her pregnancy, her face was a little thinner than usual, imparting an ethereal quality to her whole appearance. He caught his breath as the impact of her beauty made itself felt on him. As she placed a final ornament in her hair, he saw the bright colors of her underkimono showing at her sleeves. She was uncomfortable under his steady gaze.

"You must have spent a great deal of money," she said, softly. "I did not expect all this, you know. I was thinking of a small, private ceremony." She caught his eye and smiled with a strange shyness. "But I *am* glad. How careful you are in watching over me!"

He laughed. "Still trying to save me money, aren't you? Don't worry about it: just enjoy yourself. This is the first time you've ever asked me for anything."

255

She seemed relieved. "I know it's early in the day for it," she said, almost coquettishly, "but wouldn't you like to take a nice hot bath now? I had it heated early because I knew you would be here sometime during the afternoon. I can't scrub your back for you in my condition, but I'll send the maid in."

Soon he was splashing himself with hot water. Then he sat on a small stool and allowed the maid to scrub his back. She was very irritating. Her hands were rough and bony, and she seemed to be scraping his skin raw.

"All right. That's enough. Do you hear me? Just pour on the hot water."

Her aim was bad, and the water hit him not on the shoulders, but on the back of his head.

"Oh, you stupid creature," he shouted. "You'll be giving me an earache. Get out of here!"

The maid fled. He looked for a towel, and observed a laundry hamper in the corner of the dressing room. He studied it dourly as he toweled himself. When he was almost dry, Ikuko slid open the glass door and came in.

"Did the maid do it wrong?" she asked.

"Don't bother about her," he said gruffly. "Come over here." He showed her the laundry hamper. "Look there."

"I don't— What do you want me to see?"

"Those tabi."

"These?" She held up a pair. The toe had been carefully mended with white thread.

"Yes. Those." He snatched them from her hands, and threw them into the wastebasket.

"I'm sorry," she said mechanically. "I was careful in my wearing of it, but, since I washed it every day, after a year the toe gave way, and I mended it. Maybe it was not my best sewing—"

"I don't *care* about your sewing!" he shouted. "Here I am, Osaka's foremost merchant in the tabi line, and one of my ladies goes and wears a pair of the things for a whole year. And then patches them. Like some hungry widow in the gutter! What do you think this does to my reputation? I'm going to send you your tabi. You are to wear a pair one day and no longer. Then you throw them away and next day you wear a new pair. Otherwise, you'll disgrace me, and I won't have it! Do you understand?"

"Of course," she said, helping him dress. "It just—I never thought of it that way."

"Just one day and into the wastebasket with them!"

She helped him into his kimono without speaking. The maid, she guessed, had made a bad job of it, somehow.

Arriving late that afternoon at Minoya's, Kikuji found Tsuruhachi entertaining some thirty proprietresses and geisha in his usual strenuous way. These former associates of Ikuko's sat comfortably behind their trays of food, enjoying the clown's jokes and tricks. Although Kikuji recalled the guest list, he found it difficult to identify any of the women: in celebration of the approach of spring, the younger women wore hairdos appropriate to an aged lady of sixty, and their kimono were the dark and dignified garments of the elderly. The older women were even more startling, for they had arranged their hair in the simple, unadorned fashion of young girls, and their kimono were the brightly colored clothes of the very young. Ikuko, however, far more skilled in these matters than he, located the senior geisha at a glance, and proceeded to make the rounds, greeting her guests formally, and asking for their good wishes. In the oldest form of this ceremony for warding off evil, Kikuji knew, the woman in her bad luck year had to offer a meal to a woman in a year of good luck who, in the process of eating the food set before her, consumed and disposed of all the bad luck. But in the Osaka pleasure quarter, it was customary for the afflicted lady of thirty-three to wine and dine all her associates who had safely passed the bad luck year. Tsuruhachi had ordered such a great variety of delicacies that it was necessary to serve each of the guests with two trays. On the second was an ornamental cake. Kikuji caught a whiff of its delicate aroma which, superstitious old women claimed, warded off evil; and he recalled the many religious ceremonies when he had been aware of it in the past.

As the guests finished tasting the varied delicacies served them, Tsuruhachi straightened his kimono, moved into the center of the banquet hall, and began chanting a "Song of the Spring Renewal" which he had learned from one of the brief, comic kabuki plays. Tsuruhachi's rendition made the old fable come alive once more in Kikuji's imagination. The clown's reedy voice caught the smooth lecherousness of the evil demon from Mount Horai who had come

257

down to seduce the housewife. And it mounted in triumph as the wife, after stealing the cloak of invisibility and the magic mallet which held all his power, sang out vigorously, "Out with the devil! Fair fortune flourish!" and scattered beans around the floor to chase away the trespassing spirit.

It was a lively performance, and, as Tsuruhachi sang the wife's magical invocation against the devil, he suited action to words, by scattering beans on the floor. Kikuji was startled to observe that the guests immediately picked up the beans and popped them into their mouths, counting as they did so until they came to number thirty-three, at which point they joined with Tsuruhachi in the chant, "Out with the devil! Fair fortune flourish!" Kikuji was the first one to appreciate a good performance, but when an audience of some of the most respectable teahouse proprietresses and geisha in Osaka suddenly joined in the mumbo jumbo of the performance and went down on their hands and knees to swallow a lot of dirty beans from the floor just because they, like Ikuko, went along with peasant superstitions, he felt embarrassed and even tempted to guffaw. But an instant's reflection told him what he had known all along: these women, sophisticated about every aspect of sociability, were nevertheless simple and acquiescent in all other matters. If he broke a chopstick in the presence of any one of them, she would promptly pull a grave face and recite a charm to ward off evil. Ah, well, if all this nonsense gave Ikuko any feeling of security, he supposed it was worth it. How much had it cost him? He began totting up the expenses: the sashes, two hundred yen; the dinner party, three hundred yen; special pay for the geisha who were present, four hundred fifty yen. With the fee for Tsuruhachi and the waitresses, getting rid of Ikuko's demon had cost him about one thousand yen. Ikuko had worried about the expense, but he had told her that it was important to spend freely during an economic depression: only so could the investors be reassured of Kawachiya's financial strength. A lesser firm would try to economize. As Tsuruhachi had aptly phrased it, driving out Ikuko's depression was also a means of chasing away his own economic headache.

As the spring advanced, however, business conditions seemed worse than ever. People were adapting to the thrifty thirties, and opening their thin wallets only for the most necessary purchases.

Kawachiya's, famed for its finely crafted but expensive wares, had come on hard times ahead of the cheaper and less luxurious trades. One afternoon as he passed a large department store, he observed a huge crowd lined up four deep. Posters on the store front announced a sale of tabi for ten sen! When he arrived home, he sent one of the apprentices downtown to buy a selection of the sale items.

"I don't know how they can do it!" he said to Wasuke. "My grade-A tabi cost fifty sen and my cheapest are thirty-five sen. The cheapest I've ever put on sale were twenty-five sen. I can't sell below that price."

Hidesuke was listening. "But you must, Master. In a few weeks everyone will be selling tabi for ten sen! They won't be much good and they won't last long. But only rich old ladies who have always done it that way will buy tabi for fifty sen from now on."

Kikuji was thoughtful. "Machine made, of course?"

"Yes, sir. Everything automated as much as possible," Hidesuke answered.

Wasuke shook his head. "Shameful, shameful," he said softly.

When the apprentice returned with the ten-sen tabi he had bought at the sale, Kikuji and his two managers studied them.

"Well, certainly they're flimsy and poorly made," he said, and to illustrate his point tore one of them wide open. "But even so they cost someone more than ten sen to manufacture. Some fellow facing bankruptcy decided to unload his stock and get whatever he could. But in the process he is setting up new price expectations. Everyone will now want ten-sen tabi, just as they have come to expect ten-sen rice balls, and ten-sen vaudeville. What a mess! Just wait: tomorrow all my retail customers will be after me to supply them with ten-sen tabi. I'll not degrade our family name by producing such junk!"

"Ah, but if you don't, someone else will," said Hidesuke, smiling dreamily at the floor.

Kikuji looked at him with a frown. "We'll not compete with street peddlers in selling rubbish," he replied.

"Of course, Master," Hidesuke answered, looking up at him. But the smile remained. It lingered insolently in Kikuji's mind for several days. So did the nagging problem of how best to meet the competition. The more he thought about it, the less he grasped it. It was like a bluebottle fly buzzing around: whenever he tensed to swat it,

259

the creature took off and flew dizzying circles around him, leaving him irritable and exhausted. He decided he needed Ikuko, and one afternoon made plans to visit her.

O-Tōki was waiting at the entryway with his footwear. It consisted of a pair of leather-soled slippers faced with a rattan mesh. He had bought them a few days earlier chiefly because he liked the ornamental nails driven into the heel. Within each nail was a moving bit of metal serving as the hammer to produce a melodious little jingling whenever he took a step. The sound was like the noise of coins. It was a rich noise, and helped to ward off depression, a tuneful equivalent of Ikuko's multicolored sash. Kikuji had noticed a few weeks before that many of his acquaintances had begun to wear these softly jingling slippers, and he had been inclined, at first, to regard the fashion as a little ridiculous. But when he walked in his own, he found that the faint "Cha-ta, cha-ta, cha-ta-rin" sound produced by the slippers made him feel cheerful. It was like windbells, whose soft noise invariably distracted him from his own narrow concerns.

Intrigued by the sound of his steps, he decided to walk to Ikuko's instead of hailing a cab. It was a quiet, spring afternoon. The sun shone on the surface of the Nagabori River, and the silvery reflection of the wavelets moved in rhythmic dance on the white rice paper panels of the houses along the river bank. The sun's heat felt good on his neck, and he relaxed. Depressions would come and go to the end of time, he supposed, but they would have no effect on the even flow of the river, the soft light of the sun, the deep satisfaction of being fully alive. Pleasantly occupied with these thoughts, he arrived at Ikuko's place in Unagidani with the speed of the absentminded. The latticed door was open and he walked in and sat down quietly in the living room. Facing away from him sat Ikuko leaning over the charcoal brazier, her arm propped on the edge, supporting her head.

"Ikuko," he said softly, "I've come to see you."

She uttered a startled exclamation, and turned toward him, trying to pull the collar of her kimono into its proper line before standing up. As she did so, he had a glimpse of a colorful fabric on the floor under her. He reached for it and lifted it: seven of the sashes were connected together like a big rope and had been folded neatly and placed under the cushion she sat on. They were warm from her body. She must have been sitting there for a long time.

"What are these?" Kikuji asked, puzzled. "Didn't you give them to your friends?"

"These were extras. There were ten of them left over," she said, her eyes downcast. "I kept them."

"Of course, of course. But why sit on a pile of the things? Aren't you carrying this magic hocus-pocus a bit far?"

She was startled by his lack of sympathy.

"I—I don't know. My friends say that in warding off evil influences, one can't be too thorough. And so—well, I wrap three of the multicolored sashes around my middle to protect the baby, and I sit on the other seven every day. Is that—all right? I mean—you don't —mind, do you?"

Her haggard, fearful eyes looked out at him from a yellowed, puffy countenance which he found hard to recognize.

"I'm concerned about your health. You don't look well. Have you seen a doctor recently?"

"Oh, no, no, no, no, no! You mustn't say such things. If we trust in the gods, they will protect us. I need no doctors. Just faith! If you have no faith, I may be—punished!"

She trembled violently. He watched her in alarm.

"Ikuko! This isn't like you. Keep your colored sashes, but do see a doctor too."

She looked at him with glittering eyes, the sweat standing out in beads on her forehead.

"You couldn't understand these things, being a man," she whispered to him hoarsely. "You don't know what it is to be frightened. To have a child in my year of bad luck is tempting fate, I think. I wish I could wear not only my multicolored sashes, but multicolored tabi as well. They would prevent the evil from coming into me at my toes and feet. Make some for me!"

Kikuji smiled at her and patted her head. "Well, we'll see about it, my dear. People just don't wear colored tabi, you know—"

She looked as though she were half-asleep. "Colored tabi would keep me warm and safe," she murmured.

As he looked at her, his sympathetic expression changed to one of wonderment. "Of course. Of course! Everyone would want them.

261

Everyone." He rose hastily. "I must go now, my dear. You have reminded me of some business which I must take care of right away. Thank you for helping me. I'll be back, I'll be back soon—"

He stepped down at the entryway into his slippers, waved his hand to her in quick farewell, and was gone.

Persuading Wasuke and Hidesuke was not easy. As soon as he had returned to the store, he had hurried them into his private office and told them of his new idea. They had sat there completely silent and expressionless.

"You're supposed to be reacting with great enthusiasm," he said with a humorless smile.

"Colored tabi, you said?" quavered Wasuke.

"Tomorrow we start on the new line. Men's tabi in blue, brown, and black; women's in red or green."

There was another strained silence. Finally, Wasuke cleared his throat. "It's certainly an interesting idea, Master. But tabi are just everyday necessities, and not meant to be items on the fashion parade. It would be safer not to engage in these experiments, I think."

"Hidesuke, you doubtless have some reaction to give to my proposal." Kikuji had noticed the quick look of contempt the assistant manager had given Wasuke, and he wished to figure out its meaning. Hidesuke smiled his tight little smile which invariably affected Kikuji unpleasantly.

"If we're going to change, Master, I would suggest that we plunge into mechanization entirely: drop Kawachiya's main feature up to now, the handmade process, and go in for the cheapest possible manufacture. For a little while we could undersell all competitors and drive them out of business. Then we could raise our prices a little, but still sell cheap stuff rather than the fancy line you now have. The colored tabi don't seem practical to me. Women's fashions are unpredictable, and, if your colored tabi didn't take their fancy, you would be ruined. You have asked for my opinion, and I hope you will find it of some use."

His voice was smooth like a woman's and he developed his points politely and logically. But somehow Kikuji felt the same underlying contempt for him and his ideas that he had detected in that quick, patronizing look with which Hidesuke had dismissed Wasuke's earnest loyalty.

262

"I appreciate both of your opinions," Kikuji said. "Here are mine. We cannot survive making high-class tabi which sell for fifty sen. And I refuse to debase the family name by making the cheapest possible product which would soon fall apart. I certainly don't want to drive the competition out of business in these very difficult times. But between the two extremes of 'too expensive' and 'too cheap' perhaps there is another way. We will move into the production of colored tabi. And we'll study the new mechanized processes, using those which do a good job, and not using those which lower the quality of our product. With careful study, I think we ought to be able to make ten-sen tabi which our house need not be ashamed of. We can start by making velveteen tabi: these are intended for home use only, and we can experiment on the manufacturing process with them until we finally arrive at procedures we are satisfied with. Are there any questions?"

He saw the very slight shrug which Hidesuke made, as though to say it was none of his affair. Hidesuke, of course, kept the books and knew how much of the firm's profits were going to support Kikuji's mistresses. He regarded such expenditures as evidence of human weakness. He had no need for the company of other people. What would he do with himself in a teahouse?

"You seem unconvinced, Hidesuke," Kikuji said quietly. "Please don't forget that it was I who thought up the organdy-lined tabi which were so successful a year ago."

"Yes, indeed, sir. It was most successful, to be sure. But, if you recall, they were made first for Miss Ponta's independence party, and they became popular with the ladies of the pleasure quarter quite by chance. That was what gave us good publicity, you know—"

Kikuji interrupted him. "You won't believe this, my friend, but my life is all of a piece. I do not forget my business when I am with one of my mistresses, and I do not forget them when I am at my business. It was not sheer chance which made the organdy-lined tabi popular. It was my careful planning from beginning to end. You can count on the same being true as we move into the production of low-priced colored tabi."

"Very good, sir," said Hidesuke, bowing slightly.

The next few days were busy ones. Kikuji studied machinery, talked with craftsmen, and calculated endlessly. Finally, he had samples of the colored tabi made up to be sent to all retailers served by his firm. When the last sample had been sent out, he had time to think of the telephone call he had received from Hisako a few days before.

She had called at one of his busiest moments. Initially, it had been a man on the phone, but when Kikuji answered, Hisako came on. Paying no attention to his concerns, she had announced that she had bought the horse, Wine Red, and that she was to be in a race soon. Her lover had been very brusque, and had finally hung up on her. She should have known better. No woman who knows what's what calls her patron at his place of business. There is a strict etiquette in these matters, and even though Hisako was not a geisha, she should have known the rules. The trouble was that she did know and didn't care. Ponta and Ikuko, both of whom had been presented officially to his family, would never have presumed to call him at home unless there were a great emergency of some kind. But, irritated as he was, he still was interested in hearing about the horse with the fancy name. So, now that he was relatively at leisure, he called her apartment. When he received no answer, he phoned the apartment house manager and learned that she had gone to the track to watch her horse's first race. Acting on impulse, Kikuji hurried to the race track. He was scheduled to hold a party for some of his craftsmen in the early evening, but he felt that he had ample time. When he arrived by taxi, he found the races already in progress. He hastened to the upper section of the grandstand, dodging around people obstructing the passageway. He arrived in the owners' section just as one of the races had been completed. The crowd began to move around, and suddenly, in the midst of the balding, gray-haired owners, he saw Hisako, resplendent in a wine red dress, wearing the darker makeup which she reserved for the out-of-doors. She seemed to him to be putting on an act of affected elegance. Since she had not seen him, he came up behind her, slapped her playfully on the back, and said, "It's me, old girl!" She wheeled on him indignantly, saw who it was, and slowly, slowly, managed a smile which became a sociable grin.

"You took me by surprise! But you came at the right time. Our horse is in the next race if you want to see her."

"That's why I'm here."

"Hah. You're improving. You for once had the good sense to come to see a horse instead of a woman. You and your geisha crew!"

They went to look at the horse. She pretended to be perfectly casual and almost indifferent about Kikuji's sudden appearance at the track, even though he had rebuffed her on the telephone earlier. She pointed to the marshaling area, where seven four-year-old horses were being walked around by stablemen.

"Ours is number five. Wine Red! Isn't she pretty?"

And he had to agree that she was: she was smallish, but supple, and the line from neck to tail was long and powerful. The arc of her neck was tight and beautiful, and her stance skittish and alert. Hisako walked toward the horse, stretched out her hand to pat her as though greeting a puppy. Wine Red narrowed her eyes, tossed her mane, and snorted in response. The stableman holding the bridle whispered something to Hisako and she nodded in an authoritative, ownerlike fashion.

When the horses were lined up at the starting gate, Wine Red was balky and, when the barrier opened, she was among the last to start. Kikuji hadn't expected much, but such a lackluster performance left him feeling depressed. He somehow felt it typified his total situation. For a long time now he had been living it up at the teahouses, giving his four women outrageously expensive presents—horses, diamonds mounted in teeth, multicolored sashes for the exorcism of devils—and perhaps losing his race for security now that the Great Depression had struck. If the colored tabi were not successful, then he would have to go in for a severe retrenchment, starting with a cutback of funds to his four mistresses. Once that happened, who could tell what sordid economies might be forced on him?

Suddenly a roar from the crowd brought his mind back to the race track. When he stood up to look, he saw number five passing horse after horse in an effort to catch the front-runner. Kikuji became excited, and grabbed Hisako's binoculars.

"You have them backwards," came her indifferent, sardonic voice. "Try looking through the eyepiece."

He gave them back to her. Without them he watched Wine Red settle into second place.

"Next year! Next year!" Hisako said with mysterious certainty. "Then she'll have reached her full growth and she'll knock them all over!"

It was the compulsive gambler's credo and he had heard it from her in varying forms many times before. She asked him to come with her to the stable, but, mindful of his party at seven, he refused, and took a taxi home. As he got out of the cab, O-Toki came running to him.

"Master, there was a call from Unagidani. The baby has been born! A boy!"

"Ah! A boy!"

He could think of nothing suitable to say. Indifferent as he was to children, it didn't really matter whether it was a boy or girl, but somehow he felt more masculine, more justified in having fathered a boy. It was better to talk about somehow.

"Grandmother and Mother know about it, then?"

"Oh, yes, sir. Miss Ikuko's maid told me to give them the message."

"Well, I must go there at once. As soon as I change."

As he put on a fresh kimono, he tried to figure the ages of his children. Hisajiro, coddled beyond belief by his mother and grandmother, was a girlish ten-year-old. Ponta's child, Taro, must be nearly five by now, growing up isolated from both parents. And now, with Ikuko's baby, a new responsibility. He felt a sudden curiosity about Taro. Ponta had had a picture taken of him and had sent it to him. Where had he put it? He opened his desk drawer, and by good luck chanced on the right envelope. He studied the picture. A totally serious boy stared up at him. He had a sturdy, self-willed look about him which Kikuji liked. His long, almond-shaped eyes were disconcertingly like Kikuji's own. And now— What would the third become? It was all very confusing.

He heard the purr of the sliding door as it opened behind him.

"Kiku-bon,"—it was Kino—"here is the fifty-thousand-yen payoff for your latest indiscretion."

"Yes. Boys are more expensive." It seemed an asinine thing to be saying to one's grandmother. But not many grandmothers were of Kino's self-taught prurience.

"Almost as though you were doing it to spite your mother and me."

It was too much. He laughed gently in her face. "That, at least, Grandmother, I cannot lay claim to."

He bowed politely to his grandmother, and at that moment the door slid violently open. It was his mother. She looked upset and tears were in her eyes.

"Oh, Kiku-bon," she began, then hesitated, uncertain as to how best to proceed.

"What is it?" he asked sharply. "Out with it."

"Oh, Kiku-bon! I just had a phone call from Unagidani—"

He felt strangely remote from them, from all he had ever known, a lost pilgrim at a way station in outer space looking down on the world of humanity. When he spoke his voice seemed to him to echo through a tunnel.

"You are trying to tell me that Ikuko—has not survived."

Sei, unable to speak, nodded convulsively.

One minute, the miracle of new life; the next, a loved one, totally intertwined with all that one needed and valued, had disappeared into the blank wall of infinity. How could anyone understand these enormous oppositions? He stared open-mouthed at his mother and grandmother, like a drunken man trying to sweep away the fog of incomprehension gathering around him.

"Please. Explain it to me. What happened?"

"Apparently her kidneys were functioning badly all through her pregnancy," his mother managed to say. "After the birth, she had a convulsion. The midwife called the doctor. She was dead by the time he got there."

Just a few minutes ago he had been trying to fit the existence of a third son into his world. By comparison that had been easy. The nonexistence of one who had stroked and loved him was infinitely harder to adjust to. He shook his head in an effort to understand. Sei's voice droned on now: once started it seemed to go on endlessly with clinical details, as though she sought to plug up this ragged opening into the unknowable with scientific jottings of temperatures and blood pressures. It could not be true. Sei and Kino were always getting things mixed up. He propelled himself into the hallway, where O-Toki sat watchfully waiting.

"O-Toki," he croaked. "Phone! Call! Quickly!"

She understood. A minute later she extended the phone to him. He reached for it as a tired swimmer reaches for a life preserver.

"Hello. Hello," he heard from the other end. It was Ikuko's not-very-bright maid. He moistened his dry lips.

267

"Please. Please. I want to speak to your mistress—"

Before he had finished his sentence a great wail broke out through the earpiece. Slowly he put the phone down. He knew. He could not understand, but he knew. He would have to live with it and digest its harsh incomprehensibility, never understanding, never accepting, but finally, conceivably, forgetting what was too big, too sharp ever to be understood.

From the dimness of the hallway, he looked out at the courtyard, illuminated now by the long, slanting rays of the spring sun, caressing the rough paving stones almost tangibly with soft, yellow warmth. From the long, dark tunnel within him, he looked out, briefly captivated by the beauty which eyes can see, fingers touch. His spirit sought the dark. He stared on, unseeing.

"Ah, poor soul, poor soul!" came an unfamiliar voice behind him. Turning, he saw Kino standing near him in the dim hallway. He stared in wonderment. There were tears on those iron cheeks. She patted him gently on the shoulder.

"Ah, my boy! You have lost a good woman! So thoughtful, so considerate—"

He found it hard to believe. The crusty, complaining voice had quite disappeared, and in its place were the soft nuances of real grief. Old as she was, perhaps she understood death better than he did. For an instant he clasped her withered hand in his, then turned to go.

"Kiku-bon. Where are you going now?"

"To—where she is."

"Dear boy,"—she hobbled toward him and took his hand once more—"forgive me for giving you more trouble, but you must remember Semba customs at such times: the master ought never to see the face of his departed mistress, nor ought he appear at the funeral. I don't know the reason for these rules; they come from a wisdom deeper than that of any one man and we should—must—obey! When the master dies, his mistress is forbidden to attend the funeral, you know. And it works the other way too. There must be good reasons."

The sun's rays had faded away from the courtyard, and the two of them stood in the darkening hallway, each thinking in his own way of the death of Kihei and Kimika's abrupt and painful exclusion from the last rites accorded to the person she had loved best.

"Very well, Grandmother," he said softly. "I'll not be present at the wake or the funeral. But I must go now to smooth her pillow one last time."

"I know it seems hard, but not even that last glimpse is permitted by our code. But we'll do things properly. Ikuko would be happy with our arrangement, I'm sure. I'll send Hidesuke to take care of everything. You just sit down here and rest."

She meant well, he knew. But the more she talked, the more her words reverberated meaninglessly on the walls of his tunnel. He resigned himself for the moment to her dictatorship. He moved back into the living room and sat down. But as he did so Kino came to him again and placed the envelope with the fifty thousand yen in his lap.

"No, Kiku-bon, you must go to Unagidani. Not to see Ikuko, but to take care of the baby. O-Toki, you go with the young master and manage things so that no one will think he is violating the rules by seeing the dead lady. As soon as he has seen the baby, you must take the child to the home of our branch manager in Honmachi. We can't leave a newborn baby in the house where a funeral is going to take place. Can you manage it?"

He went slowly to the firm's offices at the front, followed by O-Toki. Suddenly he remembered the seven o'clock party for the craftsmen. Hastily, he phoned Wasuke and asked him to act as his representative. This done, he left by the front door with O-Toki following him.

The street was bustling with activity on this Saturday night. Produce wagons squeaked as they moved slowly on their way, like worker ants plodding along, while the bicycles and motorbikes darted hither and thither like mosquitoes. How vigorously they pursued their varied missions. From his tunnel he looked out and saw them all scurrying about, each concentrating myopically on special plans for tonight. Nothing isolates and separates like grief, he thought. No one sees me. Whenever I felt the need of her love and comfort, it was always ready for me. But in her hour of need, she was alone. I was at the race track, flitting around meaninglessly, like one of these mosquitoes bicycling around the street. Even in her fear and illness she had managed to give him a useful business prospect: the colored tabi had originated in her multicolored sash. But when she, in her tunnel of fear and sadness, had needed him, he had been like these busy, self-centered people hurrying in all directions around him and had not entered into her need at all. The multicolored sash had not worked, perhaps because of his utter disbelief in its efficacy. Would the experiment of the colored tabi also be doomed to bad luck? Very possibly so. She had said that he must have faith in her rites of exorcism and he had had none. The doom might carry o er to all that he tried to do from now on. And justly so.

Although he wanted to see her face as soon as possible, he resisted the urge to take a taxi. He needed time to get hold of himself so that he could face catastrophe without collapsing in tears. Also, an arrival by taxi would be easily observed by the neighbors. It was soothing, somehow, to be so completely alone in the midst of the Saturday night shoppers and pleasure seekers. He looked at the lights of the houses across the Nagabori River as they were reflected in its waters. How many times had he contemplated the same scene as he walked to Ikuko's house, secure in the certainty of her delight at his coming, her many endearing little mannerisms, her dedication to his happiness? And now—what was there at the end of his walk? Something which reminded him of her, but which kept saying by its coldness, its remoteness, its indifference, "You are cheated. What you sought is gone. You should have valued it more when you had it. What you see now is the illusion, the costume, the dregs. What you sought is gone, gone, gone, gone!" If only he had been with her instead of making that meaningless trip to the race track—

"Master!" It was O-Toki tugging urgently at his sleeve. He realized that they had come to the quiet alleyway leading to Ikuko's small, tidy house.

"Please wait here a moment. I'll see if you can see her in privacy."

She darted in, and returned almost immediately.

"Our timing is good, sir. The doctor left a few minutes ago, and only the maid and midwife are there. In a little while the undertaker will come, so let us hurry in now—"

Kikuji entered the alleyway, feeling every paving stone to be familiar and precious. He opened the latticed door; the entryway was dark. From the main room a little light shone and the smell of incense came to him. As he took off his slippers, he noticed Ikuko's clogs with lavender straps placed neatly side by side, pointing outward, ready for the wearer to slip on. He placed his beside hers and stood up. Ikuko's maid sensed movement in the dark antechamber, and, coming to the door to see who it was, burst into a loud wail. O-Toki stepped up to her and escorted her upstairs.

Ikuko was lying with her head to the north. Her face was covered with a light white kerchief. Kikuji knelt beside her and removed the cloth. As he did so it seemed to him that her nose had moved slightly. He closed his eyes and clenched his teeth, knowing it was an illusion but willing it to be real. He looked again, more calmly at her face. The powder which she had carefully put on in the morning still remained. The cord which kept her *marumage* hairdo in place was still fresh and neat, and the hair still glistened with oil. The candle near her head on the sutra stand flickered. He replaced it with a fresh one. He could see her relaxed, peaceful features better now. For a long time he sat there, thinking nothing, glad to be with her. There was a sudden step at the door; O-Toki came hastening in, sitting quickly to speak with him.

"There is an undertaker at the door, Master. Come. You must leave with me out the back way."

"Not so fast. What about the baby?"

"Don't worry about him," she replied. "I'll come back soon and take him to the Honmachi branch manager's house, as the lady of the house suggested." They went out through the kitchen. The board over the drainage canal was poorly fitted; it lurched under his step, and dirty water wet the hem of his kimono. Upstairs there was the sudden shrill scream of a baby and the voice of the midwife, quieting it.

A week after the funeral, Kino asked Kikuji to come to her rooms for a conference. When he got there, he found Hidesuke awaiting him. The assistant manager bowed to him and Kikuji nodded coldly. This reptilian individual had taken care of his mistress's funeral! Far from being grateful for the service rendered, Kikuji could only feel detestation at the unsuitability of the servant who had performed it. Hidesuke had been wandering around for the past week looking solemn and sepulchral. His attempts at sympathetic understanding of the bereaved were completely ridiculous. Kikuji couldn't stand the man.

Kino began the meeting by praising Hidesuke's work on the funeral. Her grandson nodded irritably.

"Now, Kikuji, I want your approval for my planned disposition of Ikuko's effects," the old lady said.

"Her effects?"

"You know what I mean. Her clothes, furniture, and the house itself. I propose to sell them and give the proceeds to her father, an old man from Yamashina. Hidesuke can be our agent in taking care of all this."

"I can do it very easily."

Kino frowned. "We have been at great pains to keep you out of public view during the wake and funeral. It would be absurd for you to come forward now. Anyway, we've almost tidied everything up. Once we've disposed of the house and handed over settlement money, we'll be in the clear."

Kikuji was puzzled. "That's the first time I've ever heard that you make a settlement when one's mistress has died."

"But of course you do. There must be no unseemly repercussions ten years from now."

Kikuji recalled the old man he had seen when, from the upstairs window of O-Fuku's Hamayu Teahouse, he had looked down on the funeral procession as it wound through the streets. Something about the old fellow had reminded him of Ikuko, but he was very old and feeble.

"There'll be no repercussions ten years hence. Ikuko's father won't last out the year."

Kino's eyes glinted. "Ah, so you've seen him." She looked for an instant at Hidesuke, and then continued, "Well, the settlement is important. We want to finish off this affair so that everything is clean and neat. Clean and neat, that's my motto."

It had been a favorite expression of Ikuko's he recalled. Maybe it was at the heart of all conservatism: clean and neat. What an epitaph to put on a tombstone!

"I have no objection," he replied finally.

"Very good," said Kino. "Hidesuke, you can go to work, then. Today you must perform the memorial service which comes the first week after the funeral. When that's done, you can begin to inventory all Ikuko's possessions so that we can sell them."

Hidesuke bowed and left.

"How did you happen to see Ikuko's father, Kiku-bon?" she asked.

"I don't know how, when, or where," he replied irritably.

"It wouldn't have been from the upstairs window of Hamayu's Teahouse in Soemoncho, would it? I'm told you watched the funeral from there. Is that so?"

"What difference does it make?"

"Oh, none at all, dear boy." She smiled maliciously. "But why did you pick Hamayu's? Don't tell me that you have already lined up *another* mistress? Oh, you must excuse me for thinking such low thoughts of you—and to think such things before the dear departed is even laid to repose. Most unseemly."

She carried the sleeve of her kimono up to her nose, and, behind its protection, she laughed. How, he wondered, could this savage virago ever have wept in sympathy at his loss only a week ago?

"Have you seen the baby?" she asked.

"Last Wednesday."

"How did it look?"

"The way babies do."

"Ah. How nice."

"Not really. Red in the face from bawling, wrinkled skin, a general impression of dampness. That was all I got." He paused moodily. "I met the foster parents: they run a general store in the vicinity of Izumi-Otsu. They seemed nice enough. If they want anything, they'll contact me through the Honmachi branch manager."

He stood up to leave his grandmother's room. Suddenly he was dizzy, and fell down on hands and knees. His grandmother supported him anxiously.

"It's really nothing. I'll be all right in a minute," he assured her.

"No, no. You look terrible. Rest a moment." She stared thoughtfully at him while he drew in a few breaths. He got to his feet again.

"You know what I think, Kiku-bon? I think you're living it up too much. Too much drinking. Too many women. Ikuko's death has beaten you down, but you don't need to adopt all the female population of Osaka. You have lost one of your mistresses. Only you can know whether you were responsible for her death. I don't mean that by making her pregnant you were responsible. Women take their chances on that. But I wonder if you were a good patron to her. There are some boys who break every toy they are given. The more they like it, the sooner they break it. If your luck is bad, you will go from one woman to another. Your mistress has died. How many more will go the same way? Maybe all women who have known the warmth of Kikuji's skin are fated themselves to become cold and lifeless; maybe each time you will grieve without being able to see your dead love's face; maybe you will each time look down from an upstairs room in a teahouse at the funeral; maybe finally your heart will become as cold and hard and unyielding as the dead bodies of those mistresses. It is something to think about, something to dream about, something to chew on and digest, before it is too late—"

Her voice came out in a rasping bass monotone, as though she were voicing prophetic truths. He stood over her for a moment shaking his head in wonderment: what did this terrible old woman want of him? She caught his look, and smiled up at him a mocking smile. He rushed off down the hallway without saying goodbye.

Eight

The end of the hundred days' mourning for Ikuko coincided with the week in October for the yearly shift to winter clothing, and it was at this time that Kikuji had determined to launch his sales campaign for the colored tabi. An old Osaka motto said, "To buy good footwear is to tread hard on misfortune." Kikuji figured that with the advent of winter fashions the new line of rich and warmly colored tabi ought to sell.

He had worked hard promoting his new product. Since Ikuko's death he had sought to lose himself in his work, obscurely thinking of the brightly colored tabi, suggested as they were by Ikuko's multicolored sashes, as an appropriate memorial to his mistress. But sometimes at night he was unable to sleep, thinking that, as the multicolored sashes had not prevented catastrophe to Ikuko, so the colored tabi might not in this depression time charm away the bad fortune conceivably inherited from this unfortunate lady. To deaden such gloomy thoughts, he worked to the point of exhaustion each day.

The night before the October sale was to begin, everything was in readiness. The retailers were all stocked. There was little more that he could do. He looked up from his ledger out the window. The long, golden rays of the September sun lingered briefly before the twilight. Earlier in the day he had made an appointment to meet Ponta and some of her friends at Kinryu's Teahouse that evening. Now he was glad that he had done so. He rose, said good night to Hidesuke and Wasuke, and walked off slowly down the quiet street. As he crossed the Nagabori River Bridge, he met Sanoya hastening on his way.

"Where are you off to, Sanoya-san?" Kikuji asked with a smile.

275

"I can tell from the look of you that you're on your way to your lady friends just as I am on my way to mine," said the old man with a knowing smile.

"Thank you for investing so heavily in my colored tabi this year," said Kikuji. "The other retailers weren't nearly as supportive. For every colored pair, they took a pair of plain white. But of course they had to protect themselves, and they are fine customers: have been so over the years. But you gambled on me by ordering only the colored tabi. It was very brave of you."

"The difference between your other customers and me, Kiku-bon, is that they have never been burned." Sanoya nodded snappishly. "Also, as you say, I am a gambler. Nothing ventured, nothing gained. And I think we're going to gain from this colorful venture of yours. But don't overdo it. Either you've been working too hard or loving too hard. Or both, maybe. You don't look well. Go home and get some sleep. Goodbye! Goodbye!"

And off he stomped down the street.

A splendidly attired Ponta was waiting for Kikuji at the entrance to Kinryu's. She chattered happily as she helped him take off his slippers.

"You asked me to bring together a bunch of the grade-A, top-flight, best-of-their-kind geisha for you tonight. I don't know why you must have Osaka's best, but I managed to get five of them for you in spite of the short notice. If that's what it takes to get you over your gloom for Ikuko, I'll be glad to help. Are you the only guest this evening?"

"Don't you think I can handle all of your friends? Of course I'm the only guest! I feel like relaxing."

"Very well. Come aboard. Relax away!" And she opened the sliding door to a roomful of geisha whom he recognized immediately as some of the finest in the profession. He sat down at the low table, and they competed with each other for the privilege of filling his sake cup as soon as he emptied it. They danced and sang and joked for him. The row of empty sake bottles grew longer on the table as he lined them up.

Ponta, he noticed, sat at one side of the table looking faintly distracted. Her sense of rivalry with Ikuko had, if anything, become accentuated by her death, and once she had allowed herself to say, stingingly, "I'll bet it was a punishment for wearing that *marumage* hairdo all the time. Imagine her making herself up like your wife!"

Kikuji had merely shaken his head and said softly, "She's dead, Ponta."

"I know, I know. And that's what's so hard for me to deal with. When she was alive she was older than I, plainer than I by far. And yet you loved her more than you love me. And you still love her more, even if she's dead."

He looked at her as she sat doing nothing, her eyes downcast.

"Hey, Sparkler!"

She looked up at him questioningly.

"Where's the sparkle tonight?"

But she wouldn't smile to reveal her diamond-studded tooth.

"Please excuse me, Master. I am struggling with heavy thoughts."

"Yes, yes. Nowadays all of us suffer from heavy thoughts. I most of all. Ladies, you must be supportive of me and make me light-hearted again!" By this time he was quite drunk, and was stretched out on the floor, leaning on one elbow.

Tamayu, the highest-ranking geisha present laughed and said, "We'll support you, won't we, girls!"

The geisha crossed their hands under Kikuji and in rhythmic dance carried him to the four corners of the room singing a little folk song asking the Buddha to look kindly on their burden. When they put him down again on the tatami mat, Kikuji sat up with a puzzled smile on his face.

"Well. That's a new experience. But since you've given me good luck, allow me to give you some, right now." He began distributing little presents of money.

"But what special event requires good luck, Master? Are you opening a new store?" asked one of them.

"No, no. But a new fashion is going to be started tomorrow morning when the stores open."

The girls shrieked. "A new fashion! We love new fashions! Oh, tell us what it is, Master!"

"Well, I'm producing tabi which are not the plain, white kind, but colored. All sorts of colors. Red, gray, blue, black."

"We can hardly wait!" said Tamayu.

He looked at her shrewdly despite his drunkenness. "Well, my

277

dear, the stores open at nine in the morning. If you wish to help me with more than words, get up early and wait in line at Sanoya's for the store to open. People seeing a line of Osaka's most magnificent geisha will certainly stop and take notice."

There were giggles and exclamations, from which emerged Tamayu's commanding voice. "Of course! We make the fashions for the women of Osaka. And the men wear what the women buy for them. Let us show how powerful we are, and make these colored tabi the rage of the city!"

Soon after, Kikuji brought the evening to an end, and was escorted by Ponta to the streetcar stop.

"Why didn't you tell me it was an advertising scheme for your new line of tabi?" she asked distantly.

"That was certainly in the back of my mind all evening. But I couldn't be sure whether or not to try it until the right opportunity came. Nobody can push these things. I didn't want to *buy* the services of the geisha. They are my friends, not my servants. If it came about that, out of friendship and sheer joy of living, they wished to help me, then I was for it. Otherwise, not."

Ponta sighed. "I'll never understand you businessmen. And even so, you're only half a businessman. Sanoya would've simply bought the services of the geisha. It costs you far more to get their voluntary help."

He smiled at her. "But it is worth far more."

Next morning he woke up early, dressed, and went out to see how the sale was shaping up. As he approached Sanoya's store from a distance, he saw in front of it a riot of color, and the thought of Ikuko's multicolored sashes flitted through his mind. When he came closer, he saw a long line of geisha in their most splendid costumes waiting patiently for the store to open. Only a few were his friends. They had enlisted the services of the others on his behalf in an impossibly short time. Tamayu was at the head of the line. Ponta was toward the rear, looking even now a little woebegone and put out. He looked at the line of magnificently clad women with a full heart. He felt a little as though he had contrived a living art exhibit by means of friendliness alone. They knew, of course, that they were helping him in business. But they were helping him as a friend, actual or potential, and, in addition, they were sure that the product

278

he had vouched for would be worth waiting for. He knew that this kind of courteous gesture had happened occasionally in the old days, long before his grandmother's time. But this was the first such occurrence he had ever heard of in his own lifetime. Even as he watched, passersby, seeing the waiting geisha, slowed their pace, paused, and then joined the line. Sanoya, recognizing the opportunity, opened his doors a little earlier than scheduled, and the rush was on. Ikuko's multicolored sash had not helped her, but it was clearly working in his behalf, perhaps because in the final moments of her life she had willed it so?

The ultimate escape from the constricting world of business was for him not the geisha and the teahouses, but Hisako and the haunted world of the race track. Here he felt completely divorced from any reality he knew. Hisako's manners were much more crude and self-centered than those of the geisha. Her independence fascinated and irritated. Now, for example, they were at the race track together. He was telling her of his financial triumph, rare in the midst of a great depression, with the colored tabi. He told her of the attention centered on his product by the geisha; and of the fact that the new fashion of wearing colored neckcloths instead of, as in the past, white ones had helped make color fashionable so that people bought tabi to match the neckcloths they would wear. Hisako merely nodded now and then, keeping her sharp eyes fixed on the race track. Following her glance, he could find little of interest there. The sky was overcast and a cold, slicing wind was blowing.

To please her, he had finally bought himself a western suit. It had been carefully tailored, and, when he looked in the mirror, he realized that it was a good fit. Unfortunately, he could not recognize the awkward human being filling those pants and that suit coat as himself. He still felt awkward, and the raw wind made him uncomfortable. For some time he had sensed that he was catching a nasty chill. Despite the cold weather, he was sweating profusely. The races, which at their best often seemed uninteresting to him, today were going badly. In the last obstacle race, the horse leading the field had fallen into a ditch, badly injuring the jockey; in the one before, two favorites had somehow run into each other and been disqualified. Kikuji was more interested in the leaden clouds hanging over the track than in the horses. Had he not given in to her whim and bought this ridiculous western outfit, he would not now be sniffling and coughing. What was a tabi seller doing wearing shoes and socks? The whole assemblage of material was damnably uncomfortable. Once out of it, he would never again be lured into it. Everything was too close, too fitted, too tight: it had none of the flowing ease of a kimono. Hisako was wearing a western outfit even skimpier than his.

"Aren't you cold?" he asked her. "I'm freezing!"

She stopped looking at the track and regarded him with surprise. "You're just not used to it yet. Western suits keep you warmer than a kimono once you are used to them."

His teeth were clicking together uncontrollably. She had turned back to her study of the race track.

"Hisako." She was looking intently through the binoculars and did not hear.

"Hisako!"

With a slightly pained expression, she lowered the binoculars and looked at him.

"I'm going home," he said. "I've caught cold."

He could feel the sweat streaming from his armpits, dampening his shirt. She looked at him with concern.

"I'm not feeling at all well," he said stiffly. "You stay on and watch Wine Red when her turn comes. I'll take a taxi home."

She looked uncomfortable. "You are all flushed! Don't you think I—" Her voice trailed off in hesitation. She did so want to see Wine Red run.

"No. You stay. I'm all right." He rose to his feet in the grandstand and felt very dizzy. He moved slowly down the steps. When he reached the open space by the ticket booth he had difficulty in keeping his balance. He suddenly felt a strong arm under his, supporting and guiding him. It was Hisako.

"I'm going home with you," she said. "I don't care to see Wine Red race today. It's such a strange day. Nothing goes right."

In the taxi he dozed, but when he occasionally opened his eyes, he saw her staring abstractedly, almost feverishly out the window. In her mind's eye, she was watching Wine Red run. A few hundred yards before the cab came to Kawachiya's, she ordered the driver to stop and got out. The cab went on and blew its horn in front of Kawachiya's. O-Toki came out, and, finding him almost unconscious, helped him to his bedroom where, spreading the bedding with practiced hands, she helped him to undress and lie down. Kino, unaware of his state, and assuming that he was drunk, came in and looked at the western clothing as it came off him.

"How could you wear such stuff, Kiku-bon? Are you all right? You're sweating so! Are you sick? That's what you get for wearing those foreign costumes. They don't keep you warm. O-Toki, when you have him in bed, call the doctor. He has a terrible fever. Here, let me put him to bed. You call the doctor!"

Kikuji closed his eyes. Kino went spinning away from him and he was left in comfortable darkness. A cold, pudgy hand touched his forehead, and he smelled antiseptic.

"You have pneumonia, young man." The words echoed and re-echoed down an endless cement corridor. He tried to move and felt himself falling agonizingly into fragments which could never be put together again, and then he opened his eyes. A great bearded man in a white gown over an army uniform was looking at him as he lay stark naked on the examining table.

"Look at this flabby, white body. What is it good for? A powder puff body, no good to anybody. Consider yourself 4-F and no good for anything at all!" The surgeon punched him so hard he fell off the table. He was indignant. He stood up, naked as he was, and began to protest this treatment. A sergeant at one side grabbed him and slapped him with a stick across the rear. The more he struggled the more hands came out of nowhere to grab him and poke, punch, or pull him. He became furious. He punched back. He shouted at the top of his voice, and opened his eyes. O-Toki was beside him, trying frantically to calm him down while she applied an ice pack to his head.

"Oh, thank you, O-Toki," he said, feeling enormous gratitude. In a moment, he was asleep. But he could never quite sleep, anymore than he could ever quite wake up. It was a trancelike state in which he floated between sleeping and waking, alert sometimes to sounds, voices, and sights, but incapable of perceiving any sequence, any time passage. Out of the nothingness came Ponta, O-Fuku, and Hisako, looking terribly intense. In their hands they carried paper scrolls. They rolled these and urged him to make his will. He took up a brush and began to write. The more he wrote, the more he needed to write in order to satisfy them. The paper expanded endlessly. His hand became numb. He could write no more. His three mistresses looked at him in cold disapproval. If only Ikuko would come to see him! He groaned and opened his eyes. It was midnight, and there was no one in the room except for O-Toki dozing in the corner. Hearing him, she roused herself and cooled his forehead with an icy cloth. But there was someone else. The disapproving mistresses? He turned his head to the other side. There sat Sei and Kino staring down at him in great anxiety. Why weren't they lively? It's terrible when sick to be bored by sad people. He yearned to shout to them, "Be lively! Sing! Shout! Have a good time! You bore me just sitting there like two old crows on a telephone wire!" But no words came. He continued staring at them, and in place of arid boredom, a great flood of gratitude filled him for these women who in their simplicity centered all their being on whether he lived or died. Their love sustained him like a good cup of hot soup. Soup! That was what he wanted. Food. He looked at them quietly, still too weak to move or talk. They somehow knew now that he was no longer delirious, and that he understood where and with whom he was.

"Oh, Kiku-bon. Once or twice we thought we had lost you. Just like your father." It was, he decided, Sei who was speaking—in a very soft, far-away voice, full of fear and uncertainty, the way people always talk to sick people, afraid that they will make them still more sick. "It will be a long time before you are back to your normal self. You must be patient. You must rest and eat—" (*Eat!* What did she have to offer? His tongue still wouldn't work for him.) "—while we take care of the business and everything else."

Eat!

"But when you're well, there must be no more of these unhealthy western suits. Really, wearing those things is as bad as being addicted to drugs! The foreigners' metabolism is different from ours. You must never risk such danger again." That, surely, seemed to be Kino. It was the sort of thing Kino said.

Eat! Were they utterly heartless with all their unappetizing advice? Suddenly, he felt an arm around his shoulders. He was being lifted up. It was O-Toki. She placed a backrest behind him. Then she took a bowl from the table: *that* was where the heavenly smell of food had been coming from. Using a Chinese soupspoon she skillfully ladled the rice soup into his mouth. In a few minutes, she removed the backrest, and lowered him once more to his pillow. Never had he felt more fulfilled, more calmly in possession of the world's best secrets, than now. He slept.

In the days of weakness that followed, Kikuji came to see his family quite differently, and as though for the first time. Everything they did was fraught with poetry. All of life under the Kawachiya roof, and perhaps elsewhere, was full of beauty, of surprise, of wonder, of delight. He had simply never noticed it before. Now he had a few of the precious moments of quietude granted to convalescents engaged in putting their lives together again. It was a time of quiet observation and joy. Nothing was too insignificant. Every morning at six he heard the slight movements of Kino and Sei as they rose in their respective rooms. The delightful splashing of water showed that they were, with the help of their maids, washing themselves. Then there was a long hour of relative silence as their makeup and hair arrangements were settled upon. When presentable, they went dutifully out to the shrine in the courtyard to chant their prayers to the fox goddess. He loved the chant, and in the silence of the day, would run it over again and again in his mind. After prayers, they would awaken Hisajiro and get him ready for school. Their rhythms were long and sweeping, like ocean swells, but those of Hisajiro were rapid and loud, like the slapping of wavelets on a lake against a pier. After nine o'clock, with the child out for the day, the work of the household began. O-Toki and her helper, Okiyo, would spread out materials for the sewing of kimono, and then would summon the seamstresses. Once the sewing was properly begun, the two maids would go off to the stores for the day's food and supplies. It was all very orderly as Kikuji observed it, like a stately dance or the ordered motions of the stars.

Every other day after lunch the ladies of the house had lessons in flower arrangement and the tea ceremony. The overheard beauty of these rituals, to which previously he had paid little attention, now delighted him. In their spare time during the afternoons the ladies would amuse themselves with Hisajiro, now safely back from school. Before his sickness, he recalled, they often went to a play or to the department store for an outing, but they abstained from such

283

pleasures now. He remembered that during his father's illness they had had no such moratorium on their pastimes. Nowadays they even omitted their lessons on the koto and samisen, lest the noise disturb him. The perfect regularity of their days, which before had seemed to him dull and unexciting, was now the principle ingredient of the beauty which he so much admired in everything they did. The smaller and less significant the deed, the more marvelous to him seemed the doing. Life to be understood, he decided, must be seen in its simplest manifestations, and preferably by a person whose own life has been cleansed of all travel stains by the heat of fever and near-death. The two ladies of the house never became really bored. Whenever they were snappish and unpleasant with each other, O-Toki would manage to organize some diversion to keep them occupied.

Communication between the business at the front of the house and the family at the rear took place during his illness in consultations between O-Toki and Hidesuke. For this purpose, they used the spare room next to the parlor. These meetings had to be properly arranged. Kino and Sei had no patience with casual conversations conducted in the hallway. Everything had to be done according to the rules established by long tradition. If the master were sick, then certain customs became operative. And again he observed, with a gradual decrease in esthetic enthusiasm, that everything in the household, from scolding a manager to repairing the rung of a chair, had to be handled with the exactitude demanded by Semba custom. As his strength increased, his impatience with blind custom increased as well, and his perception of the beauty hidden in all things declined.

The minute processes of daily activity which in the early phases of convalescence had filled him with rapture gradually became simply boring. He stared in exasperation at the inoffensive walls of his room. He wondered why Sei and Kino had not ages ago bored each other to death with their unchanging line of routine trivialities. He yearned for the subtleties of teahouse conversation. He dwelt nostalgically on the visits Kimika had made to his father during his last illness, and wished that Ponta might come to him in the same way. A mistress must not call at her patron's home except in great emergency, he knew, but a little creative subterfuge wouldn't hurt anyone. As he thought about it, the idea disintegrated into absurdity.

Ponta masquerading as a practical nurse in order to hoodwink Kino and Sei would be like the sun pretending to be the moon. In desperation, he asked O-Toki to send for Tsuruhachi.

Late in the afternoon, the jester quietly entered the sickroom. "I would have come sooner had I followed my inclinations. But people of my sort must wait till they are asked," he said solemnly.

"Good lord. You sound and look like the chief mourner at a funeral. I sent for you to cheer me up. Get on with it! Cheer away!"

The great sad eyes in the desolate face grew round in elaborate surprise. "Ah! What wonder have we here! A sick man who rejects our sentimentalities, our hypocritical sympathy. Instead, he asks only that we make him cheerful. A hopeful request, don't you think, young lady?" he said, swirling in his seat with a magnificent gesture to O-Toki. She stared at him for an instant in surprise, then, unable to repress her giggling, rushed to the door to get some tea for the bizarre guest.

When she had gone, Tsuruhachi turned back to the patient. "Master, you sent for me. What is on your mind today?"

"Tell me about my friends."

"On my way here, I passed Hamayu's Teahouse and saw O-Fuku. She reminded me of the proverb 'When the master suddenly stops seeing his lady for as long as ten days, she'd best pray he is recovering from a sickness.' She has been worried about you. She gave me this for you."

When he undid the package which the jester placed beside his pillow, Kikuji found a good luck charm which O-Fuku had obtained at a Shinto shrine. It was wrapped in thick paper, and, on it she had signed her name. Like everything else she did, the sweep of the brush strokes had about it a verve and ease. He looked at it absent-mindedly.

"Tsuruhachi, I am being bored to death. But I'm not strong enough to get up yet. Any suggestions?"

"A random assortment, sir. I suppose that in this case the mountain must come to Mohammad."

"I'm not Mohammad and I'm not interested in mountains. But it surely would be pleasant to talk with O-Fuku, Ponta, or Hisako."

"That can be arranged, sir. How would it be to have a party by telephone?"

"Please, no jokes. The phone is in the hallway, where everyone can hear what I'm saying. Besides, I must stay in bed yet awhile, so the doctor says."

"Ah, sir, you live in the 1930's. Science is waiting to serve us. If you say the word, I have a friend in the phone company who can put a telephone extension right at your pillow."

Several hours later, Tsuruhachi's friend finished putting in the extension, packed his tools, and left. Kikuji waited for a few minutes to be sure that the ladies of the house would not interrupt, then picked up the phone. Talking to Ponta was like reentering the real world. After a few moments of talk about his health, she said, "And now we have a surprise. Tsuruhachi was here and arranged it."

"What is it?" he asked, with faint irritation.

In reply, he heard a chorus of geisha voices singing one of his favorite songs. When the piece had ended, Ponta came back on the phone.

"Did you like that? We're having a party for you here. Now I'll sing you a song."

She had no sooner started than the crisp voice of Hidesuke could be heard on the wire. "Hello, hello! Operator? Is that you? Would you please take my number?"

Kikuji roared into the telephone. There was a click, followed by cautious silence. Finally Ponta said, "Now, do I dare start again?" This time she sang through to a lilting conclusion. Kikuji became sleepy, and his hand holding the receiver was numb. Tsuruhachi relieved him of the telephone, spoke a few words to Ponta, and hung up. Kikuji looked at him sleepily.

"You're a good fellow, Tsuruhachi. My family tries to keep me locked up in this tomb, but you have brought me into the world again. Only by telephone, of course, but it's a start in the right direction."

"With the telephone at your bedside, Master, you can call up O-Fuku and Hisako, as well as Ponta.

"I'm afraid not." He shook his head impatiently. "Protocol, you know. They haven't been presented to the family. And, besides, a patron doesn't call his mistress directly. Maybe from a restaurant or a teahouse, but never from his own home. Don't ask me why: Semba custom! For all Semba customs there are reasons as old as the earth and stars. And just as dull. Good night."

But he was tempted to call Hisako. After she had brought him back to his home from the race track had she rushed back to see the next race? Had she thought of him as anything but an encumbrance? Did she feel anything at all for him? He inclined to think not.

The next afternoon, when Tsuruhachi called to visit him, the jester found him sitting up staring out the window. Tsuruhachi looked too, but could only see the maid hanging clothes on a line to air.

Kikuji called her and she came running to the window in small, kimono-restrained steps.

"Okiyo, bring me that gray flannel western suit hanging under the eaves of the storehouse."

She looked at him, startled and hesitant.

"I'm not going to dress up in it and go out. I just want to see it."

When she came in with the suit, he turned to Tsuruhachi and said, "It's yours. Try it on."

The great eyes in the sad face widened in surprise. "Mine? Why, Master, it's a brand-new, imported, expensive suit! Don't you want it?"

"I hate it. I feel like a fool in it. I want you to wear it to the Polka Dot Cabaret for me."

Shaking his head doubtfully, Tsuruhachi went out into the hall to change into the suit. When he reappeared, the long trousers trailed behind him like the ceremonial garments of the forty-seven ronin. His hands were hidden in the sleeves.

"I don't blame you for feeling like a fool in this suit," he grumbled. "I make my living by being a fool, but I've never felt *this* foolish before."

Through his laughter Kikuji said, "It looks better on you than it did on me. Can you wear it that way to the Polka Dot?"

"No, no, Master. A joke is a joke, but we can't ruin a perfectly good suit just because you got pneumonia wearing it, now, can we? Let me shorten it."

He obtained a sewing box from Okiyo and with the skill of a professional tailor quickly shortened the sleeves and trousers. Then he took a tuck in the sleeves of the white shirt Kikuji had given him, and put on his new costume.

"How do I look, sir?"

"Like an avenging spirit straight out of a ghost story. And that's exactly what I need. I want you to go to Hisako. Look even gloomier than you normally look. Tell her that you were given that suit by my family as a remembrance when they were trying to decide what to do with all the clothes I had worn and would never wear again. And then sniffle and wipe your eyes. Let's see if she goes on studying the racing charts after that!"

Tsuruhachi bowed respectfully. "You have given me my chance, sir. I have always, after the manner of many clowns, I think, wanted to star in a tragic role. I shall give a performance so moving that in spite of herself she will cry out, 'Encore, Encore!' I must commit myself to it so fully that I do not contemplate the beauty of my own acting, lest I break down and weep at the tragic masterpiece I am in process of creating, I shall—"

"Oh, get on with you!" interrupted Kikuji, half in amusement, half in irritation. "I'm not going to hire a theater for your performance. The Polka Dot will have to do."

"The Polka Dot *will* do, sir. Its patrons will remember this night!"

After Tsuruhachi had finally left on his peculiar mission, Kikuji picked up a book and tried to read, but his mind was so taken up with Hisako's reaction to the strange vision of his western suit that he paid little attention to what he was reading. He ate his dinner quietly. Sei and Kino had gone out for the evening, and, save for an occasional noise from the servants' quarters, the house was very still. At around eight, there was a sliding of doors at the entryway, and Tsuruhachi entered. Only a small lamp on the floor at Kikuji's side illuminated the room, and Tsuruhachi at first was in semidarkness.

"How did it go?" Kikuji asked. "Was she surprised?"

Tsuruhachi advanced into the circle of light cast by the lamp.

"Why, you're all wet! What on earth happened? You stink of beer!"

Slowly, Tsuruhachi crumpled into seated posture before his employer.

"Ah, sir. It was quite a performance. Not mine: hers. She never gave me a chance to open my mouth. As soon as she saw that suit, she knew you were just a heap of ashes in a jug, and she sounded off like an opera singer trying to hit high C. Everybody in the Polka Dot was staring at us, and the manager came running over to see what I was doing to her. I think maybe she really loves you, sir, if you'll excuse my being personal. All that wailing must mean something. The manager kept offering her smelling salts and beer. She took the beer. Lots of it. I think maybe she was drunk when I came, but she drank enough in fifteen minutes after seeing me to make even a skilled toper see double and triple. And then she began to throw things. I got in the way of three mugs of beer filled to the brim. I got only the beer; the mugs, when they were emptied, she threw at the manager. Then she put her head down on the table and cried and cried and cried. I couldn't allow her to feel like that, so I sat down next to her, and said, 'Now, now, it's all a misunderstanding. Just a joke! He gave me the suit to wear here. To scare you, that's all.' Well, you've never seen such a change. She reared back and stared at me through those red eyes, and if looks could kill, I would myself be just a heap of ashes in a jug. Oh, that was certainly the most powerful joke I have ever participated in, I'll tell you that."

"And did she calm down then?" Kikuji asked.

"Calm down! Ah, well, you might say so. She kept on staring at me, and I kept trying to think of good conversation, but couldn't, and finally she said to me in a low, nasty voice I could barely hear, 'He has a low opinion of me and of all women. I'll not tamely submit to his nonsense. If he didn't know how to die, I do. I do!'

"A waiter helped me escort her back to her apartment. I left her there and came here right away. I am uneasy. It seems to me quite possible that she will really do what she hinted."

"Oh, come, now, Tsuruhachi. She was excited and angry, that's all."

"But excited and angry people do strange things, sir. And the waiter who helped me bring her home said that he had heard her at the entrance of the cafe giving money to one of the errand boys and telling him to buy her sleeping pills."

Kikuji thought for a moment, then rose from his bed. "Call Okiyo. I shall want my clothes. We are going to her place."

Tsuruhachi helped him dress. They left hastily by the side entrance, and, on reaching the street, signalled a taxi.

"You really think she's capable of suicide, then?" he asked Tsuruhachi.

"Ah, sir, I don't know. We are all capable of despair," replied the jester, looking straight in front of him.

289

Kikuji shook his head and exhaled, as though to expel thoughts too terrible to be formed. At last the cab came to a stop in front of Hisako's apartment house. While Tsuruhachi paid the bill, Kikuji climbed out and stared anxiously at her windows on the second floor. They were dark. He raced up the stairway. The little glass inset in her apartment door showed no light. He pounded on the door, but there was no response. Tsuruhachi, panting with the exertion of rushing up the stairs, looked at the door.

"I know the light was on when I left her here," he said.

Kikuji pushed hard and the lock gave suddenly. There was a faint light under the sliding door to the inner room. He called her name, and, when there was no answer, rushed to the sliding panel. On opening it, his eyes widened in horror. On a white sheet spread on the tatami mats lay Hisako, an empty pill bottle near her hand. She was still in her wine red gown. The image of Ikuko on her deathbed flashed vividly in his mind. That had been the unbearable sadness of great loss; this was nightmare, wildly irrational as only Hisako could make it. This dead woman before him: had he ever really known her? He felt the tears running down his face, less for her than for himself and his reputation, about to be dragged through police courts and public scrutiny. Why couldn't she behave like a lady and less like one of those passion-crazed western women? He bent down reverently beside her. Her full, red lips were parted. He stroked her cheek. It was warm still. He touched those lips with his finger— There was a great shout of pain.

"What *is* it, Master?" asked Tsuruhachi. But he saw soon enough. Kikuji was holding a bleeding finger tightly with his other hand. And Hisako lay looking up at them with a satisfied smile on her face.

"Don't play games with Hisako," she said lazily. "I fight back!"

Suddenly, he began to laugh. He could not stop. On and on he laughed, the tears still dropping from his eyes. Tsuruhachi excused himself and went downstairs to wait.

"Why pretend like this?" he asked dully.

"Ah, you want the real thing?" She tilted her head and rolled her eyes. "You pretended to be dead first, and you scared me half to death with your nonsense."

"I hated that suit. And I half hated you. You left me when I was sick and went rushing back to the race track."

290

"So that is what you think of me! I haven't been to the race track since you were ill except to provide for the horse."

He had intended to go home to resume his convalescence, but when her lips trembled, he bent down to solace her; she reached possessively toward him; he closed his eyes in a shiver of surrender at the heat of her hands.

"Oh, you rascal," he sighed softly. "You made me ill and now you have made me well again. Turn off the light. Let us prove the question of my health together."

When they had finished, she lit a cigarette, and puffed thoughtfully. "I want to change my life," she said at last.

"Change? Why?"

"No more racing. No more Polka Dot. I want you."

"Oh, come, now. In a day or so you'll feel different—"

"No," she said quietly. "You don't understand. I'm tired of all that. When you were sick, I knew. I thought I had almost lost you through—oh, through a kind of neglect. No more horses. No more night life. Just—you."

She pulled him to her again.

It was past ten. Slowly he stood up, dressed, gently kissed the sleeping Hisako on the forehead, and went downstairs. There in the parked taxi sat Tsuruhachi, hunched up in the back seat. Kikuji wakened the driver, climbed in, and gave his home address.

"I thought you were going to wait in the coffee shop," he said with a touch of embarrassment to his assistant.

"I tried, but I think the proprietress thought me some sort of western alcoholic. She wasn't at all used to beer-soaked western suits, and she kept making remarks about me to her daughter loud enough for me to hear. I left a very large tip, thanked her for her courtesy, and left." He yawned. "Even a clown has his dignity. Don't you agree?" He turned full on Kikuji, looking at him earnestly.

"Of course, of course. It was my fault, letting you wait all that time."

Unexpectedly, Tsuruhachi snapped his fingers and smiled. "I had a good nap. It was all right. But maybe the ladies of your house will not think so?"

"They needn't know. They've taken Hisajiro to a kabuki play. After the play they'll visit with their friends to show him off."

When he arrived home, he walked quietly into the courtyard toward the side door, but as he did so, he saw that the lights were on. He had been caught once again, like some schoolboy with his hand in the cookie jar. He sauntered into the hall and then to his bedroom. The ladies of the house sat with stern expressions on their faces. Okiyo was sniffling in the corner. Hisajiro looked apprehensively from one to another, not knowing what to expect.

"Good evening, Mother, Grandmother," he said with a bow to each. "I was out celebrating my recovery. It's my heredity: we are a family of night owls."

"If you keep on like this, we'll be a family in mourning," snapped Kino. She looked grimly at Tsuruhachi.

"What's the matter with Funny Man? Did he help you celebrate by jumping into a beer vat? Where'd he get your imported English suit?"

"You dislike the suit and so do I. I gave it to him."

She ignored his answer and continued staring at Tsuruhachi. "I thought you would be good for my grandson in his sickness. You are not. Leave!"

"Now, see here, Grandmother—"

"No, no, sir! The worthy lady is quite right. I apologize. Tomorrow I shall return the suit." Tsuruhachi vanished.

Kino sent Hisajiro off to bed.

"Well." He looked at them with an ironic smile. "Shall we begin?"

"The minute your temperature is down to normal you go rushing off like a tomcat on the prowl. Have you no dignity?"

"Not when I hear my own grandmother talking so disgustingly."

She gave a hard laugh. "I just name what you do. Who's disgusting?"

"Grandmother, nothing can be as bad as your imaginings."

"Okiyo, help the master get ready for bed."

The maid, who obviously had taken the brunt of the scolding before he came, hastened to help him into his night kimono. She started to fold the kimono he had worn to Hisako's, but Kino grabbed it from her, opened it up, and began to sniff at it. Like some ridiculous bloodhound she sniffed at the collar, and downward. Reluctantly, she put it down.

"Very well. The woman you were with didn't use perfume, that's clear."

Kikuji was amused, although he didn't show it. How fortunate that, before lying down with Hisako he had stripped off his clothes. There was no perfume on the kimono.

"Grandmother, you have it all wrong."

"You went to visit a sick friend, I suppose."

"A drunk friend. Kishida. I told you about him, Grandmother. Remember?"

He knew she would never admit it if she did not remember. She nodded uncertainly.

She apparently gave it up. She relaxed and sat more comfortably on the tatami next to his bedside.

"Well, just don't do it again as soon as your grandmother's back is turned. It's for your own good—" Her voice trailed away. She tilted her head and looked at him significantly. "We met two people at the theater you would be interested in."

"Ah. Who were they?"

"The first was Hiroko, your ex-wife."

His face was impassive. Eleven years! Without the mother and grandmother they would have made do with each other well enough.

"She sat in a box across from us with her new husband and his family."

"Her second husband. He isn't 'new.' They've been married at least seven years."

"Yes, yes. There were six children in the box with them. The man is a Tokyo wholesaler in foodstuffs. He must be doing well. There were three maidservants with them."

"Did they see you?"

"How could they help it? She bowed to us from where she sat."

"You returned it?"

"Kikuji! How absurd! I stared right through her."

"But why?"

"She should have come around to the entrance to our box, and sat there in the hallway, bowing with her hands on the floor. But she's too modern and rich to have good manners."

He was glad for her. She had escaped from these two vengeful creatures to a normal family, which accepted her as a human being, honored her, took her to plays, along with all her children. He was glad he had divorced her. She had deserved better than to be beaten down by Semba custom.

"Also, we met Mr. Sanoya," said Kino with a conspiratorial air. "He wants to give you a get-well party. Such a nice man!"

Poor Sanoya. How had he been maneuvered into such a mistake?

"He is very good-hearted, certainly."

"No more than he ought to be, of course. You saved his business for him. Maybe it was the right thing to do. Anyway, he wants to give us a party—at Hamayu's in Soemoncho. You like that place, don't you?" Her eyes glinted with curiosity.

"I'm sure it will be very nice there," he replied casually.

"Yes, yes. Very nice, I'm sure," the old lady cackled, overcome with an odd fit of amusement.

"It was good of him to think of it," he said again.

"Yes, yes. Wasn't it? And at Hamayu's too!" He noticed with alarm that she was exchanging looks of mysterious understanding with his mother. The bloodhounds were after him again. A get-well party with Sanoya, O-Fuku, his mother, and his grandmother all together in the same room would certainly bring on chills and fever all over again. What on earth was Sanoya thinking of? Or was he thinking of anything?

The afternoon before the party was a small domestic nightmare. Kikuji was so nervous that he had the greatest difficulty in hooking the clasps of his tabi. From across the hall he heard his mother and grandmother getting ready. It was one of their great occasions. Their hair, set the night before, was now being plaited into imposing masses by the beautician. They chattered to each other like schoolgirls awaiting a dance. How could Sanoya do a thing like this to him? He swore under his breath as he twisted his fingernail on a button. He drew on the *haori* coat which O-Toki held for him. While he was tying the cord in front, the sliding door opened and Sei and Kino looked at him with scarce-concealed impatience. With the jade ornamental pins in their hair they looked, he had to admit, magnificently festive.

"Hurry, hurry, child!" said Kino. "Mustn't keep your host waiting."

On their way to Hamayu's in the taxi, the two women kept talk-

ing excitedly to each other while Kikuji remained silent. It had begun to rain by the time they arrived at the teahouse, and six men
were lined up between the cab and the entrance, holding large
straw hats shaped like umbrellas over the guests to keep off the rain.
The ladies tucked up their magnificent kimono with their fingers
and hurried in. At the entrance stood O-Fuku, directing operations.
The quaint straw hats used instead of umbrellas had the stylish
quality of most of her innovations.

"Welcome, honored ladies of Kawachiya," she said, bowing low
on the tatami mat.

"Ah. You are the young lady we saw with Mr. Sanoya the other
day at the play, aren't you?" chirped Kino.

"Yes, my lady. Excuse me for not presenting myself at that time. I
am O-Fuku, the receptionist here at Hamayu's." She bowed again,
unhurriedly and with the flowing grace that only she was mistress
of. Then she rose and with the ease of long experience escorted the
ladies into the teahouse. She had looked at Kikuji only long enough
to acknowledge the fact of his existence. They walked down the
long hallway and, coming to a sliding door, she knelt at the entrance, announced the ladies, and opened the sliding panel. Inside
sat Sanoya and a large assemblage of business associates, each with
a geisha sitting in front of him. Their host came bounding to the
door, his red face beaming with pleasure.

"Come in, dear ladies, come in. No, no, not there. Here. In the
place of honor. Near me." He turned to Kikuji, "It is good to see you
well again, my dear fellow. I have missed you at business as well as
at leisure. Welcome back!"

Kikuji smiled wanly. "I hadn't realized— I thought it would be
just a small affair. It is good of you."

Sanoya waved an admonitory hand like a fan in front of him.
"Na-na-na-na-nah! A get-well party must be loud and full of friends
to chase away the horrors once and for all." He looked quickly at
the ladies, who were talking with O-Fuku, came close to Kikuji, and
said in low tones, "It's O-Fuku's doing. Very resourceful, that young
lady."

They were interrupted by a shriek.

"Oh! My! Look, Kikuji!" His grandmother pointed over his head.
"It's the tiger god of good health!"

She held her hands prayerfully in front of her and clapped them

295

at a papier-mâché tiger artfully arranged among bamboo branches in the art alcove. She looked severely at Kikuji. "Make your obeisance to the god of health before you get sick again, you naughty boy!"

Repressing a sigh, Kikuji went through the motions. He was about to sit down when he realized that Sei and Kino, in sitting next to Sanoya, were also looking across the table at O-Fuku.

"Grandmother, perhaps I could change places with you and sit next to Mr. Sanoya," he suggested.

With a rather exasperated gesture, she raised her sake cup to him. "No, no, my dear boy. You would drink too much. Besides, I want to alk with this charming young lady." She turned to O-Fuku. "When it comes to holding my liquor, as they say in the novels, I guess I can show my grandson a thing or two." She gave a raucous laugh. Sanoya made a short speech welcoming Kikuji back to the world of health, and followed this with several toasts. Kikuji bowed at the appropriate times, but his attention was taken up with O-Fuku and the conversation she was having with his grandmother.

"I understand our Kiku-bon quite likes Hamayu's and comes here more than to any other teahouse," said the old lady smoothly as she sipped her sake.

"Indeed yes, my lady. We have been greatly honored by his special preference." O-Fuku smiled amiably. She spoke simply and with assurance.

"Special preference! Yes, yes." Kino leaned forward conspiratorially and her voice dropped so low that Kikuji almost missed what she said. "And I can see why, too. Sometimes I forget that this grandson of mine isn't a little boy any longer. Children are such a worry! But a fine fellow in his prime should step out a bit and have his fling, eh?" Again the jarring, scratchy laugh. And again she leaned forward to pass a secret from one woman to another. "He's had his troubles, you know. Lost his mistress a little while back. Poor thing wasn't thirty-four when she died. He's been feeling lonesome since then. So he needs to step out. See what I mean?"

Managing to look cheerfully attentive, O-Fuku occupied herself with skillfully removing bones from the fish before offering it to Kino. The old lady studied her sharply for a moment, then continued, "All we care about is his well-being. That and doing things properly, don't you know. No substitute for propriety, I always say. So if he ever gets another mistress, I hope he'll have the good manners to present her to his family and to our family goddess—"

"Ah? Who is the family goddess, my lady?" asked O-Fuku.

"We worship the fox goddess. Every day. We have a shrine to her in our house. We are very, as you might say, religious." The old lady washed down a mouthful of fish with sake.

She waved her chopsticks erratically at O-Fuku. "No matter how old a grandchild is, my dear, we have to worry about him. You'll find out how it is someday. We have to protect ours, and find him the right playmates."

By this time she was talking in a voice loud enough so that Kikuji could see others were beginning to listen to what she was saying. He bowed his head in embarrassment, and at that moment realized that he felt ill. Quietly he rose to his feet. A young geisha who had been serving him noticed that he seemed to be wavering, and she rose to escort him out of the room. In the hallway he said to her, "Find a room. Let me lie down for a few moments. I'll be all right."

She spread quilts on the tatami mats of a small room and he lay down to rest until the nausea passed. Was it the exertion or his grandmother's wisdom which had made him ill? With a serious and slightly wistful expression, the youthful geisha carefully placed a cold, wet cloth on his forehead. He looked at her and smiled his thanks. At that moment the door softly slid open and O-Fuku was beside him. She dismissed the geisha and looked at him anxiously.

"I am so sorry, Master. I couldn't pay attention to you if I were to manage the ladies of your house. They are very famous; I was determined to manage them."

"And did you?" he asked in a low voice.

She tilted her head slightly and smiled. "I think so. But to do so I had to neglect you, and the whole reason for the party was to enable me to see you again."

"But you *did* enjoy managing them "

She looked at him and smiled again. "Of course," she said shyly. "One always enjoys what one does well, don't you think?"

"You do everything well."

"Don't be angry with me. I hadn't seen you for such a long time. Ponta could call you and talk with you because she had been presented to your family. For over two months I couldn't even call you to hear your voice." She hesitated, then went on. "And even that—even Miss Hisako of Polka Dot—even she—saw you—"

Tsuruhachi had been talking too much.

He took her hand and kissed it. "Forgive me. I have been neglectful. But always I've been thinking of you. Especially when I wake at night I think about you on and on and on—" He lay looking up at her. Both of them listened to the rain beating down on the eaves.

"Come to bed with me," he said.

"There isn't time tonight. Anyway, in your condition I'm not at all sure it would be what the doctor would prescribe."

There was a soft tap at the door.

"The guests are leaving, and I think they'll need you at the entry-way, O-Fuku." It was the young geisha.

O-Fuku rose immediately, straightened her clothing, opened the door, and walked across the courtyard in the rain to the hall near the doorway. The geisha assisted Kikuji as he slowly rose and walked through the halls to the room where his mother and grand-mother were saying their farewells. At the entrance, O-Fuku was bowing to each departing guest. When it was Kikuji's turn, she reached into the cupboard and drew out a new pair of slippers. Turning them over, she cut the sole in a special way with a knife. She bowed low to Kikuji.

"Master, with my knife I have slashed off the feet of the demon of sickness, which is the only right way to conclude a get-well party. Here are your new slippers. The old, sick slippers are not good for you who are cured." She bowed again.

"What a fine girl that is!" exclaimed his grandmother once the cab door was shut and they were on their way home. "She has a fine sense of what is proper. And she looks so healthy and bright. Just the sort of woman to bear a man's child, I should think."

Kikuji looked at her warily and with some amusement. "You sound like an experienced go-between." he said.

"I know how things go in the world," she replied with her peculiarly discordant snorting laugh. He forbore to sound her out further. The imaginings of that bitter mind might affect his stomach again.

Her words, however, kept ringing in his head: "Just the sort of woman to bear a man's child." What on earth did the old lady

298

mean by that? Was she about to spring some new and fantastic Semba custom on him? The doctor had declared him healthy and well again. He was free to go where he wished. But from the time of Sanoya's party he felt weighed down by the prying curiosity of his mother and grandmother. Never before had there been so many knowing looks, so many half-hidden smiles. He felt himself strangely naked as these two voyeurs of the imagination speculated on his every night out. As a result, he felt ill at ease when he visited with Ponta or with Hisako for any length of time. Nearly always, he began fidgeting after an hour or so, and restlessly returned home.

Hisako, to his surprise, had made good on her vow to quit the Polka Dot Cafe. As far as he could tell, she no longer visited the race track nor did she have the betting sheets around the apartment. The transformation to quiet mistress seemed so complete that it made him a little apprehensive. Too many things were changing too rapidly. It made him feel insecure. Her apartment nowadays was always clean and spotless. When he called to tell her that he was coming, she would rush to the store and, by the time he had actually arrived, she would be busily cooking some delicacy for him. It was a puzzling and vaguely upsetting transformation.

Ponta, meanwhile, had begun to study the art of Japanese drums. She would hold them up to her shoulder and thump on them patiently by the hour. Kikuji tried it a few times and found it unrewarding. Nor did he much like listening to her as she practiced. But it represented no sudden change in her. It fitted in with the diamond in the tooth, the rings, and the general exuberance which was her most delightful characteristic. Like Hisako, she assumed that his insistence on going home after short visits was simply the result of his physical weakness after the illness, and she waited patiently for a return of his normal desires.

He avoided going to O-Fuku. He knew she was waiting for him, but he knew too that Kino had something in mind in connection with O-Fuku, and he liked the Hamayu receptionist too much to see her hurt.

One day as he was working on the books in the accounting room, he was aware that Kino was standing at his shoulder. He looked up sharply. She was not supposed to invade the business in this fashion.

"Kiku-bon, I must talk with you. I'm sorry to interrupt, but it's important."

299

Reluctantly, he closed the ledger, stood up, and followed her into the family section of the house. Kino led the way to his mother's room. Sei greeted him as he entered. All three sat down.

"Now. What is this important matter which could not wait till supper?" he asked.

"Kiku-bon, I have just been to see O-Fuku," said Kino.

He looked at her, his eyes sparkling with anger. "Grandmother, why is it that you just cannot mind your own business?"

"She did it for your own good," speedily interposed his mother. "O-Fuku is a fine and honorable person. I won't have her harassed by you."

Kino threw back her head and laughed her snorting laugh. "Of course she is, my dear boy. I didn't go to make trouble. I went to make a deal. You need a good mistress. Your mother and I suspected that you and O-Fuku had been the best of friends for a long time. But nothing happened. You hadn't been to see her since the get-well party. I lost my patience and went over to see her."

"Why do you feel compelled to meddle in this way, Grandmother?"

"Kiku-bon, surely you know that both your mother and I have been glad that you have had your mistresses? Any prosperous businessman without a few mistresses is either stingy or hankers after young boys. In the big firms even the managers have mistresses. It's a status symbol. So that's all right. But your mother and I haven't been very pleased with your choices thus far: they're either hoydens, like Ponta, or too obedient, like Ikuko. You need a woman of spirit."

"But what on earth business is it of yours?"

"Ah, you don't realize that a mistress isn't just for a man's pleasure. Don't they say, 'A child from a mistress is a sturdy supporting post to a house'?"

"I'm sure I don't know what they say," he returned peevishly. He sipped at the tea O-Toki had just brought. "I am to assume, then, that my grandmother visited a girl I am friendly with, and asked her to become my official mistress. What did she say to this incredible proposition?"

"Oh, I like her very much." said Kino. "Some women in such a situation would have bowed and wept and made a great to-do, either overwhelmed at the honor or outraged at the notion of being an easy catch. But your friend just looked at me calmly and smiled, and said it was an unusual situation. Then she poured me tea. A perfect hostess, she is."

"But what did she say?"

"Well, but you see I had told her we particularly wanted her to have a child—"

"We?"

"Your mother and I. Much as we love Hisajiro, we aren't foolish. He hasn't the toughness needed to run a business. He's the artistic type. We thought that, if O-Fuku had a daughter—it must be a girl —then, when she grew up, she could marry an adoptive husband just like your father. He could run the business and we'd all be very secure."

"A son of O-Fuku could run the business and there would be no need for adopted husbands."

"Oh, Kiku-bon. You always miss the point! Kawachiya's is the great firm it is today because there have been three generations of heiresses, each of whom took in a sure, able man as husband and manager. We are a matriarchal family. You are an exception. Fortunately, you are also capable. No, we must have a girl."

"Are you going to order her to have a girl and not a son?"

"No. No. We won't do that. But I'm sure that, if we pray with a pure heart to our benefactress, the fox goddess, she will take care of us. It must be a girl."

"Very well. The fox goddess is in on the plan. That leaves only O-Fuku. What did she say?"

"Well, she said that usually the young man's family didn't want any children from the mistress at all, or even any mistress, so that she guessed she was fortunate in that respect. Then we talked about other things for a long time: about the history of Hamayu's Teahouse, mostly. Finally, she turned to me and said, 'I confess that I feel very deeply for your son and would be happy to be his mistress except for one thing. I enjoy being the receptionist here at Hamayu's, and I would not be happy if he bought me a house and left me in it, the way men do. Perhaps he can buy me a small house, but I will continue to work here at Hamayu's until there is a baby. Then I will stop, at least until after the child is born. Do you think we could agree to that?' I told her that we could. Doesn't that make you happy?"

Kikuji shook his head in bewilderment. "I'll never understand. For me she would not!"

"Ah, but it's different. With you it appeared that she would have to give up her freedom just to wait and be your plaything. With me, it was a business arrangement. I wanted a granddaughter. I allowed her her freedom to continue work at Hamayu's. It isn't a bad bargain for her. Besides, I don't know why she should, but she loves you, you young scamp!" She patted him fondly on his arm.

Kikuji continued to shake his head in puzzlement. His grandmother looked at him quizzically. "What you don't understand, Kiku-bon, is that O-Fuku is a full woman. The others are dolls by comparison. She is full-blooded. Her skin is soft and lustrous like mine—"

He looked at the old creature in astonishment.

"Ah, my boy, when I was young, I was—different. Even now!" And suddenly, to his consternation she drew aside in one great gesture the folds of her kimono. The breasts of the seventy-year-old woman hung down, but they were of a lustrous white texture, a consistency very like O-Fuku's.

"So you see what I mean," Kino said simply, covering herself again. "We are kindred spirits, she and I. A daughter of hers, supplemented with your blood, would be a person of great character."

Kikuji threw up his hands. "Well, it's up to the fox goddess now. You'd better pray hard!"

That night he went to see O-Fuku.

It was a long, difficult talk, hovering at times on the brink of catastrophe.

"I know," he said finally, "that you have a strong character, and you have always shown it with a physical grace that I love. But when my grandmother says you are like her, then I begin to be uncertain. I don't want you like her. She would give her soul to the devils in hell for a material advantage in the Semba District. It's all she cares about. I don't want you to make a business deal. I want you to come to me because you want to come to me."

"We must both need each other," she said softly. "I need you very much. These last few months have shown me. But please don't try to make me a plaything filed away in a house to await your pleasure. What you like about me would not last if you did that. I need to be busy and sociable. But I want you."

The next day they bought a small, old house in the Shitadera-machi District, where many of Osaka's well-known temples were situated. It was a long, quiet house, appropriate to the temple district. Kikuji wished to modernize it, but she wouldn't allow him to alter the old-fashioned charm which it had for her. He thought it rather gloomy, but he acceded to her taste. She settled in the five-room house without a maid. When she went to work, the lady in the neighboring house kept an eye on the place for her.

Looking back on the events of the past few months, Kikuji found his world changed beyond belief. The severe illness seemed to have altered all the pieces on the chessboard. Hisako had ended her career as gambler and cafe hostess. O-Fuku, his secret mistress, had tried hard to keep her affair from the prying eyes of the grandmother, and Kino had instead admired her competence and ability so much that she had pushed the liaison vigorously forward. Kikuji was used to running his own life, but just now he felt himself a creature of fate.

303

Nine

"What do you think of the Manchurian Incident, Sanoya-san?"

The old man put down his sake cup and frowned thoughtfully. "Who can say? It has been two years now. I know our young men fight bravely, and it is for the peace of Asia that we do this. But sometimes I wish our government would let the depression end before spending our resources in this way. Government can't be very different from business. This is no time for expansion."

"But you're expanding. You won't be able to be at the Osaka Tabi Sellers' Association banquet because you'll be away opening a new branch."

The old man grinned. "Yes, I've advertised that. But no one knows that I closed two other outlets which were losing money."

They were seated in a conference room between the business area at Kawachiya's and the family quarter, planning the annual banquet of the Tabi Sellers' Association.

"Sometimes, Kiku-bon, I feel very old and wish for the peace and quiet of the old days. You probably have even forgotten when we could call up the geisha houses and tell them to send their best girls to us for the evening."

"But we can still do that."

"Nah, nah, nah. It's all different. Now we economize. All they'll send us is a preselected package. Three geisha for an hour. At the special economy rate of one yen. And at the end of that hour, off they go, even if they're in the middle of a sentence."

Kikuji laughed. "I rather like it this way. A new group will replace the ones who leave, and the fun starts all over."

"It all depends on your luck. Some of those packaged geisha look like—like—well, have you ever bought a package of apples because it's cheaper than selecting your own from the pile, one by one? And then you get that economy package home, and you open it looking for a fine, chewy apple, and the first one you put your hands on has a brown spot with a worm waving his head in the center of it? Well, that's the way some of those packaged geisha affect me."

"Variety is the spice of life, Sanoya-san."

The old man grunted and lit his pipe. "Not at my age, it isn't. Sometimes I think we in Japan would be a great deal happier if Emperor Meiji hadn't sent his ministers to Europe to find out how the world was doing without us. Sometimes I think that we Japanese would be infinitely happier without variety and foreign luxury. We want too much."

"We want to make the most of our lives. Everyone does: the tribesman in New Guinea, the scientist in London," Kikuji reflected. "It's just that sometimes I think that the politicians think in other terms and will start wars to get themselves promotions."

"A fat lot of promotions they deserve for the present mess! Nothing but drought and poor crops from Hokkaido. That was the place which was going to be Japan's special food supplier. Inflation all over the place! Nobody's buying anything they don't absolutely have to have, these days. Wherever you look you find economy packages—with rotten apples. The pleasure quarter needs to be renamed. When you go there looking for company, you find the streets and houses deserted. It's very depressing. And I can't even call up the geisha house and tell them to send my favorite geisha. All I get is a one-hour package of three ugly old hags. How is a man to have any fun?"

"But it has brought the geisha entertainment system within the reach of the less wealthy classes, Sanoya-san," replied Kikuji.

"Good for them, but not good for me. If I do happen to like one of those packaged geisha and want to keep her for another hour, the fee goes up to double. It's discrimination against rich old men!" He looked sharply at Kikuji for an instant, then smiled. "Excuse me for being such a grouch. I'm just annoyed because I can't be at the Tabi Sellers' party, I guess." He knocked his pipe out on the ashtray. "No, that isn't it, really. When you're young, change is exciting, but when you're old, it is very confusing."

"I'm sorry you won't be at the party tomorrow. You need a party to cheer you up."

"Well, maybe if I finish early with my new store I'll look in toward the end of the evening and say hello to all the packaged geisha. But don't count on it."

Next evening, as he was enjoying the excitement of the party, Kikuji recalled with wry sympathy the old man's words. There were five "packages" of three geisha each, and, at the end of the hour, when everyone had become accustomed to the girls and their songs and dances, they packed up and went away, presumably to another party. They were replaced by five more "packages" of three, and for an instant, Kikuji found this rotation irritating. But then he participated in the formal introductions of the new groups, and he found the renewed socializing stimulating, all the more so when in one of the threesomes he recognized the serious and careful young geisha who had taken care of him during his brief spell of illness at his get-well party. She saw him and came over promptly to greet him. Then she returned to the far section of the room to which she had apparently been assigned, and poured sake. One of the merchants observed him watching the girl.

"Isn't she delightful?" he asked. "Like a flower about to bloom. She comes from a mountain village quite far from here. Rated the top performer in her geisha school. Korin will be a wonderful geisha if only she can preserve that country-girl earnestness. But in Osaka it won't be easy."

When asked to sing, she sang a melancholy song Kikuji had never heard before in a clear, haunting soprano voice. The guests applauded generously and asked that she dance. Fan in hand, she conducted herself with stately precision in an elaborate dance. Then she came over and seated herself gracefully in front of Kikuji.

"You work so hard and so well at being a geisha," he said smiling. "Did you learn all this at your geisha school?"

"Oh, geisha school is very demanding, sir," she replied earnestly. "We practice samisen music and singing and dancing, and we learn how to present ourselves to guests and how to serve the food and pour the wine and how to enter and exit from a room. It is a very complicated science, this being a geisha."

"And did you learn how to be a nurse to an ailing guest, as you were to me the other day?" he asked.

She looked at him in wide-eyed seriousness. "Oh, that. No, sir, I didn't learn that at geisha school. I just did what I thought you needed to have done—and what I thought O-Fuku would want me to do. I am glad you are healthy again, sir."

"Thank you. When you finish with the party here, Korin, perhaps you and some of your friends will join me and we'll go to some of the other night spots?" The two geisha on either side had been listening, and at this suggestion, their eyes sparkled, and they moved toward Kikuji chorusing, "Can we come too?" He smiled noncommittally at them.

"As I understand it," said Korin slowly, "we must have permission both from the teahouse and from the main geisha office before going off like that on a new assignment. Also, we would have to remain at the old assignment until replacements had arrived."

"Oh, you recite that straight from the book you studied at geisha school," teased one of the geisha who wished to come along. "Relax, Korin. The best student at geisha school must learn that first of all."

"Well, I don't know. Unless these things are done just right, one can't hope to be an A one geisha."

"She's thinking of her report card instead of having a good time," said the teasing geisha.

"It's all right," said Kikuji. "It takes time to apply all the lessons you pick up in geisha school, I suppose. Korin's all right."

She looked at him and a smile slowly overspread her face. "Thank you, sir," she said.

A waiter came to Kikuji at that moment and told him he was wanted on the telephone. The call was from Hidesuke. He was characteristically demonstrating his zeal even after hours, trying to arrange a meeting for his boss with one of the retail sellers. Kikuji hung up the phone with an exasperated smile. If he should scold the fellow, he might stop doing all sorts of useful things. He looked down the dimly lit hall. The noise of the party came from the banquet room at the end. On the way to it, he passed the garden, and, on sudden impulse, stepped down from the hall into a pair of garden slippers. He was overheated with too much sake, and the night air was cool. He lit a cigarette and inhaled, but the humidity had got into the tobacco grains, and even in its shape the white cylinder looked wilted. He threw it away and walked on. The lively sounds of the party receded until he could distinguish only occasional gusts of laughter. The quiet of the garden suited his mood. Another noise impinged on his consciousness: the shrill, earnest voice of a woman talking rapidly on the telephone. He moved toward the sound. Rounding the bushes, he saw Korin standing on her tiptoes to reach the mouthpiece of the phone suspended high on the wall. Whenever she gestured or nodded, the two long halves of her stiff decorative sash swayed behind her: the butterfly wings of the apprentice geisha. How graceful, how helpless she looked. After hanging up the receiver, she searched busily in her pocket and long sleeve for something.

"You have doubtless lost your *Young Geisha's Guide for Every Occasion*," said Kikuji as he came up behind her. "May I help a lady in distress."

She looked at him with a smile of surprise and puzzlement. "I must pay for my phone call, and I can't find the five-sen piece I had just a moment ago—"

"Five sen is no great matter, and the teahouse proprietor won't go bankrupt if you don't pay, even if times are hard. Forget it."

She looked half-shocked, half-uncertain because he seemed to be joking. "Oh, no, sir. This teahouse is a good customer. And there are rules. I must pay!" She spoke with quiet certainty, and he did not interfere further. Instead, he placed a five-sen coin in her palm.

"How serious you are about all your rules," he said, looking into the intense delicacy of her upturned young face. "Here are five sen for the phone call. And here are five yen for taking care of me the other night when I felt unwell. Your presence helped me greatly."

He saw the protest forming on her lips and forestalled it. "No, no. Your rule book—you must show me your rule book sometime—says nothing about taking tips from men grateful to you for a humanity and care required of no one. I give this to you not for being a talented geisha, which you are, but for being you."

She hesitated an instant, then shook the head now bent down so that he saw only the lustrous black hair with its decorative combs. "Please, sir. I mustn't."

He restrained his impatience. Was it utter purity or a species of perverse stupidity? "Very well, then. I'll do it through the proper channels: notify the geisha house so that they can take their cut, and pass it to you through the teahouse. Is that what you want?"

There was another second of silence, and again that strong-willed head shook out a negative sign.

"What, then?"

"You will be shocked," she whispered in words which he could barely hear.

"Perhaps. But I don't shock easily. Try me."

"I want to go with you when you take O-Fuku out for a night."

Kikuji's eyes widened in amazement, his fatherly smile suddenly replaced by open-mouthed astonishment. She looked up at him apprehensively, then suddenly giggled.

"I *did* shock you, didn't I?"

"Tell me more, young lady. What idea do you have of O-Fuku and me?"

"Well, everyone knows you are lovers." She looked at him with demure trustfulness.

"Oh?"

Suddenly her eyes bore into his and her complexion reddened visibly under her heavy makeup. "I want to learn—about life—everything a geisha needs to know."

He laughed in an attempt to fend her off. "And so you want O-Fuku and me—two famous lovers—to set up a sort of demonstration. Is that it?"

The head was down once more, the words barely audible. "I have offended you."

"No, my dear, you have not. I suppose that maybe you have given me the ultimate compliment. Ultimate for a man of my age, anyway." He looked at her speculatively. "Have you thought of what you're asking? O-Fuku and I are, in fact, lovers. If you come with us some night, you may find yourself at certain moments terribly isolated, and even, perhaps, embarrassed. Can you take that?"

"I need to know, I need to know," came the whispered words from the head bent at his chest. And then suddenly she was looking him full in the face with a faintly impudent grin. She stuck her tongue out at him and laughed.

"All girls need to know these things, but geisha especially. You see I come from way out in the country. Exept for what they teach in geisha school, I know nothing, nothing! You know the way Japanese schoolchildren are always taking study trips with their teachers?

309

I've never been on one. Until I came to Osaka, I had never even been outside my little village. So—is it all right? Will you take me with you and O-Fuku the next time?"

He shrugged his shoulders and shook his head. "Very well. We'll do it. If it isn't educational, it will certainly be memorable. And I guess all memorable things are ultimately educational. So, we'll try it. Maybe you will earn an advanced degree at an early age."

She bowed before him. "I must return now to the party." She turned and moved away, the train of her full kimono sliding softly over the moss on the path. He stood contemplating the gracefulness of the departing girl. Even in walking through a garden in the dark she seemed determined to give the best performance she could. Part of her charm was the sheer beauty of a child who with furrowed brow and tongue between teeth tries desperately to do as the grown-ups do. He smiled to himself. And part of her charm too was that she was far more grown-up than she seemed to realize.

As he returned to the hallway and knelt to remove the garden clogs, he noted out of the corner of his eye someone coming by. He looked up and saw staring at him familiar, sad eyes deep-set in a memorably ugly face.

"Tsuruhachi!" he exclaimed. "I haven't seen you in months. What are you doing here?"

"Eh, Master, every party needs the services of the likes of me. I am here to wake up your guests with my ready wit, my legerdemain, my imitations, my impersonations, my philosophic asides, my—"

"Tsuruhachi, don't tell me that you are one of those economy packages of geisha?"

"Precisely, Master. What I lack in sexual availability I more than make up for in general usefulness. To be quite exact, tonight I have been asked to help the lady geisha with their costumes and makeup. It's not my usual line, but the depression can't last forever, and food is food."

"I'm sorry."

"Thank you, Master, but I am all right. My mind is no longer weighed down by too much food or befogged with drink. How did the philosopher say it? I hunger; therefore I am. A fine slogan for a fine depression! But now I must get on to the party, with your permission."

310

He watched the jester in his threadbare kimono shuffle off down the corridor. The contrasting image of Korin, as she had left him in the garden came unbidden to his mind. He shook his head in confusion. She was so young. What a miserable time in which to grow up.

"I feel like a goldfish in a bowl," growled Kikuji. "Absolutely everyone in this train is staring up at us."

"Relax and enjoy it," O-Fuku replied with a slight smile. "Look at this one." She made a slight gesture toward Korin who sat with her face glued to the window. "She ignores her fellow occupants completely."

"For the present, yes," he replied with a meaningful look at O-Fuku. "She never went on a study tour. You and I are her mentors."

Indolently, he looked over the others in the railroad car. Their only common characteristic seemed to be a variety of curiosity, salacious or puritanical, as to the ultimate objectives of the rich-looking gent in kimono with the two women at his beck and call. To the pimply salesman across the aisle, who had been staring open-mouthed and unrestrainedly until he had met Kikuji's quiet gaze, the two women, different as they were, were equally attractive. The old grandmother a few seats ahead looked them over with a contemplative tolerance born of years of experience. Finding that Kikuji was staring at her, she smiled amiably and looked out the window at the terraced farms. The fate of the world did not rest on her shoulders.

He looked again at Korin. "I'm glad there is glass between you and the countryside," he said. "Otherwise, I think you would escape into it and never be seen again." She nodded, but he doubted that she had heard. As the train swung to the coast near Shirahama, she vented her excitement by chattering incessantly to him and to O-Fuku. Occasionally she punctuated her comments with almost childish shouts of joy. It was the sight of this very youthful geisha's apprentice, adorned in the finery of colorful silk kimono and ornate decorative sash, which caught all attention finally. Wealthy men with their beautiful mistresses were not uncommon; but here was a man with his mistress and, in addition, a youthful and rather delightful young geisha. Her hair was done up comfortably, like that of a young city girl, but the heavily powdered makeup was that of a woman of the quarter. O-Fuku somehow seemed even more distinguished by comparison with Korin. Her kimono was subdued but fashionable. Korin amused her, and she replied to her from time to time with a slight smile and a nod. Kikuji leaned his head against the seat cushions and closed his eyes. When he opened them a few minutes later O-Fuku and Korin were looking at him in shared amusement.

"I was right," said Korin. "You weren't asleep. What were you thinking about with your eyes closed?"

"That I was fortunate to be with two such pretty ladies."

"But that only takes a second to think. What after that?"

"Why—um—well, let me see. I was thinking about my new line of tabi, the ones with colored soles, which I have just finished sending to the retailers."

O-Fuku laughed in triumph. "You see? You thought he was dreaming about the countryside, Korin, but, when he isn't thinking about women, he's thinking about his business."

Kikuji straightened up in his seat and coughed. "Well, but of course," he said grumpily.

O-Fuku put her hand on his arm and smiled, looking into his eyes. "But of course," she agreed. "You've been very much overworked recently."

She started to say more, but the train had begun to slow down and suddenly Korin, looking out the window, said loudly, "We're there. It's Yusaki!" Hastily, they reached for their bags and belongings and prepared to get out. The guide was at the station and he drove them quickly to the rustic inn surrounded by trees, overlooking the sea. As they were shown to their rooms, they were told that the bath was ready. But they were hungry and asked to eat first. They put on the cotton lounging kimono provided by the inn. While the meal was being served, Korin rested her chin on the windowsill and watched the twilit sea below them. She noticed the two of them watching her, and ducked her head defensively.

"It is so beautiful," she mumbled indistinctly.

O-Fuku allowed herself to be drawn to the window, and stood beside Korin for a moment in silence, looking out over the dim seascape. The soft thud of the sliding door caused her to turn, and she saw the maid bringing in the food.

"Come, Korin," she said briskly. "Time to eat."

The girl awakened suddenly from her trance and walked eagerly to the table, where she knelt down and abruptly took the hot sake bottle from the maidservant's hands.

"Oh, come, now, Korin," said Kikuji. "You're on vacation. Let the maid do the pouring and serving."

"But that is not what I am supposed to do," she said earnestly.

"Oh, but it is, my dear," said O-Fuku with her usual unhurried calmness. And yet—was he imagining?—Kikuji sensed for once in her the faintest vestige of impatience. "You are supposed to relax and enjoy yourself because that will encourage the master and me to relax and enjoy ourselves too."

Korin looked at her for a moment with troubled eyes, then nodded, seized some chopsticks, and began eating voraciously. But then, just as suddenly as she had begun eating, she recollected the manners she had been taught at the geisha school; the ravenous child became in an instant the poised geisha, delicately keeping her mouth pursed as she took in tiny morsels of the shrimp tempura and swallowed them without visibly chewing or opening her mouth.

"Try some of the steamed clam," O-Fuku suggested to her.

"Perhaps not, if you don't mind," said Korin. "It is too hard to chew . . ."

O-Fuku laughed. "Too hard not to chew, you mean," she replied. "Relax, Korin. This is a geisha's night off. An apprentice geisha's night off."

"Yes. Well—maybe—" she agreed, but still she avoided the clams.

After Kikuji had finished his cigarette on the verandah, the maid came to usher them to the hot bath. They walked along the inn corridor to its end. The maid ushered them into a room with a pool of steaming water set in natural rock. Looking at it from the dressing room, Kikuji said, "Ah, that looks fine!" and began taking off his kimono. O-Fuku began to help him undress.

"Excuse me," said Korin shyly. "Is this—the only pool?"

O-Fuku looked at her in disbelief. Hadn't the girl ever been at an inn before? "It's a family-style pool, Korin. There are only the three of us. It's perfectly all right."

Kikuji had stripped down to his shorts.

Korin lifted the hem of her kimono and ran out the door. Kikuji stared after her in amazement. "Now, what do you make of that?" he asked.

313

O-Fuku took off her clothes. "Come into the pool and I'll tell you," she replied.

When they had soaked for awhile in restful silence, O-Fuku said, "That girl hasn't had the defloration rite yet."

"The what?"

"She's still a virgin. She wants not to be. It's one of the qualifications of a geisha."

"Not to be, that is."

"Of course."

"It's one of the qualifications of being a woman."

"Of course."

They fondled each other lazily in the hot water.

"She wanted to watch us tonight so that she could learn from us," Kikuji said.

"Not tonight. Get her a separate room. She'll be relieved."

"But still curious."

"Yes." She paused for a long time. Then, her voice echoing oddly in the rocky bath chamber, she said clearly and distinctly, "I find that I cannot have your baby. Or anyone's."

Kikuji seemed not to have heard. He lay face upward in the steaming water and drifted a little distance from her.

"It has been over a year now since your grandmother asked me to have the baby. I intended to, of course. It was part of our agreement, and anyway I wanted it. But I've been to three doctors. I am unfertile ground for your seed."

He looked at her in the water. That magnificent body: unfertile! It seemed an incredible contradiction, one of the gods' meanest ironies.

"Did you know about this when we made our agreement with Grandmother?"

"No, no. Not then. Only recently."

The clear reply lingered in the steamy air of the cavernlike bath. He said nothing. Only the dripping of the water faucet interrupted the heavy silence.

Suddenly he thrashed out of the water and sat on one of the wooden stools. O-Fuku followed him slowly and stood behind him to scrub his back with a rough towel. From the communal bath chamber across the courtyard came the thin wail of an infant. She

314

stopped massaging his back and stood in front of him quietly, in the easy simplicity of her nakedness.

"Let Korin have your baby."

He stared at her. "You must be mad."

"No. She regards the experience the way some mystics think of conversion. It is part of her religion. She doesn't want love. She yearns to be of service. She is like an uncancelled letter. She yearns to be canceled! She goes to sleep dreaming of a man in bed beside her. Not necessarily you. Any man who is virile and kindly. So you would be doing her a great favor."

"So I am to be the cancellation machine!"

"I am told by those who know that men set great store by sleeping with a young girl and relieving her of her virginity. I don't know why they should, and I take it on faith. Perhaps it has something to do with purity and tenderness. I don't know. But the rite of defloration"—she turned her face away from him—"I know from my own experience. Beforehand it was terrifying and bizarre. Afterward, I wept with gratitude and reserves of passion which I had not known I possessed. I would have followed that man to the ends of the earth—"

"And for him—?"

"He was a gourmet, a connoisseur. He knew the delicacy and freshness of what he was getting. Only the connoisseur is allowed, with his odd combination of sensuality, kindliness, and disinterestedness, to participate in the rite of defloration. I am told that those so honored dream happily of the event to their dying moment."

The two lovers sat gloomily contemplating each other's nakedness.

"I owe you a baby, Master," she urged. "What do you say?"

"O-Fuku, you are in my blood and I shall never be cured of you. Still—that day when I was sick at the party—it was almost as though you had sent her in to me, as though you had appointed your substitute then, just in case you couldn't keep your part of the bargain. I think you get some kind of pleasure in contemplating this substitution. I don't know that I want to be a mere cancellation machine."

"I didn't plan this scandalous expedition," she reminded him. "You did. You were willing to have her watch us. I was surprised

315

that you agreed to her suggestion, but I think you understand her very well. She claims to be adapting to traditional ways, and maybe she is. But maybe she will adapt to any and all pressures. Maybe she is not an echo of the past, but a wave of the future. She will adapt. Let Korin have your baby. I will help her. I can, I think, stand to have her as my substitute. I too have feelings—"

"Feelings? Who cares about mere feelings?" said Kikuji, standing up. "We are not talking of feelings, of love, but of rituals." He sank into the pool again. "Very well. I shall participate in the rite of defloration for Korin. Does she know it is in prospect? But what difference does it make? Rituals take place on schedule, whether they mean anything or not. Is a ritual necessary to produce a baby? And why do I need another? I have three already. One a legitimate, rather frail sort. The other two? Who can tell? So by all means, let's have a ritual defloration for a young woman who wishes to be attuned to the rhythms of the universe."

In a fury he splashed water on O-Fuku, and sank thunderously back into the pool.

When they returned to their room, Korin, having completed her ablutions in the communal pool, sat in front of a mirror, braiding her hair.

O-Fuku looked at her. "How old are you, Korin?" she asked.

"Sixteen. I'm sixteen. When I was thirteen, I began studying at the geisha school. I went directly from elementary school. But I'm sixteen and in a few months I'll be seventeen." She lowered her head apprehensively. "Is that all right?"

"Of course it's all right," answered O-Fuku. "But tell me, have you ever thought about the time when you are to be mastered?"

The girl's head was lower still. She looked with reddened cheeks at O-Fuku. "You mean, about when I must take to myself a master?"

"Well—yes, I guess I do mean that."

"I've thought about it," she said in a low voice.

"Does it bother you?"

"Of course, but it excites me too. Then, when I am, as you say, mastered, I shall be a real geisha. Now I am just a chrysalis. Then, with the magic touch of the master's wand, I shall be all butterfly, I hope. That is what our lady principal at the geisha school says anyway. She says we should prepare a trousseau just like a bride, and wait in hope for the master's magic wand."

Kikuji couldn't sleep well that night. In the half-darkness of early dawn he was awakened by the wind in the leaves outside. A crack of light filtered in from Korin's room, where she slept with the light still on. O-Fuku slept soundly at his side. He puzzled over these two women: one, whom he loved, wished to give him to the other with almost perverse generosity; and the other was dreaming dreams. If he did not lead her on her way someone less humane would do the job. And she wanted it to be done. Poor child. How utterly puzzling women could be. Gently, he freed himself of the covers, and went out on the verandah to watch the sun rising over the calm gray sea.

O-Fuku handled all the arrangements smoothly and efficiently, asking him only the most necessary questions lest he should change his mind.

"I have conferred with the lady who manages Korin's geisha house. The basic cost to you for the ceremony will be one thousand yen. Two hundred of that amount will go to the senior geisha, Koyoshi, who acts as Korin's sponsor, another hundred will be used for tips and presents to the maids and the other geisha of the house."

"By the time they've taken their cut, there won't be anything left for Korin," he grumbled.

"The rest is hers," replied O-Fuku. "This is an act of religion for her. Money couldn't buy her. Now, tell me: do you want the ladies of your house to be informed?"

He looked ironically at her.

"No."

"Very well, then. We consulted both of your horoscopes, and decided to have the ceremony on January fifteenth, three days from now."

"On the Women's New Year," he said smiling. After all the work of the regular New Year's celebration was over and done with, the women quietly celebrated the end of their labors at their own little festival.

"I hope it goes well," she said, her voice oddly uncertain.

"Yes, of course," he replied. "I will see to it that this—that her—her religious rite will measure up to her expectation."

317

"Yes, of course," she echoed vaguely.

Three days later, when he showed up at Hamayu's ahead of the designated time, O-Fuku was there, waiting.

"I didn't expect you so early," she said. "Be kind to her, Master. Gratitude sometimes grows into love."

"You want that? Don't worry: I'll do my part." He looked at her curiously for some sign of emotion, but there was none. Under her superbly crafted kimono, her breath came regularly and slow. Whatever the effort, it must have been behind the scenes. Now, as she sat quietly looking at him, she was in complete control of herself. She had promised a baby, and there would be one, sponsored by her, cared for by her, in the body of her protegee.

She turned toward the door, and, still kneeling, held it open for him. He stood up and moved toward the opening. A lock of her hair hung down enticingly on her neck. He leaned forward to touch it, but she reared suddenly backward, away from him.

"Stop it! Korin is pure and undefiled; keep yourself so today out of deference to her."

She followed him at a distance, and waved as the taxi drove off with him to Yamatoya, where Korin awaited him. There to greet him were Sanoya, who was visiting the proprietress, and a number of geisha from Korin's house. Tsuruhachi appeared and disappeared as he busily arranged the affair. Sanoya clapped him on the shoulder as he entered.

"Always busy, always busy," he shouted. "Who else would've scheduled a defloration ceremony on the Women's New Year! What a perfect way to reward them, when you come to think of it. It has all the hallmarks of the *bonchi* of Kawachiya's."

Kikuji, however, felt no exultation. Korin, to be sure, was attractive and delightful, and he liked her. He had agreed to the defloration ceremony, however, only because he had been annoyed with O-Fuku and had sought to punish her for her cool and distant way of manipulating people. He had waited for her to retract the infamous offer, and instead she had persisted, calmly and even eagerly. So here he was, an old goat of thirty-eight travel-stained years, about to commit rape under the guise of a religious ceremony on a seventeen-year-old child. He felt a complete fool.

At that moment, Korin entered the room. He stared at her for a moment and his confusion disappeared. Behind her trailed a long

318

black train of her exquisitely patterned kimono. The underkimono, showing at wrists, neck, and hem was snow-white. The swinging pendulum of her silver hair ornament was the only indication of her still-childish state. When she saw Kikuji, her eyes narrowed, and she bowed to him stiffly. She moved carefully, schooled in the behavior of a bride. Koyoshi, the senior geisha of her house stood at her side and gently urged her forward.

"And now, my dear, would you like to exchange cups with the master?" she suggested.

Almost as though sleepwalking, Korin moved forward, knelt, and with head bowed offered Kikuji a lacquered ceremonial bowl, holding it gracefully in her cupped hands. Watching her, Sanoya lost all his boisterousness. He picked up the ornately lacquered sake bottle and moved to serve them.

"Permit me. I shall be your Cupid, your sponsor in this complex art," he said almost paternally as he poured sake into her cup.

Following the toast, the proprietress clapped her hands sharply, and the two geisha came in to dance "The Crane and Turtle," a dance of long life. Tsuruhachi followed their stately performance with a quick and lively burlesque of it. Then, while the guests settled back to drink and talk, Korin was escorted off by one of the waitresses to a hot bath, while Kikuji soaked himself in another of the steaming pools. When finished, he dried himself, put on his cotton night kimono, and threw his silk robe over it before walking to a quiet detached chamber far from the guests. The sliding wall panels were open, revealing a small courtyard. By the faint light of a paper lantern, he saw the thick quilts of the bed spread out on the tatami mats. He took off his robe and stretched out on one side of the bed, looked upward toward the ceiling as etiquette prescribed, and waited. The soft thump of the sliding door panel announced Korin's presence. With small, correct steps she moved to his bedside and sat. Placing her hands before her on the floor, she bowed low before him.

"Pray, guide me in my inexperience through the intricate dance. Help me to be worthy and effective," she said earnestly.

She straightened up once more and he looked at her. Her eyelashes trembled slightly and, after one quick look at him, her eyes were downcast. The ornaments were gone from her hair now, and she wore a kimono of bright red silk with a stylized wave pattern

running through it. Koyoshi, the senior geisha, who had been standing in the doorway, moved forward and began removing the silk
basting thread from the collar of Korin's kimono. "Sreeee!" shrieked
the thread as it was pulled loose from the kimono. Expertly, Koyoshi
removed it from collar, from sleeves and skirt. "Sreee, sreee, sreee."
The piercing sound hummed insistently in the quiet room, announcing in its shrillness the purity of the body it protected. Korin kept
her head bowed and her eyes closed as she sat passively listening to
the sound which signaled the end of childish innocence. Koyoshi
wound the thread around her fingers, and bowed to the lovers.

"May the gods smile on the two of you tonight," she said quietly,
and was gone.

The shrill sound of the basting thread lingered in Kikuji's head.
He looked at Korin, who had by now stretched out on the bed beside him. Her face was expressionless. He raised himself on one
elbow and looked down at her.

"Korin. Are you sure?" he asked quietly.

She nodded, opened her eyes and flashed a quick, nervous smile
at him.

With his hand he touched the red kimono at her neck, and it fell
away, revealing the slenderness of her body. His hand lingered for a
moment at the hollows of her shoulder, moved down to the firm,
well-formed breasts, and on to the rhythms of the rib cage, the
rounded softness of belly and navel. He threw off his kimono and
clasped her to him . . .

Eons later, sated and sleepy, he relaxed his hold on her and lay
back to yawn. She sat up, found her kimono, and put it on. Then she
placed one hand on the tatami mat and held her skirt in place with
the other while she bowed and said formally, "Please pardon me for
my disorderliness and my shortcomings."

"Huh?"

"Please pardon me for my disorderliness and my shortcomings,"
she repeated.

He was wide awake now. He sat up and looked at her. In all the
many times he had slept with women, he had never before received
an after-intercourse salutation. It was as though she had served him
a meal and, at the end of it, had bowed and apologized for her
scanty menu. He struggled to control himself: wildly lascivious re-
plies suggested themselves, but he restrained his impulse to laugh at

her. She looked so serious and so earnest, kneeling there on the floor beside him.

"You were beautiful," he said gently. "Now get in bed here and go to sleep. You have earned it."

She smiled and picked up her sash from the basket tray on the floor. As she did so, Kikuji heard the dry sound of paper sheets falling. He looked to see what it was, but hastily she hid something under her kimono.

"What's that?" he asked lazily.

She seemed terribly confused.

"Oh, it's really nothing at all, Master, nothing at all."

He heard the crumpling sound of paper again. He laughed. She had prepared herself with "spring pictures," the obscene drawings which in the old days were hidden under the pillows of young brides for the purpose, he thought, not of educating them about sex but of exciting them to try it. He reached out his hand.

"Still waters run deep. I wouldn't have thought you would have gone in for sexy pictures, Korin. But since you have, you ought to share them with me."

She tried to prevent him, but he grabbed a sheaf of papers from her hand. It was a small booklet, about the same size and appearance as some of the very explicit picture guides for young brides which he had seen. He turned it over and frowned in puzzlement as he studied the title.

"*The Geisha's Handbook*? Do they have a handbook, actually? Like the boy scouts? Incredible!"

"Oh, please. Give it back to me," she said in a small voice. "You shouldn't be reading it."

"Is it obscene, then?" he asked.

"No, no. Nothing like that. But it isn't for men at all. You mustn't."

"Ah, but I must! I am a great scholar of all learning that isn't for men at all. This sounds like quite a find, Korin. You just look the other way and be as embarrassed as you like while I read."

She laughed and pulled the blanket over her head. Kikuji moved the lamp closer to his side and opened *The Geisha's Handbook*. He read it slowly aloud so that he might involve Korin in the material and ask her questions whenever he needed additional explanations.

" 'I. A geisha should take each day's task seriously,' " he read.

321

"That sounds like a good rule. Let's see what they mean by it. 'She must always get up by 10 A.M. in the morning, clean her room, and take care of her clothes. By 3 P.M., she must have completed her bath and be ready for calls any time thereafter.' Well, that sounds reasonable. Except for the time scheme, it sounds more like a schedule for a private in the army than for a lady. But let's proceed with the goings-on of the geisha world."

There was a groan of protest from under the blanket.

"Item II," said Kikuji, reading ahead swiftly, "deals with hair and makeup. It says here that 'Hair and makeup should be done carefully according to the rule. A geisha's hair must be set every day without thought of economizing on the fee. Unless she is going on an excursion or is to attend a play, she should on no account wear her hair swept back in the new style. Waiting at the beauty shop for treatment can be tedious, but a geisha must remember her professional dignity at all times, and resist all temptation to engage in gossip about her patrons, the mistress of her house, or her fellow geisha. When one's turn comes at the beauty shop, the beautician will doubtless wish to have you try all the latest fashions. Ignore such salesmanship. Stick to Kyoto powder and Kyoto rouge: they have proved their worth to our profession over the years. Study the result of your treatment carefully in the mirror before paying. Remember that blotches of powder in the wrong place—on the ear, for example—can make even the most refined geisha look amateurish and countrified.' "

Kikuji looked at the form under the blanket. "I suppose you have memorized all this bilge."

There was no answer.

"Very well. Let us get on with our lesson." He turned a page. "Now we come to Lesson III: 'The Curriculum of the Geisha School.' Maybe this will be the meat of the matter." And he began reading once more in a schoolmasterly fashion.

" 'Dancing, singing, and the playing of various instruments, particularly samisen, strings, drums, and flute, should be emphasized. A geisha should not concentrate so much on one art that she becomes overspecialized and is forced now and then to say, "I am a dancer, not a musician." Such a confession of limitation is damaging to the profession. To avoid the danger, the apprentice geisha should use her time wisely, and practice during intervals of enforced leisure, as, for example, while waiting to be served at the beauty parlor.' "

Kikuji put the book down for a moment and poked at the form under the blanket. "Come on out," he urged. "It isn't at all what I had thought it was. You don't need to be that embarrassed, do you?"

Her face appeared, swathed in heavy folds of blanket. "You are not supposed to be reading the secrets of my profession," she wailed. "It isn't—it isn't proper!"

"But the secrets of your profession seem thus far to be quite tame."

"Ah. Thus far. You must give it to me!"

A gleam of interest appeared in his eye. "Well, let's read the rest, shall we? Then I'll give you back your boy scout manual."

But the face had disappeared once more under the covers.

" 'IV. On the Way to the Party: A geisha should regard walking to a party as part of her grand entrance to the social drama, as important to her as an actor's entrance on the elevated walkway of the kabuki theater. When a great actor suddenly emerges onto that platform, the action stops, all eyes are on him, wondering what marvelous gesture he will make next. So it should be with the geisha on her way to a party. She must never forget her audience so much as to chat informally with her fellow geisha, or walk casually side by side with her male attendant. She can never tell who is looking. Today's passerby may well become tomorrow's patron. Every casual action must be performed with studied dignity and grace.' "

Kikuji looked at Korin under her blanket. "Gracious. If one works so hard just going to a party, I should think that by the time one got there one would be all tired out. But I suppose a true geisha never gets tired—except, perhaps, with studied dignity and grace? On with the party! To think that I always thought parties just opportunities for talking and singing and having a good time. And now I find that while I was having a good time, all my geisha friends were putting on a kind of grand opera performance and I didn't even realize it. But let me read on, with studied dignity and grace. Here we are. 'Item V. Entering a Party: A geisha's entrance to a party must be made strictly according to the rules of etiquette.

When going to a teahouse in the winter, she will first remove her shawl and coat, quickly take off her wooden clogs, go to the room where the party is being held, open the sliding panel ever so slightly and, from a sitting posture, with hands extended at the doorsill, greet the guests, being sure to maintain a bright and infectious smile while doing so. After they have responded to your greeting, go in.' This book covers absolutely everything. Without geisha school, you might be tempted to keep on your shawl and coat and clogs, I suppose. But I still am not in the party yet, as I follow my geisha there. I have smiled a bright and infectious smile, and I have gone in. What do I do now? Grab at a sake bottle or stuff my mouth with tempura? On with the party! Are you listening?"

A muffled assent came from under the quilt.

" 'VI. Locate Guest of Honor: Immediately after entering the room, look for the guest of honor. (You should have made appropriate inquiries about him before going this far.) Although it is the host who has hired you, your function is to entertain his guests. To do so is to entertain the host as well by making his task easier. Do not ignore the guests in the lower seats. In the future they will all become very important people who may possibly become patrons. Many a geisha has ruined her future by snobbishly paying attention only to the most honored guests and ignoring younger ones who five years from now will have arrived at positions of importance. A geisha should also keep in mind that the younger ones may be very lively and pleasant to have around.' "

Kikuji looked up from the book. "I think that on that score I would give you a high grade, Korin. At my get-well party, I noticed particularly how assiduous you were to the younger guests, even though you seemed to have a weather eye out for all the rest of the company. You were probably the most popular—and busiest—geisha there. Now—shall we continue?"

He picked up the book once more.

"Where are we? Our geisha has made all the old wrecks with money and all the young animals who may one day earn lots of money very comfortable. What does our book prescribe next?" He turned a few pages. "Here we are. 'Section VII. A Geisha Should Not Beg.' I should hope not. Is it necessary to say so? 'No true geisha should ever beg her patron to take her to a play or on a shopping expedition. Furthermore, she must never at parties try to sell tickets to her recitals. To do so is gauche. Such conduct befits a peddler selling her wares at a bridge, but not a geisha. Abstain from such cheap and inappropriate conduct.' "

Kikuji smiled at Korin, whose face had once more appeared from under the quilt.

"But don't worry too much about all this: if you ever really want me to buy a ticket to your recital, I shall be happy to contribute. Let us continue our education. 'Begging for food is worst of all. The most shameful thing a geisha can do is to keep asking her patron to order her a special dish or, after he has left the party, to order it herself.' So if you're hungry right now, you must keep it to yourself, my dear. And now the party seems about to end. 'VIII. Leaving a Party: Always consult with the teahouse proprietress or the home office before leaving a party. You are not free to follow your own inclinations and go to another party just because one of your favorite patrons is there. In the case of absolute necessity, call the home office and leave after another geisha has been dispatched to take your place at the party. Duty to profession should come before friendship for a patron.' And just in case you have any naughty ideas, my love, you mustn't sneak off and telephone your patron either. It says so here. 'IX. During a party a geisha should not use the telephone except in extreme emergency. To leave the room and engage in a long phone call is to cheat your patron who expects you to entertain him. If, however, you must make a phone call to the home office, get permission from the teahouse proprietress and leave the price of the call. Some unscrupulous people are a disgrace to the profession and cheat by not paying for their phone calls. To do so is as shameful as begging for food. Never, never forget to leave the price of your phone call.' Ah, well, Korin. I am glad to see that you have taken that warning to heart." He began laughing and couldn't stop even after the tears came to his eyes.

Korin sat straight up in bed. "Why are your laughing, Master?"

He wiped his eyes. "Oh, don't mind me, Korin. Just lie down and go to sleep."

"How can I sleep while you are laughing like a madman over my book? What is so funny?"

"I was just remembering your great worriment when I saw you

325

telephoning in the garden. You couldn't find the money to pay, and you were ready to hang yourself. All because of Article IX of *The Geisha's Handbook!*"

"Well, but you have read far enough, Master. Let me have the book so that we can both go to sleep. You must not know all our secrets."

"Ah, but these are important secrets. You wouldn't deprive me of my education, surely?"

Laughing, she darted forward, trying to snatch the booklet from his hands, but he fended her off with his shoulder and continued reading.

" 'X. A Geisha's Private Residence Is Off-Limits to Patrons: Inviting favorite patrons to one's own house has been the end of many a promising professional career. The teahouse needs the geisha and the geisha the teahouse. Neither can prosper without the other. Never forget that the patron who prefers to visit you at your own home is usually a most unadmirable person concerned more with having his fun cheaply than with honorable dealing. The geisha who cheats the teahouse in this way will sooner or later herself be cheated by her economy-minded patron. The teahouse is the only appropriate setting for the flowering of a geisha's many delicate talents.' "

Kikuji lowered the book for a moment to look at Korin, who by this time was lying resignedly, her head on the pillow, listening to his reading. "I think that in fairness to your customers, there ought to be a companion volume of instructions called *The Patron's Handbook.* These economy-minded fellows should be instructed in proper teahouse behavior. And now, what's next?"

He turned a page, and frowned attentively. "Ah. Now we get to the heart of the matter," he said softly. "Listen to this."

"Hmh," came the reply from Korin.

" 'XI. Servicing the patron is to be performed with no dimunition of respect and politeness.' Oh, Korin! Can you never escape from etiquette? Not even in bed? 'For the period of time that a special patron seeks her favors, a geisha must regard him as a husband and lord. He must be serviced with utmost care. Performed with requisite skill and delicacy, the dance of the sheets is the very acme of the geisha's mysterious art, at once sensual pleasure and spiritual revelation. The geisha may at times find the experience less rewarding than this, but she should remember that it is the ultimate aim of her professional training to make it so for the gentleman she services. After the climax, an interval of complete peace and quiet should be allowed, at the end of which the geisha should take the initiative, tidy herself up, put on her night kimono, and apologize prettily to her lord and master for not having been more skillful. Do not lie around naked. To do so may seem to be pleading for more, and your lord has already given you his best efforts. Sporting your charms in this manner is vulgar and unprofessional. A fully effective geisha forms and organizes her conduct with skill and foresight even in the heat of passion. Only so can she service her lord so that he will always remember the experience with rich emotion.' "

Slowly, he put the book down. Korin lay with her eyes closed.

"Poor child," he said pensively. "Did you go through—all that, just by the book? You did it just as the book said you should: the interval of peace and quiet, the tidying up, and even that marvelous bow when you asked me to forgive your inexperience. Did you do it so that, had your teacher been present, she would have given you a perfect grade? Didn't you enjoy it?"

As he sat over her, he could see the tears forming at the corners of her eyes and rolling down her cheeks. With his hand he softly wiped them away as fast as they formed.

"No, my darling. No cause for tears. Let's continue with that interval of peace and quiet, shall we?"

He flicked open her kimono and devoured the subtle variations of the human figure which expressed her youth and intensity: those small, firm breasts, the soft undulations created by the ribs, the lovely swooping fall of the inverted V where the rib cage ended, the delicacy of pubic hair. He stretched out beside her, feeling her warmth as it swept over him in its usual surprising way, at toes, lips, chest, groin.

"Books are good, of course," he said dreamily. "Lots of good books have lots of good theory. But if all the boy scouts followed the manual exactly, they would all be alike, and geisha are nothing if not individual. They learn by living. Let me be your teacher. Learn by loving. In my arms. The first lesson: mutual need."

Hours later he woke up. The lamp at the bedside was still on. He rolled over intending to turn it out. As he did so, he was overwhelmed with a sense of utter exhaustion. He was a fragile empty shell of a man. Korin slept the comfortable, intense sleep of the young beside him. He stared perplexedly up at the ceiling. What was the matter? That beautiful child must have taken it out of him. And yet he had had two women of a night many times before. Many times. When was the last? He couldn't quite recall. Almost forty, he thought. From twenty to forty: those were the good years. Maybe better at twenty than at forty though. This child beside him had twenty good years of loving to give. How would it be from forty to sixty, he wondered? Like Sanoya, maybe: puttering around with the ladies out of nostalgia, buying their good will without, when you got right down to it, any ability to put it to good use— Still, he supposed, if one couldn't go on making love, he could still make friends and enjoy companionship. Like Sanoya. Poor old Sanoya.

Idly he picked up the geisha manual again and leafed through it, reading here and there. It no longer seemed as hilarious as when he had read it to Korin. He thought of waking her up again, but before he could act on the impulse, he fell asleep himself.

But the ladies refused to leave him alone. Exhausted as he was, they wanted more. Here was Ponta, the diamond in her tooth flashing light around her eerily. But now it was Hisako looking at him in that brooding way of hers as though awaiting the final, superb tip on the final, superb horse race. What more did she want of him? He had given her a horse. What more? But it wasn't Hisako after all; it was O-Fuku, beautiful, calm O-Fuku, trailing her fingers in the waters of Lake Biwa, looking both calm and expectant. What was it she wanted? A baby, of course. Korin was only her substitute, and she wanted a baby of him. She looked at him insistently: it was his duty, she seemed to say. And then he realized that all three were looking at him in the same way. It was his duty.

Like an insubstantial shadow play the three faded away. The various commandments of the geisha manual were pronounced by a formidable voice in the deep recesses of his mind, and after each he had a vision of Korin dutifully performing what was required in her earnest, heart-rendingly earnest, fashion.

He was sitting up in the bed, his nakedness drenched in sweat. Korin was anxiously holding his arm. He looked at her, puzzled.

"What's the matter?" he said confusedly.

"You were shouting. I had to wake you up. It was a nightmare."

"What did I shout?"

"You said, 'No. No. No. Korin! You must help me!' What did it mean?"

"I don't know," he replied grimly. How could you tell a teenager whom you had just deflowered that you had for the first time realized that you were on the way to being old? Tears formed in the corners of his eyes. Her dextrous fingers wiped them away, one by one.

Ten

He sank back into the bath and felt heat reaching inward to the tight muscles of his neck, back, and legs. He closed his eyes and relaxed. It had been a hard day. Who would ever have thought a few short years ago that things would get so complicated? The depression, of course, had been bad enough, but businesses should be able to survive such disturbances, and his had, everything considered, ridden the waves of financial stress very well. It was this damnable war that was causing the trouble. From the beginning of the great campaigns in China in 1937 his options had been steadily curtailed, so that now, two years later, he had to use his wits just to make ends meet.

When in December the Association of Tabi Merchants had been formed to preside over the rationing of materials, Kikuji had been elected to the governing board. All today he had been arguing and discussing at a meeting of the board. At the beginning a majority had been in favor of a complete reorganization of the system so that goods would go from manufacturer directly to retailer. Had Kikuji not been present, the motion would have passed, and Kawachiya's would have been ruined. He had pointed out that this was no time to try crazy experiments, and convinced them that they should stick with time-tested methods. When he emerged from the often-stormy session, it was growing dark. He had hurried home for the welcome rest provided by a hot bath.

Slowly he stood up, stepped out of the tub, and toweled himself dry. As he did so, his eye fell on the little wooden box for torn and worn-out clothing. He frowned irritably, dressed, and opened the sliding door to the outside court where O-Toki was adjusting coal in the furnace under the bath.

330

"O-Toki, please ask my grandmother to come here for a moment."

A few minutes later Kino appeared, her face red from the heat of her charcoal brazier. She opened the door with a puzzled look.

"Is something wrong? Why do you summon me to the bath chamber?" she asked.

"Grandmother, these tabi are yours, I think?" he said, picking up a pair of white tabi from the discard box. "They are your size."

"Why, yes, Kiku-bon. They're mine. I threw them away because they were worn out. Can't have that in a tabi manufacturing family."

"But they are as good as new."

"Oh? They can't be. I've worn them often. Look here. See? By the big toe there's almost a hole."

"No, Grandmother. There is a lot of wear left in these tabi."

"Oh, Kiku-bon. Would you want the grandmother of a great and successful merchant to go around wearing worn-out things? We have our reputation to protect."

He passed his hand through his damp hair wearily. When would she understand that times were changing?

"Grandmother, I used to throw away underwear after one wearing. I scolded Ikuko for sewing torn tabi instead of getting new ones. But that was all in the old days. You must understand. Everything nowadays is tightly rationed. What you throw away so casually cannot be replaced. Just a week ago I told you and Mother that you could have only four pairs a month. My other women protegees get five pairs every two months. Japan is straining to win a war. Sometimes I wonder if, even with a great empire, Japan can afford your spendthrift ways."

"Oh, dear, it's all so upsetting. I know. You told us. I forgot, that's all." She beamed radiantly at him as though to close the incident.

"Three weeks ago, when I came home from a session with my customers, I found you and Mother talking to that slick salesman from Mitsukoshi Department Store. Your room was covered with magnificent silk material, all embroidered with gold thread."

She pursed her lips reflectively. "I know, dear. He's holding them for us still, you know. Really an extraordinary bargain, and he's offering it to us because we have been such loyal customers. Just a little while ago those pieces sold for three hundred yen, and now he's

331

willing to let us have them for only fifty yen each. We really ought to stock up with ten bolts of the stuff. It will be hard to find soon."

He groaned. "But don't you see? The reason the price came down is that the government edict prohibiting the use of luxuries has made silks like that useless. If you wore them, you would find yourself attacked and criticized in the streets. That salesman knows that you and Mother are so lost in the old days that you alone of all his former customers would go right on buying goods which you couldn't use."

"Don't be angry, Kiku-bon."

"I'm not angry. But I repeat what I said then: you cannot buy those silks and you simply must learn to economize in these difficult times."

"Oh, this ridiculous war won't last long. You'll see! You're too young to remember. The Russo-Japanese War and the old Sino-Japanese War before it were both over in a jiffy. So when we win, we'll need nice clothes to celebrate. We don't want to go out and cheer in the streets looking like perfect frumpy horrors, now, do we?"

He closed his eyes and sighed in despair. "Please wait until the victory sirens sound before you go off on any more of your buying sprees. The only reason you haven't felt the full impact of the scarcity is that our warehouses are loaded with goods. Every time you splurge I give up what cannot be replaced."

He threw the tabi down and started out into the hallway, but she caught his sleeve.

"Kiku-bon. Please don't be so upset. These are difficult times for us, too. Nothing is the same any more. You must be patient with us. We do try, oh, so hard." She was the image of repentance. Humbly she knelt down and picked up the tabi. Then she followed behind him as he went to the room where his mother sat, impeccably attired, waiting for supper.

"Ah, how tired you look, Kiku-bon," she said as he came in. "Is business so bad?"

"No worse than that of everyone else, I suppose. If only they would stop drafting our clerks and apprentices."

His mother smiled absently. "It was such fun at first. Remember when the first two were drafted? I forget their names—"

"Muramoto Kenshichi and Sato Matsukichi."

"Oh, yes. Very nice boys they were. We held a ceremony for them at our shrine, and your mother and I made a little kit for them to take along, plus a good luck present, a thousand-stitch belt and other things. And the morning they left we had everyone out lining the street cheering them and waving flags. It was such fun!"

"We have lost nine more since then, Mother."

"Yes. It is a nuisance."

"You knew that Muramoto had returned a few months ago from China? He's the clerk without a left arm whom I'm training to keep accounts."

"Oh. I didn't know it was the same boy. Still, half a man is better than none at all, isn't that so?"

"Yes, Mother, that's so."

"If only Hidesuke were here, everything would be all right."

Hidesuke. What sort of spell had he cast over the family? Kikuji shook his head as though to wake himself up. Even he had always assumed the man's infallibility. His father had appointed him assistant manager, and his father, uncertain with women, knew men.

He thought over once again the events of the night a month ago when, just after supper, O-Toki informed him that Hidesuke had asked permission to speak with him in the main office when he had time that evening. He had walked along the long corridor to the office, chewing on a toothpick. As he slid open the door, he saw Hidesuke bent almost frantically over the books, making notations. At the best of times the man never looked healthy; now he looked pale and feverish. Although it was a cool spring evening, beads of sweat stood out on his forehead. From the corner of his eye he perceived his employer and he wheeled around and stood up. Kikuji motioned him into a seat and sat down himself.

"What's the trouble, Hidesuke?"

"I was—just trying to straighten up the books a bit while I was waiting for you."

"There's plenty of time for that during the regular business day, isn't there?"

"Ah, Master, if only there were!" It was a genuine cry of pain from this impassive, rocklike man. He turned his head away so that Kikuji could not see his eyes. In a moment he had regained control of himself. "I only found out this afternoon. I tried to tell you then, but you were busy with customers." He looked unseeingly at the floor.

"Tell me what?"

"Ah, Master, they have drafted me!"

Behind the rimless glasses the eyes looked searchingly at Kikuji, as though imploring him for the help no one could give. There was a long interval of silence. To have said he was sorry might, perhaps, have been the appropriate consolation for this miserable man, but it would not have been patriotic. To have congratulated him on having a chance to serve his country would, under the circumstances, have been insupportable irony.

"We'll miss you here, Hidesuke," he said sincerely. "You are very nearly irreplaceable." Suddenly he laughed harshly and shrugged. "But I guess in these terrible times just about everyone is irreplaceable, when you stop to think about it."

"Yes. Yes. It is a great inconvenience to you," he said, his eyes darting nervously around the office. "I shall try to get the books in order before I leave on Thursday—"

"Thursday? Why that's only the day after tomorrow."

"Yes. I must leave Thursday morning."

"Very well. But you must spend your last day with your family. Tomorrow you must come here to dinner with your wife and children. Till then, you are free. Forget the business. There are more important things."

The assistant manager drew himself up. "I cannot do that. I must set the books in order before I leave. Don't worry about me, please."

He had left the clerk toiling over his figures, and returned to the family quarters to tell the news to Sei and Kino. They were much upset, and he realized what an important factor Hidesuke had been in their lives. Through him they had exerted more influence on the business than he had suspected. He was their man, and now he was to be gobbled up by the war machine. They had acted almost as though Hidesuke had been guilty of an impertinence in allowing himself to be taken from them.

"You may be sure, there was nothing he wanted less. He had his future figured out to the infinite decimal point. And the war has uprooted him. Let us hope it doesn't uproot us all."

The farewell banquet the next night had been strained and artificial. Hidesuke's wife and children were delighted with their sukiyaki, and they chattered and joked as much as their enormous respect for the ladies would permit. But Hidesuke's sharp eyes, alert as ever, seemed nevertheless to be clouded by gloom and despair. He was strangely restless, spoke only when he had to, and left as early as good manners would permit.

"I've never seen him like this before," said Kino. "You don't suppose he's a coward?"

"No more than the next man," replied Kikuji. "But he certainly does seem terribly worried."

"Ah, Kikuji. They'll be after you next."

He laughed to reassure them.

"I doubt it. Although I am as healthy as a horse, my physical examination, by army standards, was poor. A number of little things weren't as the army wants them: flat feet, for instance, and varicose veins. Also, I'm listed as a person essential to wartime industrial planning in the Osaka area. Do you have flat feet, Hisajiro?"

His nineteen-year-old son, who had been paying little attention, was startled at his father's question. "I—no—I have nice feet."

Sei gave a loud wail. "How can you say such things, Kiku-bon? Your own child, your own baby! We mustn't let Hisajiro go into the army, ever. He has the soul of an artist. You can't wish such a dreary life for him?"

"Or for anyone else. It's the samurai class who are kicking up the dust right now. It's not good for business. But, of course, if they win, we'll have a great empire. That would be good for business! I must tell Hidesuke that. It will make him try harder at soldiering. He'll do anything to improve business."

"If only Hidesuke were here . . ." His mother's complacent trust in the fellow irritated him.

"If only he were," he smiled bitterly, "I would be very much inclined to break his scrawny neck."

Kino stared at him severely with a touch of her former authority. "What a terrible thing to say! About your father's trusted employee! About a soldier of the Emperor!"

"Yes. Well, I know now why this soldier of the Emperor was so worried just before he left for the army."

"Ah, the poor man. I think maybe he's like Hisajiro: just too delicate for that rough kind of life."

"Too delicate. That one? Grandmother, I think you would exempt all your friends and acquaintances as too delicate. But Assistant Manager Hidesuke was not too delicate to pocket 34,200 yen which didn't belong to him."

The two women stared speechlessly at him for a moment. Then Kino whispered hoarsely, "Mercy on us. It cannot be!"

"I've been over the books again and again since he left. I can't be mistaken. He has been stealing from us for years, and doctoring the books to conceal the thefts. But he was drafted so suddenly he had no chance to alter the accounts of the past six months. That was why he insisted on spending the last day-and-a-half of his free time before going into the army working on the books. He was trying to hide his tracks. But he was so nervous and upset, he made a bad job of it. Once I had figured out his methods, I could trace his thefts way back, almost to the time of Father's death. 34,200 yen. That's a lot of money for an assistant manager on a salary of 260 yen a month. When he started stealing, he was making 55 yen. He was twenty-seven at the time of Father's death. He's been skimming off a percentage for fifteen years."

Kino pulled out her pipe and began tamping tobacco into it.

"I thought I was a good judge of character and I got your father to promote that man. How glad I am you have found him out. But shouldn't we have him arrested?"

Kikuji laughed. "Ah, Grandmother, he is a soldier now. If I bring charges against such a samurai, people will begin to snarl at me and ask, 'Why aren't you in the army? Why do you persecute our brave soldiers?' No, there is nothing to be done. The matter is closed, and I shall tell no one. Not even Wasuke. If he saw how stupid I've been, then he might think of getting his share too." He saw the fear and protest forming in their eyes, and held up his hand with a laugh. "No, no: he's quite honest. I'm sure of that. I was just—making a joke."

As he looked at the two women, he was suddenly quite unexpectedly overwhelmed by a wave of pity. Sei sat weeping quietly. She cried nowadays at the slightest excuse, and oftentimes for nothing at all. Kino was made of sterner stuff. She sat holding the worn tabi in one hand, her head upturned, and those oddly youthful, alert eyes of hers fixed on his. Enigmatically, she shrugged her shoulders and turned to the younger woman.

"Come, come, Sei, my daughter," she said. "Times change and old people must adapt or shut their eyes. For fifteen years we managed to live a good life, even though we trusted Hidesuke as our protector while he was stealing from us. Kiku-bon will see us through. Your son is a great merchant of the Semba, and we have been remiss in not acknowledging his skill. Even after ten years of uncertainty and depression, our house is still one of the great Osaka firms. Kiku-bon will see us through."

Sei smiled faintly and tried to brush away tears with her handkerchief. "Maybe so," she said faintly. "After three generations of women controlling, perhaps it is best in these war-confused days to have a man in charge. Every time I venture outside the house I find that the world has changed unrecognizably since I last went out. These are strange times. I hope you can deal with them, Kiku-bon. You are the only one we have to depend on."

Kikuji rose and prepared to leave the room. Kino frowned. "You're not going off and leave us alone tonight, are you?"

He steeled himself. "I had promised Ponta some time ago that I would visit her tonight. I haven't seen her for weeks."

She surprised him by nodding amiably and even producing a half-hearted smile. "It's all right, my dear. You have many responsibilities, I know."

There was a tap on the door, and Wasuke showed his head. "I'm sorry to interrupt, sir, but there is a call from Echigocho on the office phone—"

He restrained an impulse to swear, and went down the hall after Wasuke to the main office. Picking up the phone, he said severely, "You should know better than to call me at my home in this way! Only in the most serious emergencies—"

"I know, I know, my dear, but, don't you see, this *is* an emergency. You see, our son, Taro—" Ponta's voice broke.

"What has happened to Taro?" he asked quickly.

"He has been badly beaten! A terrible gash on his left cheek almost to his eye. It took five stitches. A slight concussion, and—"

"But what happened?"

"A gang of boys after school followed him shouting out, 'Taro the bastard! Son of a whore!' He turned around, swung his schoolbag, and knocked down the ringleader. Then he jumped on him. But the other boys grabbed him, and—oh, it was terrible! When the police got there, he was unconscious, lying in the dirt. They took him to his foster home and called the school doctor. That was about an hour ago. Oh, Kikuji, you must go with me to see the boy. You must!"

In the cab on the way to pick up Ponta he added up the many responsibilities his grandmother had mentioned: not only many women, but children too. One must count one's blessings. At least his venture with Korin, despite all the care and deliberateness of O-Fuku, had not paid off in the form of yet another damp, squalling responsibility. He wondered idly what Hisajiro, he of the nice feet and artist's soul, would have done if his classmates had called his mother a whore. Poor Hisajiro. All individuality smothered by women. And now he was going to acknowledge responsibility for the child he had officially disowned, declared illegitimate, and lodged with foster parents. He pulled out his wallet and extracted a snapshot of a boy wearing the school cap of a seventh grader. Ponta had sent it to him some months ago. He seemed a big, lively boy, the face essentially Ponta's transformed by the mystery of genetics into one of male sturdiness. Looking at the picture, he could understand that this child could be expected to fight back.

Ponta was waiting for him when the cab arrived, and during the short ride to the home of the old couple who were raising Taro, she said little. Taro lay on the bedding in a small room, the left side of his face heavily bandaged.

"Is the eye all right?" whispered Kikuji to the old man. He received a quick nod in reply.

The boy turned his head to look at them with his one uncovered eye, and then tried to sit up. Ponta hastily knelt and pressed him back to the pillow.

"Oh, Mother, I'm glad you came," he said in a loud, healthy voice quite at odds with his injured appearance.

"Taro, your father came to see you too," she said, smiling so that her diamond-studded tooth glittered.

A long silence followed. Taro stared curiously and unblinkingly as only children can. Only the one eye showed, and its remorseless inspection made Kikuji uncomfortable. The boy glared at him like Tange Sazen, the one-eyed samurai.

"Are you my father?" slowly came the question in the high-pitched tones of childhood.

338

"That's right," Kikuji responded gruffly. "And if you're going to grow up with both eyes and a head that works, you're going to have to stop fighting. You're a sad sight, young fellow."

The boy giggled. "I gave them a few good wallops, though. There were eight of them and only one of me." He stared again for a long time at Kikuji. "You are a tabi manufacturer," he said flatly.

"That's right."

"I am going to be a tabi manufacturer when I grow up. I'm no country yokel like those kids who beat me up, and they know it."

Kikuji remained silent.

The child continued staring at him and Kikuji looked away.

"I know what I am. My mother tells me that you can have only one real wife and only one real son. She says I mustn't ever ask you for money or for help. But she says you love me and will be proud of me if I do well. I will try, my father. Is that all right?"

Kikuji knelt beside Ponta and took the boy's hand in his, smiling at that small bandaged head. "It is very much all right, Taro. You are a good boy."

The child looked at him in silence. He squeezed his father's hand, smiled, and closed his eye. Kikuji looked away and rapidly blinked his eyes. Welcome the responsibility, he thought.

"We must go now," he said in a low voice to Ponta. "The child is asleep."

"I will spend the night here," she answered. "He may wake up and need me."

Slowly Kikuji rose to his feet. As a token of sympathy for the pain of sickness, he placed a sum of money on the table. "When he's better, use that to buy him a treat of some sort," he said to the foster parents. He said good night, and climbed into the waiting cab.

"All right, driver. Take me back to the Semba. Or—no, wait a minute. Drive to Izumi-Otsu station."

At Izumi-Otsu, he got out and asked for directions to the Maruno Sundry Store. It was in a narrow alley off the main street with only a six-foot frontage. Kikuji located it by the sign in the window designating it as a store authorized to sell the ration of tabi. He looked at his watch. It was ten o'clock. There was some light showing between the slats of the wooden shutters. Perhaps they had not yet gone to bed? He knocked gently on the door and waited. It speedily opened. Mr. Maruno became excited on seeing who it was.

339

"Wife! Wife! Come here! This is a great honor, sir, a great honor indeed. Wife! Come here!"

"Oh, please don't bother her. It is very late, and I apologize."

But they escorted him in, and the wife, who must have been getting ready for bed, came in to greet him and pour tea.

"Please, I am sorry to cause you inconvenience. I happened to be in the neighborhood, you see. I haven't seen you for eight years— not since the third year memorial for Miss Ikuko was held in Kyoto. And tonight I began to think of her son, whom I have never seen since he was born—"

"Ah, of course. Please, let me wake him up and bring him to see his distinguished father." The old lady was almost out of the room before he could stop her.

"No, no. Don't wake him up, please. I just—well, might I just look at him as he sleeps?"

Instantly they were on their feet to lead him to the boy's bedroom. The door slid open, and there, in a confusion of heavy quilts slept a ten-year-old, his face turned away from the door. On the floor beside the bedding was spread an assortment of comic books. Kikuji carefully stepped over them and around the child to look at his face. The Marunos turned on a lamp. As Kikuji knelt down to study the sleeping form, he received a shock. It was Ikuko's face. The same finely sculptured nose, the same small mouth, the same high cheekbones. After looking at him for a few minutes, Kikuji stood up and went back to the living room.

"I should thank you for the good care you are taking of him," he said. "The room is a very nice one, and the bedclothes look uncommonly expensive to me. Is he a good boy?"

"We are very fond of him, sir," replied Mr. Maruno. "You don't intend to take him away with you, do you?"

Kikuji smiled sadly and raised his hand in protest. "Nothing like that. Let us say that, at my time of life, I am counting up my assets. Ikuro looks like one of the best."

"I'm glad you think so, sir. We have tried to make him so."

He thanked them, and escaped from their hospitality as quickly as courtesy permitted. He walked to the mouth of the alley, where his taxi was waiting. He climbed in and ordered the driver to return to the Semba. It was a cold December night, and the icy air came through the crevices of the doors. He felt spent and anxious. He stared into the darkness but could see only an occasional branch looming into the headlights. He had just completed a pilgrimage into the past, and also into the future. Those bare branches reaching out at the car as it passed: they were like the reaching hands of all the women and children he had made himself responsible for. He felt tired and old, anxious to flee those hands. But there was no possibility of escape. What a terrible word, this responsibility. How is it that one becomes responsible for another? And how was the burden to be discharged? There were so many. At home, there were Kino, Sei, and Hisajiro; outside, there were four women, plus Taro, who fought back when called a bastard, and Ikuro, who looked just like his mother. It was a big family to take care of. If only the war would end. It would be easier then.

"A lot of cowardly people want the war to end so that they can pick up their old, dissolute, wasteful habits again. It will never end until we have forced our enemies to cry out for peace. We have bloodied the noses of the Americans. We have sunk the British fleet. And those at home must make sacrifices to support our brave boys at the front."

It was Kaneda Yatahei, the president of the Neighborhood Association, reciting the monotonous cliches which were the wartime substitute for real meaning. It was as though for Kaneda there were no fearful air raids to keep one shivering in stifling bomb shelters all night. The war had given this obnoxious man the status he had never had in peacetime. He had built up a wholesale industry specializing in the production of felt, and, as a recently successful businessman, he hadn't much use for Kikuji, the master of a firm with a tradition of centuries behind it. He came now and again to Kikuji's office with some official unpleasantness to communicate. The worse the war news, the nastier Kaneda's imperiousness. Kikuji sipped his tea and waited.

The visitor's eyes narrowed and he smiled mirthlessly. "The ladies of your immediate family are so old that they needn't worry about being forced to do war work in some factory. But in an old, established firm like yours, I know you have traditions to uphold, and women aplenty to take care of outside the immediate family.

341

Eh?" He laughed soundlessly as he tapped his cigarette on the ashtray. "Those lovely ladies—you wouldn't want them to soil their pretty hands with hard, greasy war work, now, would you? So probably you will be making arrangements for them? Like all the other masters of the great traditional houses? A fat lot of use they are in winning our war!"

"We are all in it together," replied Kikuji evenly.

"Hmmmmm. Maybe so, maybe so. But some people sweat for the cause more than others."

"The air raids afflict all of us equally."

Kaneda laughed with harsh satisfaction. "Yes, yes. Even your lovely ladies must sweat a bit when the bombs begin to fall."

Clearly, he would be delighted to see Kikuji's women drafted into war work. It would be a personal triumph for him.

Soon after his unpleasant visitor left, Kikuji climbed into one of the charcoal-burning cabs of wartime and drove in it to the other side of town. He got out in front of a recently constructed factory. He presented the secretary with his card and was immediately ushered into the office of the plant manager.

The man at the desk rose when he saw Kikuji and limped painfully forward to greet him.

"Kishida, old fellow! It is good to see you improving," said Kikuji.

"Well, yes. Last time I saw you I was in a wheelchair at the army hospital. Now I'm practically an athlete," replied the manager, patting his bad right leg gently. "What can I do for you?"

"I hesitate to ask a veteran this—"

"Ask what you want," said Kishida. "You have been a good friend to me. I hadn't behaved very well to you, and yet, when I went off into the army, you were there at the train station to see me off. Only you of all my business college classmates. And my wife has told me how helpful you were to her all the time I was away in China: getting clothing and various scarce items on the black market which she and the children needed. When I got her letters in China and read about your kindness, I resolved then to be just as good a friend to you if ever I had the chance. And now, apparently, I have the chance."

Kikuji hesitated. If only the man weren't a veteran. But, of course, if he weren't a veteran, he would never have been made manager of this new war industries firm, and so could never have helped him.

"I have a dear friend, a lady that is—"

Kishida smiled amiably. "Of course. Only one?"

"N-n-n-no. There are four, to be perfectly exact. But this one I am especially concerned about. You know her—"

"Ah. It's Hisako of the Polka Dot Cafe, isn't is? She used to be crazy about the horses."

"She still is. Once she tried to stop betting on the horses at my request, but she just couldn't do it. I made it worse by giving her a horse. She loves the creature—"

"Is he any good?"

"Oh, so-so. It wins a second or third place now and then, but never a first. A very handsome animal, though, and she takes care of it as though it were her child. It's incredible!"

Kishida nodded. "Hisako always was a little incredible. More European in her ways than Japanese perhaps."

Kikuji smiled. "I shouldn't tell you this, but since you know her, you will be amused in the right way. I went to see her a couple of weeks ago. She has a house at the top of Uemachi Hill, a little apartment. I knocked on the door: no answer. I knocked again. Then I pushed it, and it opened. I called in to her. She appeared at the door, her eyes all red with weeping. I asked what was the matter. So then she cried some more, and finally got around to saying. 'The draft card came.' I was horrified, you know. When they draft women, they send them to all sorts of dirty jobs in all sorts of places. I tried to comfort her. And she stopped crying completely, opened her mouth, and stared at me in complete puzzlement. 'It isn't me, you dope,' she said, 'It's my horse. They're drafting Wine Red! They can't take her away from me! What will I do when she's gone? And surely they don't really need her.' So, you see, you're quite right. She is incredible. She wanted me to get a draft exemption for her horse! I laughed and asked if it had flat feet and varicose veins, and she was furious with me. She has a whole photograph album filled with nothing but pictures of that horse. We looked at them together that afternoon. It was like looking at a baby's album!"

When he had stopped laughing, the wounded veteran looked

shrewdly at Kikuji. "But you didn't come to me to find a job for the horse so that it could be exempted?"

Kikuji smiled. "It's the horse's mistress—and mine—that I'm concerned about. She is an experienced entertainer. The people in your factory must have their rest periods organized, and she could do that. I just wondered if you couldn't use her."

Kishida pulled thoughtfully at his pipe.

"My friend, a long time ago I threw beer in your face and called you a decadent loafer and womanizer. I thought you would never come to terms with the realities of life. I was wrong. Yours are the realities of life; mine—well, mine were the militant slogans which young men throw around when they have one beer too many." He patted his wounded leg affectionately. "I like your realities better than the bullet that shattered my thighbone. You are living your life your own way, with principles born of your own feelings. That makes sense to me. Most of us go through life half-alive. Not you. You have enough love and affection for twenty ordinary men. You help everybody. I'll be honored to return the favor. If your friend Hisako wants a job as an entertainment organizer in a plant manufacturing wooden airplanes, she is welcome to it."

Later that afternoon, chatting with Sanoya over a beer, Kikuji laughed ruefully, and said, "You know, it's funny thing about Kishida. He really hated me at one time and would have done anything to destroy my reputation."

"What happened to change his attitude?" asked his old friend.

"It was very odd. A business friend of mine was leaving for the army, and I went down to see him off at the station. As I was slowly walking down the side of the troop train, I heard someone calling my name. It was Kishida. He thought I had come down to see him off. He was profoundly moved that I would do that after his bad behavior to me. And so I stayed with him and cheered him on his way. He introduced his wife and children and waved a small flag and cheered until he was out of sight. And now we are the best of friends."

Sanoya laughed. "Wartime changes everything around. So now your lady of the race track is taken care of. What of the other three?"

"They're a great worry to me. I tried to get them to go back to

344

their home towns in the country, so that they wouldn't be in danger in the air raids, but they won't go."

Sanoya laughed. "What magnetism you must have!"

"If they stay on in Osaka, I'm just not sure what may happen. O-Fuku's boss at Hamayu was smart enough to convert her teahouse into a recreational club for factory workers, so I doubt that O-Fuku will be drafted for war work. Hisako is now taken care of. Ponta I'm not sure about. She has three geisha in her house now, and they work hard at entertaining the soldiers through the Service Men's Recreational Clubs. She may need something more official than that if she is to escape dirty work in an assembly line. I'm working on it."

"Ah?" asked Sanoya, just before emptying his sake cup.

"You recall Tsuruhachi?"

"Our sad-faced jester? Of course."

"He's working in a steel mill in Amagasaki. He was drafted for it two years ago. Recently I asked O-Fuku to get in touch with him for me. She set up a lunch for us at one of those restaurants which serve black market beef to trusted special guests in private rooms on the second floor. Poor Tsuruhachi. He was wearing a not-very-clean, oversized factory uniform. He seemed almost to have lost the habit of laughter. But after some sake and a huge beefsteak, he was his old self. I asked him if his factory had organized its workers' recreational facilities, and he said that they wanted to, but hadn't been able to get the right person for it yet. So I suggested Ponta, and he thought maybe she would do. The head lady of a geisha establishment must not only have class but a good deal of organizing ability. He said he would do what he could, and yesterday he called me up to tell me that Ponta would be interviewed and he thought her chances good. Behind that sad-eyed caricature of a face is a shrewd and kindly mind. He's a good fellow."

"I see. You have been busy on behalf of your flock." He snubbed out a cigarette and looked appraisingly at his visitor. "That leaves Korin. How is she?"

"Not pregnant, if that's what you mean," replied Kikuji shortly.

Certainly they had tried. But with all O-Fuku's special diets and aphrodisiacs, nothing had happened, and he was just as glad. Still, he had grown fond of Korin. She appealed to his protective in-

345

stincts, and he had bought her a small house. Sooner or later she would undoubtedly be drafted for war work unless he found a haven for her. The neighbors in the Sennencho District where she lived were already gossiping about the former geisha. Although she had stopped going to the hairdresser every day, she still retained the dainty elegance of her profession. And yet she would poke around among the vegetables at the grocer's for the best bunch, and then haggle interminably about price with the proprietor while the neighbors listened. Kikuji, having heard the gossip, scolded her for being so stingy, but she had promptly pulled out her geisha manual, and read the appropriate rules from it in a stern voice:

"A geisha must keep her daily expenditure within the limits of her allowance. She will please her patron by spending carefully on clothes and all other needful items. If her allowance is one hundred yen, she should save at least thirty-three. Pay promptly and exactly when you have to but avoid needless spending. A thrifty person knows the relative value of all the things she might buy and limits herself accordingly. The merely stingy person hoards her money blindly and in so doing sacrifices all dignity and self-esteem. A geisha must, therefore, know the difference between thrift and stinginess. And she must keep the importance of careful management in mind at all times, whether actively pursuing the profession of the geisha or backed by a patron in her own establishment."

It was like a reading from a holy book. She closed her treasured text with reverence and finality. Kikuji gave up the argument.

"What is she doing these days?" Sanoya's question pulled him back to the present.

"Nothing, I regret to say." Kikuji shook his head. "I'm worried about her."

"She's a fine girl. I can take care of her," said Sanoya.

"Pardon?"

"I'll make her secretary for the Retailers Association office."

"She's no good at typing and working with figures, you know," said Kikuji doubtfully.

"I don't hire a geisha to do typing and addition!" laughed Sanoya. "I'll want her to arrange meals, drinks, and some small entertainment for special clients. But she'll have to maintain a modest and even plain appearance. None of the trappings of a geisha. Not till the war's won, I'm afraid."

346

"I am most indebted to you for your help," said Kikuji, placing his hands before him on the tatami mat and bowing low to his friend.

"We are each indebted to the other, and that's the way it should be. I don't want my best business associate to be so worried about his collection of women that he mixes up my orders. Drink down, drink down!"

Next day, the head of the Neighborhood Association, Kaneda Yatahei, stopped him on the street, greeted him politely, and began to talk about the work of the Tabi Regulatory Association. He started to leave, and then, as though thinking better of it, came back and whispered hoarsely, "I know it will pain you, but I think you should know. They are closing the pleasure quarters for the duration of the war. All the geisha must store away their fine kimono and put on working clothes like the rest of us! Isn't that depressing?"

The older man's eyes gleamed with restrained malice as he studied Kikuji's face. Kikuji looked at him quietly and smiled.

"On the contrary, it is necessary and right. You don't really think it depressing, do you?"

Kaneda was caught off guard. "N-n-n-o, I guess not," he replied cautiously. "But it's a bit of the old Japan gone forever, and you're so tied in with the great traditions, well, I thought you might just possibly—be a little upset."

"You and I differ on the great traditions, Mr. Kaneda. Our glorious samurai tradition is one for which we must sacrifice everything at present. But when the war is won, the other traditions will remain and blossom forth once more to give our country the greatness in the arts and in cultural matters which it has always had. Don't you think so?"

Kikuji leaned forward earnestly as he spoke, staring intently, even piously into Kaneda's face.

"Yes, yes, I suppose that's so. Of course, of course." Kaneda looked around him nervously. "But you—don't you have—won't you, that is, won't you miss the geisha, now, really? Won't you?"

"Of course. Just as much as I miss all the great traditions of which you speak so well. But we are simply putting them into the closet for this bitter, difficult time. When peace returns, they will return too, Mr. Kaneda."

347

Kikuji smiled an almost beatific smile. Mr. Kaneda stared at him for a moment, then bowed abruptly and walked off.

Kikuji looked thoughtfully at the receding figure. "He'll be after me again as soon as he can think of some new rule to use as a weapon," he thought. "How fortunate that all four of my women are safely placed for the duration of the war."

But, although he expected some form of retaliation from the self-important Neighborhood Association president, he was surprised at how quickly it materialized. Within two days Mr. Kaneda was in his office, briefcase in hand, looking very official. Kikuji escorted him into one of the parlors behind the offices and ordered tea.

"I have little time for socializing," said Mr. Kaneda. "I have been studying the results of our third drive for precious metals, which we need, as no doubt you and your family already know, for the manufacture of—of airplanes, torpedoes, and, uh, artillery, and, uh—"

"Tanks?" suggested Kikuji.

"Yes. Just so. Tanks." He glared at his host. "Some people think more of their jewelry than of the lives of our brave soldiers. They hoard."

"I know," replied Kikuji earnestly. "What can I do?"

"I tell you this, Master of Kawachiya's: you can do more than you have done." With a flourish, he opened his briefcase. "I have here a detailed listing of contributions made by families in our neighborhood. I have taken the liberty of checking the register of your holdings in jewelry, and I know that if your family and the ladies associated with you were to contribute what they actually possess, it would add up to one of the largest totals received from any Semba family or firm."

"But they have contributed," said Kikuji, thinking mainly of Kino and Sei.

Kaneda sneered. "A gold watch, some silver cups, a few medals. Where is the diamond sash clip mounted in platinum which your grandmother purchased ten years ago? The diamond ring your mother bought twenty-three years ago? I can read the whole list, if you want. It will take some time. After I finish with the ladies of the house, there are the possessions of your other lady friends to add up."

Kikuji thought for a moment, and then nodded slowly. "You are quite right, Mr. Kaneda. The ladies of the house are elderly, and they do not fully understand the war and the necessities of wartime living. I have reminded them from time to time, but now I shall insist. I shall see to it that they contribute fully if, as you say, they have up to now been holding back.

"Please do so," snapped Kaneda, officiously closing his briefcase and rising. "As the head of a home front regulatory organization, you should be setting an example for the citizens of the Semba instead of needing special reminders like this."

He nodded curtly and departed.

Kikuji walked furiously into the main hall and down to his grandmother's detached rooms, where Kino and Sei were talking. Angrily he told them of his meeting with Kaneda, and of the demands that had been made.

As Kino listened, her head gradually went up and her shoulders back. "In the old days," she said majestically, "when there was a fire, the man of the house would grab the ancestral tablet and the woman would be responsible for rescuing the jewelry. A family's honor and reputation depend on these two things. And do you now tell me that the Emperor will confiscate these trinkets which are more prized by us than life itself? It cannot be!"

Sei broke into tears, and in frustration Kikuji retreated. Four days later, however, he received a notice from the chief of police: it noted that platinum and diamonds were necessary for the manufacture of fighter planes, and that anyone concealing such materials could be brought to trial as a traitor to his country. Without a word, he gave the notice to Kino. As she read it, her eyes widened, and her hand began to shake. She passed it on to Sei, and before she had finished reading it the old lady was on her feet standing at the door.

"Come, my daughter. Let us get our wonderful possessions out of the storage vault and give them to the people who make airplanes." She turned a flashing look on Kikuji. "When we have won the war, you must get all these lovely gems back for us. Don't forget."

He nodded, and set off to make Ponta give up her rings and bracelets. O-Fuku, Hisako, and Korin presented no problem, since none felt especially possessive about jewelry.

But Ponta, when he showed her the notice, lowered her head sullenly. "I wish the war would end" was her initial reaction.

She remained stubbornly silent in response to Kikuji's urging. Finally he stood up and prepared to leave. She jumped up as he slid the door open. "Wait, wait!" she cried. Then in an oddly muted fashion, she said, "Do you really think they might—arrest me if I don't give them what I have?"

He nodded gravely. "Often in these matters one small offense uncovers another. They are very likely to decide that you are working for Tsuruhachi's company just to avoid a draft that would put you into the middle of a lot of hard work. You know, of course, that the recent decree closing the geisha establishments has all those professionally trained women making parachutes and army uniforms. You might end up doing that twelve hours a day. I don't want that. I hate the thought of the women I am fond of being rounded up like so many horses and sent off to do any old job that needs doing."

"Very well," she whispered in a voice he could scarcely hear. "I'll give them up." Then she raised her head assertively and said clearly, "But you must get all those lovely things back for me when we have won."

Kikuji laughed. "That is exactly what my mother and grandmother said to me. I'll do my best, though. I'll get you twice as many if I can."

"Good. Then here they are." And with the greatest gaiety she began emptying various chests, throwing bracelets, necklaces, and rings on the table. Soon there was a large pile.

"How's that?" she said when she had finished.

"It's fine. Except for one missing item," he answered.

She looked at him for a moment, and then shrieked angrily, "I'll go to jail first! They can take me out and shoot me! It's the only way they'll get it!"

"Calm down, calm down."

"I won't give it up. Tell me, are they asking for gold fillings from teeth? Or silver fillings? Or platinum false teeth? Why should they want my diamond-studded tooth? How disgusting to see a tooth mixed with a pile of precious jewels. Especially when it is my tooth!"

Kikuji laughed. "Well, keep it then. But don't ever wear it outside or you'll be in trouble. Promise?"

She beamed at him and nodded vigorously. "Let them take all the rest. When I'm depressed, I need to look at myself in the mirror

350

wearing the diamond-studded tooth. And after the war, please get me twice as much as I have given away."

As he walked slowly home in the late afternoon, he looked at the passersby. It was depressing. Everyone was wearing work clothes: the women in those horribly baggy linen pants which only farm women had ever consented to wear before, and the men going around in dingy khaki uniforms with puttees wrapped around their legs. Was it absolutely necessary for Japan to forsake all its fine esthetic traditions to win the war? His grandmother and Ponta had a point; it was the one he had made to Kaneda earlier: after the war, Japan would have to bring out of the moth closets the culture and beauty of centuries which had been stowed away. In an emergency, beauty and grace had to be shelved. But only for the duration of the emergency.

"It is for your own good, Grandmother."

"I know, I know, Kiku-bon. I hate the air raids more than I can say. But Osaka is our home. We've never left it except for short visits. We wouldn't know what to do with ourselves out in the countryside."

"I can't have you and Mother running night after night to the air raid shelter in the courtyard. Even if no bombs fall, your health is impaired by staying awake hour after hour in that badly ventilated hole in the ground."

"Oh, it's better than that, Kiku-bon. As air raid shelters go, it's one of the very best in the neighborhood." She looked at him and smiled wryly. "But I do hate it!"

It was the spring of 1944. Enemy planes were flying in to attack the cities with increasing frequency. He had been trying for some time to persuade the ladies of the house to go to the country. With his mother and grandmother safe, he would have much less to worry about. He had wanted them to go to their ancestral town of Kawachi in Wakayama Prefecture. The Keimyoji Temple of Kawachi was their ancestral temple. When Kikuji's grandfather had died, the family had donated a lecture hall to the town. It could easily be converted into a suitable habitation for them. But they would have none of it. They wanted to stay in Osaka, where they knew everybody and were comfortable, except for the air raids.

"How would it be to go to Arima Hot Springs?" Kikuji asked.

351

Kino's expression brightened enormously. "Oh, that would be very nice! We've been there so often on visits that we know everyone there. Much better than Kawachi. Don't you think so, Sei, dear?"

Sei nodded agreeably, and the matter was settled. Kikuji sent Wasuke to Arima to find a place for them, and he located a small inn whose owner and son had been drafted. There was little business for inns at hot springs in wartime, and the place was for sale. Kikuji bought it quickly and made plans for the ladies to move in January. He was delighted to find them amenable. He knew they had enjoyed visiting Arima many times in the past, and, as a consequence, had many friends in the little resort town. In these terrible days it was essential to have acquaintances around who could help out in an emergency. Moreover, socializing with their friends in Arima, the ladies would not grow bored and wish to return to Osaka quickly.

Kino and Sei joined in the preparations for moving with their usual energy. Chest after chest was packed with the elaborate kimono they treasured, but were unable to wear during the wartime emergency. Kikuji obtained two trucks for the move. Sei and Kino tirelessly supervised the loading. Their goods would not fit, so they had the trucks unloaded in order to experiment with a more precise disposition of the available space. But even after the second loading, a number of chests could not be fitted in, and they persuaded Kikuji to provide an additional cart for the surplus. Tired, but triumphant, they watched the moving vans pull out of the yard and disappear down the street, their freight covered with the heavy crested curtains of Kawachiya's, incongruously festive and gay in the drab, colorless streets of the war-stricken city, like a rich bride's trousseau caught up in a funeral procession.

That night they had a quiet family dinner at home. In preparation, O-Toki had prowled tirelessly in the black market district, and, as a result, was able to serve a meal such as they hadn't had in a long time. On the black lacquer tables in front of each of them the servants placed five courses of very scarce delicacies, each served in the finest family bowls. They ate slowly, savoring to the full the taste of sliced raw fish fresh that day from the waters of Akashi, sauteed red snapper, steamed clams, broiled swordfish, and clear soup. For this meal Kino and Sei had reserved from the Arima shipment their most richly embroidered silk kimono; they sat before their trays as though participating in a teahouse party. Not the least objectionable part of the war to them was that they were expected to forego their carefully selected, beautifully sewn garments and dress like farmers' wives in drab, utterly unfeminine shirts and baggy trousers. To avoid this humiliation, they hardly ever ventured out of the house, and continued in the privacy of their home to wear sumptuous kimono with skirts so long they formed magnificent trains that brushed the tatami mats behind them as they walked. And tonight their faces were carefully powdered, their hair perfectly set and gleaming as though lacquered.

Kikuji studied them in silent admiration as they ate. How stubbornly these esthetic anachronisms of another age clung to their customs and ways. Their powdered faces showed few of the wrinkles of age. The two of them, Sei at sixty and Kino twenty years older, seemed to have stopped aging ten years ago; they looked like two sisters in some kabuki scene as they sat, nodding and chatting quietly to each other. As they picked delicate morsels up with their chopsticks, they occasionally looked at each other and giggled, like schoolgirls on an outing. The older they grew, the more youthfully they behaved. They were esthetically perfect: caught in a time bubble from an earlier, aristocratic age, untouched by the fierce pressures and demands of an industrial nation at war. So much the better. There was enough of uniforms and uniformity outside the doors of the family mansion. And yet, for all that, he couldn't help but feel that there was something unnatural and unhealthy in these two old women so inflexibly wedded to past custom. It was his responsibility to see to it that the protective time bubble did not suddenly pop, as bubbles will, leaving them exposed to the harsh realities of the present.

Then too, sitting beside them was Hisajiro, waving his delicate hands in kabuki actor's gestures. What would become of him? Every day before going to school he put on the shapeless khaki uniform and wound the puttees around his legs. But the minute he returned, he always changed into a stylish kimono and sat around chatting with Sei and Kino, absorbing their ways.

As the meal ended, he noticed that Kino had suddenly become silent and restless, her eyes roving around the various objects of the room.

"Is there something wrong, Grandmother?" he asked politely.

"Oh, Kiku-bon. Of course there is! We're leaving our ancestral mansion forever, I'm afraid," she said gloomily.

"Just for a while, Grandmother," he answered. "Till the war ends."

"Kawachiya's without women," she said, staring somberly at the floor, "that's the way we'll be leaving it. Without women. After three generations of women in control."

She drank her tea, and looked at him in silence.

"Your mother and I had hoped," she said at last, "that you and O-Fuku would have had a baby girl, and then she could have taken an adoptive husband, as I did and as your mother did, and that way the women would have continued to manage things. But it didn't work out that way."

"What about me?" asked Hisajiro petulantly.

"Maybe it's best as it is," Kino went on. "Only men count, nowadays. You stay behind to run things. We women get bundled off into the mountains until everything is settled one way or another—"

She covered her face and her shoulders shook with suppressed sobs.

"But, Mother," said Sei, "it's just the war. It will end soon. The family business is as good as ever."

Kino stopped weeping and stared unseeingly past her daughter. Suddenly she lurched to her feet and lunged like a madwoman. Kikuji tried to hold her, but she pulled away from him and wrapped her arms around the polished post decorating the alcove where a flower arrangement had been placed.

"This house is my life," she gasped, clinging to the cherrywood pillar, smoothed by the hands of generations. She ran her fingers lovingly over its contours, rested her cheek on its surface. "This is where I belong!" It was intended as a stern assertion, but came out as a pitiable wail. Sei from her sitting position slid over to the post and caressed it near the floor. Kino sank down and the two women embraced each other with the post between them, their voices rising to a crescendo of hysterical weeping. Hisajiro drew back in horror. Kikuji watched icily with an eye made cruel by long custom. He was watching, he knew, a pathetic ceremony marking the end of an era in his family's history. But he found himself obscurely irritated with what he could only regard as self-indulgent playacting by the

354

two women. Of course it was a house full of memories as durable and polished as the cherrywood pillar, and he was as fond of it as they were. But need they go on like this, kissing posts and wailing as though at a funeral? Always when these sheltered ladies experienced genuine emotion, they set to work embroidering it until their sentimental excesses had made it a parody of itself.

Next morning, when at last the charcoal-burning taxi drew away from the curb and sputtered its way down the street, Kikuji drew a long breath of relief. Even after the cab had come, the two ladies had lingered tearfully in front of the house. At Hisajiro's exasperated urging, they had finally climbed in. Kikuji had leaned down at the window and urged them once again to take O-Toki with them. But they were adamant. Apparently they felt that she was their representative and agent at the family mansion. Feeling conventional and almost foolish, he had gravely urged Hisajiro to take care of the ladies, and Hisajiro, doubtless feeling the same, had nodded solemnly. As the cab began to move, the two women took out their handkerchiefs and waved brightly out the window until they disappeared down the street.

He turned with a light heart, and, feeling exhilarated in his freedom, went wandering through the familiar rooms, emptied now of their occupants, but filled with their personalities. The fine sense of being free to do as he wanted lingered with him all day, and that evening he decided to visit O-Fuku. He called Hamayu's to ask her if she could get off from work to see him. Since Hamayu's had been converted into a club for industrial workers, he had never been sure that she could get time off for a social visit. She told him to wait, and, after a lengthy pause, she returned to the phone to say that it was all right. Ponta, Hisako, and Korin, since they now worked by day and were free evenings, were much easier to visit. But he hadn't seen O-Fuku for a long time. He changed into the khaki uniforms which he hated, but which was the prescribed attire for all men nowadays. O-Toki had wrapped up a fresh fish for him to give to O-Fuku. With it in hand he walked to her house in Shitaderacho. She was waiting for him. The sake was warming on the charcoal brazier, and she had set out some hors d'oeuvres for him to munch on. He looked appreciatively at her preparations.

"Until the war ends, there can be no entertaining at the pleasure quarter, of course. But you always manage to make your house seem as comfortable as the Hamayu Teahouse."

She laughed. "I made Hamayu's comfortable; I make this place comfortable. My skills don't desert me when I come back home."

He looked at the hors d'oeuvres. "Where do you get such delicacies as these in wartime?"

"I traded some of the tabi you gave me for them on the black market, Master. The black market operators are just as eager to get tabi as I am to get little delicacies. But it isn't easy."

"And sake too!"

"That especially. I can't do without it any more than you can."

It was true, he realized. She enjoyed drinking more than any of his other mistresses. He poured her a cupful and enjoyed as always the especially graceful way in which she drank it. They kept pace with each other, cup for cup, and soon were both in a delightful state of carefree intimacy.

"You never change," he said, looking at her affectionately.

"Why do you say that?"

"The things that bother the others don't bother you. They complain all the time about wartime shortages and inconveniences. You adapt. They get worn down by worry and change. You ride out the storm. You are imperturbable."

"As long as there is sake." She regarded him placidly. "Sake—and you."

"Even I get worn down. I wouldn't admit it to the others, but I do. You have no idea how hard it is to hold a business together in these times."

"The others?"

"You know. Ponta, Hisako, Korin. And my mother and grandmother when they're around. I sent them off to Arima today. Did I tell you?"

"They'll be safe in Arima. And you will be spared their complaining."

Suddenly he kissed her passionately, and they stretched out on the tatami mats.

"Oh, it has been such a long time," she whispered as they fiercely caressed each other.

It had indeed been a long time. He was at a loss to say why. Was it too much concentration on his business? the war? advancing age?

or perhaps a combination of all of these? O-Fuku shrugged off her kimono, and Kikuji stripped off his clothes. Slowly, almost lazily, he moved closer to her until he felt the softness of her belly under his. Her warmth flowed into him; slowly, luxuriously, she stroked the length of his back with her hands. He closed his eyes in a trance of delight.

But suddenly he was wide awake. There was a shouting outside and the discordant shrill of a police whistle. "Air raid alert! Air raid alert! Take cover!" The air raid wardens could be heard from far and near.

Kikuji began to withdraw, but he felt the urgent pressure of her hands on his buttocks, pushing in. "It's all right," she whispered to him. Her hand reached the lamp, and they were in darkness. Her legs twined around his, and her hands roved insistently.

"Who wants to go into a hole in the earth like a mole?" she whispered. "A bomb landing on us would add power to our sex! I can't think of a finer way to die, a little drunk and overflowing with love."

Kikuji closed his eyes again and submitted to his sensations. In the distance he heard the determined throb of airplane motors. He listened with a deep sense of fear and panic. It was a strange sensation. The sound of the planes increased steadily along with his physical ecstasy. Just as the planes were directly overhead, he came in a strange and delightful mixture of terror and passion. He fully expected that at the same instant a bomb would smash through the ceiling and explode . . .

Slowly the noise of the airplanes faded away.

"How was it with you?" he whispered.

She moaned sleepily and he realized that she had climaxed along with him. Had she too felt the terrible, wonderful emotions of terror and passion, inextricably intertwined? He felt somehow cleansed, purified of the burden of care which had been, without his being quite aware of it, weighing him down. How marvelous just to be alive, alive, alive!

He walked lightheartedly down the street just freed from the air raid, swinging a bundle. He had decided to stop by Korin's place before going home. As soon as he had mentioned his intention to O-Fuku, she called Korin to tell her that he was coming. Then she sliced the fish that he had brought, and wrapped up the larger half for Korin. The indefinable happiness which had swept over him during the air raid remained with him. For the first time in many months, he felt in perfect control of himself and of his destiny. Korin lived a little beyond O-Fuku. A few blocks after her apartment was Ponta's house, and finally Hisako's place. All of them lived approximately on a straight line from his house. If he had set out for Hisako's apartment, he could have stopped on the way to visit Ponta, Korin, and O-Fuku. The entire walk would not have taken more than an hour. As he turned in at Korin's house, he saw her dark silhouette waiting for him at the entryway. She escorted him in. Plates were on the table. He was not hungry, and told her so, so that she would not waste food on him. But she served him a bowl of soup anyway. He began to ask about her work at Sanoya's firm, but just as she began to answer, the air raid sirens sounded deafeningly. Korin covered her ears until the sound died away. Then she hastily spread ashes over the charcoal and stood up.

"Quickly! Enemy planes will be here soon. The shelter is in the lot back of the house."

Kikuji hesitated. "It's only a warning alert," he said. "Let's just sit here in the darkness until it's over."

"Oh, Master! It is against regulations. And even in daytime I get to the shelter at the office faster than anyone else. It is much more dangerous at night. Come!"

She led the way and he followed, hating the situation in which he found himself. As they reached the entrance to the shelter the red alert roared, and they expected any minute to hear the drone of enemy planes. Five or six people were jostling for entrance at the door. Instinctively, Kikuji drew back, but Korin pushed from in back and he entered. The smell of bad air was stupefying. He was moved by the pressure of bodies behind him toward the rear of the shelter. It was hot, uncomfortable, and crowded.

"Where are the planes?" shouted someone near the entrance.

"What planes?" came another voice. "They're just trying out their new sirens to see if they work."

"Hah! They work enough to scare me out of my warm bed into this filthy cesspool," cried an old woman with a shrill voice.

"Patience, people, patience! Is everyone here? Let me take a head count, please."

The beam of a flashlight stabbed into the darkness of the shelter. This was what Kikuji had dreaded. To be caught in this ridiculous situation, visiting his mistress in the middle of an air raid. He flattened himself against the wall of the shelter, feeling like a lizard on the run. The gentle beam of the flashlight moved inexorably until it fell on the back of his head.

"Well, well. We have an extra dividend tonight," said the head of the area's Neighborhood Association when he had finished his count. "Maybe somebody had a baby? There are eighteen here instead of seventeen."

"It's all right! It's my—my patron, you see" came Korin's clear, bell-like voice through the dark.

"Ah, I see. Your patron, sure enough," said the Neighborhood Association head dryly. "You picked a bad night for a visit, boss!"

With the light shining straight into his eyes, Kikuji could see nothing, but he could hear the scornful laughter all around him. Finally—mercifully—the light was turned off, and he was allowed to slip into the darkness once more. His uniform was damp with sweat. There was a low buzz of talk in the shelter, but no indication of any enemy planes. At last the all-clear siren sounded, and the people in the shelter hurried out into the night air, grumbling about official stupidity as they went.

Kikuji's lighthearted mood had melted away in the beam of the official's flashlight. He wanted now only to get home.

He spoke a few hasty words of farewell to Korin, and walked off into the darkness. The blackout in the city was absolute, and he walked slowly, feeling his way along the uneven pavement. Surely the airplanes were gone for the night? A little light wouldn't hurt anyone. He recalled that the city was in the process of confiscating all manhole covers as part of the metals-for-war drive. On his way to Korin's place he had noticed some of the flimsy sawhorses around the open holes which would later be given wooden coverings. A fine end that would be for a Semba master. He reached into his pocket for a small flashlight; from time to time he used it for a quick look at the terrain before moving ahead in the darkness.

He was leaning forward peering into the night when without warning he was knocked off his feet by someone moving rapidly in the opposite direction. There was a great clanking of metal, as though a kitchen pot had fallen on the street, followed by a number of curses uttered with savage intensity. Slowly, Kikuji picked himself up and turned on his flashlight. Framed in its beam sat a soldier wearing the sword and armband of a military policeman. He reached for his helmet, still rocking on the pavement, and stood up, glaring in the direction of the light.

"Turn that damned thing off, you imbecile," he shouted. "Can't you watch where you're going? Flashing lights just after an air raid. Knocking down a soldier of the Emperor!"

His own light flashed on, and he studied Kikuji for an instant.

"Who the devil are you, you simpleton?" he asked.

"I'm a merchant," stammered Kikuji, "a wholesaler of tabi."

"I'll bet you are. Selling tabi at midnight in the dark! Why aren't you in the army?"

"I'm classified as home guard, sir."

"Hah! Home guard. Another coward trying to save his skin. The country's full of them. All sneaking out at midnight with flashlights to sell tabi. I could break your neck."

Kikuji could think of no suitable reply.

"And where have you been with your flashlight, you simpleton? Come on! Where have you been? Near some munitions factory, I'll bet, flashing that light to show the enemy planes their way to the target."

Kikuji bowed his head in confusion. "No, sir, nothing like that. I was visiting a sick friend for a while, and I—uh—lost track of the time . . ."

"Sick friend? Sick with what?"

"Oh, nothing much, sir. Uh—fainting spells, mainly. And diarrhea."

"Fainting spells. Diarrhea." The M.P. repeated the terms with a barking judicial solemnity. "And for this you are out in a blackout just after an air raid at midnight?"

"Well, sir, the sick person has no living relatives, and so—I really had to see how things were going."

"And this sick person with no living relatives is a he or a she, Mr. Home Guard?"

"Yes. Well, it's a lady."

"I'll bet. Address?"

"Sennencho, sir."

"Now we're getting somewhere, my fine simpleton. All the

whores and geisha live in Sennencho. This one is your mistress, and you got hot pants and had to go see her. Men dying in foxholes—and filth like you running around at midnight with no thought of helping the war effort. You're disgusting! And you're probably a spy whenever you can take time off from bedding down your whores. You're coming along with me to the police station, my fine creep. My fat home guard. I've caught a good one this time."

He seized Kikuji by the arm and propelled him forward. Kikuji dug his feet in and tensed his muscles to resist. Then suddenly he bowed his head and walked along submissively. He realized that he was in great danger, and that this strutting fellow might well egg him on to attempt some violence so that he could kill him in self-defense. The white armband of the M.P. was a powerful sign to him as to all other citizens. He bowed to its authority without protest.

At the Shiomachi Police Station, his captor took him into a small curtained room for interrogation. The questions, Kikuji felt, were less for the purpose of gaining information than for sadistic gloating. Kikuji watched the M.P. as he picked up a glowing piece of charcoal to light his cigarette. It was the characterless, unformed face of a minor clerk, a dullard of forty who, having all his life resented and bowed to a succession of bosses, now for once found himself in an exhilaratingly powerful position, conferred on him by a sword and white armband. Kikuji was overwhelmed and humiliated by the man's leering interrogation. Just as he felt that he could take no more, the door opened and a policeman entered. Stiffly, he saluted the M.P.

"Have you an incident to report, sir?"

The M.P. attempted a cynical laugh. "This guy here: he was flashing lights just after the air raid. Could be a spy. Says he was visiting a sick friend, but it turns out that he was really after a piece from his whore. He'll say anything, this one."

The gray-haired policeman adjusted his spectacles in embarrassment and cleared his throat. "But, don't you see, sir, you have arrested the master of Kawachiya's, one of the oldest firms in the Semba. I was once stationed in that section, and I have known the master these twenty years." He turned to Kikuji. "How do you do, sir. I am sorry to see you here."

The M.P. tried to look unconcerned. "Well, you don't say. You know this man, do you?"

"Yes, sir. Didn't he identify himself as the master of Kawa-chiya's?"

"I hadn't got that far." The M.P. tried to cloak his imcompetence in an air of mystery. "I was busy checking up on his clandestine activities during the air raid."

"Yes, of course," replied Sergeant Kondo. "But I can vouch for the master of Kawachiya's."

The M.P. frowned weightily before giving his verdict. "Very well. Maybe by now the master of Kawachiya's has learned his lesson and we can forget this little indiscretion. In this time of national emergency one must conduct oneself uprightly at all times to avoid suspicion of treason. You *have* learned your lesson, haven't you?"

He stared sharply at Kikuji, who nodded his head curtly, and said in a low voice, "Of course, sir."

The M.P. continued staring at him, moving a toothpick in his mouth at the same time. "I didn't hear that," he said evenly. "What was it you said?"

Kikuji inhaled deeply, smiled courteously to the M.P., and replied distinctly, "I have indeed learned my lesson and I thank you for helping me."

The M.P. looked at him meditatively.

"Yes. Well, I'll let you go this time, but regulations say you've got to have a civilian guarantor in such a situation. Can you give me the name of someone to call who can come here and identify you?"

"Sergeant Kondo won't do?"

"It must be a *civilian* guarantor."

"It is two o'clock in the morning."

"Yes."

"Very well. There is Sanoya Rokuemon . . ."

Half an hour later, Sanoya bustled into the police station, camel's-hair coat over his wartime uniform. He looked cold but thoroughly ready. After greeting Kikuji, he turned severely on the M.P.

"Now, what further must be done to secure the release of my good friend and business associate, the master of Kawachiya's?"

The M.P. drew himself up in all his authority. "Since the merchants of the Semba have been praised officially many times for their great cooperation in the war effort, since they have donated from their own pockets money for our much-needed airplanes, I am inclined to overlook tonight's great indiscretion."

"Very good of you, I'm sure. I'll take full responsibility for my friend," replied Sanoya, politely insolent.

Kikuji thanked Sergeant Kondo, and walked out of the police station with Sanoya. The two of them walked for some time in silence. The chill in the night air was piercing.

"The world must have its quota of sons of bitches," said Sanoya finally. "Don't let that simpleton get you down."

Kikuji laughed grimly. "Simpleton! That was his favorite word for me."

They continued to walk in silence for a time.

"I am ashamed and embarrassed to have got into this mess, but I can't tell you how grateful I am to you for coming to my aid."

Sanoya slapped him lightly on the arm. "Forget it. We do for each other." He laughed. "I must confess this little mix-up is the last thing I ever expected of you. You're human too, Kiku-bon. But, you know, we humans don't have much place in the world any more. Too many goblins chattering about self-defense forces, emergencies, crises. The good old days with their teahouses, their leisure, their graces—they're gone for good, I'm afraid. When they lay me out on my bier, I'll still be wearing this damnable khaki uniform. And the obituary will say I was a good man because I gave money for an airplane. You thought you were in our world of humanity tonight, but you weren't. You strayed into the territory of the goblins who talk and eat abstractions. And believe them, alas!"

They were back in the Semba now. The familiar shapes of buildings loomed up at them through the predawn darkness.

"Remember this street before the war?" asked Sanoya. "At this time of year and this hour of the morning all the lights would be blazing, and the various houses would be humming with overtime work. And now—look at them!—lifeless, dormant, waiting, waiting for the dawn and the end of this dreadful night. Only in the art of killing and dying is our country still proficient. When will it end, Kiku-bon?"

They had arrived at the entrance to Kawachiya's. Observing the overwrought condition of his friend, Kikuji made a quick decision to invite him in to spend what remained of the night. The old man made no objection, and soon they were in the guest parlor, sharing a bottle of sake while O-Toki stoically prepared the bath and the guest room.

"I could not wake up my housekeeper at three in the morning as you have just done. She would not take kindly to that at all," said Sanoya, sipping his cup of sake. "You have a treasure in that O-Toki."

"I guess so," replied Kikuji. "Her mother was with the family when my father was alive, and O-Toki grew up here. She's about the only one left now. All our fifty clerks and apprentices have been drafted, and their dormitories are gathering dust. The ladies' maids have fled back to their home towns rather than get drafted for war work in some factory here in Osaka. My family is gone for the duration of the war. In all this huge house, only the store, my room, and O-Toki's room are in use, apart from kitchen and bathroom. Wasuke, the manager, commutes from his home in Tamade."

"You must be very lonely."

Kikuji toyed with his sake cup. "Yes," he replied. "Very lonely. That was why I went out tonight. There'll be no more of that, of course. Discretion was what the M.P. called for, and by God discretion he'll get. More sake?"

Sanoya held up his cup and Kikuji poured.

"Still, there are times, you know, on these winter nights when I lie listening to the squeaking of the trees in the courtyard as they bend in the wind, and the lapping of the waves on the Yokobori River—sounds which I've heard all my life—and, well, I feel I'd be better off in the army, mindlessly obeying someone rather than having to plan and think for myself."

Sanoya, who had wanted to complain, was rather taken aback by Kikuji's complaints. "Yes," he responded sleepily, "it's a hard life."

"I work at the Osaka Tabi Rationing Association in the morning doing work one of my subordinate clerks would've done in the old days. I come back and work on distributing my own merchandise to the retailers. I quit early, take a bath, have dinner, and wait for the next day. I feel as though I'm just marking time, waiting for something special to happen."

"Yes. I hate this way of living. It's the same with everybody."

"It will get worse before it gets better," said Kikuji half to himself.

"Will it ever get better, do you think?" asked Sanoya.

"We must hope so if we are to go on living," said Kikuji.

Wasuke said good night and left. It was still early, but business was at a standstill. Kikuji saw his manager to the door and stood there looking out into the empty street. Wasuke held onto his hat and leaned into the wind as he walked. The sky was heavy and gray. A scrap of newspaper blew down the street. With a sigh, Kikuji closed and locked the door. He went into the family quarters, bathed, dressed comfortably, and was served his supper by O-Toki. In the general decline, she at least remained unfailingly efficient, performing her allotted tasks silently and well. For a short time after supper, Kikuji listened to the communiques on the radio. Then he went to the kitchen where O-Toki was finishing her chores.

"I am going to bed, O-Toki," he said. "Please lock up and take care of the charcoal fire for me."

She nodded and murmured good night to him. He went to his room. She had already spread his bedding on the floor. He put on his night kimono and moved beneath the thick quilts. He was tired and after he turned out the light he expected to fall asleep immediately. Instead, he lay listening to the shriek of the February wind and the creaking of the heavy tree branches. The noise of the waves slapping with insistent monotony against the stone walls of the shoreline normally lulled him to sleep. Tonight it kept him awake. He turned on the light and read a magazine. Gradually the noise of the wind died down. He closed the magazine, turned off the light, and adjusted himself for sleep. Just as he was dozing off, he heard a sharp noise, and was instantly alert. A hammer blow? The breaking of a lock? It came from the direction of the courtyard. He jumped up, put on a lounging robe over his sleepwear, and went into the hallway. In the courtyard the wind gently ruffled a few dead leaves. He hurried toward the storehouses at the rear of the house, and, as he came out in the yard, he stopped dead. Standing under a shrub was O-Toki, in her night kimono with her hair flowing down.

"O-Toki," he called in a low voice.

"You heard it too, Master," she said as she aimed a flashlight beam at the storehouse.

"Stand back, O-Toki. I'll take a look."

He moved cautiously toward the storehouse. A stab of the flashlight was enough for him to see that the lock had been broken and that the door was ajar. Standing a little to one side, he looked in and turned on the flashlight. There was no one there, and, at first glance, nothing seemed to have been touched. On the cement floor near the door were some muddy footprints. Kikuji recalled the tough-looking freight handler who had delivered materials in the storehouse that afternoon. He had been wearing straw slippers when making his delivery, but bare feet would be better for burglary. O-Toki came into the storehouse and looked around with him.

"The only shortage I can find," he said slowly after making a thorough inspection, "is in this bundle here: the wrapping is torn and perhaps there are thirty pairs missing. We must have scared him away before he could do any real damage. It's just a sneak thief. So you mustn't worry."

He realized that she was trembling with fright. He looked at her for the first time. She had been around like a piece of furniture ever since he could remember. She had dressed him, scrubbed his back, fed him when he was sick. He could never recall looking at her. Her hair was hanging in long, lustrous strands down to her waist, her kimono was loosely fastened, so that he could see the rise and fall of her breasts.

"Don't be frightened. Sit down. Lie down."

He took her in his arms and placed her on the bales of tabi. He sat beside her. On a sudden impulse, he turned the light off and kissed her. He swept open her kimono; she, with a knowledge born of long experience, easily unfastened his. As he lay in her arms, feeling her warmth permeating the centers of his being, he realized how great a deprivation the M.P. had forced upon him. They said not a word in the storehouse as they lay together. When he left her and went back to his room, he felt comfortably elated. Her smooth skin reminded him of Ikuko. But in the back of his mind there was also a sense of shame, which grew with the passage of time.

After the night of the storehouse incident, he called her into his room almost every night. Despite the changed relationship, she served him as assiduously as ever. If anything, she worked still harder at being a good housekeeper and servant, as though to insist that in her daytime functions lay her real worth. Much of her time she spent searching for food, which was getting increasingly scarce. She would go off sometimes in the morning, traveling by train into the country, carrying a supply of new tabi with her. In the evening she would return with bags of vegetables and fish.

When he finished dinner, she would come in to clear away the dishes. He would look at her and say, "O-Toki, perhaps later?"

Without looking up as she gathered the dishes, she would reply, "Yes, sir." Then she went back to the kitchen to have her own meal and clean up the various utensils before bathing, dressing in her night kimono, and coming to tap delicately on the sliding panel of his room. There was nothing informal about her: when he opened the door always he found her sitting politely at the sill, awaiting his permission to enter.

"Come in, come in," he would whisper, in a flurry of trembling anticipation. She would enter, close the door, smile at him, and await his commands. Sometimes he would seize her ankle and draw her gently to the bed; sometimes he would simply repeat, "Come in, come in," holding open the folds of the quilt for her. When he had had enough, he would dismiss her gratefully but matter-of-factly, as the owner of a cat lets it out for the night. They talked no more than absolutely necessary. He was amazed at her fund of passion. She was prompt and skillful to try out sexual experiments which he had heard about but never dared try with his other mistresses. She played her part in the game of sex with unfailing attention and vigor. When he allowed her to do so, she would gently stroke and caress his body almost like an artist playing an instrument, and imperceptibly draw him to tumultous climax, which she watched with a strange gleam in her eye.

One night at supper he sat silently with a frown of depression on his face. As usual she served him in near-silence. At the end of the meal as she was about to clear the table, she asked in her usual neutral, impersonal fashion, "Would the master like some sake? I have been able to get some."

He smiled and refused politely. Then he looked at her seriously and took her hand. "Even when I'm depressed, you know. You have done everything for me except change my diapers. Maybe even that! And I have violated all the Semba rules governing the master-servant relationship. Even between employees in a household sex is taboo. In the old days a clerk caught in bed with a ladies' maid would be driven out of the house barefooted. There's even a proverb about it: 'Those fleeing with naked foot from out a house have bared their all to each other inside.' And here I, a master, have taken advantage of a faithful, loyal servant in a shameful way. It is very bad."

She looked at him in enigmatic silence for a moment.

"The master must know," she said slowly and with difficulty, "I have watched that body for these many years, bathed it, and dressed it, even bandaged it sometimes. I have seen it change from the body of a child to that of an adolescent to that of a man. For as long as I can remember I have wanted to stroke it in affection. Now I am having that experience. I know that my good fortune will end sometime, and to the world it will never be known. But I shall remember."

She sat for a moment with her eyes cast down, and then, as though suddenly recalling her duties, began again to clear the table.

"O-Toki?" he asked.

"Yes, Master. As soon as I have straightened up the kitchen, I'll be there."

And that night, as on the others, she came with the punctual politeness of the skilled servant, and played upon him in whatever way he wished, acceding to his every whim. He had a feeling that she was never fully satisfied and could have gone on, her intensity rigidly controlled and rationed, with sex play forever; but, when he was sated and utterly exhausted, she put everything back in order, bade him a courteous good night, and padded silently back through the long hallway to the maid's room. Her leaving never failed to excite in him a strangely pleasurable sensation, one which he had never experienced with the other four women, and which he could only suppose to be sadistic in origin.

Gradually, however, he was consumed with self-disgust. Bit by bit his association with O-Toki seemed increasingly evil to him, precisely because he, and, behind that servant's facade, she, enjoyed it so much. The sense of guilt, like radio static in the midst of fine music, destroyed the pleasure. And now he discovered that even when he visited one of his mistresses, he was unable to recapture fully his pleasure in her arms. The jaundiced face of the military policeman would flash to his mind at the most unexpected moments. All the frustration and hatefulness of the war-torn world seemed to have moved into his heart. On many evenings, he would return from work, stretch on the mats of his bedroom, and stare dully at the ceiling.

On Girls' Day in early March there came a message from the ladies in Arima: both were unwell with colds. Could he spare O-Toki, and, if so, would he send her immediately?

He summoned her and read the letter. When he finished, she said nothing. A long minute passed. He cleared his throat.

"They seem miserable without you, O-Toki," he said.

Her gaze fell. She bowed her head.

"As you wish, Master."

She packed her bags and left quietly that afternoon.

Kikuji wandered around the vacant house after she left, absorbing the emptiness of the house. He came back to his own room, and stretched out on the tatami mats, staring up at the ceiling.

"Empty! After sheltering so many generations it is empty of the people who are its meaning," he thought. "Like me after only forty years: empty, hollow, meaningless. Women gone, business at a standstill, nothing to look forward to except the next air raid."

He stood up and went back to the office. Wasuke was getting ready to leave for the day.

"Wasuke, you might as well move in here with me." he said. "Your family has been evacuated to the country just as mine has. You might as well save yourself the long trip home."

The old man thanked him and next day came back with a suitcase.

"Yes, yes," he said, his reedy voice breaking into a faintly senile chuckle, "We will keep each other company. Yes, yes. Until the war ends."

One afternoon a week later, Sanoya burst in on him as he sat doing nothing in his office. The old man's presence filled the room with vitality, and his voice boomed out at Kikuji.

"Ah, the patient is suffering from boredom this afternoon. When the next war comes, I prescribe that you get into war production,

Kiku-bon. Soldiers can't use tabi. And so"—he pulled off his shoes, and sat down beside Kikuji—"you're bored. Naturally. I'm bored. We're all bored."

Kikuji smiled weakly and shrugged.

Sanoya leaned forward toward him conspiratorially, and shook a warning finger at him. "But the bored ones of the earth are about to rebel. No more parties, says the government. So we'll get together and bore each other to death. We shall celebrate the end of the world, but secretly. It will be our Dead-end party, our Doomsday banquet!"

Kikuji laughed. "What *are* you talking about?"

"I've told you! We're going to have a spree to cheer us up and forget this endless, chronic, dreary emergency. Sogawaya has a fine house he bought out in the country: it's away from everybody; on a mountainside overlooking the sea; almost like an inn; big and comfortable. A perfect place for a party. He's inviting only old, established Semba merchants: the slow and retarded fellows too stupid to get their share of the war production goodies: you and me, Someichi, and Omiya."

"But—"

"Forget that military policeman! We have a perfectly safe arrangement. You must take your best kimono along with you, and you can change into it when you get there. How does that sound? You'll come?"

The next day at two, a charcoal-burning cab stopped at Kawachiya's, and Kikuji, carrying a satchel, climbed in to be greeted by his four friends. Sogawaya explained lengthily to the driver how to get to his country estate: they were to drive along the sea on the Hanshin Highway through Kobe to the town of Maiko. There they were to turn into the mountains for a short distance. Soon they were on their way, with the ocean on their left. All five of the passengers, warmed by the spring sun and cheered by the placid beauty of the sea, felt a sense of release. Too long they had been shut up in their empty houses in the war-torn city. The cab resounded with rapid conversation and laughter. At the end of an hour's drive, the car came to a stop at the top of a steep wooded rise. Led by Sogawaya, they carried their bags and bottles along a path through the woods. Soon they came to a hedge over which could be seen at a distance an expanse of tile roof. On the other side of the gate dogs began to bark furiously. Sogawaya opened the gate and with a few sharp commands quieted his pets. Kikuji counted six huge Akita dogs milling affectionately around their master. Sogawaya observed the respectful attention his dogs were receiving from the guests.

"They won't hurt you," he said, laughing. "But they are very effective in keeping out intruders in these dangerous times."

At the entryway were three geisha in colorful kimono to greet them. They ushered the guests into the main room, where a great banquet of seafood delicacies had been set out.

"Now, that's what I call a party!" shouted Sanoya. "No rationed canned food. I haven't seen food like this since the war began. Or women like this. Let's get out of these damned monkey suits and dress like gentlemen. Remember, now. Put everything you have into this session. This is a kind of a funeral banquet: a funeral for our kind, our world, our way of life. But it's a good way of life, so let's do it up just right and go out in a blaze of glory!"

"No speechmaking, Sanoya. Get into your kimono and start drinking!"

"Gentlemen, Gentlemen!" shouted their host. "Please feel free here in my house. I bought it as a refuge from the bombing for my family, and it is completely isolated and private. Those Akita dogs will keep out all strangers, including police and M.P.'s. Before changing into your kimono, you would doubtless like to take a hot bath. It is ready and waiting for you."

After the bath, dressed in their resplendent kimono, some of which smelled faintly of camphor, the men relaxed in the spacious living room. The sliding panels leading to the verandah had been removed so that they could look down over the trees to the sea. Sanoya became pleasantly drunk, and began to sing a melancholy song to the rhythm of the samisen. Others followed his lead and sang favorite songs. With the more familiar ones, the guests joined in. The geisha danced and sang.

Kikuji sat down beside Sanoya, who was watching the lengthening shadows hovering over forest and ocean. The old man looked at him with a sad smile. "What a fine way to come to the end of things," he said. "It's like being released from prison."

"No philosophizing from you," laughed Kikuji, jumping to his feet. "Now I shall do a solemn dance while reciting a sutra, kabuki style. I don't do this often: just for Doomsday parties, and Doomsday doesn't come very often. But I can't do it alone. All of us must join in. Tuck in the hems of your kimono. Tie a handkerchief over the lower part of your face. Ready? Samisens, play! Dancers, dance!"

And so, with Kikuji leading them in kabuki fashion, they danced feverishly round and round, singing the sutra to the rhythms of samisen and gong. Round and round the circle of dancers went, louder and louder grew the song, mingled with drunken laughter. After a great crescendo of singing, they halted and stretched out on the floor, exhausted.

The night had fallen. The servants replaced the sliding panels and closed them to preserve blackout conditions. Comfortably weary, the five friends with their geisha sat quietly drinking sake until nine. Sogawaya urged them to stay on for the night, but, with the thought of air raids on their minds, they preferred to go back home and guard their properties.

"I don't know what good you will be, though," said their host, laughing. "You have so much alcohol in you that if the enemy planes drop a lighted match near you, you will go up in flames! Better stay here and sleep it off."

But they climbed tipsily into the cab which they had hired for the day, and drove back toward Osaka. When he got in front of his house, Kikuji solemnly wagged a finger at his friends.

"This outing proves to me that the Semba never surrenders: not to boredom, not to bureaucrats, not to bombers! Before tonight we were all nearly bored to death. It is good to know that there are still close friends to count on . . ."

"Good night, Kiku-bon! Go to bed! You're drunk!" yelled Sanoya as the cab pulled away.

Wasuke helped him to his room, tried ineffectually to take off his party kimono, and finally left him sprawled comfortably on the bedding.

There was a terrible noise in his head. But, of course, this was his dream. How pleasant to dismiss a nightmare by turning over and sleeping more soundly still. But the noise began again, louder, more insistently. He opened his eyes, threw off the covers and slowly rose to his feet. Above the shriek of the air raid siren he could hear overhead the steady drone of the bomber engines, and the noise of pandemonium in his beloved city. The room seemed brightly lit; looking out the window, he saw why. The sky over Osaka Harbor showed tongues of flame flaring up through a curtain of smoke, and, as he watched, new fires burst forth in infinite numbers, and they were moving nearer and nearer, red flowers of destruction speckling the night, and, growing larger, effacing it. The noise of the planes faded, but the siren kept up its frantic wail. He turned on the radio, but the announcer described only his own confusion in the emergency. Hurrying to the front door, Kikuji found the midnight streets full of people running, shouting, giving orders, asking questions which no one answered. Some were busy loading their possessions onto carts, but in the eerie half-light cartwheels clashed together and stopped, blocking the street. Air raid wardens were running about frantically, giving orders to which no one paid any attention. As he turned back into the house, the electricity was cut and the blare of radios ceased. How would O-Fuku, Korin, Ponta, and Hisako manage in all this confusion? There was no way to find out. He ran to the air raid shelter in the back yard.

From a distance he heard the steady, inhuman throb of the second wave of bombers. Antiaircraft guns were shooting steadily and deafeningly at them. Looking out the door of the shelter, he could see new red flowerets of fire blooming. Wasuke stood at his side.

"Master, do you think we'll be all right?"

"It's anybody's guess. Right now they're bombing the Taisho District where there are many factories. It's only a mile from the Semba. But the Yokobori River will protect us from fire coming from that side."

He tried to sound confident for the benefit of the old man, but he felt in his heart that all was lost. The next wave of bombers would surely attack the Semba District. He looked up at his five stone storehouses standing in a row along the river. The one on the far right held furniture; after it came one holding clothing, another for merchandise, a small one for valuables and, last of all, a storehouse for grain. The one in the middle, the merchandise warehouse, had the most space around it on every side.

Suddenly Kikuji jumped out of the shelter.

"Wasuke, help me! The big storehouse! Get water inside it! Without water vapor, the goods will ignite if the temperature goes high enough. Help me to put enough water buckets inside so that everything does not become drier and drier, until there is nothing left but a charred ruin!"

Together they dragged many five-gallon tubs from the storage shed and placed them under the water faucet. Water pressure was low, however, so they resorted to the pump of the old well and with its help filled the containers. As each filled, Kikuji carried it inside and placed it at one of the corners. Just as he had finished bringing in the water buckets, the neighborhood air raid bell rang frantically. Kikuji ran back into the house to get his emergency case, a bag packed with essentials for just such a raid as this; he picked it up and threw it into the storehouse before closing its door. As he neared the shelter, he heard the sound of something scattering on the roofs of the storehouses, and an instant later a fire bloomed forth on the ground near the main house. The shrubbery burned in an instant, and the flames spread to the eaves and the hallway of the old mansion. Cut off by the fire from reaching the air raid shelter, Kikuji grabbed Wasuke's hand, and jumped with him into the Yokobori River. Kikuji could barely touch bottom with his toes, so, still holding Wasuke, he half swam, half walked to a cluster of stakes where boats were occasionally tied. The two of them held on to the stakes and listened to the cyclone roar of the flames. Great tongues of fire shot out over the river.

"Nobody can survive such a firestorm," said Kikuji.

But Wasuke, softly saying his prayers to himself, did not respond.

The air grew so hot that they sank lower and lower into the river, keeping only their noses exposed, and then only at intervals, for they kept ducking their heads to keep cool. Even so, the water which preserved them grew warm. Burning fragments moved slowly down the river.

When the heat permitted, Kikuji watched his home. First, the walls flared up and burned furiously, the flames curling tenaciously around the eaves of the tile roof. Once the walls were consumed, the inner frame of the structure was exposed, and gusts of wind blew the flames inward toward the structural columns and beams. Firebombs meanwhile fell in a continual hail on the roofs of the warehouses, and finally the clothing and grain storehouses began to burn. The whirlwind of flame from these buildings swirled into the interior of the family mansion. The beams were obliterated in a curtain of darting, crackling flames, and soon, with a horrible, lingering explosion, the roof caved in, leaving only one post upright: the smooth cherrywood pillar which Kino and Sei had embraced the night of their departure. Now it stood sharply outlined against the flames for a few minutes before being hugged to their fiery embrace.

As he watched, tears came to Kikuji's eyes. Two hundred and eighty years of living so suddenly, violently erased. He restrained a sob.

"The raid is over, Wasuke," he said gently to the old man, who was shivering despite the heat of the water around him. "The fires are growing smaller. Let's get out of this river before we are hit by some of the debris floating downstream."

He helped the old man over the retaining wall. He rested for a minute, then turned to look at the damage. Of all the buildings on the Kawachiya property, only the merchandise storehouse still stood. As far as the eye could see, the city was burning. The flames nearby were weakening now, and white smoke was curling from the ruins. In the distance he could see a few other white storehouses looming over the ashes and rubble, ghosts of a city cremated. Threading his way through the debris in the courtyard, he reached the warehouse and touched its wall. To his surprise, he felt no trace of heat. Could it be that this most valuable of all the storehouses had been preserved from burning by means of the water tubs he had loaded under the roof? If only a portion of the goods remained, it would be something to start with in the difficult task of restoring the family's holdings. Cautiously, he went to the thick door, turned the latch, and, standing behind it, pulled it ajar. After testing the outdraft with his hand, he threw the door wide open and poked his head in. As far as he could see, the materials for his tabi as well as the many bales of finished goods had survived the firebombs with no harm at all. He turned to inform Wasuke. But the old manager was sobbing quietly and, paying no attention to the condition of the warehouse, threw himself flat on his back just inside the door with his arm over his eyes.

Kikuji turned to stare at the ruins of the family mansion, anger contending with despair within him. He drew a deep breath and his thoughts turned again to O-Fuku, Korin, Ponta, and Hisako. Had

375

they survived? For some time it would be impossible to find out. He turned to the inert form stretched out on the storehouse floor.

"Wasuke, when you are rested a little, perhaps you could bring out some of the rice we stored in the shelter and cook some rice balls for emergency use."

The old man sat up and looked in puzzlement at his boss. "Eh? Rice? Is the master hungry?" he asked from the depths of his exhaustion.

"It's best to keep busy, I think," he replied. "Besides, Ponta, Korin, O-Fuku, and Hisako are sure to come here, assuming they were burned out, as almost certainly they were—and, of course, assuming that they survived. But they are resourceful enough. I give them more than a fifty-fifty chance. In any case, we must be ready for them. Rice balls would help."

Wearily, he went to the well in the courtyard and pumped the water. As it came from the pump, it steamed like tea being poured from a kettle. He washed the mud off his face and arms. Suddenly, he felt exhaustion lowering upon his muscles like some great weight. He dragged himself back to the storehouse, and fell flat on the mats of the small room beside Wasuke, who, despite his intentions, had not yet been able to get up to make rice balls. For some time he lay there half-asleep thinking about the four women. He had told them to come to him in case of emergency. But were they still alive?

Wasuke's voice came to him as in a dream. "Master, she's here! Miss Ponta!"

He opened his eyes at the sound of slow, dragging footsteps. Ponta stood at the doorway, her face smeared with soot, her collar open, a heavy knapsack hanging from her shoulder. Tears streaked the grime on her face as she saw him.

"Oh, Master, thank heaven you're alive!" she whispered hoarsely.

Kikuji stood up, took her knapsack from her, placed it on the floor, and put his arm affectionately around her shoulder.

"Thank heaven anyone's alive, after that," he said softly. "I don't know how the other women made out yet."

"I was so worried about you. I dropped everything and rushed here without a second thought, bringing only myself. Just the clothes I had on!"

She smiled, and the whiteness of her teeth showed strangely through the soot on her face.

"But you saved your bank account, Ponta."

"Bank account? No, I didn't. I don't understand."

"You've got your fortune in your mouth. You're wearing your diamond-studded tooth. And what about the backpack?"

"Yes, well, you see, the tooth was all I managed to save. The pack isn't mine. I grabbed it where it lay on the street and put it on my back to keep off the heat of the flames. I did have a knapsack of my own, but it caught fire after I left the air raid shelter."

"But why did you leave it?" he asked.

"Oh. It was so crowded! And it got hotter and hotter until I felt like a chicken in an oven. I pushed to the front and got out. But Echigocho was so crowded, and I was so frightened by the fire. I had a devil of a time getting out. I came right to you, just as you told me to do. Without anything at all!"

She protested too much, and he had a feeling that she had hidden away all her valuables, her kimono, and many of her precious stones long before the air raids became severe. Ponta would survive anything but a direct hit from a bomb.

"Never mind. We'll talk about it later. There's some rice in there. Let's make some rice balls. I'm hungry."

As the three of them sat on the floor of the storehouse eating rice balls, they heard the heavy, slow scraping of wooden clogs on the stones of the courtyard. Kikuji looked out and saw Korin tottering wearily under the weight of a huge backpack. She spotted him at the doorway and with a glad cry came toward him. Then, behind him, she saw Ponta, and stopped.

"Ah, Korin. Come in, come in. Thank God you're safe and unharmed!" He saw the two women staring hard at each other, and said with more assurance than he really felt, "You know each other, I think. Korin, this is Ponta." Korin removed her wooden clogs before stepping up onto the tatami matting, then bowed silently. Ponta smiled her great lady smile, and for the first time Korin saw the diamond-studded tooth. Her eyes widened and her mouth opened in complete astonishment. Kikuji had mentioned Ponta's famous decoration, but now, faced with it, she found it disconcerting and totally outside her narrow range of experience.

377

"Come on, Korin. Take off that enormous pack," ordered Kikuji. "Don't just stand there staring."

"I brought along everything I had stored in the air raid shelter: rice, underwear, my three kimono, some canned food, and other things." She hesitated, looked apologetically at him, and added in a low voice, "I don't wish to be a nuisance, so I brought my own supplies."

"What's that for?" Kikuji pointed to a fashionable red silk handbag dangling from her wrist.

"It is my engagement handbag. I take it with me when I am decked out in my geisha costume and am going to a party."

"You won't be needing it here for awhile, I shouldn't think," he said with a wry smile. "I'll bet I know one thing that's in it, along with your combs and perfumes and fans: you'll never be caught without your geisha manual!"

She smiled shamefacedly and drew it out of the bag just enough for him to see.

"Well, once a geisha, always a geisha," he said philosophically. "But I can't see why, with the world coming to an end, you take just these items with you into your exile."

"But I need them," she said primly, with her eyes downcast. "Without them I wouldn't know who I am." She looked at him apprehensively. "In such a world one must have something to believe in. Don't you think so?"

"Of course. I wouldn't criticize you. Take care of your engagement bag. You'll need it someday." He looked at Ponta, who was smiling rather arrogantly at Korin. "Just the way Ponta has that tooth to believe in and store up for the future."

He looked at his watch. It was already two in the morning. Now that the women had begun to gather at his house, he felt a great sense of relief mingled with his exhaustion. He could hardly keep his eyes open. Thinking back, he realized that between his return from the party and the beginning of the air raid he had had no more than an hour's sleep.

"I suggest all of us get a little rest now. The other two will be joining us soon. Wasuke and I will take naps down here. The two of you can have the upstairs room. There is bedding there and here. I had all the storehouses stocked with necessary items in case of just such an emergency as we are now facing."

378

Ponta and Korin eyed each other uncomfortably. Kikuji stared at the two of them with rising impatience.

"This is no time for nonsense," he said firmly. "We're lucky to be alive, and you two must get along with each other and with the other two when they come. Do I make myself perfectly clear?"

Korin bowed her head and went upstairs obediently. Ponta sighed as she stood up and with slow, weary steps climbed the steep stairway. He listened for a while to make sure that they were not quarreling, but, after the sounds made in spreading out the bedding, he heard nothing. They were, he guessed, going to sleep without speaking to each other. So much the better. He smiled to himself. It was like something out of a comic tale. Here he was receiving all his mistresses by candlelight in his warehouse, surrounded by a vast wilderness of charred timbers and ashes. These pampered darlings were his art works: graceful, esthetically pleasing, fit ornaments for a rich and easygoing civilization. But of what use could they possibly be from now on? "Still," he thought as he was dozing off, "I am responsible for them. I'll see them through, if I can. I have no choice."

"Click. Click. Click. Click." The sharp tapping noise brought him out of his sleep, and he lay for a minute trying to place it. Then he realized that it was the special sound of high-heeled women's shoes on the cement walk of the courtyard. Wasuke heard it too and started fumbling, as an old man does, to get up. Kikuji put a restraining hand on his arm, and the manager immediately went back to sleep. The heavy door was pushed open, and there, framed in the opening, stood Hisako, wearing slacks and carrying a backpack.

He rose and went to her. "I'm glad you're here! You had me worried. Why didn't you come sooner?"

"Well, I started to, but then I forgot something, and went back to get it."

"With all of Osaka burning to nothing, you went back to get something? What?"

She slung the backpack off her shoulders and deposited it before him. As it hit the floor there was a sound of paper.

"That," she replied. "My stock certificates."

He looked at her with a puzzled expression. She smiled vaguely. "They're all textile stocks. Since the race track closed down, I've transferred my talents to the stock market."

379

He pushed the bag away irritably. "So now you have a bag full of waste paper. The textile factories—all factories—will end as heaps of ashes on the streets of Tokyo, Osaka—"

"Probably so. But it wouldn't do to leave them behind. I didn't think of them till I had walked to the financial district. Then I remembered my broker saying that, once the war was over, there would be a time for peacetime stocks. And I looked at the flames for a minute and then took the chance. I gambled my whole dumb life for these stocks! As you say, they may be totally worthless. But that's another gamble, and we'll just have to wait and see."

With her head she gestured toward the debris behind her. "Only the storehouse remains?"

He nodded. "Better than nothing. You must be tired. Ponta and Korin are upstairs, sleeping. You had better join them. But—no cat fights! Understand?"

She stared moodily at him for a moment, then shrugged her shoulders. "It's a roof over my head. I'll be a good girl," she said in her usual fashion. Then, with a cold look at him, she went upstairs to sleep.

The rest of the night passed somehow. There was no noise from upstairs, and the women, apparently exhausted, slept. Kikuji, however, tossed on the surface of sleep, his mind toiling with worries, the most constant of which was O-Fuku. Throughout the night he twisted and turned feverishly, recalling her earlier unwillingness to go to the air raid shelter when he had visited her, and her desire to die in a state of pleasure and tipsiness. Had she, perhaps, again taken needless risks, and this time been burned to death? Oppressed by his thoughts, at the first sign of dawn Kikuji rose, took a bottle of sake out of the supply he had had placed in the storehouse, and began to drink.

All night long he had been saying to himself, "If only the door would open and O-Fuku were standing there . . ." He was exhausted with willing her to come to him, to remain alive. So now, when the door creaked slowly open, and she stood there, saying softly, "Master, I am here," he could not react. He swallowed a few times to control his emotions. Finally he recovered his tongue.

"O-Fuku. Are you hurt?" he asked in a hoarse voice quite unlike his own.

She entered, graceful and poised as ever.

"I am sorry to be so tardy, Master," she said in her usual, unhurried way. As he approached her, he smelled sake, and suddenly realized she was quite drunk.

"You're as drunk as can be," he said bitingly, doubly irritated not only because his sake bottle and half-empty glass were in plain sight, but because he now realized that much of his exhaustion and grumpiness came from a hangover.

"Oh, please, Master, not so judicial. I just got tired of the damned blackout curtains, don't you understand? Every day looks like a funeral, these days. So my friends and I—you know them, I think—the priest of the Shotokuji Temple across the street from me, and the blind masseur who comes by every so often to give me a massage? Anyway, we decided to have a let-come-what-may party and forget the war and the bombing and rationing and the dreary uniforms all of us have to wear. You know? So they came over to my place and we began to drink and enjoy ourselves. Don't be mad at me for drinking. As we drank the three of us agreed that we loved drinking more than anything else in the world. You know? Anyway, I was having the most marvelous time I've had since—well, since that wonderful air raid alert when the planes came over and you and I were together and we were getting drunk and loved and bombed all at the same time! Remember? So I was enjoying myself listening to the masseur's gossip and the priest's confessions of youthful escapades. It was a grand party! Then all of a sudden some old fool of an air raid warden began shouting outside and blowing his whistle, and we could hear the neighbors leaving to go to the shelters. But we were having such a nice time. You know how it is, Master. The only party I had had in weeks. So we just sat tight and drank some more. I forget who first noticed the red shadows flickering on the blackout curtain. Not the masseur, I guess. But he heard the crackling noise. I opened the curtain, and all we could see was the fire leaping up. I was terribly scared, Master."

"Naturally. What did you do?"

"Well, first of all, we sat down and drank up all the sake. I don't often have enough, but, oh, Master, I had enough tonight, all right. I felt just fine tonight. Or maybe I should say this morning, I guess. You know?"

"You're drunk as a lord, O-Fuku. I can't imagine how you ever got through it all safely."

"This was good sake, Master. Good sake, you know, well, good sake, it inspires certain special drinkers like me so that when we get drunk we always do the right thing. Good sake bathes and purifies my mind, I think."

She had been sitting beside him, her eyes half-closed.

"Have some." He poured out what remained in the bottle, and she drank it in long sips.

"And now," she said, standing up, "I may go upstairs and sleep? The others are there, I suppose?" She raised a hand to prevent him from speaking. "I don't mind a bit, not one bit. Just as long as they leave a place for me to lie down in. Good night, Master. You are the most understanding man I've ever understood!"

And with that well-intentioned, obscure compliment, she climbed the stairs and disappeared.

O-Fuku had left the door ajar. In the stillness of the morning, he heard the faint music of a windbell. Occasionally he would hear the sound of embers exploding into flames again. Once there was a great crashing of lumber, followed by a splash and a hiss. A house had apparently collapsed into the river. He didn't want to see the burned city. His own mind was as desolate and empty as the city itself. What was he to do with these four women brought together in a storehouse surrounded by acre after acre of ashes and charred beams? He knew his limits: he could not live with four women. How strange that all four, after having been burned out and having lost all their possessions, seemed perfectly calm and unworried. For good reason, probably. They hadn't worked hard to get what they had; he had always given freely to them. Now that it was all burned up, they would expect more from their unfailing provider. O-Fuku worried so little about the future that she kept drinking through the air raid and then brought only herself to the storehouse. At another time such reliance on him might be flattering, but now it made him feel bankrupt and inadequate. What was to be done?

He rose suddenly on impulse and, holding his candle, went silently upstairs to where the four women lay sleeping. In the dim light he watched them. Nearest him was Ponta, her face, roughened from excessive use of makeup, twisted to one side. In her half-opened mouth he could see the diamond. O-Fuku, her mouth wide open, snorted drunkenly as she slept beside Ponta. Korin, her engagement bag placed neatly next to her, rested her head on a box-pillow, which she must have had in her pack. Hisako, in apparent disdain for the other women, slept up against the wall. His candle began to flare and dim erratically as the wick was slowly overwhelmed by the fluid wax. Was this the sad reality of all he had worshipped and loved? These thoughtless, faded creatures lacking any capacity to understand and deal with actuality? At various times each in her own way had transported him to a heaven of delight; there they lay in disarray on the tatami: fallen butterflies, their colors faded, their wings no longer flickering in the spring sunlight. Here, he thought, is all that I have to show for twenty-five years of living. These bedraggled creatures have relied on me, but in a much more essential way I have relied on them.

Suddenly he stamped the floor in a fury and shouted, "Wake up! Wake up!" He dashed downstairs, picked up a box placed in the storehouse for emergency use, and with it ran back upstairs. He sat down in front of the sleepy women and opened the box. It was filled with money. Quickly he divided it into five approximately equal piles without even counting it.

"That's all I have," he said, talking rapidly. "It's about one hundred thousand yen. I've divided it into five roughly equal piles. Each should contain about twenty thousand yen. That should be enough, even with wartime inflation, to take care of you for a little while. I want all of you to go right away to the family temple in Kawachi-Nagano. I rented a building there just in case I might need it. The temple houses nuns, so you'll find it convenient in many ways. Do you understand?"

The women were stunned by his rapid-fire explanation, and said nothing.

"Very well. Wasuke here will act as your guide. I have made up my mind that this is the best thing to do, so please do not ask questions. Just—go!" He held up his hands as though he were pushing them out the door.

In the silence that followed, he heard the breeze blowing faintly outside, and the strange scratching of the broken electric wire as it blew now and then against the side of the storehouse. The draft from the wind coming in under the door swayed the flame of the new candle which he held; he cupped it with his other hand, and it grew straight and bright again. Korin watched Kikuji with the unblinking seriousness of a child studying some mysterious event. Ponta sat with her eyes cast down, quickly sizing up the piles of bills on the floor and occasionally darting an appraising glance at Kikuji's face. Hisako, her legs to one side, faced away from the other women as though to ignore them. O-Fuku rested her head against the wall, lazily surveying the scene through a comfortable drunken haze. Her face and neck were red.

There was a great wail, and Korin threw herself forward on her face. "Out of a blue sky you suddenly throw us away," she sobbed. "We are to go off to some distant nunnery in the country! What is to become of us?"

Her shoulders shook in tearful protest. Kikuji breathed deeply. This was what he most wanted to avoid.

"I won't abandon you at such a time! So stop the crying. Can't you see that already it is difficult to get out of Osaka? You've seen the condition of the city. Soon it may be impossible to escape. You must go right now, before it's too late. Obviously, I'm not going to let you suffer for want of money. I'm thinking only of your safety."

Hisako stood up, slung her pack over one shoulder, and started down the stairs.

He wheeled around. "Hisako, where under the sun are you going?"

"You said, 'Get out.' I'm getting out," she said icily.

"But you can't just leave without somewhere to go, Hisako. There is no more Osaka! There is no place to go, and nothing to eat. If you go to Kawachi-Nagano with the others, you'll be safe. How about it?"

She hesitated for a moment.

"Besides," he added, "You can't survive without money. You must take your share."

Without saying anything she took off the knapsack again, stonily returned to where she had been sitting, and picked up a pile of the bills on the tatami mat. Ponta's calculating eyes watched sharply, and she pursed her lips.

"I think we should take the money and go to Kawachi-Nagano as the master suggests," she said. And with that, she reached over several piles of money to one not near her, taking the pile which she obviously had decided was the biggest. Korin slowly dried her face with her handkerchief and picked up her heap of banknotes.

"O-Fuku! Wake up!" Kikuji said sharply. "Take your share of the money."

Sleepily, she picked up some of the bills in front of her and tried to stuff them between the layers of her waistband.

"Thank you very much, Master," she said, her words blurring into each other.

"No, O-Fuku. You can't carry twenty thousand yen in your waistband. Haven't you any handbag?"

"Here, Sister." Korin held up a cotton scarf she had fished from her knapsack. In it she wrapped O-Fuku's share and gave it to her.

Kikuji reached for the remaining pile. "This is my share. It will see me through. Who knows what will happen to our bank deposits at such a time?"

A faint smile of appreciation and sympathy appeared on the faces of some of the women.

"And so, if you are ready—?" he said questioningly. They gathered up their belongings. "Come this way, and I'll let Wasuke show you how to get out of Osaka. It won't be easy."

He led the way downstairs, where they found Wasuke busily packing an emergency knapsack with the remaining rice balls, rice, salt, canned goods, and finally a supply of tabi which he could exchange for food.

"I'm sorry to have to ask this of you, Wasuke. I know how very tired you are. But if you take my friends to the Keimyoji Temple and ask the nuns to take care of them, you would be helping me greatly, just as you always have." He looked with concern at the old man.

"There's no need to worry, Master. I am glad to get out of Osaka even for a day. Besides, the abbess in charge is an old friend of mine. She is very old, but still hale and hearty. She has been there ever since your family gave the detached lecture hall to the temple as a memorial to your grandfather. Your family is remembered with honor and affection at the temple. And your ladies will be comfortable there."

As always, Wasuke spoke simply, practically, and utterly without

385

pretense. As he talked he put the finishing touches on a separate bundle he had put together to give the old abbess. The women stood, hesitant about leaving, bearing the same bags and packs they had arrived with. O-Fuku by now had sobered up and looked pale and unwell.

"Goodbye, Master. We'll wait for you in Nagano," one of them said tremulously, and all bowed, speaking their farewells in low, tearful voices. Wasuke opened the door, and, silhouetted against the dawn, they followed behind him on the blackened stepping stones. The sky was covered with a heavy black smog. No sunlight came through. White smoke still rose slowly from many places. He watched as the five picked their way through the debris and the smoke, weaving in and out of the vapors like phantoms. From time to time they looked back at him and waved as he stood in the doorway. He waved back, wishing they would hurry. Every muscle in his body ached. A sudden gust of wind puffed the smoke into a dense curtain, and the five silhouettes disappeared. Kikuji went back inside the storehouse to rest.

He woke up with a start. Someone had been knocking at the door. He looked at his watch, but it had stopped. Looking out the latticed window, he saw that it was growing dark. Wasuke could not possibly be returning this early, even if he wanted to. Quite possibly gangs of looters were going from one surviving structure to another in the vast wasteland of ashes and charred beams. The knocking resumed. Cautiously, Kikuji called through the door, "Who is it?"

The low, indistinct voice of a woman answered. He swung the heavy door open immediately.

"Mother! And Grandmother too! Why, oh why didn't you stay safe in Arima?"

Behind Sei stood Kino, supported by O-Toki. The bottoms of their work pants were dirty and their hair was all in tangles.

"Come in, come in," he shouted at them. "You are crazy to risk coming here. I wanted you in Arima!"

Sei's face began to twitch tearfully, but Kino answered angrily, "We are not crazy, young man! Our place is at our home. As soon as we heard that the Semba had burned, we managed to get a ride in the back of a truck in exchange for our last twenty pair of tabi and so somehow we jounced our way here."

386

She turned in the doorway and looked at the place where the family mansion had been, seeing the ruin fully for the first time.

"So it is, it is, indeed, it is—gone," she said gently, almost inaudibly. Tears made little paths down her face as she surveyed the scene, head held high and shoulders back. Then she began to collapse. Her shoulders sagged, her head was bowed, her knees gave way. On the tatami mat, she sobbed uncontrollably.

"Our house, our house . . ."

Her eyes still glinted angrily, and the voice sounded more fierce than he would have thought possible in a woman of her years faced with such catastrophe.

O-Toki tried to make her more comfortable. "Come, my lady, let me help you—"

Kino shook off her extended hands. She sat up, her eyes hard.

"Kiku-bon, why did you let it burn? With the Yokobori River behind it and large open spaces on either side of it, how could it have caught fire?"

He was silent, trying to think of how to explain the firebomb attack to his grandmother.

"Kawachiya's has survived dozens of fires in the neighborhood over the centuries. Big fires! It didn't burn!" She leaned forward craftily and whispered to him, "You weren't satisfied with just kicking us out, were you? You had to burn it up because you knew we loved it. You had to show us who was boss."

Her eyes glittered madly close to his, and she smiled a victorious smile at having found him out.

"Grandmother, no. You don't know! You're very tired and need rest. We'll talk about this later."

"That will give you a chance to invent lies!"

"We did everything we possibly could, Grandmother. We were lucky to have saved even the storehouse. Wasuke and I put tubs of water inside, even while the bombs were falling. We never went to the shelter at all. We had to jump into the river to escape the flames. It was worse than anything you can imagine!"

Sei too tried to calm the old lady. "Mother, don't say these things! Our Kiku-bon could never do anything to hurt us. He loved the house just as much as we did."

Kino looked sardonically at her. "Hah! You, my daughter, are a bit of a sucker and always have been. That's why you've had to depend on me all your life. Don't let this Kiku-bon deceive you!" Her eyes narrowed as a sudden inspiration struck her. "I tell you what! We'll ask the fox goddess whether I'm right or not."

"The—the fox goddess?"

"Certainly! The shrine is right out here. Come!"

She led the way into the ruined courtyard, and found her way to the headless statue of the fox. Kneeling in the debris before the stone figure, she recited a sutra, and then went on mumbling indistinguishably. Finally she raised her head, eyes wide, staring sightlessly into space.

"Ah," she said. "Ah! Just as I thought! Did it burn nicely, Kiku-bon? Did my beautiful cherrywood beam sparkle with lovely red flames before it collapsed? And the roof tiles: did they twist and snap with pain as will our bones on the day of cremation?"

She picked up a charred fragment of wood at her knee and looked at it for a long minute.

"My lovely home," she said dully.

With O-Toki's help she rose to her feet. Suddenly she wheeled on Kikuji with a contemptuous smile.

"And where are the concubines hiding?" When he didn't answer, she continued, "Are they still alive?"

He nodded.

"Congratulations! You still have your women." Then the vigor of her rage drained from her face and in seconds she became an old, old woman again. "But I am left with nothing. Nothing."

She started to walk uncertainly in the wrong direction. Sei and O-Toki reached out their hands to support her, but, feeling them at her side, she suddenly straightened up proudly, shook them off, and walked unsteadily by herself to the storehouse. She stood for a moment looking at the blackened front of the building, and collapsed in a faint at the doorway. Kikuji held her head up and forced a little sake between her lips. She opened her eyes feebly, and closed them again. When he was sure that her breathing was regular and peaceful, he carried her to the second floor. Sei and O-Toki went up to sleep on either side of her, leaving Kikuji at last the opportunity to be embarrassed and ashamed once more of his past behavior with O-Toki. Since her arrival he had not paid attention to her except as another willing hand at a difficult time.

By the next morning, Kino had undergone yet another change. It was as though the spirit of rage which had possessed her had now departed, taking with it all her willfulness. With Sei and O-Toki she quietly helped to organize the various materials which had been stored in the family air raid shelter.

"How fortunate that we had the foresight to build this shelter," said Sei.

Kikuji, who remembered that Sei and Kino had objected to defacing the property with such a construction until the air raid defense officials gave him what amounted to a written order to build one, merely nodded. Once it had been built, however, they had taken an active interest in it, and stored it with various essential items, including extra bedding, clothing, and foodstuffs. Now, however, upon inspecting the shelter, they found that a water pipe near it must have been broken in the air raid, for water had seeped in. It was necessary, therefore, to bring out all their supplies and equipment to inspect for water damage. Wasuke, who had returned from Nagano the night before with the report that the four women were comfortably settled there, helped Kikuji carry the various items, while Sei, Kino, and O-Toki sorted them. The women efficiently opened and examined the canvas bags containing the bedding, the mothproof boxes containing their kimono, the cartons of canned goods, the bags of rice and other staples. Anything ruined by moisture was discarded; wet clothing and bedding were spread out to dry; the supplies still in good condition were taken to the storehouse.

"Here, Grandmother," said Kikuji, coming out of the shelter with a large wooden box in his arms. "This one has your name on it."

Eagerly she opened it. The smell of camphor came out strongly. It was filled with her best kimono. She took one magnificently brocaded garment from the box and spread it out on her shoulder. Then she stood gazing down at it for a long time, as though in a dream.

"Come, Grandmother," said Kikuji kindly. "Let me take that box into the storehouse for you, and then you can look over the kimono in it. Why not put one on?"

She meticulously folded the kimono she had admired and returned it to the chest. He lifted the box and deposited it on the tatami mats by the entrance. Docilely she followed him. When he left to go back to the shelter for more materials, she was sitting placidly beside the box, taking the lid off.

Returning to the shelter, he found Wasuke working at the electric switchbox. The floor at the rear of the shelter slanted downward, and the water was knee-deep there. The switchbox was at eye level, but the moisture had crept up through the concrete. Wasuke was trying to prevent a short circuit. It was hot and humid in the shelter, and the two men were bathed in sweat as they worked.

Suddenly he heard a high-pitched cry of terror. It was O-Toki. He rushed to the door. "My lady, my lady!" she was shouting.

"O-Toki, what's the matter?"

"It's your grandmother, sir!" Not trusting herself to speak, she pointed frantically toward the river.

"Quick! Where is she?"

"Oh, Master, she has fallen into the river!"

He raced to the bank, where Sei was wailing and pointing toward the middle of the river. He caught a momentary glimpse of a white kimono borne down by the current. He tore off his shirt and pants and jumped in to swim vigorously to midchannel. But he could see no trace of the white kimono. He heard voices, and turning his head, saw a small boat approaching. He swam toward it and, grabbing the edge, looked into the faces of Wasuke and their neighbor, the owner of the lumberyard, who had also managed to save his storehouse but nothing else.

"Can you see her?" he asked.

"Not now. I think she's downriver from here."

They gave him directions and he swam off to search further. Sei and O-Toki stood like statues on the bank waiting. In the ruins along the river, there were no other people around to help. Kikuji felt cold and numb in the water. He kept a wary eye out for floating wreckage, and once was barely able to get out of the way when a partly submerged assemblage of charred beams and corrugated roof tin came floating past. Urged by the lumber merchant, he climbed into the boat. They rowed upstream a little, and then down again, toward the bridge at Shinmochi.

"There! Go over there! I thought I saw— There! Under the bridge! By that upright stake!" Kikuji shouted.

In the shade of the bridge, the whiteness of the kimono sleeve caught on the stake was like a little flag. She was face down in the water, her kimono billowing in the water around her, bobbing up and down as the wavelets caught the body. Rather than pull her indecorously into the boat, Kikuji knelt down on the flooring, thrust his arms deep into the water, and, curving them around his grandmother, drew her gently on board. Even with the stones that she had placed in the sleeves of her kimono, she didn't weigh much. He studied her face. It was smooth, calm, even beautiful in death.

"She hasn't the look of a drowned person," said the lumberman. "She must have died of shock when she jumped."

"She jumped?" said Kikuji in an agonized voice as the realization came to him that she had taken her own life.

"Yes, sir. She jumped. I was at my place poking around among the ruins for anything I could salvage, and I looked up to see her sort of skipping along the road to the upstream bridge, light as a butterfly in that white kimono. From a distance, I thought she was a young woman. Every so often she would bend down and pick something up from among the ruins. I know now that she was picking up those same stones you found in her sleeves, poor lady! When she got to the bridge way upstream there, she stood in the middle of it, leaning against the railing, staring into the water as it went swirling under the bridge. She stayed like that for a long time. Then, all of a sudden, she ran across to the downstream side, and fell, all white, into the water . . . It was then, when she fell, that she gave up the ghost."

The boat headed in swiftly to the Kawachiya landing. Sei embraced the wet, pathetically small figure, and wept. O-Toki, her face glistening with tears, bowed low and apologized abjectly for not paying proper attention to her aged mistress. But Kikuji kept gazing at the placid, beautiful face of the dead woman, trying once again, for nearly the last time to understand the mystery of her life as it had always seemed to him. He recalled the night before her departure for Arima, when she had embraced the cherrywood post, and he had been offended by her histrionics. But she had been quite genuine. The spirits of many generations inhabited that house and found their expression through her sharp and agile tongue and mind. She had prospered in the tradition which the house represented. And so it was fitting, even necessary, that she should perish on the same day that the family mansion ceased to exist. Looking at her now, he thought that there was something about her that reminded one of a young girl: the smoothness and luster of her skin, for one thing, made her look much younger than her eighty years. And her eyebrows formed neat, straight lines, unlike the shaggy brows of most old people. Under her finely formed nose, her lips were slightly open, the lips of a connoisseur who had tasted and digested all the good that fortune could give her, spitting out all the sourness of misfortune or defeat. In her aristicratic countenance one could read the two-hundred-and-eighty-year-long history of her Semba family.

Kino, had she had her say, would simply not have tolerated such a skimpy funeral. But there was no help for it. They did the best they could. Had there been no war, no devastation, they would have taken the body to their ancestral village of Kawachi-Nagano and held the funeral and cremation there. It would have been a great ceremony of the sort that Kino loved. Diligently and affectionately, Kikuji sought to make do with what could be scraped together out of the ruins. They held the funeral in the storehouse the next day, presided over by a priest from the temple of Kohoji in the Nakadera District, which had survived the bombing. Some of the managers of branch stores and their families attended, dressed in the drab uniforms of wartime. By good luck, Kikuji had happened on a box containing the white mourning kimono required by Semba tradition which the family had used at the time of Kihei's death, so he and Sei were properly dressed for the occasion. The air raid siren sounded once during the service, but the all-clear sounded almost immediately after, so that Kino's last rites were not marred by one of the many raids which now came by day and by night to distract, weary, confuse, and, of course, occasionally kill the inhabitants of Osaka. When the service was over, they carried the coffin to a dilapidated hearse, long ago stripped of its gilt and silver ornamentation.

Sei and O-Toki stood watching quietly. As the door of the hearse shut on the casket, Sei turned her tear-devastated face to her son. "I depend on you, now."

He patted her hands and murmured, "Of course, of course." He was thinking of Kino's last half-hour of life. After the funeral was over he took his mother back to the storehouse, then walked up to the bridge from which Kino had jumped. He looked down at the currents into which only yesterday she too, standing just here, had stared. Yesterday had been obscured with smog; today the spring sun glinted from the water. He heard her voice once more.

"And where are the concubines hiding? . . . You still have your women. But I am left with nothing. Nothing."

It was a gloomy, wretched voice, reverberating from the grave, striking his sun-warmed ears, as he stood looking down on the darting ever-changing currents of the river.

Epilogue

When the train pulled into the station, the chaos surpassed his expectations. Only one car had glass in its windows. Looking in as it passed, Kikuji saw five or six huge occupation soldiers lounging comfortably in it. The other cars were crammed so full of people that he wondered how the sides kept them in. As the farmers and black marketeers with their bulging bundles passed by him, he kept a sharp eye out for his friend. Finally he saw him at a distance: an aged man, standing very straight, dressed in a dark kimono, a stray from another age. He called and the white-haired old man came to him and bowed.

"It was good of you to come," he said simply.

"Welcome back," said Kikuji. "Did you enjoy your stay at Himeji?"

"Too long, really. While the bombs were falling, I was glad to be there. But after the peace came, I wanted to get back. It took me seven months to break loose from my relatives."

They took a cab to a small restaurant Kikuji knew in the black market district. The manager showed them to a corner room on the second floor overlooking the busy marketplace. The window panels were open and they sat comfortably on cushions, warmed by the April sun, watching the busy crowds below them in silence.

"How different from a year ago," said Sanoya with a nostalgic smile.

"The people or the place?"

"Both. The place was a heap of ashes. And the people were shivering in their air raid shelters waiting for the next bomb—and invasion. I thought we had lost all spirit, all will to live. And now look at them. Busy as bees building a hive."

He drank his sake thoughtfully.

"And how is it with you? Is Kawachiya's finding its way back to prosperity again?"

"It will take time. The Semba as you knew it—and all of Osaka for that matter—is gone. In its place a few buildings are beginning to sprout up like mushrooms. One of my storehouses was saved. I've turned that into a small factory-workshop. I sold a few lots I had downtown, and with the money, built a makeshift store with an eighteen-foot frontage on the site of our old home. We live in the rooms above the store."

"One must start somewhere."

"Exactly. That's what I told myself after the bombing and my grandmother's death. If the war had gone on long after those— those almost incomprehensible erasures of everything I've known, I think I would have given up in despair."

Sanoya grunted assent. "That's the way everyone felt. Giving up that impossible war made so much sense. Now we can rebuild."

"We can try, anyway. But, you know, Sanoya, some of my friends wanted me to make stockings, or go in for black market operations. They don't understand. I'm going to rebuild the family business as a tabi wholesaler. That is basic. Given that one absolutely necessary limitation, I'll go along with the times. I've already done so: I'm beginning the manufacture of tabi-style sneakers—you know, the rubber shoes that farmers and workmen wear because they have a separate space like tabi for the big toe. They like sneakers of that kind; they're sturdy and they grip the rocks and unstable places very well. I can't keep up with the demand."

Sanoya laughed. "You're always the *bonchi!* Even in your sleep, you plan your business campaigns like a general. But are you equipped for such a line of goods? It sounds too ambitious for my taste."

"Look, this is what I've done so far: I bought rubber soles from Kobe, set up a shoe-sewing machine in the storehouse, and put my craftsmen who returned from the war to work putting soles and insteps together. At first it didn't work well, and I thought I was going to have trouble. So I went to Kobe and hired three skilled workers away from a highly respected shoe manufacturing firm by offering them three times the salary they were making there. They trained the rest of my workmen, and the retailers have been delighted with the result. I have made it a package deal: with each pair of the tabi-sneakers goes a pair of my best quality white tabi. So business is expanding faster than I had thought possible. But it is still very small compared with the old days. If my grandmother looks down on us now, I'm sure she sniffs scornfully at our ridiculous little store perched on the ashes of the family mansion."

"I wish I had your energy," the old man said.

"I don't have much of it any more, either," answered Kikuji lightly. "Just about enough to get through each day as it comes."

"And your family? How have they adjusted to your grandmother's death and this new world of peace and prosperity?"

"My mother without Grandmother is really quite different," he said reflectively. "No more arrogance, no love of fashionable ceremony. She does everything I ask or suggest without argument." He laughed shortly. "I liked her better the other way, even if she was more trouble."

Sanoya nodded in polite agreement.

"Hisajiro is—not strong, you know. He hasn't gone back to college since the war, and he doesn't help with the business. Mostly he sits around the house listening to the radio."

"He'll take hold eventually, I'm sure," said Sanoya commiseratingly. "It's the same with all youngsters nowadays. Then, all of a sudden, they catch hold, become serious, hard-working fellows. He'll shape up in time."

"I doubt it," said Kikuji flatly. "In any case, he has two half-brothers I'm thinking of bringing into the firm. There's Ponta's son, Taro. He's twenty now. And Ikuko's boy, Ikuro, is fifteen. I've kept in touch with both of them during the last few years. They're good boys, and they would take care of Hisajiro . . ."

He drank a quantity of sake from a water glass, and stared moodily out the window. "Then there's our housekeeper, O-Toki. You wouldn't believe how she has changed: all gray-haired and wrinkles under the eyes. She wants to retire."

"Ah?" said Sanoya, slightly puzzled. "But there are plenty of women around nowadays who would be glad to have her job. Why not let her retire?"

"Yes, I suppose so," replied Kikuji enigmatically.

"And your ladies?" asked the old man curiously.

"I evacuated them to the family temple grounds in Kawachi-Nagano during the last days of the war. They're still there."

"I should think they would be tired of the country, even country as beautiful as that."

"They are. They keep writing me they want to come home. Here's the latest."

He reached in his pocket and tossed to Sanoya the letter from Hisako which he had received that morning. Sanoya read it slowly aloud.

"We greatly enjoy the new bathhouse you ordered built for us. But we would very much like to see you soon because we wish to discuss our future with you. As it is, we feel that we are imposing upon the temple authorities by staying on endlessly in this fashion. You have said that you do not wish us to come to Osaka. Please, then, come here to Kawachi-Nagano so that we may talk frankly with you about the future. We think we ought to have one."

He folded the paper after reading it and returned it to Kikuji. "Her brush strokes are very beautiful," he said cautiously.

"That's more than she is!" The outrageous sentence burst from Kikuji's lips without his intending it.

"You are experiencing some trouble, I gather," said the old man.

"The universal difficulty. They are old. Old and ugly."

Sanoya poured himself a drink.

"It happens to women too, you know," he said gently. "Sometimes the fault is in the eye of the beholder."

"I have given my life to these people. Night after night, year after year, I have sought them out at all hours, loved them, sheltered them, treasured them—"

"—And they had the unparalleled impudence to grow old and fat and wrinkled. Is that it?"

"They were an ideal, the opposite of my grandmother and my mother. With them I escaped."

"Escaped what?"

"The Semba—"

"—Which you love, and which you represent perfectly."

"—All the fakery and ceremony which my mother and grandmother went in for."

"You have it wrong, Kiku-bon. Like the ladies of your house, your protegees were themselves superb examples of the traditions of Japan which vanished in the light of the firebombs. Do not now, because they are old, think that you were misguided and wrong in loving them. If so, they were misguided and wrong in loving you. You saw them as an ideal, and all ideals, no matter in what tangible, visual form they are objectified, have a truth of the spirit to them. These old women have left you with two fine, very effective boys on whom you pin your hopes. Give the women their share of the credit. Revere the past; don't dismiss it as meaningless if the present moment fails to match your dreams. But excuse me. I talk too much."

"Well, I must see them, I suppose. I've been sending Wasuke up there once a month to pay their stipends to them. Now I had best go and make final accountings with each of them. Ikuko was the best of the lot."

"You say that because she died still young and beautiful. These others were as rare and lovely a group of women as I can imagine. Venerate them for what they have been. And for having loved you faithfully. And for having grown old and ugly in your service. Prince Genji did not dismiss the lady with the red nose because she was ugly and ridiculous."

"Ah, Sanoya," said Kikuji with an odd smile, "I never knew you were so philosophical."

"Nor I," said the old man grimly, reaching for the bottle. "You may not have known it, but I was in love with one of your four, ugly ladies once. I knew I was too old and ugly for what she deserved, and I helped you to befriend O-Fuku. You knew that?"

"In the back of my mind, yes, I suppose I did, old friend. I have never considered it squarely until this minute."

"Well, forget it now. I shouldn't have mentioned it. But be nice to your four women. They have lived their lives for you."

"I'll have to do something soon, I suppose. It's been dragging on too long."

"What will you do?"

"Go up there, say goodbye, and give each one a whopping big severance check." He drained his glass and stared moodily out the window at the crowd below.

"Ponta, Hisako, Korin: I kept them for old time's sake and because they were incapable of taking care of themselves. O-Fuku I valued most. And I still do. But I'm no longer in love with her."

Two days later, he took the train toward Wakayama, and got off at Kawachi-Nagano station. From there he sat uncomfortably in a bus as it bounced and crawled its way along a dusty mountain road. After an hour's ride, the driver pulled up at a tiny intersection, pointed up it, and said to him, "Keimyoji Temple is a half-hour's walk up that road."

It was a hot day and with each step the white dust blew up to his sweaty face. He rounded a curve and saw the small temple gate ahead of him on the right. He stopped and mopped his face with a handkerchief. He hadn't seen them since that terrible night when, after the air raid, he had almost chased them out of Osaka. It would not be easy now to make a clean break. He moved under a tree and sat down for a few minutes to cool off. He loosened the collar of his kimono. The four checks which he had put in the pocket of his cotton waistband were damp, and he held them in the breeze to dry out. Slowly, almost unwillingly, he got up and walked up the hill and through the gate. He hadn't told them that he was coming, so there was no one around to welcome him. The path, lined by cedars, was shaded and cool. Through the trees in the distance he saw the outlines of the stately main hall of the temple. On the right was the detached building which his family had contributed in memory of his grandfather. It was here that the four women were staying. To the left of the main hall was the abbess's residence. He wanted to see her to express his gratitude and to give her a considerable donation, so he turned toward the cedar-bordered path leading to her door. As he did so, however, he heard shrill feminine laughter through the shrubbery at his right. He turned at once in that direction and walked to the dirt wall surrounding the memorial hall. Going through the small door in the fence, he found the shrubbery still very dense on both sides of the path. On the right side, he heard again, and much closer, the sound of women's voices and the splashing of water. Kikuji stopped, and found an aperture in the hedge through which he could see the new bathhouse. The sliding door was fully open. The women were secure in their isolated location and had opened the door to allow the sun to come in. The four of them were seated in a circle on the scrubbing floor. The one bent over washing her hair was O-Fuku. Korin rubbed a cake of soap in her friend's hair, and blew soap bubbles from it into the air. They landed on the wet bodies of Ponta and Hisako. As the two laughingly protested and brushed away the bubbles, Korin blew another gale of bubbles at them. Kikuji looked at them with the studious

399

sympathy of an artist analyzing a painting. "The fault," Sanoya had said, "is sometimes in the eye of the beholder." And so it must have been. These women were not old or ugly. From arm to hip their skin was smooth, lustrous, well rounded. Protected from the confusion of a postwar era, they looked well fed and happy.

They had stopped their lighthearted play and had begun chatting lazily with each other.

"What will you do if you go back to Osaka, Miss Ponta?" asked Korin.

"I'll rebuild my geisha house, hire qualified girls, and go back into business. I can manage. And you?"

"Oh, I am trained as a geisha. I'll have no trouble. I'm puzzled by the master's long silence, though."

"Nah," came Hisako's drawling voice. "By now he must have faced the fact that he has no more need of us. He's had two weeks in which to reply to our latest letter."

"I'll bet that nasty old lady, his grandmother, has something to do with it. What a samurai she is!" said Ponta.

"Well, we can't wait here forever for him to make up his mind while the world passes us by," answered Hisako. "I've got my textile stocks, and from what my broker says in his latest letter, I'm not doing at all badly. So I'm going to Osaka soon and take charge of my money."

"I hope he has enough—" said Korin.

"Of course he does. He's a moneybags," answered Hisako.

"Oh, how I envy you people. Miss Hisako has her stocks and Miss Ponta has her diamond in her mouth and lots of rings and a beautiful son. When is he coming next to see you?"

"Ah, Korin, that's a secret. If people find out I have a twenty-year-old son, they won't find me very seductive any more." Ponta rolled her eyes and laughed. She looked at O-Fuku, who listened amiably, but said nothing. "And how about you, O-Fuku? What will you do if it is clear that the master has lost interest in us?"

"Me? Oh, I don't know. I've been thinking I might just stay right on here, if they'll let me."

"Here! Why would anyone stay here?" All three stared at her.

"Why not? I can still get along very well on the money the master gave me when we left Osaka. I don't need much. I love the peacefulness of the country, and every night I have my nice hot sake. As for the distant future—hmm, well, let the distant future take care of itself. It's no concern of mine."

She stood up, climbed into the hot bath, and sank back contentedly with the water up to her chin.

"Well, what a bunch of clowns we've been!" came Hisako's strident voice, sounding over the noise of the running water faucet, "Nobody snagged that guy after all these years of trying. He should've been able to pick a wife from four women as different as we are from each other."

The others smiled a little in response to this forthright verdict, but said nothing.

"The water temperature is perfect right now," said O-Fuku at length. "Why don't all of you get into the pool and soak?" She sat with one arm on the edge of the pool. Her skin from shoulder to neck was reddened by the hot water.

"Hey, hey, hey! Look at that red skin. Like maples leaves in fall. The skin you love to touch!" shouted Korin. She jumped into the pool and, stretching out her hand, tweaked O-Fuku's breast.

"Oh, you abandoned women," shouted Ponta in mock disgust, and she flailed into the pool so violently that she splashed a shower of water over both O-Fuku and Korin. Hisako joined in the water fight. As they threw the hot water about, steam rose thicker and thicker until he could see only the outlines of the women.

He watched them with the intense absorption of a moviegoer watching a screen. In their frolic, regardless of their age, they seemed eternally youthful, even O-Fuku, who was already past forty. They were charming and springlike, and he had been unjust to them when, after the horrors of the air raid, he had stood in judgement on their ruined beauty. Venus herself would be a little the worse for wear after an air raid. He recalled vividly his sensations that night as he stood contemplating the sleeping women. Fallen butterflies they had seemed, their wings all ragged and useless, the meadows in which they flourished forever burned away. But now these same butterflies danced and played as vivaciously as ever, lighting gracefully now on this flower, now on that, never dreaming that the day would end or that leaves would fall. They were creatures of beauty. He admired the scene as he would have regarded a great painting. They had not changed; he had changed. Before the air raid, they had been amorous ideals whose charm and presence had made him fully human; they had enabled him to be himself in defiance of the strictures of his grandmother. Still they were beautiful, exquisite; but the magic of lust was gone. Feeling benevolent, nostalgic, pure, and a little old, he turned away from the scene of springlike celebration and walked slowly back down the cedar-lined path. As he went through the door in the fence surrounding the ladies' dwelling, he stopped. Then he bent down and studied a scrawl on the wall. It was a beast with the heads of four women, and underneath was the caption "Temple of the Concubines." It was a clumsy picture, but strangely lively. He couldn't tell whether it was the work of a child or a grown-up. Obviously, however, it reflected the mocking hostility of the villagers toward his ladies. There was a country wit, a practiced obscenity, and the moral judgement of laboring folk on the leisure class involved in that captioned picture. "The Temple of the Concubines." He spoke the term aloud. It was a fair judgement, not on them, but on the blind romanticism which had for twenty-five years made him equate masculine independence—from Kino, from Sei—with amorous adventurism. His was the offense; he had constructed this crazy temple of concubines; he had made all these women and O-Toki too, the idle, obedient servants of his whims. He studied the four-headed creature once more, and, with a smile of self-contempt on his face, walked back the way he had come toward the bus stop.

He came to the main road just in time to see the bus speeding off in the distance, stirring up a cloud of dust. He was not bothered. He was satisfied to walk a little and organize his thoughts. He was glad he had heard the women as he had, speaking freely their real thoughts without any notion of being overheard. They had seemed healthily unsentimental about their long association with him. They were left with no special grudges, and, to be sure, no special appreciation, either. And, quite clearly, they were perfectly capable of managing their own affairs without any supervision from him. Better, he thought, to send them the severance checks in the mail, along with a pleasant and friendly letter of parting. They would prefer that to a romantic display of emotion, and it would be more honest. He would tell them he hoped they could remain his good friends. That ought to be about the right line to take. He would write tonight and send Wasuke in the morning.

The rich tones of green, yellow, and brown of Mt. Izumi became suddenly indistinguishable with the approach of evening. The mountain loomed, dark and formidable, to the left of the road, its profile clear against the sky. In another hour all would be swallowed in the shades of night. On sudden impulse, he turned off the main road, and walked along a grassy road sloping toward the mountain. It ran into woods. Beyond was a meadowland, and in it he found a narrow trail which headed circuitously up the mountain. He climbed, sweating and puffing, tucking his kimono up so that it did not impede his rapid steps. He climbed like a man possessed, and yet, had he had to explain to a policeman just why he was doing so, he could not have said. After a half-hour of steady climbing, he came to a flat grassland; the evening breeze made the overgrown grass and weeds rustle and sway. He turned and saw in the distance the faint twinkling lights of the burned but still vigorous city. Though his tabi were wet with evening dew, he stood contemplating the scene. Those faint lights from blackened Osaka were sparkling and cold, as though coming to him from the ocean depths. Never had he felt more completely and utterly alone, but, far from being depressed, he experienced a calm sense of liberation and acceptance such as he had never known. Osaka had been burned away, but was still there. Those lights would be joined by others, newer, better, brighter. And so with his family. Three generations of women, armed with the tradition of centuries, had controlled him and his father obsessively, and they were gone. And the women he had turned to in rebellion for love and sympathy were, on their own initiative as much as on his, about to vanish from his world. What was left? He was left. As Osaka was twinkling and gleaming tentatively in the distance, he would raise the family fortunes once more—and to a level of success which his forebears would never have conceived of.

He had, all these years, he realized, been a man on a quest for a happiness which he had never defined. Perhaps, had he been mature enough and independent enough, he could have achieved it with Hiroko. But after the divorce, his womanizing rebellion had never been more than partially effective. That was why he kept adding new women to the group. And the more he added, the less the possibility of achieving what he sought. He had been well on the way to destroying his ability to love at all, for he had begun to detect, not ecstasy, but sameness and repetition no matter how much he sought for the unique experience. And now, after roaming for years with an illusion of complete freedom, he realized suddenly that he had escaped from a quicksand of sensual dependence and essential frivolity. And the fault was his, not theirs. He would treasure the memory of these women, so different, so alike in trusting him. But he was free. Like the lights of distant Osaka, his mind and spirit sparkled and danced. With a glad smile, he raised his eyes to the heavens.

"Time to get going," he said aloud in the darkened wilderness.

And with the lights of Osaka to guide him, he walked with firm steps down toward the road, toward the city and the future.